The Sound of Butterflies

The Sound of Butterflies

Rachael King

WM
WILLIAM MORROW
An Imprint of HarperCollinsPublishers

THE SOUND OF BUTTERFLIES. Copyright © 2006 by
Rachael King. All rights reserved. Printed in the United
States of America. No part of this book may be used or
reproduced in any manner whatsoever without written
permission except in the case of brief quotations
embodied in critical articles and reviews. For
information address HarperCollins Publishers,
10 East 53rd Street, New York, NY 10022.

HarperCollins books may be purchased for
educational, business, or sales promotional use. For
information please write: Special Markets Department,
HarperCollins Publishers, 10 East 53rd Street,
New York, NY 10022.

FIRST U.S. EDITION

Designed by Nicola Ferguson
Map courtesy of the Library of Congress: São Paulo:
Secção Geographica Artistica da Compa. Lith.
Hartmann-Reichenbach, 1910.
Gift of Mrs. Kermit Roosevelt.

Library of Congress Cataloging-in-Publication Data
has been applied for.

ISBN: 978-0-06-135764-0
ISBN-10: 0-06-135764-2

07 08 09 10 11 WBC/RRD 10 9 8 7 6 5 4 3 2 1

This book is dedicated to the memory of my father, Michael King. Miss you.

CARTA DA VIAÇÃO FERREA
DO
BRASIL
ORGANISADA POR ORDEM DO EX.ᵐᵒ SNR
Dᴿ MIGUEL CALMON DU PIN E ALMEIDA
MINISTRO DA VIAÇÃO E OBRAS PUBLICAS
no Escriptorio da Administração Geral da Commissão de Estudos
e Construcção de Estradas de Ferro sob a direcção do Engenheiro chefe
ERNESTO A. LASSANCE CUNHA
Auxiliado pelo Engᵒ Militar
ALIPIO GAMA
e por
EUGENIO DHERMANDO E LUIZ PRIVAT

Escala de 1:5.000.000
1910

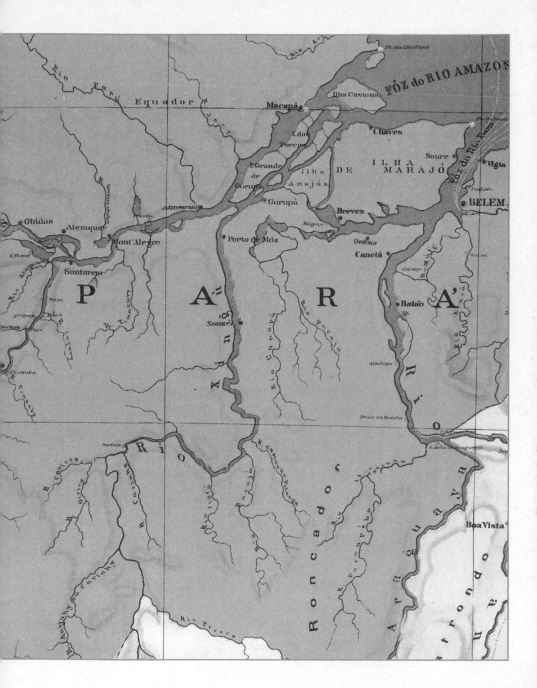

The Amazon

The Sound of Butterflies

Manaus, Brazil, January 6th, 1904

Dear Sophie,

We have finally reached Manaus and are now being accommodated at the home of Mr. Santos—a man who has so far proved to be full of surprises, as has the city itself. After spending so long in the rain forest and on the river, to come across a city such as this is nothing short of astounding, with its paved roads and trams rattling by, its fancy tailors and the smell of fresh pastries wafting from cake shops. On the way here from the docks by horse and carriage, I caught a glimpse of the opera house's magnificent azure and gold roof tiles shining brilliantly in the sun. I fancied if I closed my eyes I would be able to hear the strains of beautiful singing emanating from within—or was it the call of the birds who had ventured in from the jungle?

Mr. Santos's house is an outrageous show of wealth, such as I have never seen in England. Lavish artworks adorn the gigantic entrance hall, too many to take in before he appeared at the top of the stairs and welcomed us. There is one that caught my attention, however, and I must describe it here, for I felt its significance even in my awestruck state.

It was a pre-Raphaelite-style painting of a woman kneeling beside an open chest. In the upper corner of the picture a cloud of moths seemed to burst from the frame. The woman had a look of fear on her face, and remorse. It was the flash of yellow and black that drew my gaze to her wrist, where a swallow-tailed butterfly—I couldn't be sure of the species—sat lightly like the jewel of a bracelet.

I realized I was looking at a depiction of Pandora's box, the moths representing the evils of the world that Pandora inadvertently released with her curiosity. The butterfly, I remembered from my studies, represented Hope—to be sent after the world's troubles so mankind wouldn't sink into despair. How like my own butterfly it was! In color and shape, if not markings. If I believed in such things, I would say it was a sign.

Richmond, England, May 1904

NOTHING IN THE LETTER suggests to Sophie that her husband will arrive home a different man. It is a strange, unfinished kind of a letter, written four months earlier and somehow delayed in its journey to her. She hasn't heard from Thomas for some time, but she has forced herself not to worry, and, after all, she knows from his agent, Mr. Ridewell, that he is at least safe, if not happy. The letter comes on the very same day she receives an unexpected note from Ridewell stating that Thomas will be arriving on the train from Liverpool at eleven o'clock on Friday. She throws open all the windows in the house—letting in the spring air and startling the vicar, who is walking past, swinging an umbrella and checking the sky for rain— and leads her maid Mary in a mission to scrub every surface of the house, driven by a mad energy that has long been absent from her body. As the day comes nearer, however, her joy is replaced by apprehension. She has to steel herself with the knowledge that something has changed; their bond, which seemed so strong in the past, is little more than a daisy chain, stretched between them, that has curled and broken and died.

The train from Liverpool shudders into the station and stops with a sigh. Sheets of steam rise and hiss; flowers of mist swirl and cling to her before thinning and melting away. She has a moment of stillness in which to scan the windows before the doors open and the platform comes alive with a sudden bustle. She braces her body against the crowd. Trunks thud as they hit the ground. A porter pushes a luggage trolley so close that she has to snatch her skirts to her body to prevent them being caught in the wheels and dragged away. Her head jerks about as she scans the faces—many of them obscured by the low brims of hats—looking for her husband. She's not even sure she will recognize him if she sees him.

A bag crashes against her leg and she reaches out to steady herself, catching a man's arm. He looks up in surprise and she pulls her hand away.

"I'm sorry," she says.

The man smiles and touches the rim of his hat with one fat forefinger. A kind smile, from beneath a thick auburn mustache, which she returns before the man spins away, his long brown coat fanning around him, to bark orders. The unfortunate porter he addresses balances several crates and cases on a trolley while struggling to push it at the same time.

Only after the throng clears—after it finally moves away, and the clatter of luggage and the rustle of skirts and cloaks evaporate with it—does she see him. He stands alone. He is a narrow figure in a cloak creased in folds, as if bought off a shelf in Liverpool that day. It swamps him but he appears to be shivering in spite of it. His head is bare and in his arms he holds a large Gladstone bag.

She has imagined this meeting: that she would run at him and he would lift her up and kiss her. She has even fantasized about the feeling of his skin against hers; she has been aching for him.

But it is not to be. Sophie feels his eyes inside her, on her face, in her hair, but he makes no move toward her. His eyebrows are bunched together and his mouth is tightly pursed. But of course, this is how Thomas's face has arranged itself every day she has known him, a permanently worried expression supported by childlike features, which have always kept him younger than his twenty-seven years.

"My darling." She walks forward, puts her hands on his shoulders and kisses his cheek. It is tough under her lips. His skin is hardened and scarred and his whiskers are coarser, darker. His eyes, level with hers, are corollas of white-blue under slim gold eyebrows. Something in them has changed. They are sharper, colder; his newly tanned skin throws them into stark relief. His pupils tremble and his breath comes in short squeezes. Red, scaly hands hold his bag tight and do not return the embrace.

This is just not how things were meant to be. Her hands still rest on his shoulders and she wants to shake him. To shake him and say, *What have you done with my husband? Where is Thomas?*

A voice comes from behind her.

"Mrs. Edgar."

She turns her head. The man whose arm she grabbed stands with his large brown bowler hat in his hands. He bows, showing Sophie the top of his head, which has only a thin coating of copper hair. "I am Francis Ridewell."

The agent. She hadn't seen him inching up to them, hadn't even heard his shoes on the hard stones.

"Yes, of course," she says. "Thank you for bringing my husband home. Your letter was most unexpected." Her hands still rest on Thomas's shoulders. She is surprised to see them there. She pulls them away, reclaiming them.

"The thing is, madam . . ."

The man pauses. He gives a flicking motion of his head as he indicates the seat under the awning. He wants her to move away, to sit down with him. She checks her husband. His eyes are closed now. She wavers, uncertain for a moment, but as Mr. Ridewell moves away she follows.

He waits for her to sit before doing so himself, and while he fusses around arranging his coat, she asks him, impatient now: "Is he all right, Mr. Ridewell? Has something happened?"

Mr. Ridewell shakes his head. "I really don't know. It's most peculiar. I received a letter from a man in Brazil informing me of the date Mr. Edgar's ship would be arriving back in Liverpool. He was like this when I met him at the dock. I spoke to the steward of the ship . . . They thought he was deaf at first. He wouldn't respond to any questions, not even with a yes or no. But they saw him turn at some commotion on board, and when there was a fire in the hold he came running with everyone else, so he heard the alarm. But they still couldn't get any words out of him."

"I see." The steadiness of her own voice surprises her. "Has he lost his mind?"

"Well, that will be for a doctor to decide, madam. I'm afraid I've had to look after him this far. His clothes were like rags when he got off the boat in Liverpool, and forgive me for saying . . ."

"Go on."

"He smelt. I took him home and gave him a bath and got him a change of clothes from his trunk."

She looks over at Thomas and sees the frayed cuffs of his trousers where they meet bright new boots.

"I bought him a cloak—he was freezing—and some shoes."

"We will pay you, of course," says Sophie. It's the only thing she can think of, under the circumstances. That she is in debt to this man.

He stops her with a raised palm. "I've seen to it that the porter has gathered together his crates of specimens. Only one was lost in the fire. There may be some smoke damage in the others. They're waiting for you at the front gate."

"What can have caused this, Mr. Ridewell?"

"I can't say, madam. I'm very sorry. The Amazon can be a challenging place, so I'm told. I've heard of men losing their possessions, their faith, and their virtue. But I've never heard of anyone losing his ability to speak."

BEFORE HE LEFT LONDON for Brazil, Thomas spent long hours in Richmond Park, and Sophie came to think of it as his domain. He scoured every inch of it, turning over rotten pieces of wood, crouching in piles of damp leaves, looking at beetles or waiting patiently for butterflies to appear. He took her on his expeditions with promises of a picnic, but she always ended up sitting with damp skirts on a rug watching him, fending off the ants that crawled up her ankles. He told her he had found more than a hundred species of beetle and thirty types of butterfly: these he had carefully brought home in jars, shutting himself in his study to do whatever it was that he did with them—some process that occupied him indefinitely and sent a poisonous odor through the house.

Insects lined his study—beetles and butterflies mostly, on the walls and crammed into drawers. Sophie felt sick when she went in there, as if they were alive, and she couldn't stand too close to the walls in case one slipped down her blouse. Thomas teased her about it, running his fingers, like tiny insect feet, down her spine until she squeaked and ran from the room, her shoulders hunched around her ears and goose bumps on her skin.

After he left, she started to walk over the hills of the park every day, at first to feel closer to him, but soon because she enjoyed the exercise. Her thighs grew strong under her skirt, which gave her an unexpected pleasure. She lost some of the plumpness in her cheeks, but she tried to make up for this by always taking an extra serving of pudding. When she emerged from the park, if she met acquaintances strolling toward her, they often turned their heads, aghast at her ruddy complexion, the sheen of sweat on her upper lip, but she didn't care.

On one of her walks, she saw a fawn up close. She was used to watching the red and the fallow deer from afar, taking care to stay away from the stags when they were rutting, but on this occasion, she startled one as she stood up from a soft place in the bracken, where she had stopped to rest. It gazed at her for a moment, its neck and ears straight and strong, its legs slightly splayed. Its breath came in gusts that shimmered against its sides. She stood for what seemed minutes. Then she saw it. It was crying. Two thick, oily tears welled in its eyes and fell down its face. It dropped its head, as if to wipe them away, before it lifted its legs in a high step and leapt toward the woods. Not graceful like a deer should be, but altogether more *animal*.

Her friend Agatha told her that if you meet an animal face-to-face, its spirit stays with you for life, inhabiting a part of your soul. Better a beautiful deer, she said, than a hedgehog, or a wild pig. Then she dropped to her knees on the carpet and performed an impression of a wild boar, snorting and tearing at Sophie's skirts with imaginary tusks. Sophie laughed so hard that her elbow knocked her teacup and sent it tumbling to the floor.

Agatha also teased her about Captain Fale, who had been a great comfort for Sophie with his visits. He would often accompany the two ladies on strolls around the town, and would come and sit with them on wet afternoons. Sophie had thought at first that he was sweet on Agatha, that she was acting as a chaperone to a blossoming romance, but Agatha dismissed him as desperate and lonely. "Besides, Bear," she said, "he's rather hoping that Thomas doesn't come back from the jungle. It's *you* he's in love with." Sophie laughed off these comments. She felt sorry for Captain Fale, she thought, because of his leg, and also because all his years in the army had meant that he still hadn't found a wife, even though he was nearly forty. And he wasn't bad company. He could be a little pompous at times, but he had a shyness about him that she found endearing.

Most of her time at home was spent sitting with Agatha. They would read, or embroider, or play whist, or imagine the rain forest and what adventures lay within it. Agatha said she would like to explore it, but Sophie's insides curled at the thought of the damp jungle, the slimy insect life, and the natives, who she was convinced were not yet altogether Christian. Sophie sat every morning before breakfast in the little chapel around the corner. Breathing in the scent of beeswax and the dark stain of the wood, she emptied her mind and sat very still. She closed her eyes and listened to the silence, broken only by the occasional clipping of a horse and carriage outside.

Then she bowed her head and prayed.

Once, before Thomas left for Brazil, she came upon him sitting quietly at the front of the church. She slipped into the pew several rows behind him and watched. The afternoon light glittered through the stained-glass window and cast splashes of color across his body. Her own hands, when she opened them on her lap, were daubed with red light. The warmth of the sun fell on them, like blood. Thomas prayed so long that she thought he was asleep. She crept into the aisle and began to inch toward him. Then he started to sway as he brought his hands up, clasped, to his chest. With his eyes still closed, he wore a rapturous expression.

She had seen that look once before, in the forest, when he appeared to go into a trance. The same intense light appeared on his features, while he squatted like a child in the foul-smelling detritus of the forest floor, a butterfly ensnared by tweezers in one hand, his magnifying glass in the other.

Sophie wasn't at all surprised in church that day when he pulled his hands apart. A small red butterfly flew out from his fingers and ascended to the ceiling of the church.

SHE TURNS TO HELP him from the carriage, as if he is an invalid, but he ignores her hand and springs down. He lifts his face to the front of the house, which is part of a long row of tidy two-story dwellings, and his eyes sweep over the windows and doors, over the trellis that

supports the climbing rose. His gaze falls on the window of her bedroom and his Adam's apple bobs as he swallows. They step through
the gate while the driver humps the first of the crates onto his shoulder and follows. Thomas's hands reach out to the lavender hedge
that lines the path to the door; his hand flinches and his fingers curl in-
ward for a moment before flattening out, becoming bolder. He keeps
his hand over the lavender as he walks, and each stalk curves slightly
under it, shivering as he passes. When he gets to the end, he grips one
flower head and breaks it off. He crushes it between his fingers and
brings it to his nose. He closes his eyes as he inhales. Sophie can't read
his expression; perhaps he's merely reacquainting himself with the
smells of England. But there is something violent in the action, and
the decapitated lavender stalk looks obscene, like a broken bone.

After directing the driver to Thomas's study, where he packs the
crates into a tight formation in the corner, Sophie pays him and then
she is alone with her husband. She deliberately says nothing, waiting for him to fill the silence. He stands at the bottom of the stairs,
one hand on the banister. His other holds the Gladstone bag. He
lifts one foot onto the bottom stair and turns his head to face her.

"What is it?"

She immediately regrets being the first to speak. He doesn't
answer, of course, just begins the slow ascent. She follows close behind him, the muscles in her arms taut, as if readying herself to catch
him if he falls.

She has kept his bedroom exactly as he left it: his clothes hanging in the heavy oak wardrobe, regularly checked for moths; his
shoes shiny and dusted every month; his brushes on the squat dressing table. The bed with the nightshirt laid across it and the hot-water
bottle waiting to be filled, propped against the pillow. His slippers
peek out from under his bed. She had expected him to take many of
these comforts with him, but he had insisted on traveling light.

The room engulfs his small frame. Its solid lines and forest green
wallpaper seem to mock him with their strength, their sureness. He

puts the bag down and sits on the bed. He pushes with his feet and bounces his mass, which seems as insubstantial as a feather. A smile begins at the corners of his mouth and he sighs. He's glad to be home, she thinks. Surely he is.

"Thomas . . ." she begins, but she finds herself trailing away and pressing with her dark-colored clothing into the wall. Anything she says will be wrong, out of place—she knows that.

"I'll leave you to rest," she says finally. She indicates the washbasin on the sideboard, a fresh towel that she put there herself, and backs out, pulling the door behind her.

WHEN THEY FIRST MET, Thomas impressed her with his knowledge about insects. He helped her cup a butterfly, a red admiral, while telling her about its habitat, the thousands of scales that make up its wings, like the shingles on a roof. He preferred its original name—"red admirable"—for there was much to admire about this little creature. But she barely listened; instead, she felt the warmth of his hand on hers and the summer sun on her closed eyes, the smell of the rain clouds that gathered just out of sight.

When Brazil swallowed him and the letters stopped, she thought she could hear the constant rumble of thunder over the horizon. Lying now in her high white bed, she feels it in her body, unsettling her. How can she feel alone again, and so unstable, with her husband home and in the next room? She has spent all this time with only her maid, Mary, for company in the night, with nobody to get up to investigate the night's noises but her. Only last week, she heard a clatter from downstairs and went down to find that a fox had somehow got inside, sneaking in from the park and rummaging for food. She tiptoed down so quietly that she surprised it—but she only saw its eyes reflected in her lamp before it skittered away, its claws scraping at the stone floor. The sound disturbed the remnants of her night's sleep, but it was the musky smell of the fox that stayed with her as she bolted the door and ascended the stairs to her room.

In the darkness it is as if he has never come home, as if she is still dreaming of him in the jungle. Her sheets are just as cold as they always were.

Still, her dried-up heart is becoming more pliable. When their eyes met in his room, there was a softening in her chest, which reminded her that Thomas was not a stranger, after all, even though he treated her as one. He had stayed in his room for the rest of the day and into the night. She had hesitated outside his door before she went to bed, put her hand on the doorknob and her ear to the cool wood. She could hear his breathing in fluttery snores. She supposed that he was overcome with exhaustion; that the bed had swallowed him in luxury after the creaking hammocks or the narrow berths he had endured over the last year.

Outside her window, a gust whooshes through the branches of the plum tree like the low bark of a dog, making her jump. Through a slit in the curtains, she sees movement outside. Earlier, when her lamp was lit, she looked up in fright at the sound of fingers tapping on the window. When she pushed back the curtain a moth hurled itself at the glass as if to break it, whirring in dark furred circles.

Sometimes she wakes at night with the sensation that something is lying on top of her, pushing her back down. Other times, when she drifts off to sleep, she starts to sink into the bed, hot hands pulling at her. Last year it got unbearably warm in September and she spent most nights naked, like Lady Godiva, keeping her curtains open so she could be awoken early by the first snatches of light and put her nightgown back on before Mary came in. Not that Mary would care. But now her stiff nightgown scrapes against her skin, and she can't take it off; not when she is so cold, and not with Thomas in the next room.

She turns her back to the window and closes her eyes. She falls asleep and dreams she needs to urinate. In the dream, she walks around town, and people offer her chamber pots, whipping them out from beneath their coats like a conjuring trick, triumphant looks on their faces. To use one, she would have to lift her heavy skirts and squat right there in the street. So she continues her walk, but every bush she comes to leaves her wide open to public view. She becomes so desperate that she takes a pot off a shrewd-faced man with narrowed eyes, who offers it to her with hands that are red and raw. She tries to use it, but the man has called a crowd of witnesses, and Sophie finds that she can't ease her bladder with an audience, with the man staring at her with his tiny eyes.

The pressure in her abdomen wakes her eventually, and she knows the only way to calm her dreams is to get out of bed. She gropes for the chamber pot and squats over it. Hot needles pierce her feet as she splashes herself, and she curses. She closes her eyes and relief spreads through her as the moisture on her feet quickly cools. When she opens them again, it is so dark all she can see is the violent purple light that presses against her eyelids. There is a tap at the window and then another, more insistent. She lurches to her feet—the moth won't leave her alone; it's taunting her now—and as she does so, her foot catches the pot and there is a moment of terrible silence before the floor is sluiced with her piss.

She gropes around for a towel and starts to cry as she mops up her mess, knowing that the smell will be appalling, that it will seep into the floorboards and stay there long after they have been scrubbed clean. She hears tapping at the window again, but when she throws back the curtain, she sees that it's not the moth but a small branch of the plum tree that has come loose in the wind and brushes the window lightly, its spring buds kissing the pane.

"GOOD MORNING," SOPHIE SAYS to her husband when he comes into the parlor. He sits down opposite her, in front of the table setting of one boiled egg, a slice of toast, and the best silver.

"Tea?"

She waits for him to answer, but instead he picks up his cup and holds it out to her. He looks directly into her face, expectant.

Sophie picks up the silver teapot and begins to pour. Together they watch the thin arc of liquid as she pumps her wrist down and up and back down again. Not a drop spilled. He bobs his head so slightly that she supposes it must be a nod of gratitude, but he might just as easily be catching an itch in his collar.

She doesn't know what to do, so she talks: about the weather; about the house repairs she organized while he was away—the back door practically dropped off its hinges one day; about the river and how it rose to swallow the fields last autumn; about who got married in the neighborhood—you won't believe who Miss Prym is marrying (only the arrogant Mr. Winchester!); about the state of her health—good on the whole. Thomas, meanwhile, slurps his tea and gulps down his egg. He drops his sleeve into the yolk, and cleans it off by bringing it to his mouth and sucking. His little tongue flicks out like a cat's. He sees her looking when she stops talking, and brings his arm down slowly, suddenly ashamed. He turns quite pink. Once he has finished his breakfast he sits with his hands on his lap, staring at them as if daring them to misbehave. He looks as though he might be listening to her, so concentrated is his gaze on his lap, but she gets no reaction to any of the information she imparts to him. Out of desperation, she tells him about her accident with the chamber pot. She puts it into the lightest tone she can muster: she will shock him into speaking to her.

"So, you see, there is still a smell about my room this morning, and I didn't have the heart to ask Mary to clean up my mess."

Nothing. He is frozen, cold as a pond in winter. She could strap on her skates and glide across his surface.

She changes tack.

"Thomas, dear. Please look at me."

He hears that, at least. He lifts his head. She detects the same look in his eyes that she saw at the train station. Fright.

"Darling. Won't you tell me what the matter is?"

He gives an accusatory stare at the salt cellar, lifts his napkin off his lap, and puts it down on his plate with a shaking hand. He pushes his chair back and leans forward as if he means to rise.

"No!" she says.

He stops and looks at her like a startled deer.

"Please don't walk away, Thomas." She reaches across the table and grasps his hand. He transfers his desultory stare to her wedding ring.

But what can she say to him? She doesn't know how to get him to speak, whether asking questions will only make him back away. Why is he making it so difficult for her?

"Why did you stop writing to me?"

Again, nothing. His hand quivers under hers. Perhaps she should try something easier.

"Are you glad to be home?" She hopes that this will elicit, at the very least, a nod; perhaps he will take his other hand and stretch it over hers, and she will see something in his face that she can grasp, something that will give her some hope. But there is nothing.

She picks his hand up a fraction, then drops it again.

Her chair tips onto the floorboards as she jumps up and marches from the room.

AT THE VERY MOMENT Sophie's chair makes such a racket in the dining room, Captain Samuel Fale, who lives a few houses down the road, closes the Edgars' front gate with a clang while humming a tune to himself that he can't quite place. It goes ta-tum-tum-titum in the most unusual of rhythms and he knows he hasn't simply made it up, so someone must have laid it in his mind—whether by accident or design he doesn't know.

He flinches as he mounts the stairs. His bad leg misses the momentum and his foot slams into the step. That fall from his horse ended his career in the army, and now his damned leg drags around after him like a heavy ax. He never likes to be reminded of his affliction, but these blasted steps do it every time. A price to pay for good company, perhaps.

Mary answers the door and won't meet his eyes. She shows him into the drawing room, drops into a poor imitation of a curtsy—impertinent girl—then scurries away to find her mistress without a word. He has been in here many times in the past six months, but he is always taken aback by how the walls seem close enough to touch each other. The heavy velvet curtains add to the room's claustrophobic air. Still, it has its advantages—in the winter it's always as warm as a furnace.

He sits down on a lumpy chair and almost immediately catches his sleeve button in the worn fabric of its arm. He curses out loud and looks around quickly to make sure Sophie—Mrs. Edgar— hasn't slipped in without him knowing and been party to his disgraceful demeanor. But he is still alone. He untangles his button, which now hangs loosely on its thread, and sits back to wait.

The door opens behind him. He adjusts his tie and stands.

It's not Mrs. Edgar. It's a man, if you can call him that. He looks more like a nervous youth. His skin is ruddy, like a farm laborer's, but his body is insubstantial; his face is thin and his head looks to be too heavy for the reedy neck that sticks out from his collar. The skin of his throat is inflamed, as if he is not used to wearing constricting clothing. Although cut short, his hair cannot contain its girlish blond curls.

But it's the mouth that draws most of his attention. Fale supposes that a woman might find it sweet, but to him it looks insolent, as if the bottom lip is forcing the top lip upward, buckling it into sharp contours, like the edges of a violin. The lips are obscenely red. He shifts his weight but flinches as he remembers his bad leg. The lips are still there. He can't stop himself from staring at them. He waits for them to move, for the gentleman—he supposes he must be a gentleman—to say something. But those lips stay like that. Pert.

Then the man turns on his heel and walks out of the room. Fale sits back down on the arm of the chair, disoriented. He knows he has seen the man before, but he can't place him. Is it some bastard friend of that maid's? Has he seen him up at the Star and Garter? Then it comes to him. He lets himself slide from the arm of the chair into its seat, his legs dangling off the side. A gust of hot air rises from his collar as he lands and he feels his armpits dampen.

His suspicions are confirmed when Mary slips in through the door and finds him sitting sideways, flapping around like a seal. He struggles to his feet, feeling foolish.

"What is it, girl?"

"If you please, sir . . ." She studies the fireplace as she speaks. "Mrs. Edgar can't come down. She has a headache. I'm to tell you that she will be in touch."

Headache, indeed. Fale jams his hat down on his head, takes up his cane and, brandishing it dangerously close to Mary's knees, finds his way to the door, where he limps blindly down the steps and out onto the gray street.

Blasted *Edgar* is back.

WHEN SOPHIE COMES DOWNSTAIRS again—when she is ready to face her husband—she finds Thomas sitting in the conservatory. Mary informs her that he has been there all morning. He sits with his chair pointed to the window, giving him a clear view outside. The heavy rain clouds have broken briefly, and a web of sunlight stretches across the garden. He sits very still, with his hands crossed in his lap, as if posing for a photograph. He doesn't lift his eyes to her when she sits down on a chair near him and takes up her embroidery.

She stabs the needle into the fabric and pulls it out the other side, while her eyes flick between her work and her husband. A wobbly rose forms under her fingers. She changes thread to begin work on the stem.

She has forgotten to put her thimble on. Just as she pricks her finger, Thomas leaps up from his chair. He slaps his palms on the large window that dominates the room. If he was speaking, she thinks to herself wryly, he would have given a shout. His body is rigid and he is looking at something in the garden, something that has startled him.

"What is it?" asks Sophie. She cranes her neck to see past him.

The vibrations from Thomas's hands on the window have dislodged a butterfly from the outer sill, and it loops a path in front of his face before it tumbles through the air to the far flower bed and out of sight around the side of the house. It's just a plain little thing— a cabbage butterfly perhaps—but the only thing moving in the garden, the only thing he could be looking at. When it has gone, Thomas turns away from a patch of mist on the window caused by his own breath. He shakes his head, as if to wake himself up, and lowers himself into his chair again. His hands on the armrests tremble.

Sophie stands and goes to his side. "Thomas. What's wrong?"

He closes his eyes and appears to be trying to control his breathing. His cheeks are marked with red blotches, which shine with a thin coating of perspiration. He takes three long breaths, then opens his eyes and looks at her. His eyes are cold, defiant. She takes an involuntary step back and holds her needle tighter. Its spindly edge digs into her flesh where she has pricked it; she lifts her thumb to her face as a bead of blood collapses and slides to the floor.

DR. DIXON ARRIVES WITH the afternoon's rain. He shakes off his hat and places it on the coatrack, then shrugs his wet cloak into Mary's hands. She flaps it and hangs it up.

The examination takes place in Thomas's bedroom. The curtains are open, but rain pummels the window and the weak light from outside is swallowed by the room's dark walls. Sophie hangs in the doorway, waiting to be dismissed, but hoping to witness at least some part of the process. Thomas has his back to her in the gloom and his head bowed, attending to the buttons on his shirt. She watches him, a new sharpness in her stare. A thrill of something like danger runs through her—or the anticipation of seeing her husband without his shirt. When it slips from his shoulders, her breath contracts and her hands stiffen into fists. Circular red welts, like small crumpets, dot his thin back. Jagged scratches on his arms are angry and inflamed, and she hadn't known until this point that he had a bandage around one arm. Dr. Dixon hears her reaction, turns with a newly lit lamp in one hand, and puts the other on the door.

"I think we should have some privacy, Mrs. Edgar."

Sophie finds herself staring at the dark-stained wood, her hot breath bouncing back into her face.

THE DOCTOR ANNOUNCES HE has put Thomas to bed for a rest. He follows Sophie into the drawing room, where she sits twisting her handkerchief into tight spirals. Mary has started a fire in anticipation of the conversation, but she has not lit any lamps; it is still daytime, after all.

Dr. Dixon tries to explain the examination to her. The welts on his back, as far as he can tell without any help from Mr. Edgar, are insect bites that have become infected. The scratches were probably caused by the wear and scrape of the jungle. None of his wounds seem to be healing.

"It may be the stress of the voyage that has done it, not allowed him to heal, but . . ." Here he leans forward in his chair and rests his elbows on his knees. "I suspect the fact is more to do with the reason why he won't speak."

"I don't understand. Why won't he speak?"

"Ah, now that I don't know. He's had a bump to his head, which may have contributed, but I've never heard of anyone losing his speech from a blow like that. He may have suffered some kind of shock, I suppose . . ." He hesitates and looks into the fire, frowning. "Yes," he says quietly, as if to himself. The next sentence is mumbled into his chest.

"I beg your pardon?" His manner is doing nothing to alleviate Sophie's tension.

"Forgive me." Dr. Dixon raises his voice and looks at her. "I said, that cut—under his bandage. It was quite filthy. I've cleaned and redressed it. Do you think you can dress it yourself? In a couple of days? Keep him in bed. Give him plenty of rest."

She nods. "And his speech? Will bed rest help that?"

"I can't say."

"Dr. Dixon. Please." The warmth from the fire falls across one cheek as she faces him. She fastens her gaze on his face and concentrates on stopping tears. He returns the look, one eye sharp in the soft light.

"Mrs. Edgar, I'm afraid I just don't know."

"Well, what is your opinion?"

"My opinion?" He purses his lips and examines the floor for a moment. Then he gives her a smile. Forced, she thinks. "My opinion is that he seems to be perfectly sound in his mind apart from this one thing. Have you seen any evidence to the contrary?"

She thinks about her husband, how he seems hollowed out, with dead eyes.

"No," she says. "Although there was an incident this morning . . ." She tells him about the butterfly on the windowsill, about Thomas's trembling hands.

"I see. Are you sure it was a butterfly he was looking at?"

She nods. "I'm sure."

"Why would he have reacted like that?"

"It seems far-fetched, I know. But he's obsessed with them. He went away to study them. He went to collect butterflies, but he also hoped to find one in particular."

"Oh? Which one was that?"

"That's just it. It doesn't have a name—it hasn't officially been discovered. But Thomas heard rumors about it, and he was determined to be the first to actually catch a specimen and bring it back to England. He even thought he would name it after himself—some Latin version of his name."

"And did he? Find it?"

"He hadn't in any of the letters I got from him. But they stopped . . ." She looks away. She feels herself blushing as she realizes it is not just Thomas she has opened to scrutiny. "I don't know if he ever found it. It doesn't really help us, anyway, does it?"

"No," says the doctor. "I'm sorry, Mrs. Edgar. He seems to be suffering from some kind of nervous dyspepsia. I suggest time and bed rest. And patience. No, please don't get upset, madam. You could always have him sent away somewhere so that—"

"No!" She drops the handkerchief and hides her face in her skirt as she bends to pick it up. This she couldn't bear—the admission that her husband might be insane. "I can't do that," she insists.

"Then be patient," he says. She sees his eyes enlarge with pity for her and it gives her a sickness in her stomach. It's a look she has seen before in others, and she has always pushed it aside. It makes her lift her chin higher; it makes her resentful despite the good that is probably intended by it. She doesn't know this man; beyond treating her for a cough last winter, he knows nothing about her.

"Don't badger him," he continues. "Leave him be. Perhaps all he needs is to be in the loving care of his wife. He has been in the jungle, Mrs. Edgar, away from the comforts of the civilized world. Try to communicate with him gently. Once he's had some rest, take him to do the things he loves. Does he like music?"

Sophie nods.

"Strolls in the park? Anything like that, Mrs. Edgar. You could admit him to a hospital if you want, to have his head examined—"

"No." She forces herself to smile at him. "I won't risk that just yet. Thank you, Dr. Dixon. I'll try to be patient, as you say. I'm sure we can find some way to communicate."

TWO

My dear Sophie,

At last the chance to write a letter. The voyage from Lisbon was shorter than I had imagined it would be, but at times it seemed interminable. I spent several days ill in my cabin when the sea was particularly rough. I can't describe the feeling very well, but it is as if you would rather die than face the rest of your days with such a sickness in the stomach—and you feel that it will be the rest of your days. However, a few days before we sighted the coast, the sea calmed down and I emerged refreshed and able to drink some water, and even hold down some food.

During the voyage I became acquainted with my new companions. I will tell you a little about each of them, but I feel that I will get to know them even better in the months to come. George Sebel is always immaculate in his appearance. Even on the morning we landed—when I confess I threw on my clothes, forgetting my waistcoat, and must have looked a shabby fright—George, whom I ran into in the corridor, had taken the time to comb and pomade his hair before leaving his cabin. I had no such patience, as I was soon to set foot on a new continent! While we took turns looking at the jungle and the river through Ernie Harris's telescope, George seemed singularly un-impressed, muttering something to himself about his African expedition last year. He even stooped down to rub at some piece of grime that had lodged itself on his shoe, quite ignoring the marvelous sight of the forest. It was sprinkled with the palms and plantains, and, had the Amazon not been a jaundiced yellow, I would have expected to see the forest reflected back in the water. A city was threaded through the jungle—white build-ings, some with domes, and red roofs, pushing up among the palms. It was all but dwarfed by the huge ships that were anchored in the port, no doubt laden with rubber, awaiting clearance.

My other two companions—Ernie, the surgeon, who is also an ama-teur but experienced ornithologist (that's birds, my love!) and a skilled taxidermist, and John Gitchens, who is a plant-hunter—seemed as transfixed as I. The steward pointed out the gigantic birds circling over the city, and when Ernie trained his telescope on them, he became quite agitated. He allowed me a small peek—they were vultures—but soon wrested the telescope from my hands again. I couldn't help but be slightly disgusted by the idea of the ugly creatures, even though from this far I suppose they looked quite elegant and graceful.

But back to George—he is a decent fellow, and has studied zoology and entomology at Cambridge. He is the official insect collector on the voyage. I feel very blessed to have been taken along as well, despite my amateur status. It just goes to show that having friends in the right places (I refer to Mr. Crawley, at Kew, of course, who introduced me to the agent Ridewell) can do wonders. George has agreed to let me collect butterflies as well as assist him—he will be more than busy with the ants and the beetles and Lord only knows what else that is lurking in this for-est! I think I can learn much from our Mr. Sebel, provided I can pene-trate the hard exterior he seems to have put up for himself.

As for the other two, I can't begin to explain the relief I feel at having a surgeon on the expedition with us. Although he wasn't much help when

I was ill on the boat (he being sick at the same time), it gives me great comfort to know that he will be in the jungle with us and has come prepared with every manner of instrument and medicine that he can carry. I don't know much about the hospitals here in Brazil, but in any case, there may be times when we are too far away from them, and diseases like malaria are rife. Ernie himself is an energetic fellow. I can't quite bring myself to call him Dr. Harris, as he has about him the boisterous manner of a schoolboy that I find alternately charming and irritating. He has started to taunt George in a way that I wouldn't dare, but I suppose he is taking advantage of George's stoic nature to have a bit of fun.

John Gitchens is something of a gentle giant, I feel. He is very quiet, and he has enormous rough brown hands and a big beard, which George complains is quite out of fashion. John doesn't talk about himself at all, but Ernie told me that he has seen many more adventures than we can hope to in our lifetime. He is the oldest of us all, nearly forty, and when he looks at me I feel as if he is reading my every thought. He has the most expressive, large brown eyes that I think I have seen, though the rest of him seems to hide behind the beard. On the voyage, when the rest of us would sit down in the evening to read, he would position himself near a porthole and stare out to sea. If we wanted to play cards, he had to be coaxed quite strongly to make a fourth for bridge, sometimes refusing altogether, at which times we had to include the captain—who treated us as his honored guests—or one of the other passengers. When we arrived at our house today, John disappeared into the forest for some hours. When he came back, the color had returned to his cheeks and he looked alive again.

Nothing has been seen of our benefactor, Mr. Santos. We were met at the dock by one of his men, who showed us to more than adequate lodgings on the outskirts of the city—close to the forest. Within five minutes we can walk into the interior and never know that we are near civilization. More on this later.

The overwhelming impression I have of the city is that it seems to be competing with the jungle for space. There is greenery everywhere—sprouting from ledges, growing out of cracks in the buildings—and there is a heady smell of fruit from the mango trees and the blossoming orange and lemon trees. It is a curious cocktail. Banana palms grow on every roof and balcony with giant leaves that are glossy and opulent. The richness of smells and abundance of nature are a heavy contrast to the poverty of human life. Even the grander buildings have fallen into disrepair. The population has swelled recently, and I don't know if the city is coping with the influx of people come to work in the rubber trade. There is a jumble of humanity here—whites, Indians, Negroes, and different mixtures of all three, all with their own name as if they are new races—mameluco (white and Indian), mulatto (Negro and white), cafuzo (Negro and Indian), and caboclo (all three). The dock was overwhelming with its crowds and its intense stickiness, as if a fire were constantly burning nearby. At least on the river there was a breeze—in the city, between the buildings, there is none.

   You will not believe, Sophie, the kind of cargo that was on board our ship, bound for Manaus, which is hundreds of miles up the Amazon. The captain informed us that there were grand pianos, paving stones from Europe, hundreds of cases of French champagne and other wines, cheese from Devon, fur coats from Paris (in this heat!), and many other extravagances. He even told us they had bags and bags of laundry, which had been sent from Manaus to Lisbon to be washed. Evidently the locals in Manaus don't trust the water from the Amazon, and they think nothing of the expense of sending it away. Decadent, certainly, but also very patient, I'd say! Captain Tilly says we will have to see Manaus with our own eyes to believe it. The city is completely isolated, with no roads leading to it, but it has a complete tram system within it. They recently built an opera house and they have extravagant parties to celebrate everything. The people who live there have grown very rich from the rubber boom and they have more money than they know what to do with. Fortunately for us, Mr. Santos has decided to use some of his to further British science and to cement his British interests. They say he is the one of the richest of them all, with a rubber plantation far up the Amazon that is thousands of square miles in area.

After we arrived in our lodgings, and had settled in somewhat, we ventured into the forest a little way after John, but we didn't find him, and he returned a long time after we did. Santos's man came with us, to make sure that we didn't get lost on our first outing. The road from our lodgings continued on only a few yards before we seemed to be deep in the forest. Almost immediately I saw several different Morphos (do you remember the beautiful blues I showed you in the museum that day?) high up in the trees, and a few other species of butterfly that I could not identify offhand. You can imagine how this set my heart racing—already within minutes of arriving there were exciting new discoveries for me! I have a very good feeling about finding my butterfly.

We had just made it back to the house when the heavens opened and it poured with rain. I couldn't believe it—it happened so quickly that I hadn't even seen the clouds gathering.

In many ways it was a welcome respite from the heat—indeed, while we had been walking, our guide informed us that he would normally be sleeping away the hottest part of the day. We noticed several of our neighbors from afar, slung in hammocks on their verandas.

Well, my little Sophie, my candle is burning down and my hand is aching with the writing. I promise I will write to you as often as I can. You can send letters to me care of the agent Ridewell, whose address you have, as he will be forwarding everything to me on a regular basis. The night is hot here, but it is cold without you, my sugarplum.

Your loving husband,
Thomas

Thomas sealed the letter and tied it up with string for extra protection. Ernie was already asleep, on his back with his mouth open under his mustache, a loud popping sound coming from the back of his throat every time he breathed out. Thomas had written by candlelight out of respect for his roommate. The room was sparsely furnished. Hammocks hung on either side, with small desks next to them for each man. Makeshift shelves waited in the corner for books to be unpacked and for specimens to be collected.

He peeled his shirt off slowly. Every fiber stuck to him with layers of sweat. He put on his nightshirt, which was crisp on his skin for a moment before it, too, was swallowed in dampness. He knelt for a brief prayer on the hard tiled floor, and climbed into his hammock. This he accomplished with some difficulty: he tried to go in with his knees first, but the wretched thing kept spinning around and throwing him out. Finally he backed in, sat down, and gingerly lay back with his feet on the ground. Then he swung his legs up, and found that he was most comfortable. It was certainly a welcome relief after the hard berth on the ship.

After four weeks on the sea, Thomas's legs had taken some adjusting to dry land. As he had walked through town, the buildings about him seemed to undulate. But for the first time since they had set out his stomach felt calm—apart from the excitement gnawing at it from the inside—and he felt the stirrings of the appetite that had well and truly deserted him somewhere in the Atlantic. He had eaten ravenously at dinner, when the deluge was just beginning to ease. John Gitchens returned soaked and smiling; he grabbed a half a loaf of bread and made a line of wet footprints to his room, where they soon heard him vigorously unpacking.

In the twilight Thomas had ventured outside again, as the mechanics of the cicadas and crickets started up and the smell of wet earth rose and permeated his clothes, his skin. The air still held its moisture from the downpour; he could feel it on his face and hands.

As night fell, the forest was outlined black against the softening sky. It seemed to suck away the last of the light. Thomas stood on the balcony with his face turned toward the jungle sounds, and a new cacophony of rhythms—booms and clacks from toads and frogs, mostly—enveloped him.

Earlier in the day, as they walked through the forest, the noise had enthralled him. The forest in England was a silent place—nothing but the sound of his feet crunching on pine needles; animals stayed out of sight. Here, the air throbbed with the screams of birds and monkeys, the distant crack of falling branches, and the scuttling in the undergrowth of creatures that could choose to be seen or sink into camouflage on the forest floor. The air was thick with heat and moisture; he felt as if he were wading through warm porridge.

When he caught sight of his first Morphos, their blue wings shining in the sun like stained glass, he felt a familiar stirring in his trousers. This was something he couldn't explain, and had long ago given up trying to. Ever since he was a young lad, his body had occasionally—only occasionally—reacted this way to the excitement of spotting and catching butterflies. This was not a problem for him when he was alone, roaming through the fields of England—and it didn't happen often, usually only during the chase of a particularly rare species—but in company it was an inconvenience to say the least. He took off his hat and held it with both hands in front of him, enjoying the sensation of his hardness pressing against his breeches as he spotted another Morpho, then a pair of buttery Pieridae.

ERNIE HAD FINALLY TURNED on his side, and was no longer snoring. It hardly made a difference to the night sounds and Thomas wondered if he would ever get to sleep. He put his hand to his groin and thought about Sophie. His dear, sweet Sophie. The way her tiny, thin nostrils went red in the cold. The way she stamped her foot out of frustration but always kept her good humor. The feel of her breasts the first time they had made love—not on their wedding night, when she had just wanted him to hold her, but two nights after. Her breasts were heavy and smooth and the nipples were cold to touch. She had been trembling that first time he entered her, but the next night she had pulled him on top of her, lifting her nightgown to receive him quickly. He remembered the square of moonlight in her hair, her eyes dark smudges in her face. By the end of the week she was moving around beneath him, little sounds escaping her. She had begun to guide his hands to the places that gave her the most pleasure, and together they learned about each other's bodies as well as their own.

He had nearly made love to her in the park once, in a discreet pocket of forest, when she had accompanied him to collect butterflies. He had brought a rug, and they sat down together well out of sight of the forest path. He remembered kissing her, and the velvet of her fluttering tongue, like the wings of the butterflies in the jars that lay beside them. One of his hands was in the earth, and as he scratched at the ground, the damp odor of mushrooms was released. He moved to lie on top of her and she opened her mouth wider, but when he began to lift her skirts, she pushed him away and sat up.

"Not here, Thomas," she said.

"It'll be fine," he breathed. "Nobody will come." But when he covered her face with insistent kisses, she turned away and got to her feet. She stood over him, with the strong trunks of oak trees stretching above her, and her blond hair wisping about her face. Her hands were balanced on her hips, and she no doubt thought she was warning him off, but it only aroused him more. He had turned away then, and busied himself with his collecting equipment, while she gathered up the rug and brushed off her skirts.

He gave a soft moan and turned on his side, bringing his hands away from where they would be tempted and folding them under his cheek.

But he couldn't sleep. After managing to steer his mind away from thoughts of his wife, he focused on the day to come, which gave him a new kind of excitement. He couldn't help but worry a little—certainly there were dangers to be met in this country. If it wasn't the snakes and the giant spiders, or the stinging ants and the prickling plants, it was the mosquitoes, or the diseases. And the alligators. Those that had gone before him had even had trouble with the people—for hadn't one explorer overheard a plot to kill him by some of the Indians who were assisting him? It was only his knowledge of the language that had saved him. Thomas vowed to learn as many of the languages as he could. There was Portuguese first, of course, but there was also a shared Indian language, the Lingoa Geral, which all of the tribes understood. But when would he fit it in? In between collecting and preserving and studying, he might not find the time. He would speak to the others about it tomorrow.

Tomorrow. He turned onto his back and crossed his arms behind his head. He imagined the forest again, its fragrant trees and twisted flowers. He pictured himself standing in a clearing with his net in his hand, while a cloud of butterflies flitted around him. He could make out some of the species he knew—a multicolored *Papilio machaon*, a transparent *Cithaerias aurorina* with its bright pink spot on its lower wings—and there, in the middle of the cloud, was *his* butterfly. The left wings were a glossy black, the right sulphur-yellow: a crazy asymmetry that went against all the laws of nature. It was larger than any of the others and it hovered with a regal presence, alone.

The butterfly had never been caught or recorded. Thomas had heard of it through Peter Crawley at Kew Gardens. He stood one day with Peter in the Palm House at Kew. He had removed his jacket and was fanning himself with a newspaper—the glasshouse was very humid to promote the growth of tropical plants. They were discussing the lecture on South American butterflies they had both attended the night before at the Natural History Museum. It reminded Peter of a rumor that had floated around Kew for some forty years, that both Alfred Russel Wallace and Richard Spruce had seen a giant swallow-tailed butterfly in their travels in the Amazon. The two great explorers had spoken of it separately, in whispers, not able to give a positive sighting of it, but both agreeing that it had the most unusual marking—on one side its wings were yellow, on the other side black. It shouldn't even have been able to fly with such markings, as the black wings would absorb more heat and weigh one side of the creature down. They conceded that it could have been a trick of the light; that the long evening shadows distort images in the jungle, much as the moon appears to be bigger when it rises over the horizon. They were busy enough with their own new species without worrying about one that perhaps did not exist.

Thomas remembered Peter's little round glasses misting up as they spoke, his awkward tongue tripping over his slight lisp, and a little girl with a blue ribbon in her hair who was standing behind him, about to pull a delicate flower from the spiky stem of one of the exhibits. Then Peter said something that Thomas immediately knew would change his life forever.

"That chap that I introduced you to. Ridewell. He was asking about you. It seems there's an expedition to Brazil being planned to collect specimens. Some fellow over there, a rubber tycoon of some sort, is anxious to pamper British interests in his company. He's funding some chaps to go over there, through the Natural History Museum. Ridewell was impressed by your comment about what little kudos there is in beetle-hunting and butterfly-chasing in England. He wondered if perhaps you might be interested in a bit of a challenge."

The rumor of the black and yellow butterfly ingrained itself in Thomas's mind. With encouragement from Peter, and from the friends he had made at the Entomological Society, he decided not only to take the opportunity to fulfill his dream of becoming a professional naturalist, but to make a mark in history by capturing, studying, naming, and bringing home the elusive specimen.

"You'll see, my love," he had said to Sophie. "It's my true calling. Our lives will never be dull!"

She had laughed then, stroking his forehead. "Well, if you put it like that, how can I let you stay here with me? You *must* go. Don't you worry about me."

Now, in his imagination, Thomas held his breath as he stole toward it. The other butterflies rose toward the treetops, while his butterfly—his *Papilio sophia,* as he had decided to call it—remained hovering just above the ground. He held out his net.

The butterfly waited a moment, then dived forward into it. He felt the thrill of the catch deep inside him.

He must have fallen asleep: the image was too perfect, too real. He woke up to find a stickiness between his legs, a chorus of birds screeching through the shutters.

A loud grunt came from Ernie on the other side of the room. Evidently the good doctor's interest in birds didn't stretch to early mornings. "Can't you shut them up?" he moaned, before he pulled up his cover and buried his head beneath it.

THOMAS'S BACK ACHED. AFTER the rigid berth on the ship, his spine protested at resting the whole night in curvature, but he was not going to let that dull throb interfere with his first day's collecting.

John and George already sat in silence at the breakfast table, eating bread rolls and drinking coffee, the smell of which enveloped them. George offered him the pot—more out of politeness than kindness, Thomas couldn't help thinking—then went back to his book, holding it away from his body while peering through his glasses and turning the pages with clean white hands. He was dressed in his usual somber black waistcoat, and his cuff links shone in the patch of early-morning sun that fell through the window. Thomas wondered how long he would remain so pressed and tidy, and whether his pomade would melt in the heat.

Thomas cradled the cup of warm liquid in his hands and took a sip. It was thick and strong, not like the weak and muddy brew served at the Star and Garter in Richmond and by his maid at home; when he tasted it he made an involuntary garbled noise in his throat and lifted his eyes to find the others staring at him. John smiled and pushed the sugar toward him. Thomas gratefully dropped three lumps into his cup and stirred. It was now a heady sweet mixture and he finished the whole cup, then another.

Ernie Harris arrived and sat down, rubbing at his face and yawning. His hair stuck up and he tried to smooth it down with his hands. Until now, nobody had spoken, but Ernie wasn't one to let a gap in conversation go by without filling it.

"Did anybody sleep with that racket going on all night?" He had moved on to his mustache, twirling the ends before reaching for the coffee.

The other men looked at each other. "What racket?" asked George.

"Bloody insects! And God knows what else. And those birds this morning. It was like being in the Cockney markets, all that shrieking!"

George was smirking at him. A scream sounded, a haunting noise that Thomas felt down his spine.

"Christ!" said Ernie, and nearly dropped the coffeepot. "See what I mean? What was that?"

"Howler monkey," said John in his soft northern accent, so quiet for such a big man. Thomas remembered being surprised by it when he had first heard him speak. He had expected a booming burr, striated as if by tobacco and whiskey. Instead, John's voice was that of a gentle soul—one who spends his life trying not to frighten children.

The doctor looked at John in surprise, as if he'd forgotten he was there, though how, Thomas couldn't imagine: the bearded man dwarfed the chair he sat on and leaned heavily on the table with his elbows.

"You'd better get used to it pretty quickly, Ernie, or you'll never get any sleep."

"I suppose you'd be accustomed to the noisy life, with your background," said Ernie. Thomas wasn't quite sure what he meant by this, but while Ernie's puffy eyes looked at George and winked, and George continued smirking, John just stared at the table and turned his coffee cup around twice in his big hands before getting up and loping from the room.

AFTER BREAKFAST, THE MEN gathered their equipment and set off in high spirits with a clatter of jars and collecting boxes. Their young guide, Paulo, had shown up on the doorstep that morning. The ever-efficient George Sebel had spoken with Santos's man, Antonio, about obtaining a full-time guide who could assist in the catching of errant specimens and who could also carry equipment, and this boy seemed to please him. He was about sixteen, with bronze skin, downy hair on his face, and long thin legs, like a deer's. His doe eyes looked at them shyly through long eyelashes.

Even John seemed to have forgotten his mood, and swung his machete as he stalked ahead of them, humming to himself. They made a racket as they entered the forest—probably scaring off any life-forms within a mile—but Thomas knew they would settle down once they were deep inside. He surprised himself by chattering to the others; he couldn't slow himself down. They must have made a curious sight—four white men and the darker-skinned guide. George Sebel and Ernie Harris each carried shotguns, and the bespectacled George's waistcoat and immaculate shirt and collar looked stiff and out of place. In deference to the heat, Thomas wore a simple light cotton shirt, with his fishing vest over the top—useful for carrying pins and boxes—and a soft felt hat. The others carried bags filled with their equipment—in addition to jars and boxes, they had wads of cotton, different sizes of paper and shot, and pincushions. From experience Thomas knew pins could leap out of a cushion and prick the fingers of an unsuspecting collector, which was why he carried his pins rolled on a piece of cotton in one of his many pockets.

"Are you not intending to catch any birds and bring them back alive, Ernie?" asked Thomas.

"Good heavens, man, not yet! I can't be bothered looking after the bloody things. Easier just to shoot them and skin them on the spot. I'm hoping our man here will help me carry them back."

Paulo walked on ahead, oblivious to the fact that they were talking about him.

"I say," said Ernie, and he tapped the boy on the shoulder with the barrel of his gun. The boy spun around and dropped to the ground, shooting his leg out and knocking Ernie off his feet. He fell heavily.

"Bloody hell!" he roared. "What did he do that for?"

"He thought you were threatening him with your gun, you idiot," said George, adjusting his glasses to peer down at the prone doctor. "You can't go around pointing it at people like that."

"It's not even bloody loaded yet!" said Ernie as he got to his feet, puffing—the wind was nearly knocked out of him. He stooped to pick up some paper that had fallen out of his bag.

Paulo's widened eyes were shrinking back to their normal size. He looked from one man to the other, saw that John had stopped and turned, and was suppressing a laugh. Paulo broke into a wide smile. *"Ele não vai me matar?"* he said.

"Não, o idiota não vai te matar," replied John, towering above the boy.

The others looked at John in surprise.

"What did you say to him?" asked Ernie. But John had already turned his back and was trudging ahead of them swinging his machete with his long arms.

"You didn't tell us you could speak Portuguese, John," said Thomas.

John paused for a moment and turned. "You didn't ask," he said, and continued on his way. The young man ran to catch up

with him, and Thomas could hear him chattering up at John, elic-
iting the odd low response.

As they left the road, the forest became as dark as dusk, despite
the clear morning. The sun fell only in thin chinks through the tops
of the trees. The terrain undulated between low patches of swamp
and drier ground. Small streams crossed their path but most of
these they could leap with one step; others had one or two stones to
guide their way across.

George Sebel struggled with all of his equipment, even with Paulo's help. He had no free hands to take his hat off and mop his brow,
so he had to keep stopping.

"Look," he said finally, "can somebody give me a hand?"

Thomas stepped forward to relieve him of his game bag.

"You *will* carry a ridiculous amount of gear, Sebel," said Ernie.
"What are you planning to catch?"

"Everything. Insects, snakes, frogs. Lizards and whatnot. The
more we catch, the more we get paid. I'm still going to study the coleoptera, I'm just branching out in my collecting."

"But you're not seriously going to try and collect all of these things
on one day, are you? The *first* day?"

"Never miss an opportunity, Ernest," said George. "You should
know that by now. What if Thomas here were to find his butterfly
out on a stroll and he had nothing with which to catch the thing? I
didn't come back from Africa with so many species by being un-
prepared, you know."

George's face was fixed as if he could smell something distaste-
ful, when the only odors present were the hot, sweet smell of the
jungle and the sandy earth. Perhaps a thin wisp of cooking from
the outskirts of the town. When George turned away from him,
Ernie grunted and pulled a face behind his back, making Thomas
smile.

They came to a faint fork in the path, and John turned around and called out to them. "Here, you three, take Paulo. I'm going on by myself." He veered off through the trees.

"Are you sure, John?" called Thomas, but the man was gone, into the shadows. Paulo fell into silence again, robbed of the one person who could speak his language. Even the boisterous Ernie was quiet, listening instead to the calls of the birds high in the trees.

Soon they came upon a small clearing. A brick well stood in the middle, strangled by creepers. Thomas tripped and reached out to steady himself on the slim trunk of a tree. Immediately his hand was covered with huge ants, tracing ticklish circles on his skin, advancing up his sleeve.

"Ants!" he cried to anyone who would listen. He jerked his hand away, cursed and shook his hands as if they were wet. Ants fell to the ground like shiny gemstones.

Ernie stood by and laughed. "I'm sure George could tell you exactly what kind of ant that is, Tom." But George had stopped behind them a distance and was crouching on the ground, trying to catch something.

A sudden sting under his cuff told Thomas he hadn't rid himself of all of the insects. An angry red mark was blooming already on his wrist. Paulo came and took his hand and Thomas allowed himself to be examined.

"*Não foi nada*," said the boy, and dropped the hand, looking bored.

"What?" said Thomas. "Ernie, what did he say? Will I be all right?"

"He doesn't look too concerned. I'm sure you'll be fine." Ernie took his turn looking at it. "Just a little sting. Nothing to worry about. If it itches I can give you something for it later."

The ants had taken all of Thomas's attention, but he soon realized that the little clearing swarmed with butterflies. With the extra light, he could make out individual facets of the forest. In the gloom the tree trunks had been columns of shadows, but now each stood out with its own shape and texture; bark by turns scaly, smooth, and gray, or with lethal spikes. Their roots—one of which he had tripped on—snaked out around the ground and climbing plants wound up the trees like boa constrictors. High above them, past the bushy wigs of epiphytes, the roof of the forest soared like the green stained-glass ceiling of a cathedral. The outlines were sharp. Thomas laid a hand on his chest to calm the quickening beat of his heart.

He became acutely aware of the sounds around him: hisses, whistles, and cries—every few seconds the distant crack of a falling branch. The floor was alive with ants and he glimpsed beetles threading themselves through the tree roots and pieces of rotting fruit. A brown snake slunk away from them in the direction they had come.

A cackling birdcall sounded and Ernie snapped his head up, attentive, tilting his head to determine its direction.

"Can you wait here for me for a moment?" He ducked off at a run into the trees.

Thomas took his hat off and fanned himself, suddenly overwhelmed by the humidity. His shirt clung to his back. Paulo was looking at him quizzically.

"Yes, go with him," said Thomas. He flicked his fingers in Ernie's direction. "I'll be fine."

The boy understood and jogged after him. George, deprived of his guide, stood and, after brushing off his still tidy clothes, followed, with barely a glance in Thomas's direction.

Thomas wiped his brow. He felt strangely awake. His heart was still beating quickly in his chest—too quickly for the leisurely walk it had taken to get there. His limbs felt restless and he shook them one by one, shaking out the kinks of a short night's sleep on a bowed bed.

He crossed to the well and, after checking for ants, leaned against it to see which of the butterflies would come to him. One or two flittered past—a bold blue *Morpho* and a brown skipper, whose mushroom wings flashed purple every now and then as they caught the light. They made no sound. He couldn't bring himself to study chirping crickets or cicadas—great winged beetles that buzzed past his ear. It was the butterfly that sneaked up on him; its soft wings produced not even a rush of air as it passed. He could pluck one out of his net and hold out his hand; it would sit still for a moment, dazed, then launch itself with barely a tickle from his hand to the nearest flower.

Then there was the excitement of the chase—waiting for its descent if out of reach, the creeping walk, net ready as it settles on a flower. He must become as silent as the butterfly in order not to startle it.

He enjoyed his moment of solitude—without the boisterous ramblings of Ernie or the terse, tight-lipped replies of George. Only John seemed to share his love of silence—amazing, really, that a man so big could move through the jungle barely snapping a twig.

The sun was climbing higher in the sky; he could see it winking through the tall palms. It was getting hotter. His wet shirt clung to his back now and he took a sip of water from his bottle. It tasted like metal. From somewhere nearby came the boom of a shotgun—Ernie's collection had begun.

A delicate, creamy butterfly—possibly an *endymion* but he couldn't be sure—flapped lazily past him, with its stardust wings catching the light. He pushed himself off the well and crept after it. When it alighted on a curved flower with clinging moisture pooled inside it, he readied his net. He swiped; the net opened out and received the butterfly.

"Come here, little thing," said Thomas. He carefully turned it out into one of his killing jars, lined with plaster of Paris mixed with a few drops of cyanide. The butterfly flicked around inside the jar. He knew it would soon be dead and hoped it didn't damage itself in the meantime. When it was still, he carefully opened the jar and

drew it out with tweezers, his cork-lined collecting box at the
ready. He settled the thorax into the groove cut in the cork and
pinned it. For a moment the butterfly seemed to rise and fall in a
sigh and he let his little fingertip linger on its soft wing.

He always felt a pang of guilt when he killed a butterfly, but he
hoped it wasn't a painful death. There was no other way to study
them, really. He could keep them in jars until they died of their own
accord, but he then ran the risk of the butterflies being damaged, of
age wearing tears into the delicate wings. This way, when he mounted
it, then identified it properly, labeled it, and sent it back to England,
the specimen would be perfect.

Before long, he had collected ten butterflies, including two more
Helicopis endymion, which he had found clinging to the underside of
a heart-shaped leaf, and a swallow-tailed *Papilio*. He sat back on the
well and gazed up at the giant *Morpho rhetenor* gliding in the treetops. As they flapped occasionally, their wings gave off a wild blue
flash that Thomas was sure he would spot half a mile away if the forest wasn't so dense. He felt a small sense of loss; a feeling that they
would never come down and he would never be able to reach them.

A crashing sound alerted him to George and Ernie's return. Harris carried several paper-wrapped parcels in his arms. Blood was
smeared across them like ink. Paulo, whose face was solemn, held
out a cone of paper to Thomas, who peered inside. Tiny dead birds—
hummingbirds—were piled inside it like sweet treats, their colors
sharp. The shot that Ernie had used was so fine there was barely a
mark on them.

"*Estão mortos.*" Paulo looked mournfully at his little package.

"He couldn't understand why I was skinning them," said Ernie.
"I think he wanted me to take the meaty carcasses with us, for food.
He got quite upset when I dumped them on the ground. A waste, I
suppose. Those ants will make short work of them. I bet if we went
back they'd all be picked clean." He stopped. "I say, old boy," he
said. "Are you *that* pleased to see us?"

Thomas realized with a shudder that Ernie was staring at his groin, a look of amusement on his face. He snatched his hat off his head and held it in front of him. George looked away, blushing, and found something interesting to look at a few paces away in the undergrowth. He beckoned Paulo to squat with him.

"I don't know what you mean," said Thomas. He took the opportunity to change the subject. "But I've been feeling a bit peculiar since that ant bite."

"In what way?" Ernie was standing in front of him now, piling the birds into his bag and adjusting his shotgun over his shoulder.

"Everything seems to be louder, sharper. I feel restless and—"

"And your heart seems to be beating faster?"

"Yes," said Thomas. "What is it? Some kind of poison?"

"Well, I don't know what it has to do with the activity downstairs, Tom, but I'd say you've had too much coffee! Not to mention—how many lumps of sugar did you put in it?"

"About three. Well, it was bitter!"

"Ha!" Ernie slapped Thomas's back and sent him forward a pace to steady himself. "There's your answer, Tom. You don't have coffee very often, I take it? Never mind, keep it up and you soon won't notice much change. I suggest you have another dose tomorrow. It wasn't unpleasant, was it?"

"No, I guess not. Just strange."

"Careful, you'll become addicted! Especially if that's the effect it has on you!" He glanced at where Thomas's hat was still clasped in front of him.

Thomas felt himself redden. "Nonsense," he muttered.

Ernie turned to Paulo, who had lost interest in George and his beetles. *"Café,"* he said to him, and brought an imaginary cup to his lips, then pointed at Thomas. Then he set his hands vibrating and jittered his head around. Paulo laughed.

"Ele bebeu café demais? Que engraçado!"

"Quite right," said Ernie. "Look, chaps, I think we should turn back now. It's going to be the hottest part of the day soon; I think you'll find all the birds and insects will go into hiding, and so should we."

Thomas took a last longing look at the blues gliding in the tree-tops and turned with his companions toward home.

THOMAS KNEW THAT HIS time in the jungle would never be as sweet as those first few days. Every discomfort—his creaky hammock, the oppressive humidity, the strange food prepared by the black cook Antonio had hired for them, and the relentless attack of mosquitoes and gnats—was overpowered by the devastating beauty of the rain forest and all that he found within it.

They quickly established a routine. They rose just after dawn, drank coffee, which seemed to be in abundance, then strolled around the forest collecting specimens until two or three in the afternoon.

Thomas liked nothing better than the peacefulness of stalking a butterfly, when he could disappear into the jungle and into his thoughts for hours at a time. He never left the established paths, but he sometimes managed to go all morning without seeing another soul. Occasionally he would pass a native hut by a stream, and a tribe of children would line up to stare at him as he passed.

Even having George near, digging into trees and squatting gingerly in the undergrowth so as not to dirty himself looking for beetles, was harmonious. Ernie would inevitably disturb their peace if he was close, ribbing them and blasting away with his gun, not caring how soiled his clothes got with blood and guts, but John also preferred to collect on his own and the men would often go all day without seeing him.

The heat in the afternoon became oppressive, and while their neighbors slept away the worst of it, Thomas and his companions rested under the shade of the veranda's awning and discussed their day's finds, drinking coffee and smoking cigarettes, which Thomas had recently taken to. It was Ernie who had started him off, when George's new team of boys—dark-eyed Indian children—began to carry things and to hunt for him. George paid them well, and there would be knocks on the door at any time of the day with shouts of *"Olha que flor bonita!"* or *"Uns lagartos pra vocês!"* which Thomas soon learned, through their daily Portuguese lessons from Antonio, was alerting them to a flower, or a handful of lizards that the boys had hunted out. One day they arrived with a boa constrictor in a cage, and Thomas reluctantly helped George lift it onto the porch.

Ernie stood by, leaning against the doorframe, smoking.

"What a magnificent taxidermy project for you, George," said Ernie. His pink lips quivered beneath his mustache. "I'll help you." George made a point of ignoring him. While Ernie was expert at stuffing, it was something George was yet to master, and he didn't like to be reminded of the fact.

"Smoke?" Ernie held the packet out to Thomas.

"You know I don't," said Thomas, annoyed that Ernie seemed to be teasing him for his discomfort. He had imagined the boa tightening itself around his chest and found himself short of breath. He could hear the creature's lungs, like bellows, a deep wheezing whistle, and its great black head seemed to be looking straight at him.

"Calms your nerves, old man," said Ernie. "Trust me, I'm a doctor." He took one out of the packet and held it out to him.

Thomas took it and rolled it around between his fingers. He didn't want Ernie to think his nerves needed calming, but the doctor was already striking a match and holding it out for him. He put the cigarette tentatively to his lips and let Ernie touch the end of it with his flame. He sucked at it, careful not to shock his lungs by inhaling straightaway. Clouds of smoke billowed in front of his face and went up his nose. He took the cigarette out of his mouth and sneezed.

They sat down while George negotiated a fee for the children, who gestured and shrieked in their excitement. Thomas inhaled carefully at first, but became bolder as a pleasant buzzing filled his head. There was something about Ernie—the way he sat with his legs crossed and the cigarette in his hand, his rakish hairstyle, which was never quite tidy, and his easy charm—that for a moment Thomas coveted. He crossed his legs as well, and studied the way Ernie held his cigarette, not scissored between his first and second fingers, but pinched between his thumb and forefinger, using them like tweezers. He did the same and inhaled once more. The smoke drifted from the end of the cigarette into his eyes and they twitched and squinted.

"Now all we need is . . ." Ernie reached into his jacket pocket and drew out a silver hip flask. He toasted Thomas with it—"Here's to us"—and took a swig. He held it out to Thomas.

The whiskey scorched his throat but seemed to make a natural companion to the smoke from the cigarette, which was burned down to a thin pinch of paper and a few curly strands of tobacco. He pulled a piece off his lips and another from the tip of his tongue.

"I could grow accustomed to this," he said.

"That's my man," said Ernie, and gave him a hearty slap on the back.

AS THE WEEKS WORE on, talk turned to speculation about their benefactor. They hadn't met him yet; nor had Antonio given them an indication of when they might. They began to imagine what sort of a man Santos might be. Ernie pictured him as a huge oaf who couldn't speak English and had more money than intelligence. He puffed out his cheeks and lurched around the veranda, grunting, to make his point. George said he was sure Mr. Santos was perfectly sophisticated; that he was a man who loved the rain forest and wanted to share its riches with the world. John concluded that perhaps he was a man up to no good; that he was only putting them up in order to placate the British directors of his company so they wouldn't ask too many questions. Thomas laughed at John's cynicism. It seemed ill-fitting in his quiet personality; but then, it was delivered as dry as the bread they ate every morning for breakfast, and he was beginning to learn that he couldn't imagine what John was thinking, no matter what his tongue was saying.

For his own part, Thomas pictured Santos as a kind and gentle if somewhat parochial man, with a handlebar mustache, who had recently come into a large sum of money due to the explosion of the rubber market, and who was putting it to good use.

The local children seemed fascinated by the idea of the rubber baron, who even wended his way into their games. One of them would stomp around with a straight back, pushing his chest out and setting his face a fierce grimace, while the other children chanted, "Santos, Santos!" But when the designated child put his fingers to his head to resemble horns, Antonio chased the little group away with a sharp word, and in their squeals Thomas couldn't help wonder if he heard genuine fright.

They always dined at four o'clock, with the cook complaining in croaky Portuguese that he had to work through the hottest part of the day for their dinner. The meal invariably consisted of beef, which seemed to be the only type of meat available to them, despite the chickens and pigs Thomas saw roaming the streets among broken fence posts. Every meal was always finished with bananas and oranges, which were in constant supply, and Thomas often went out walking with two or three pieces of fruit stuffed into his bag among his equipment. He found that a blackened banana, squashed and left on a log, so that its fermented aroma was released, was useful in attracting certain lofty butterflies that until then he had only gazed at from below.

They spent the evenings preserving their collections and making notes, often while the last of the afternoon deluge—which struck most days—faded away, and they received regular invitations to dine with other British citizens in Belém—traders mostly, but the British consulate also put on a formal dinner for them.

They walked into town down a long avenue lined with silk cotton trees, heavy with balled red flowers like Christmas decorations. Many of the larger houses had fallen into disrepair; stucco crumbled from whitewashed walls, and red roof tiles lay shattered on the ground where they had fallen off. A kind of faded grandeur had settled over the city. Thomas drank too much wine at the consul's house and had to be put to bed by Ernie. He had a dim recollection of his half-walk back through the sandy streets of Belém, past low houses with no windows, and the jeers and laughter of the people who sat outside them. He woke up the next day with a heavy weight in his head. He was appalled to find that he had vomited on himself, made worse by the fact that Ernie lay in his hammock and complained about the smell.

The little house was beginning to resemble a museum. Ernie's stuffed birds crouched on top of the bookshelves; others lay neatly in rows in the boxes he had brought with him, their feet tucked under them and their bodies in a sleek diving pose. Although he preserved most of his smaller specimens in jars of formaldehyde, George had also stuffed some iguanas and other lizards, inexpertly. They had so much stuffing they appeared fatter than they should have been, and all their wrinkles were smoothed out, like old women with babies' skin. Ernie offered to help him, but he refused, and concentrated on his beetles instead.

Thomas awoke one morning to find that his first batch of butterflies was smothered with ants, and there was little left of the pristine insects he had caught. The others had already had trouble with rats and mice, so a complicated system of booby traps was set up, with the aid of George, who said he had lost many a specimen in his early days.

They hung drying cages from the rafters, and covered the ropes that held them with a bitter vegetable oil to deter the ants. This didn't stop the mice from running down the ropes and attacking whatever was in the cage, so they hung inverted bowls halfway down the ropes. This prevented the rats and mice from having a decent running surface, and they had nowhere to go but back up the rope.

Sometimes they pulled their tables outside and worked in companionable silence, pinning insects or painting intricate likenesses of their collections for their journals. The garden was alive with dripping flowers; hummingbirds flitted between them like fat bumblebees; dark-haired girls adorned with gold earrings collected blossoms on the side of the road and waved to them. George, still clad stiffly in his waistcoat and jacket, when the other men had long since stripped down to simple flannel shirts, turned his back to the women when they walked past, but Ernie was quick to smile and wink. Even John, on the few occasions he joined them, would call out one or two words of greeting in Portuguese. Thomas just watched, feeling the warmth of the coffee spread through his blood, and the tingling in his face from the cigarettes. On afternoons such as this he couldn't imagine ever leaving Belém.

One evening, they were caught in the daily downpour, and the rain came down in impenetrable sheets. They huddled under the branches of a low tree beside a great tract of cleared forest that had been burned away; what remained of the charred trunks of trees protruded like cancerous bones from the brown landscape. Great muddy pools lay like dark stains on the earth. Thomas could only stand and stare through the roar of the rain and hope that all of the life inside had escaped from the torching, but even as the rain began to ease, he saw a small, torn red butterfly floating a delicate circle inside a blackened puddle.

Belém, November 15th, 1903

I've not written in this journal for a few days. Between collecting, preserving, and documenting, there seems to be little time for writing in here, even writing letters. Poor Sophie must be hungry for news of me, but other than a description of my catches, which I fear will bore her, there is little to tell.

I have told her about the boa constrictor, but have left out my shameful experience with too much wine.

It is imperative, I know, to keep this journal up, for didn't the great explorers and collectors keep meticulous records not only of their bounty, but of their personal experiences on the Amazon? Perhaps one day my experiences will be published. Edited, of course. Perhaps I will be considered to be a pioneer of natural history, too. But no. I must not say perhaps. I will be a great explorer. I will make my name on this journey or be doomed to an insignificant life, my only excitement a little roast beef on Sunday. I am not stupid. I am aware of my shortcomings in the field of scientific knowledge. But I will rise above them as soon as I bring home a magnificent *Papilio sophia.*

We have been here now nearly four weeks. I could easily stay here for a year—there are about 700 different species of butterfly around Belém, compared with only 66 in the whole of England! I estimate that I have caught and documented only half of these so far. I have had better luck with catching some of the high fliers—one of the boys that hangs around and helps us showed me how a bright blue rag is most useful in attracting the male *Morpho rhetenor* (but not the female, strangely). I leave it draped over a plant and it comes down to investigate, whereby I step out from my hiding place and voilà! It is mine. My hands were shaking so much the first time that I missed it, so excited was I at seeing it up close.

I have also fashioned a long-handled net, but this is terribly awkward to carry around with me. It is twenty feet long, and I can't walk through the forest without banging into things and inevitably bruising myself. When I do use it, it is cumbersome to wave about, too, although I have managed to catch one or two slow-moving female *rhetenors* with it. How dull they are compared with their mates! No iridescent blue for them, but a turgid brown. On their own, they may be considered attractive enough, but with a mate so beautiful, they cannot help but feel like the dowdy wife of a handsome dandy, I'm sure.

When I first arrived, I thought that I should never be able to catch one of these lofty species. Now that I have, I see that anything is within my grasp. Anything!

John is anxious to move on. Last night he put into words what we all knew in our hearts—Belém is not the Amazon rain forest. We are too close to civilization. My walks through the forest are often interrupted with the cloying presence of man, whether in the sounds of shouting from some neighbors' dispute, or the devastating rape of the beautiful forest to make way for the progress of the city. While John has found more than twenty specimens of palms alone, all with distinct native names, he often stands very still and looks to the northwest, as if listening for the depths of the forest calling his name. While I am not sure that I will necessarily find such an abundance of lepidoptera upriver, I do know that the only sightings of my giant butterfly have been near Manaus, not down this far. Therefore, as much as I am stimulated here, I am impatient to move on also.

Ernie, too, complains that the most exotic birds do not exist so close to a city, although he has learned where to find them. When we first arrived he seemed to catch only the smaller and more common birds. Now he brings back exotic parrots and toucans and macaws. He is establishing a fine collection.

We have prepared our first consignment to send to Mr. Ridewell—at last count we had 323 species of lepidoptera (butterflies mostly—I confess that moths hold little interest for me, and George collected most of them), 400-odd beetles, 32 different species of bird, some lizards and snakes, and nine chests of plants, with countless dried seeds. Ernie plans to take live specimens back at the end of the trip. He wants to be able to accompany them, and he will dispose of them at various zoos with which he is in regular contact.

Nobody has taken to collecting the numerous great spiders that are about the place. There is one—a ghastly hairy thing it is—called a mygale, of which there are many different species. One of them spins a thick web between two trees and catches small birds in it. I have never seen such a thing as a finch, quite dead, covered with some kind of venom, while another struggles to free itself. One wants to help, but we know that we can't interfere with nature in this way; besides, who knows what state it would have been in had I freed it? I can't help but feel ill when I see these spiders, and whenever I do it takes me longer than usual to get to sleep at night. I have taken to greasing my hammock strings with the same vegetable oil we use to deter the ants. I haven't spoken of this (rather irrational, I know) fear, but I suspect the others feel the same, otherwise why have none of them caught any?

When Antonio arrived to give us Portuguese lessons this afternoon, we talked to him about our desire to move on. He has agreed that it is time, and that we are ready to meet our benefactor. We are to leave for Santarém next week, where we will at last meet our Mr. Santos, who lives in Manaus, and then we will progress into little-charted depths. We would have met Mr. Santos earlier, said Antonio, but he has been delayed upriver by some troublesome native rubber workers.

I sense that it is only a matter of time before my beautiful butterfly comes to me. I will hold it in my hands more gently than I would a lover. It will be my key to greatness; more important, it will belong to me.

THREE

Richmond, May 1904

B Y T H E S L A N T O F the sun, Agatha judges that it is
nearly eleven. She clutches her elbow with a gloved
hand as she inhales the last of her cigarette, then tosses
it into the scrubby part of the flower bed where it will
never be found. Her other glove is in her pocket; she
takes it out and bangs it on her dress to rid it of any
tobacco smells, then returns it to her right hand.

She promised Sophie she would visit today, but the
thought of running into Thomas again repels her. That
first time she saw him, after his long absence, he seemed
to slither along the walls. His newly rough features held
a chilling vacancy. She wanted to steal Sophie away
from the source of her pain.

No—she is being cruel. Her grandmother would
have said that Thomas had been taken by spirits. Agatha has heard of it happening before—people moving
around as if they live on this earth, while their ears and
hearts are focused on another realm. And he did have
about him the air of one who is not fully occupying the

world. He stared off into the corner of the room, as if watching something there. But when she forgot herself for a moment and made a light joke, his eyes found hers and quickly looked away; he heard her, all right, but something prevented him from reacting to the world around him. Poor Sophie looked at that point as if she might cry.

Maybe she is not imagining his snakelike quality. Just as she told Sophie that the deer she encountered in the park would stay with her, perhaps Thomas met with a snake in the jungle. They probably crossed his path willy-nilly—there would have been no getting away from them. But no. Her grandmother led her to believe that animals are good spirits, not bad ones that would rob a man of his ability to speak and thereby devastate his wife. Unless he has done something to deserve it.

She shakes this thought off immediately. Not Thomas—he wouldn't hurt a fly. She smiles. Because he *does* hurt flies, doesn't he? And beetles. Even the butterflies he professes to love so much. The first thing he does when he catches them is pinch their little bodies until they die, or drop them in a jar with poison until they suffocate to death.

She sighs and closes her eyes to the strengthening sun. She *has* always liked Thomas, if just for the fact that he makes Sophie so happy. Despite his murderous tendencies toward insects—she isn't naive, she knows it's all in the name of science—he has a light touch with his wife; when they are together his hand on her waist seems to make Sophie float. He brings out a maternal instinct in the women around him—even in Agatha. She was with him one day when he tripped on the road and she had an urge to kiss the graze on his palm better. Thomas mistook her hand on his and the look in her eye for something far more inappropriate and jumped to his feet, his face exploding with color. She laughed at him then; she couldn't help it.

Agatha hides her cigarette case in her little purse, adjusts her new hat, which she decorated herself last week with silk flowers, and sets out for Sophie's house. She feels a little guilty that she doesn't plan to stay long; she has used Sophie as an excuse to leave the house, but she plans to spend the afternoon with Robert.

Mary answers the door and shows her to the parlor. Sophie's cheeks are pale when she looks up. Agatha wonders how long it has been since she has taken one of her daily walks. She wears her dowdiest blouse and skirt of coarse cotton that verges on hessian; Agatha supposes she has recently returned from church. Her knees are probably rubbed raw from kneeling and praying for her husband. Her hair is scraped into a tight bun, quite out of step with the current fashion, and it gives her the look of a cruel schoolmistress. Agatha feels quite shocked; it's as if her friend is punishing herself.

Sophie seems too lethargic to even stand and welcome her, so Agatha bends to kiss her on the cheek and sits.

She leans forward. "So where is he?" she whispers.

"He's still having bed rest," says Sophie. "He gets up in the evenings and we dine together. But the doctor said he's to live quietly. To see if it . . ." She raises a hand to rub at an imaginary spot on her forehead. "To see if it helps his condition."

Agatha slumps back in her chair and lets her arms dangle off the sides. Sophie is enormously distracted; she hasn't even commented on her new hat. She usually teases her about whatever she wears.

"Sophie Bear. My Sophie Bear . . ." She doesn't continue.

Sophie nods, as if in answer to an unspoken question. "I'm fine. Just a little tired, that's all." She manages a weak smile, which broadens, falsely, as Mary brings the tea things in. "Thank you, Mary. Down here, please. I'll pour."

Mary backs out of the room. She seems to be trying to make herself as unobtrusive as possible and it's working. Agatha shoots her a sympathetic look and takes a cup, turning her attention back to Sophie. "What are you going to do? Do you have a plan?"

"Dr. Dixon said I should try to communicate with him by taking him to do the things he likes. Take him to the park."

"He hasn't been yet? But he was always there . . ."

"Yes, he was. But no, he hasn't been."

"And what about his brother? What about Cameron?"

"He's abroad. I've written to him, but as yet I've had no reply. But look, there's this." Sophie pulls a folded sheet of paper from the pocket of her skirt. It amazes Agatha, the things that Sophie produces from her pockets: a handkerchief, a letter, a book—she once saw an umbrella appear from seemingly nowhere and was inclined to think that Sophie had been keeping it hidden in her skirts.

It is a letter. Sophie hands it to Agatha, who immediately recognizes the mean, tight writing. "From your father," she says. "Did you tell him Thomas is back?"

Sophie nods. "I had to, really. He might have heard about it from somebody else. I wrote to him straightaway."

"And have you told him?"

"No! Heavens, no. Give him something else to disapprove of? Ugh. I couldn't bear it."

"So what did you tell him?"

"Well, naturally I told him that I had moved out of your house and back here."

"Ah yes, the White Lie." They thought of the lie—that Sophie had moved in with Agatha's family—as quelling Mr. Winterstone's anxiety. He wouldn't stand for having a daughter abandoned by her husband to live alone. But Agatha and Sophie both knew that if it was Sophie's welfare he had been concerned about, they wouldn't have lied to him; Sophie was convinced he was more worried about appearances than anything else. The thought of his daughter keeping house alone might enrage him. Anyway, it wasn't a complete lie: Sophie did spend a lot of time with Agatha's family; she even spent Christmas with them.

"But here's the problem, see." Sophie leans forward and taps the final paragraph of the letter. "He wants to visit. The day after tomorrow."

Agatha reads it out loud. *"I am interested in discussing Thomas's expedition with him."* She looks up. "Oh hell."

Sophie flinches.

"Sorry," says Agatha. "What are you going to do?"

"I don't know. I didn't expect to have to deal with this so soon. I mean, he *never* visits. Kingston is only a few miles away, but he just never seems to have the time."

"And he never issues invitations to you."

"Precisely."

"What will he do?"

"If Thomas still isn't speaking?"

Agatha pauses. How naive Sophie can be, how optimistic. That she even thinks there is a chance Thomas will be speaking in two days' time makes her want to jump up and hug her. "Yes," she says.

"Well, in the worst situation, I suppose he might order me to come home and insist that Thomas goes to a hospital. But then again, what kind of a scandal would that cause? I doubt he would tolerate that. Perhaps he will ignore the problem. Maybe he will turn his back on us forever." She takes the letter back from Agatha and begins to fold it into smaller and smaller squares. Her hands shake and some color is creeping back into her face.

"Don't be angry with him yet," says Agatha. "You don't know that he'll desert you."

"Yes," says Sophie. "I'm letting my imagination run away. It seems too real sometimes. You're right. Perhaps he'll turn out to be kind about Thomas after all."

"What'll you do in the meantime?"

"Follow Dr. Dixon's advice, of course. I plan to take him for a walk this afternoon."

"And you think this will help?"

Sophie sighs again. It settles over Agatha. The weight of it presses on her shoulders.

"I don't know, Aggie. What do you think?"

Agatha sips her tea and takes a bite from a muffin. "I think . . ." Her mouth is full, but she presses on. "What about dancing?"

This elicits a smile from Sophie. "Thomas didn't dance very well before!"

"Well, there you go!" says Agatha, pleased she has at last raised some mirth. "He'll probably be much better at it now!" She reaches out and touches Sophie's knee. "We'll get him to talk, darling, don't you worry."

"I don't know if it's just a matter of getting him to talk, as you say. There's something that has silenced him, and I need to find out how to get him back. To get my Thomas back." Her face becomes suddenly red, and the tears follow.

Agatha realizes she has been uncharitable in thinking of Thomas as a snake. It's not his fault; the man is very ill. She only identified him as the cause of Sophie's suffering and reacted badly. He is more like an infant, a burden on her poor friend. She must do everything she can to help.

But not this afternoon. She is already walking toward Robert in her mind, planning the secret route he showed her from the park, which will take her past the ugly old crows that loiter by the wall and through a rotting gate into his garden. She knows that Sophie saw their exchange in church that day, and Agatha has waited for her to say something, or to start asking questions. She might even have told her if she wanted to know. But now her friend has too many other things on her mind.

Besides, the room is oppressive. There is no hint that it is a beautiful morning outside; the curtains are nearly closed. "It's no wonder you're feeling so gloomy, Bear." Agatha stands and crosses to the window. She tugs at the drapes, letting a wash of light fall into the room. "And now I really must be going. I promised Mother I would help her with her sewing."

And she will. Later.

. . .

SOPHIE STANDS OVER HER sleeping husband. His tanned skin is reverting back to its paleness—too pale, really, but it could be the gloomy light of the bedroom. He sleeps on his back, with a pile of pillows beneath his head and shoulders, so that his body is bowed. His arms lie outside the bedclothes, and below the sleeves of his nightshirt his hands are still red and callused. The wound on his arm is beginning to heal, and soon she will remove the bandage altogether. His face is turned to one side. Even in sleep his lips are neatly pursed. His hair is beginning to curl awkwardly around his ear, which protrudes less obviously now that his face is filling out somewhat. He hasn't lost his appetite at least; he eats the soup she brings him every day, and in the evening has been devouring a good-sized plate of meat and cheese and bread for supper. And yet he still looks deflated somehow, hollowed out. There is an air of sadness about him, even as he sleeps.

She misses him more than she did when he was in Brazil. At least when he was there she knew he was thinking about her—to begin with, anyway—and she could imagine him moving through the rain forest with strong legs, his face crinkled with concentration. The day she saw him off at the station, he pulled her onto the train with him and embraced her in his empty compartment. When the whistle blew, she had to disentangle herself from his arms; the train had started to move as she opened the door and jumped back onto the platform. She was left with the smell of peppermints in her hair and the sight of his bright face at the window.

Thomas jerks awake and for a moment she thinks he is going to smile at her, but his face remains expressionless, his head fixed to the pillow. Only his eyes dart about, as if looking for the other people she might have brought into the room with her.

"Let's go for a walk in the park," she says. "It's a lovely afternoon."

Her husband draws back the bedclothes to let himself out of the bed. His thin legs, she notes, are also scarred from the insect bites. The golden hairs are caught in a chink of light from the window and they seemed to sparkle. He stands firmly on his feet—he has been kept fit with a turn around the garden every evening before supper. Sophie will not have her husband a cripple as well as a mute.

"I'll leave you to get dressed," she says.

AS THEY STROLL UP the Terrace, toward the park entrance, Sophie becomes aware of another problem; one she hadn't even thought of before now. People nod at them as they pass. Some of them avert their eyes. She dreads meeting somebody they really know: not just polite strangers, or those who have heard about the strange, silent young man who has returned from the Amazon, but people from church. She's glad they live in a reasonably big town, not a tiny village. She can sometimes go days without seeing people she knows, and on the weekends, the place is full of Londoners, so she can further sink into the background.

They make it to the park without seeing a familiar face. Thomas's gait is slow at first, a shuffling amble, as she imagines a sloth might move. As they pass through the gate, walking without touching, Sophie feels a cool breeze on her face. It reaches inside her and lifts her spirits. She feels it like a finger tracing circles in her abdomen. She leads him up the path toward the shady wood, where Thomas used to collect beetles and where she knows they are less likely to come across any people.

Thomas has picked up his pace, and she feels her muscles stretch as she keeps in step with him. She misses her own walks. She doesn't like to leave him for too long, in case he needs her, or in case he decides to speak and there is nobody there but Mary to hear him. She spends only a few minutes in the church, early each morning, before he wakes up. Mary is under instructions to come and get her if he shows any change, but so far her visits have gone undisturbed.

I need to talk to him, she thinks. What can I talk about?

"Do you remember, Thomas, the first time I went beetling with you?" She doesn't wait for an answer. "And how bitterly I complained! You promised me a picnic that day, but you got so excited about finding that one—what was it, a stag?—that you forgot to eat, and you left me sitting there in the shade getting cold! But I soon learned, didn't I; I brought a book the next time."

They pass the fork in the path that winds around an oak tree and leads to the hidden hollow where Thomas once tried to make love to her. She places her hand on his arm again and lightly steers him down the path. Twigs crack and the sponge of rotten leaves springs under their feet. Sophie reaches out a hand and trails it over the brittle bark of the oak. Her fingers find tiny gorges and riverbeds in its texture, a landscape for a thousand insects. She pulls him to a stop in their secret spot. With the sound of their feet on the forest floor withdrawn, the silence rises up to meet them. Thomas closes his eyes, seeming to breathe it in through his pores as a frog might. The air is cool in the shade, the pillars of the forest trees robust and strong. Sophie realizes they have achieved absolute quiet. Always there is something that produces noise in their lives—whether the clipping of a horse and carriage, or the animal roar of a motor. Even in the sedate paths by the river, the water sluices the banks, licking at itself or the edge of a pier.

She kisses his cheek. It reminds her of when she was a girl and would kiss her father good night. There is a slackness to the skin, and yet the flesh is unyielding, and doesn't press itself to her lips as she has learned that a lover's would, or even a friend's. Nanny would bring her into her father's study every evening—the only contact she had with him all day. She stood by his chair and told him what she had learned that day, before leaning forward with her warm breath and planting her offering on his waiting cheek. He would turn his back on her then and it was time for Nanny to take her hand and lead her away. She would look back, hoping that her father would turn, just once, and give her a secret smile to hold on to and to carry to her bed. But all she saw was the cold mountain of his back bent over his desk, his hand scribbling madly, his daughter forgotten.

Thomas has not shaved for some time; a few red bristles poke through his skin, but his face is mostly covered with a fine down. It is the closest to a beard she has seen on him. When she pulls back from the kiss on his cheek, he will not meet her eyes; he is the same new frog—Thomas, not a prince. But he blushes a little and for a moment reverts back to the shy young man she first met at the fete on the river. There was a tea dance at the Star and Garter, where he stood on her foot, twice, during the waltz. Later that evening, the riverside was lit up with lights and he asked to see her again. The lights were reflected in the ambling river. When he laid his hand over hers she felt as weightless as the Chinese lanterns lifting and turning in the summer breeze.

She decides to leave him for a moment and wanders over to the clearing in the trees, which gives her a view down the valley. She stood in this very spot once when she was a little girl and Nanny brought her to Richmond for the day. She accidentally got "lost" and found herself here as the sun sank behind Windsor Castle. She looked out at it, knowing that she was destined for great things—to marry a prince and live in the castle, perhaps. The Thames was a silver ribbon winding toward her. Now it is a river again, with rowboats dotted on its surface. She can make out the chimney of the Sunbury Waterworks and Eel Pie Island, where Nanny told her all the eel pies in England are made. To the left of the view, the smoke of Kingston-on-Thames, where she grew up, mingles with the blue haze of the distant Surrey Hills.

And now her father is coming to visit. She doesn't want him to find Thomas like this; she knows her father will be disappointed in her and see her once again as a burden. Her father has never taken much interest in her husband; he was anxious to marry her off early but hoped she would marry Thomas's older brother Cameron, who was the heir to their father's fortune. As the second son of a semiwealthy man, Thomas was provided with an allowance that was more than enough for them to live on, but modest. Sophie knew that her father thought the only way to be rid of all responsibility for her was to have her marry a man whose money would allow her to be surrounded by servants, and to have her every fancy catered for.

She turns and finds Thomas where she left him; he has sat himself down and is leaning against a tree with his eyes closed. She realizes as she walks toward him that for the first time his face appears to be relaxed. There is even a contented curl at the edges of his mouth. He is cured, she thinks. This is all he needed—a stroll in his beloved park.

She rushes to him and the rustle of her skirts and the crack of twigs beneath her feet make his eyes jerk open. He glares at her. It stops her in her tracks. Surely he isn't angry with her? She feels a stab of guilt that she has disturbed his peace. She has trampled on his domain. Sophie stands up straight and puts on a bright voice.

"Are we feeling better?" She immediately regrets her patronizing choice of words. "Are *you* feeling better, Thomas?"

She expects him to look away, despite her hopes. Instead, he stares up at her for a moment, and the glare softens. Then, she's not sure, but she *thinks* he gives a small nod.

"Darling!" She falls beside him and puts her arms around his neck. She expects him to mold to her shape. His cheek against hers is burning; she has forgotten the fire held in the body of another human being. But he remains stiff and Sophie realizes too late that she has made a mistake. She draws back. He is blushing and his hand grasps a handful of bark and dirt from the ground. He says nothing.

But it is a start, she tells herself. Isn't it a start?

. . .

TWO DAYS LATER, SOPHIE opens the door to her father. Charles Winterstone stands stiffly on the doorstep and, despite the warm day, wears a coat over his pale suit, and gloves. He pulls off his hat and nods.

"Sophie."

"Father. Please come in." She stands aside and he passes into the hallway. She catches a whiff of soap as he passes, is close enough to see a fresh shaving cut beneath his neatly trimmed beard.

"And where is Thomas?" asks her father as he deposits his hat onto the stand. "And that girl of yours?"

"Mary," says Sophie. "She has the morning off. The tea's all made." She could have set her clock by her father's arrival at eleven; she has never known him to be either late or early for any appointment. She had no fear of the tea getting cold while she waited for him.

In the drawing room, she finally answers his question.

"I'm afraid I have some bad news, Father. Thomas has been called away on urgent business. A telegram came for him this morning and he has had to go up to London to see somebody at the Natural History Museum."

"Oh, that is a pity," he says. "I don't think I can be back here for a number of weeks."

His voice seems light but his eyes accuse her. She shifts in her seat. A few weeks. She has bought some time, then.

"And Agatha's father? How is he?"

"Yes, good, I think."

"Did you thank him for letting you stay with him for so long? Perhaps I should thank him myself."

"That won't be necessary. The family knows I had a lovely time with them."

This is not a complete lie. She has spent plenty of time at their house, and Christmas was one of the most pleasurable holidays she can remember. There is a warmth in that house: a bond between Agatha, her parents, and her younger brother and sister. Agatha teases the young ones mercilessly, and the house is filled with their shrieks and shouts, and inevitably Mr. Dunne yelling after them to be quieter, but there is never anger in his voice. They never expected Agatha, once she was out and had courting prospects, to lose her wild ways. Sophie knows that many people in the neighborhood disapprove of Mr. Dunne and his half-Gypsy wife and their band of raucous children, but they are too tight-lipped to do anything but accept them.

Mr. Winterstone has to make do with asking Sophie about her husband's travels. Sophie, as best she can, makes up stories, based on the early letters she received from him.

"And did he find his butterfly? The one that would make him famous?" He leans forward eagerly. Hungrily, she thinks.

"No, he didn't."

"I see," says her father, and he leans back in his chair. His hunger appears sated. Sophie realizes with a plunging heart that this is what he wanted her to say; he has been waiting for her husband to fail in some way.

"At least," she blurts, "not that he has told me about. But I feel that the business he is attending to in London may be somehow related. He is quite secretive about it. Perhaps he is on the verge of an announcement and has had to keep it quiet."

"Perhaps." Her father strokes his beard and will not meet her eyes.

She remembers cold days in their house in Kingston, when they would tiptoe around each other, the hard hand of Nanny pulling her away from his study door. She always wondered how a woman so sinewy could have such a soft demeanor. She had no bosom to speak of, but when she pulled Sophie into an embrace, she fit as snugly as a key in a lock.

They finish their tea in near silence. Her father faces the fireplace and his gaze flicks up at the only photograph Sophie has of her mother. The woman has the look of one whose favorite rosebush has just been cut down; she is biting her narrow lip to will herself not to cry, but her eyes are defiant, planning revenge. The only memory Sophie has of her mother is a word; she can remember the feeling of "Mama" on her lips as a toddler, but she had nothing to apply it to. Eventually it lost all meaning and faded from her vocabulary.

Sophie tries to chat, but her father sits fortified behind his tiny cup. It is an inadequate defense, but somehow he uses it as the largest and strongest shield. On no account must any of her warmth penetrate him. She has an urge to laugh, but she stifles it and stands.

"Well, thank you for visiting, Father." She registers the relief in his face.

"Yes, yes," he says as he stands also. "I do have some business to attend to."

The business of brandy, she expects, up at the Star and Garter. She releases him from his misery. No—she releases them both.

After he has gone, she moves slowly up the stairs, a cup of tea in one hand, the other dragging itself on the banister. Thomas is asleep in the dim room. She pulls the curtains open and sets the tea down beside him.

"He's gone," says Sophie. "Thank you for being so quiet."

CAPTAIN SAMUEL FALE ALIGHTS from his cab at the entrance to the Star and Garter Hotel. He is meeting his old friend Sid Worthing, but plans to get there a little early to knock back a sly whiskey or two to help him cope with Sid's banter about his wonderful life. Not that Fale begrudges his friend his good fortune—Sid had taken some options in a Brazilian rubber company and is now enjoying the fruits of a remarkable boom—but he doesn't need to hear him drone on about it. About that, and about his pretty new wife, a silent Frenchwoman he picked up in his travels. She is a gorgeous specimen, no doubt about it, with a sweetly puckered face like a marigold; but Fale can't work out how he has made her so damned quiet—after all, aren't those Mediterranean types supposed to be hot-blooded and noisy? He rather thinks this is their attraction. Not that he wants one for himself—give him a straight-backed English girl any day—but he can't help but wonder what the point is. Perhaps her demureness is just for show and all that passion is repressed all day, to be let out at night.

He chuckles to himself at the thought of Sid—not the most agile of men now that his wealth has gone to his belly—wrestling under the sheets with a golden beauty. What a waste.

He pays the driver, who grumbles at the short distance from Fale's home. The captain feels his eyes on his back as he limps away, and he exaggerates the stiffness in his leg to rouse some sympathy from the rough young man. Surely he can see that he isn't about to walk here from his house with his injury. He hears the driver click his tongue to his horse and drive away.

The dining room is filling slowly, but it is nowhere near capacity. On the weekend, which had been unseasonably warm for late spring, there were close to six hundred for dinner. The Star and Garter is the fashionable place for Londoners to venture for the day—they often spend the morning at Kew, then make their way to Richmond and be home on the train or boat by suppertime. Fale missed out on his favorite spot and took tea on the terrace overlooking the river, which he found to be most pleasant. He closed his eyes and felt the sun beating down on his lids. When he opened them a fraction, and tiny slits of Italian Romanesque architecture loomed above him, he could fancy himself somewhere on the Italian Riviera, a place he had never been but had always wanted to go.

Fale takes his seat and orders a drink. The clinking of cutlery and the murmur of sparse conversation nibble at the edge of his consciousness. The smell of roast beef feeds his stomach's anticipation. He nods at the man at the next table, who nods back and returns his attention to his newspaper. He seems a very tall fellow; his long legs jut out the side as if he can't quite fit them under the table. His pale suit is crinkled and a black bowler sits on the table beside his elbow; a coat is draped over the back of his chair. He reminds Fale of a colonel he once served under, a huge man with an even larger voice and the same neat beard, who died under the hooves of a runaway horse when he pushed a young private out of its path. This resemblance gives Fale a respect—irrational, he knows—for this stranger, and suddenly he cares very much what the man thinks of him. He sits up straighter in his chair and, with his finger, checks his mustache for crumbs.

The waiter puts his drink down and moves on to the stranger's table.

As Fale takes a sweet sip of his whiskey the waiter says, "Will there be anything else, Mr. Winterstone?" The man, Winterstone, orders a brandy. Fale is disappointed to hear his voice, which is not booming as his colonel's was, and has no pretensions in the accent—pretensions that Fale himself maintains at all costs.

Winterstone, Winterstone. He knows the name, but can't place it. Fale takes in the long legs again, which put him in mind of a stork's. His shoulders are broad but fine, giving him proud, upright air. And those long legs . . .

Sophie.

He leans back casually and takes a cigarette from his silver case. He taps it twice on the tablecloth and lights it. He realizes he has been staring when Winterstone looks up and returns the gaze. Yes, there in his eyes is a further resemblance. They stare over the half-moon reading glasses, into Fale's heart, analyzing him. Fale feels a curious sense of regret—for what, he can't be sure. He sees that he is going to have to speak to justify the scrutiny. He exhales his lungful of smoke and addresses the man, maintaining his nonchalant stance.

"Excuse me, sir."

Winterstone says nothing.

Fale presses on. "Are you by any chance related to Mrs. Sophie Edgar?"

The man folds his newspaper slowly and deliberately. He places it neatly at the corner of the table, lining up all parallel and perpendicular lines. He removes his glasses.

"She is my daughter," he says at last. "And you are?"

Fale surprises himself by stuttering. "F-forgive me, sir. I couldn't help overhear your name and make the connection. My name is Fale, Captain Samuel Fale. Mrs. Edgar is an acquaintance of mine."

"Is she? Surely you mean her husband, Mr. Edgar?"

Fale takes a breath. He knows he could make a fool of himself and put Sophie at risk with whatever comes out of his mouth. He must act carefully, deliberately. And fast.

"Yes, of course." He can't remember Edgar's first name. What is it? "He . . . he and I are old friends," he lies. He realizes too late that he is digging a hole for himself, and possibly with both hands. "That is, we have known each other for some time." This is not completely untrue—Fale met Edgar's father once, when—Thomas! Of course, it is Thomas—was just a lad. The boy accompanied Mr. Edgar, Sr., into town.

"I see." The man's face softens, and he does not go back to his newspaper. "Would you care to join me, as we are both drinking alone?"

"Well, I am expecting someone . . ."

"I see," Winterstone says again.

Fale must remember that this man is not his sturdy colonel. He has embarrassed him, and he can see the older man's hands shake slightly as he goes to take up his glasses and newspaper again. He must make amends. "But my companion won't be here for another twenty minutes. I would be delighted, sir."

A slow smile spreads over the older man's face.

Fale starts to rise, but Winterstone spots his walking stick and his stiff leg and bids him sit, instead picking up his drink and moving to join him.

It turns out that Winterstone dines at the Star and Garter whenever he is in Richmond on business as a barrister. The two men discuss the history of the hotel; Winterstone visited it as a young man, when it was another building altogether, before it burned down in 1870. He recalls his excitement when he first visited the hotel without his parents. Captain Fale attended an engagement for the Indian officers who had arrived for the queen's Diamond Jubilee. He doesn't tell Winterstone, but he made up a few stories that night—made out that he had been fighting in the Boer War when he damaged his leg. Nobody had any reason to disbelieve him.

"You must see something of your daughter, sir," says Fale, "if you come to Richmond so frequently."

Winterstone looks away, and his jaw tightens.

"Not very much," he says. "I am usually too busy."

"Ah," says Fale. "That is a shame."

The man smiles a watery smile. "I did see her today, however. I had tea with her this morning."

Fale nods. "It's a terrible shame, isn't it? About her husband, I mean."

Winterstone's head snaps up. "Whatever do you mean, sir?"

Fale pauses to read the man's voice. He detects an icy tone creeping into it. He must proceed with caution. "Did you not see Mr. Edgar today?"

"He has been called to London on urgent business. I had hoped to meet with him and discuss his journey to the Amazon. It was all planned, but he had to leave at the last minute. He will be away for some days."

Fale realizes he has made a mistake in mentioning this, but then myriad possibilities swim before his eyes. Mr. Winterstone does not know about Edgar's condition. Sophie has lied to him, surely. Or perhaps Edgar has recovered. Since his return, Fale has kept his distance, but Sophie confided in him only yesterday, when he had met her on the street. He could tell that she was putting on a brave face; she stood so tall and strong. Beautiful. She asked him not to tell anybody—not yet, anyway—and he complied for her sake. But here is a chance to do some good, perhaps. Surely if her father only knew about his son-in-law's muteness, he would be able to help her. Perhaps he could arrange for some top-quality care in some hospital, somewhere far away.

He realizes he has not spoken for some time. Winterstone searches his eyes. "What exactly are you saying about my daughter's husband, Captain Fale?"

Such an elegant man. Even when he suspects something is being held from him, he keeps such a strong composure and good posture. He was so considerate when he spotted Fale's walking stick. A real gentleman, Fale thinks, and it comes to him, the nature of the regret he has been feeling.

He should have liked this man for a father-in-law.

FOUR

Santarém, December 6th, 1903

My dearest Sophie,

Thank you for your last letter, and for sending me my beloved peppermints. I ran out a week ago, and have not been able to find any like them in Belém. I'm glad you are coping without me, my lamb, but I still fret and have some regrets about leaving you alone for so long by yourself. I trust you are surrounding yourself with good company.

We have left Belém, as our journey up the Amazon must continue. We boarded another ship bound for Manaus, which arranged to drop us off at Santarém. We are fortunate that there is currently a rubber boom, because it affords easy mobility up the river. I think about the times that naturalists before us had to reach their destinations by small unreliable trading vessels and canoes, at the mercy of who knows what type of scoundrels and heathens! We may yet have to take such a boat if we wish to go further into the interior, but for now I'm happy not to experience the genuine article.

We were all a little sad to leave Belém, despite our impatience both to see more of this wondrous country and to meet Mr. Santos. It will not surprise me at all if our time at Belém turns out to be a golden period of our stay—despite small discomforts, life was very easy there. It was there I began to think of myself as a collector, not just one who dabbles, meandering around the countryside, picking up the odd pretty insect.

I have not much to report about the 400-mile journey up the Amazon. After leaving Belém, and the stretch of tributary before the main river, the huts of caboclos, those people who are a mixture of all the races of Brazil, thinned somewhat. I encountered some of these settlements in my walks when I had ventured some miles from Belém. The caboclos live by gathering from the forest and fishing in the river, and off the produce of a small plantation. Many of these people are also rubber gatherers, and the men are lured by the promise of wages and drink away from their families. The women are left to take care of themselves. I was struck by how miserable the plantations were, and there were always plenty of small children whose mouths, no doubt, needed feeding. Once or twice I confess I succumbed to my pity and gave the children some coins. More often than not they looked at them as if they didn't know what they might do with them.

Continuing up the river, it becomes so wide in places one cannot see the other side. The view became monotonous once we were accustomed to it, a steady but not unpleasant draping of green above the ocher of the river. Every now and then we saw some creature or another rise out of the depths. The crew tossed out scraps to see what would pick it up, and pointed out alligators and pirarucu, one of the fish here, which grows to the size of a small dolphin.

We arrived at Santarém and what a welcome sight it was—I am anxious to continue with my collecting. Santarém is a pretty town at the mouth of the River Tapajós, which flows into the Amazon, set on sloping ground, with whitewashed houses that have red roofs. It is quite European in its appearance, disarmingly so. The inhabitants are mostly Roman Catholics, and the church, which stands in a large grassy square, is quite impressively large, such as something you might find in Spain or Portugal. Walking at first through the streets I might have been inclined to forget I was on another continent were it not for the oppressive, moist heat and the forest encroaching on all sides. The forest is quite different here from in Belém. It is sparser, and the hilly ground is marked by wide-open spaces of clumpy, dried-up grasses. In the height of the dry season, the locals tell us, it rains less than once a week.

The house in which we are staying—once again arranged for us by Santos's man Antonio, who has accompanied us—is at the outskirts of the town, toward the banks of the Tapajós, which has broad, white, sandy beaches, graced with tall javary palms, and water of dark green— a welcome change from the monotony of the yellow Amazon with the forest trailing into the water.

We have been here scarcely a day, but have already discovered the pleasures of swimming in the river. I prefer to run in and straight out again, thereby avoiding any nasty creatures (water snakes, or piranha, or a particularly nasty tiny fish that swims into one's most intimate places and makes a home!) while still enjoying the cooling benefits of the swim. John is a strong swimmer, and uses the opportunity to take some exercise, pounding the water for several hundred yards before turning and swimming back against a rather strong current (indeed, the current is what keeps us safe from alligators). Not that I want to worry you, my dear. I assure you I am perfectly safe! Ernie stands about up to his waist, smoking a cigarette, and George doesn't go in the water at all, save taking his boots off and dipping his toes in. The local Indian children, who live in thatched huts nearby, come down to the water and lie very still in its shallows. I became curious after I heard them giggling to themselves, and when I approached saw they were attended to by tiny fish, which seemed to be kissing them all over. Antonio explained to me that the children lie very still in the water and the fish come and eat the ticks and jiggers and other parasites that have burrowed into their skin! I assumed this act would mean the children would get regularly nipped, but from their laughter it appears it tickles them more than it hurts them.

The house is pleasant enough, though a step down from the house in Belém. Again we are sleeping in hammocks (I have resigned myself to the fact that as long as I am on Brazilian soil, I will not have an ordinary bed). We are only staying in town for a week. We were to have met Mr. Santos and have him accompany us to Manaus, but he has been further delayed. Instead, we have been promised an excursion into the interior, where we will stay for as long as suits us. We will be taking the cook that Antonio arranged for us; Antonio himself will be our guide, as it seems he knows this area well, and George managed to persuade young Paulo from Belém to accompany us, at least as far as this, if not further. So we have plenty of help. I believe we may even be traveling by canoe, in which case we will have one or two Indians to steer us and to help us by catching food for us to eat.

I have developed a taste for the local coffee, my love, of which I enclose a sample. It is refreshing in the extreme when taken first thing in the morning, and what seemed bitter to me at first is now aromatic and bracing. I advise you to take it quite weak to begin with, then build up the strength as you get used to the taste. I assure you it is much better than the coffee we usually drink at home. I look forward to sitting in our parlor together, little Sophie, and sharing this pleasure with you. I am also hoping, my darling, that you can send me some more pepper mints. By the time you get this, and then send them back to me, months may have passed. How frustratingly slow letters can be!

I think of you always, my love, and look forward to the day when I will again be

Yours,

Thomas

Thomas found he relied on his peppermints more and more to disguise the taste of smoke in his mouth when he went to bed. He enjoyed it while smoking the cigarette, but it did turn to an almost brassy sensation on his tongue—from where it came he couldn't imagine. His fingers were beginning to develop a yellow stain, which occasionally wore off after a lot of scrubbing, but mostly sat on his fingers reminding him of his new vice. But Ernie Harris had the same stains, and despite himself Thomas thought of the mark as a brand of brotherhood between them. Of manhood.

He took the folded packet of ground coffee, wrapped it with the letter in brown paper and tied it with string. His hand shook slightly as he wrote his own address on the front—it was only in moments like this, when he had imagined his conversation with Sophie and written it down, that he felt the bruises of homesickness.

On the other side of the room John Gitchens—his new roommate—made scratching sounds as he sketched the shrubs he had found that day on the campos. Every now and then there was a "gloop" as he dipped a brush into a jar of water and added some color to his sketch.

The house was smaller than the house in Belém, and had no balcony, so they either had to sit outside in the sun, or inside where it was dark. Thomas had made this corner his own as soon as they arrived, even though he knew they might not stay for long. The house was at their disposal while they were away on their expedition to keep the belongings that were unnecessary and difficult to carry. He had been furnished with another wooden table, the same size as the one in Belém, and he had stacked up his books and journals and laid out his tools. A silver-framed photograph of Sophie gazed at him as he worked.

He took great joy in cataloging his finds through drawing and painting—the one thing he excelled at. He had watched George trying to paint—his lines smudged and he more often than not ended up with a swirling puddle of brown water, which ran off the side of his page and onto his trousers. George had rebuffed him when he offered to help.

"It takes more than a few painting skills to be a scientist, Thomas. I'm very happy for you that you could always take a job as an artist if you needed to."

Thomas already cringed at his own clumsy knowledge in comparison to George's without the man taking pity on him and all but patting him on the head. He knew it wasn't necessary to make studies of the butterflies—they had already been done by those who had gone before him—but he liked to keep a log for his own satisfaction, and of course it was a way of keeping track of the hundreds of specimens he would be shipping back to Ridewell to sell for him. With each consignment that was sent back, he asked Ridewell to reserve an amount for his own collection.

John stirred behind him, and Thomas turned to look at him. He was leaning back in his chair, his arms stretched up and back over his head. The chair tipped onto its back legs and for a moment Thomas was worried it would break under the big man's weight. But he finished his stretch and let the chair back to the ground without a sound.

John, too, had piled books up on his desk, and there were tins lining the wall, in which he kept his seeds. Propped beside his desk were his botanical press and a pile of brown paper, in which he wrapped the plants before pressing them. John appeared to be packing up for the evening, so Thomas ventured to ask him a question. He had observed that John carried no photographs with him. Even Ernie and George, whom he knew to be unmarried, had pictures of their parents and brothers and sisters.

"Tell me, John," said Thomas, "are you married? May I ask?"

John turned in his chair and looked at Thomas from beneath a solid, high forehead. His beard was becoming unruly, and his cheekbones were squared and sharp above it.

"No, I'm not. I see you are, though. I couldn't help but notice your pretty wife." Again, Thomas wondered at John's soft northern voice in one so large and rough. "And how long have you been married?"

"Two years," said Thomas.

"It must have been hard for you to leave her behind."

Thomas nodded, but he was suddenly gripped by a feeling he realized with panic was something like guilt. That he had left her alone like that. She had said she didn't mind, was excited for him in fact, but still, what if he hadn't made sufficient arrangements for her? Wasn't taking enough responsibility for her?

"That's why I could never marry," said John, as if reading his thoughts. "Someone of my profession. It wouldn't be fair on a woman." He ran his hands over his face. He was a statue, larger than life-size, his edges hewn with a rough chisel. He sighed. "When I fall in love one day, perhaps I will. But who will feed the hungry mouths if I'm killed in a jungle somewhere?"

Thomas shuddered. "Is that something you think about?" He realized he hadn't thought of danger like that, had let excitement push away all thoughts for his safety.

"Of course." John stood up, blocking the light from the lantern momentarily before moving aside, causing an occlusion that fluttered in the air like a moth. "But you can't let it stop you living. I just see it as inevitable that when my time comes, I will go. I would rather go in the jaws of a tiger than in some quiet corner of England." His lip curled as he said "England" and a drop of spit launched itself from his mouth, disappearing before it hit the floor.

Thomas sensed that it was time to stop talking, but his curiosity was getting the better of him. "And what of your family? Your parents?"

"I haven't seen them since I was a lad. My lot was to go down the mines like my father. I wanted to learn, but do you think opportunities were there for someone like me?"

"But you seem to know so much, John." Thomas meant his knowledge of the rain forest, his fluent Portuguese.

"Aye," said John. "Well, it's not from working down any mines, I can tell you. I got out when I could. I hitched a ride down to Liverpool and jumped on the first ship I could find. Met a man; a collector he was—a botanist. Took pity on me—they were going to throw me off at the next port—and took me on as his apprentice. Took me all over."

"How wonderful," said Thomas limply.

John just stared at him. The jut of his brow cast his eyes in deep shadow, but still there was a glint there. He shook his head.

"Wonderful, terrible. It's all the same. I've seen some things. I wouldn't be sitting here talking to you if it wasn't for that man."

"And where is he now?"

"Gone." John rose again and screwed up his mouth as though it had filled with saliva. He crossed to his water jug and poured some into the bowl. He sluiced his face, his back to Thomas, who decided to leave the man alone for a few minutes.

Outside, the chorus was softer than in Belém. A light breeze cooled the sweat on his face and arms. The scent of some flower— John would be able to tell him what it was—filled the courtyard and once inside his lungs made him nauseous. He took his tobacco from his pocket, quickly rolled himself a cigarette, and lit it.

He thought back over the past days' events, about how much he had told Sophie and what was left unsaid. There were many ladies on the steamer, bound for Manaus, and most of them were unac-companied. They seemed to be traveling in a tight-knit group, pooling together in the evening and playing loud rounds of whist. Their voices were shrill, like macaws, and drifted across the room in clouds, along with the smoke from their cigarettes.

These women, though elegantly dressed, were of questionable vir-tue, he knew. One had even tried to solicit his attentions. She was a fine-looking woman, no doubt, and there was something in her coun-tenance that reminded him of Sophie—her height, perhaps; her strong shoulders. But her hair was red, not blond, coiffed into an elaborate nest on top of her head. Sophie would never take such pains for her ap-pearance. As he had sat alone, reading, he was alerted to her approach by the rustle of her skirts. His polite smile became forced when she sat down beside him and laid one gloved hand on his bare wrist.

"I am Lillie," she said with a strong French accent. "As in Langtry. That is, my name is not Langtry, but I have the same name as that famous English beauty. You are English, no?"

Thomas removed his arm from her reach and attempted to turn his shoulder to her without appearing too rude.

"English, yes. My name is Edgar, miss. Thomas Edgar."

"Well, Monsieur Ed-gar." She drew out the final syllable of his name and rolled the "r" deep in her throat. "What do you think of the Amazon so far?" She leaned toward him with her elbows on the table, exposing more of her cleavage than necessary. The action caused her breast to plump up even more, and it was a wonder the woman could breathe at all, her stays must have been so tight. A smattering of freckles dusted her décolletage. The edge of one areola, an edge of the palest pink shell, drew his eye and held it. For a moment he felt his jaw slacken, a physiological reaction, he knew, to the hidden beauties of the female flesh laid bare for his own witness. Her breast suddenly rose, as if she had been holding her breath and was taking a difficult gasp of air, and Thomas's eyes slid to the table. He felt himself begin to color. She had asked him a question. God would give him the strength to answer it.

"Yes. Yes, quite interesting, thank you, Miss . . ."

"Lillie."

"Miss Lillie, yes. I only wish my wife were here to share it." There, he had said it. Surely this would give the young lady the idea. But she only laughed softly.

"Yes, I'm sure your wife would have a fine time here, Monsieur Edgar. There is much for a girl to see and do in Manaus, I am told." And with that she stood, and with a sideways nod of head, which flexed her white neck, she floated back to the other side of the room to her friends. They leaned forward hungrily as Lillie sat. She had said no more than a couple of words before the table erupted in more shrieking laughter and glances were slung his way.

Humiliated, Thomas turned his back on the spectacle and tried to focus on his book.

After a few minutes, the giggling stopped, and Thomas, assuming the women had gone, turned to check. Ernie Harris stood at the table, making elaborate sweeps with his hands. Several of the women's mouths hung open or their hands were clasped to their chests. Then Ernie gave a slight bow and crooked his arm. Lillie stood and took it.

Thomas realized with a lurch that they were walking toward him and he turned back to his book, but the words were just a line of furry caterpillars on the page.

"Ah, Thomas," said Ernie. "Lillie and I are just taking a turn about the deck. Then I'll come and join you for a drink." He winked. Lillie's eyes met Thomas's for a moment and looked away as she arranged her lips in a pout that she no doubt thought alluring.

The pair exited the games room and Thomas fixed his eye on the porthole, expecting them to pass by at any moment. The lamps were lit outside, draped in a cloud of insects. A large moth hurled itself at the porthole in a frenzy. How tenacious they were. He stared outside for some time, but Lillie and Ernie did not pass by, so he continued with his reading.

After about twenty minutes, Ernie reentered the games room alone. He adjusted his collar by hooking his finger in it and stretching his neck forward like a starling as he walked. He dropped heavily into the seat next to Thomas with a sigh. His cheeks were quite flushed and his lips were moist. Despite this, his tongue kept darting out from beneath his neat mustache to wet them further. He let out a sound, a sort of "hooeey," and patted his chest.

"And where is Miss Lillie?" inquired Thomas.

"Oh, she wasn't feeling very well, so I accompanied her back to her cabin where she could lie down. She was attacked by mosquitoes outside; they went berserk over all that tender young flesh so ripely exposed! I told her the new theory about mosquitoes causing malaria and she went quite faint. She's resting comfortably now, though."

"I see," said Thomas. He felt a stab of something and realized with horror it was jealousy. That Ernie could do as he pleased, and held little regard for the consequences, either in this world or the next.

"As for me . . ." Ernie rubbed his hands together, "I'm quite done in, old man. Think I'll hit the hay."

NOW ON FIRM SOIL in Santarém, Thomas ground the end of his cigarette into the dirt with his heel and took a peppermint from his pocket. He felt the cool vapors rise up through his sinuses and the pleasant tickle of a distant sneeze. It built and built until he let a gigantic explosion bend him over double. It was one of the side effects of his peppermints that he was not at all averse to.

"Bless you!" He heard the voice from inside the house, from the direction of Ernie and George's room, and he chuckled.

There were relatively few mosquitoes in Santarém, and if Ernie's new theory proved correct, he had found another reason to avoid them beyond the intense irritation and discomfort they caused with their incessant whining in his ear and their sharp bites, which left his arms red and raw. There were still gnats and sand flies and ticks to worry about, of course. Thomas pictured himself lying naked in the shallows of the river, as the boys had been that day, with their penises floating and waving in the current like minnows. He had omitted the fact of their nudity in his letter to Sophie, but he had become quite used to the sights of the human body in Brazil, mostly of the small children and the odd older native woman with pendulous breasts exposed. George, whom Thomas expected to be the most tenacious with his prudery, spent a long time standing by the boys in the water, practicing his Portuguese on them, and seemed quite disappointed when their mothers called them out of the river.

John was about to get into his hammock when Thomas returned to his room. The ropes gave a moan as he put his substantial weight on them, but the hooks held fast. Thomas said nothing but smiled a little at the other man before crossing to his own hammock.

"Thomas," said John. He looked as if he had something important to tell him: he was sitting up as much as the hammock would allow, with a look of earnest concentration on his face.

Thomas began to remove his boots. "Yes, John?"

"Only that . . . about what we talked about before . . ." He sighed, and the hammock creaked again. "Only, could you not mention it to the others, about how I got started in this business? About the mines."

"Of course I won't, John. Not if you don't want me to."

John seemed satisfied with this answer, and lay back down. But with his eyes on the ceiling, he spoke again. "It's only that they already treat me as their inferior. I don't want to give them any more reason to do so."

Thomas paused. *Did* Ernie and George treat John badly? He tried to remember any interaction he had witnessed, and recalled their first morning in Belém, when Ernie had made some comment about his background and John had left the room. None of them had spoken much to John, but Thomas had thought this was because the man was so dark and quiet, not through some conscious choice to snub him. Did this mean Thomas had also exercised some superiority over him, an unconscious recognition of their class difference? He couldn't remember. But surely John's willingness to share his past with Thomas meant he was an ally, not a threat.

"Of course," he said again. "I'm sorry." He didn't know why he was apologizing, but John didn't answer, and by the light of the one lamp that was left, Thomas could see that his eyes were closed. Thomas was pleased to be sharing a room with John, if only for the fact he didn't snore the way Ernie did. The new pairing was much more harmonious—Ernie had little consideration for others.

Thomas had even woken one night to the sound of Ernie pleasuring himself. He was sure John would not be so indiscreet.

He removed the rest of his clothes and put on his nightshirt before kneeling on the mat by his hammock to pray. As he finished, he again remembered the scene on the ship when Lillie had leaned forward. He caught his breath at the vivid detail of her areola, as soft as a moth's wing. He shuddered.

And please, God, he finished, *grant me the strength of my convictions*. The closer they moved to Manaus and the more Thomas learned about the city, the more uneasy he was becoming.

IN THE WEEK THAT followed, the four men explored together, rising at six to cloudless days, their breakfast prepared by the cook in the little hut that served as a scullery while they readied their equipment. Then they set off with Paulo and an Indian guide, once again arranged by Antonio, along seldom-used paths that took them across the bare campos, peppered with rocks and low shrubs, and into pockets of forest. Some days they wandered for miles along the riverbanks, where there was no shortage of lepidoptera. George's hunt for beetles continued, but he found plenty of other varieties of insects to keep him occupied as well—wasps and mason bees of a kind; crickets and ants. He had also taken it upon himself to further his collection of snakes and lizards, finally using the gun he carried everywhere with him in shooting a *jacuarú*, a fat lizard that ran with little grace and much noise. Thomas didn't fancy its chances of making it out of Brazil expertly stuffed, and he drew some satisfaction from the idea. George still barked orders at him if he thought Thomas was doing something wrong, if he thought he was being too rough with a butterfly, or too timid.

Often they would split up and go in different directions, then meet up for lunch in some shady wood, where they would sit out the hottest hours, smoking cigarettes and lying on their backs, while the creatures of the rain forest lived out their lives overhead. Blue and black Morphos, some as big as blackbirds, patrolled the canopy, and Thomas was satisfied to lie on his back and watch them dipping and gliding, with no itch in his feet to try to chase them or lure them down. He had a prize to keep him satisfied for days—a rare *Callithea sapphira*, with a dusting of black spots on its gray lower wings, and brilliant orange bands on its upper. He had already captured a female, which flew lower than the male, but the male had required him to climb a tree, dodging stinging insects. With his makeshift pole net, he had managed to snare the beautiful creature, after waiting for nearly an hour for it to come into reach. If he didn't catch another butterfly the whole time he was in Santarém he would still be happy.

Birds called to each other: glossy black *anús*, bright trogons of varying species. A toucan came dangerously close. Thomas marveled at its heavy curved beak and was dismayed when Ernie picked up his gun and shot it. It wavered a moment, and Thomas swore that it looked at him just before it tipped back and lost its grip on the branch. A dreadful sadness slopped in his belly, spreading through his insides like ink on a tablecloth. The bird was dead when it hit the ground and Ernie bounded over to claim his prize. Thomas knew he was being hypocritical—after all, the first thing he did when he saw a beautiful specimen of lepidoptera was to catch it and kill it— but he felt that the process of setting the butterfly meant that it would live forever. There was something dreadfully forlorn about Ernie's stuffed birds. He had opened up one of his drawers to have a look one day and the birds were lined up, stuffed, lying like bullets, their bodies fixed as if they were diving: wings tucked in, eyes closed, feet back. He remembered feeling shock at how *dead* they looked, not unlike his beautiful lepidoptera: cadavers, lying in a row, waiting to be studied. Which, he supposed, they were.

On their way home, they would bathe in the river again, and Thomas began to relax about the amount of time he spent in the water. Their guide and Paulo took off all of their clothes when they were away from the town, and when Ernie and John did the same, Thomas did too. The first time, he removed his clothes slowly while John threw his off and ran in, folding himself into a graceful dive before he swam out with strong strokes. Ernie walked in and hesitated as the water reached his groin. His flat, white buttocks quivered a little, before Thomas saw him decide to push on. Ernie let out a sharp whistle. "Christ!" he yelled, then turned, grinning. He hunched his shoulders and stroked the surface of the water with one hand, a cigarette in the other. "Sorry, Thomas! Didn't mean to do the name-in-vain thing, but you should try getting river water on your bare cannonballs!"

"Coming in, George?" asked Thomas as he ran toward the water. Paulo already stood by him, naked, trying to pull him to his feet by the hand.

"Not me, Thomas! You know me! Can't stand the stuff!" He waved Paulo away, laughing. His tone was more jovial than Thomas had heard for a long time. Santarém was obviously agreeing with George.

Thomas hit the water running, and felt his legs slow as the liquid engulfed them and dragged them back. The touch of the water on his uncovered genitals made him gasp before he relaxed into the freedom of weightlessness it gave him.

He slid into a slow breaststroke, taking in the pleasant scene around him—John off in the distance, while Ernie smoked and picked stray tobacco from his tongue, peering into the water. Paulo and the guide floated on their backs, calling to each other. Paulo waved at George, who waved back. A cluster of butterflies gathered on the shore downriver, appearing as a bed of dandelions, which broke apart and rose into the air at some disturbance. They were the same butterflies he had seen from the ship, migrating from north to south in buttery wafts. One of the swarms had crossed the ship, and men and women were suddenly picking the lepidoptera from their hats, from inside their drinks; a chaotic moment of butterfly-induced madness crowded the passengers and Thomas lay back on his deck chair and watched with a smile.

A pleasant tightness fell across the skin of Thomas's shoulders from the hot sun. He dropped under the surface. He had forgotten the sound of silence. Even in the forest, which he had come to think of as a quiet place, there was always the screeching of a bird or the distant roar of a howler monkey. Wind rustled branches and fruit thudded as it fell, ripe and bursting, to the forest floor. But under the water, Thomas was stunned by the lack of sound. He opened his eyes, but the water was murky, with detritus from the forest drifting before his face. He stopped moving his limbs and hung in the warmth and stillness of the water until his chest ached.

AN ABUNDANCE OF GOOD food was at their disposal in Santarém—there were good bread makers, meat was in steady supply, and they feasted on watermelon every evening when they returned from their day's work, waving to their neighbors, who gathered outside their own houses to smoke and gossip and play checkers. Always men, Thomas noticed, for the women seemed to be kept indoors in this town.

When the time came for them to leave on their journey up the Tapajós, Thomas felt a momentary hunger pang; he was sure his stomach would not be as well catered for deep in the rain forest away from a town. Antonio arranged to accompany them—he knew the area well. He brought with him the silent Indian cook they had employed in the house, and two others: João, a small but tough and strong man of about thirty who spoke English and had been their guide around Santarém; and Paulo, who threw himself enthusiastically into his role as the men's right-hand man—carrying supplies and taking on hunting and fishing duties. Thomas overheard Paulo ordering João about, and the other man's terse replies, which in Thomas's limited Portuguese translated to something like "When did you become my father, boy?" With any luck, and with the skill of the natives, they would not starve. Ernie took precautions by stocking up his medical supplies, particularly quinine. George had already scared everyone when he woke up with a slight fever one morning, but by the end of the day he was well again—a passing ague only. They began to take a small dose of quinine every day as insurance.

Their mode of transportation was finally the rustic affair that Thomas had been expecting all along. They took two large canoes, each of which had a small cabin for shelter, where hammocks were strung and equipment and supplies stored. Antonio arrived on the morning of their departure with crates of salt and tools.

"I say," said Ernie, "do we need that much salt? Won't it weigh us down?"

"For trade," growled Antonio. "You will thank me when you have fresh chicken to eat."

"I was rather looking forward to sampling the meats of the jungle," replied Ernie. He nudged Thomas. "Sloth and monkey, Thomas. I've heard they're delicious."

Thomas grimaced and even George raised a smile.

"I bet John's tried all of those, haven't you, John?" said George.

John paused from helping Paulo load crates onto the canoes. He wiped his forehead with his sleeve.

"Well, I've never had sloth, but I've eaten monkey, all right, and snake. There's no need to starve in a place like this."

"Yes," said George, "I expect you'd be used to scavenging for what you can find." He waved his handkerchief in John's direction before flattening it on the back of his neck. John turned away and continued in his work, but Thomas saw Ernie shoot George an amused look, and the two men shared a moment that Thomas had no wish to be a part of.

"Here," he said, and bent to help John with a large crate of books. George's, he noticed, and he tightened his grip as they passed it over the strip of river between the dock and the boat, in case John decided to drop it. Their eyes met for a moment and Thomas saw in John's that the solid man was letting the comments go. His shirt was open and sweat rolled freely from his neck into the tangle of dark hair on his chest, where it gathered to be washed off later in the river. Suddenly Thomas thought he understood what lay behind John's vigorous swimming action: that it was how he cleansed himself of ill feeling, and how he could arise fresh each morning and work alongside two men who did not respect him.

"Thank you, Thomas," said John as the last of the crates disappeared into the cabins. They both glanced at the other two, who stood on the dock talking. George waved his hand at a mason bee that was bothering them and Ernie, as always, was smoking. Ernie glanced up as Thomas approached them.

"Have they finished, then? Ah, good. I think that's us, then, isn't it? Time to go?" He dropped his cigarette butt into the river and produced his silver hip flask from his pocket. "Swig to see us off?" He took a nip, then passed the bottle to George, who handed it to Thomas without taking any.

The flask held a potent new smell, not unlike paraffin, and when Thomas knocked it back it burned his throat and left a bitter taste in his mouth. He screwed up his face. "What is *that*?"

Ernie chuckled and took the flask without offering it to John, who stood a little apart, staring up the river. "It's *cachaça*, some local spirit. Made from sugar. It'll strip your stomach lining, I'm sure, but it's all I could get hold of. The Indians are addicted to it— give them this and they'll do anything for you." John made a low sound in his throat and stalked away. Ernie watched him go, then said, almost wistfully, "I've enough to last us until Manaus, when we can get the finest brandy Europe has to offer."

THE LADEN CANOES LISTED dangerously once they came to a gusty expanse of river that crooked south. Only the skill of the men saved them from tipping over and losing their precious collecting and preserving equipment. Thomas tried to sit still, but every time the canoe lurched to one side he cried out and grabbed hold of the edge with one hand and his Gladstone bag, which contained his journals and his letters from Sophie, with the other.

They did not intend to travel too far into the interior—Antonio had pinpointed a site where a disused rubber settlement would be at their disposal. It was less than a two-day journey from Santarém, and they would be there by the afternoon of the next day, all going well. They planned to stay only two weeks, depending on their success. They were within easy traveling distance of Santarém should something go wrong or should their collecting prove fruitless. Every tributary of the Amazon yielded different plants and wildlife, and the men were grateful for the variety offered to them—had they gone straight to Manaus on the River Negro, their collections would have been limited.

Once past the worst of the wind, they put in at a small village to gather their nerve and to rid themselves of some of their heavy cargo. Thomas suspected that Antonio had overloaded them in order to make some kind of profit from the goods they were carrying, but he kept his thoughts to himself, telling himself that the man merely hadn't expected the collecting equipment to be quite as weighty.

They were received with interest by the villagers, a mixture of Indians and *mamelucos*, who were those of both Indian and European blood. The settlement was presided over by Captain Arturo, a Portuguese seaman who had arrived some ten years earlier and had never left. He invited the Englishmen to dinner, cooked by his Indian wife. Thomas watched with interest as a parade of golden-skinned children came in to say good night to their father, who lifted the little ones high over his head before planting a kiss on each of their cheeks. The older ones contented themselves with a kiss on the forehead and stared silently at their visitors. After dinner the captain produced a bottle of local spirits, made from mandioca root, and George and John excused themselves to return to the canoes and their hammocks.

"I am glad there are some *real* men to join me," the captain joked. "Although *you* . . ." He squinted down a pointed finger at Thomas as though aiming a rifle. "You look like you need a good drink and a bit of fun! Look at you, so young and untouched. Like life is yet to show its face to you, heh? So delicate, you are!" He laughed at this, and Ernie joined in. Thomas smiled and shifted in his seat. The captain went on. "What has the forest thrown at you so far? Have you been sick yet? You look like you would get sick easily."

"No," said Thomas. "None of us has been."

"Hmph," said Arturo. "Yet. And you will be the first man down, I think!" At this he slapped Thomas on the back, spilling drink onto the table and his hands. Thomas pulled out a handkerchief and wiped his hands while the captain poured him more.

When his glass was full, Thomas raised it, shaking off the captain's comments. They were meant in jest, he knew, but he could have let them eat at him. "To the Amazon!" he said in what he hoped was a robust voice. The three men banged their glasses together and knocked their drinks back. Thomas's trickled down into his stomach and caressed him there, promising things to come.

The drunker Arturo got, the more his already limited English slipped into slurred Portuguese. Thomas understood some of what he said, but the more drunk *he* got the less his own comprehension. Finally, he had to lay his hand on top of his glass and his head on the table as gibberish whirlpooled around him.

Ernie nudged Thomas. "Don't you just hope that our Senhor Santos is as hospitable as the captain here?"

"What did you say?" said Arturo. "Santos? The rubber man?" Thomas heard this reaction, but he could not focus on Arturo's face.

"Yes," said Ernie. "He's the reason we are in your gorgeous country, my man."

Thomas didn't hear what was said next, because Arturo banged his fist on the table so hard that Thomas's ear, which had been resting quietly near his glass, was now roaring. The shock of the noise had propelled his head upward, and he was momentarily sobered enough that he could see Arturo's bulbous nose pulsing as his nostrils flared in and out.

Ernie was staring at the captain in disbelief. He raised both palms and started to nod. "Time for us to go, Edgar." He stood unsteadily and pulled Thomas to his feet also.

"Yes, go to the devil!" yelled Arturo, then some more in Portuguese.

The door of the house banged behind them and they were left standing in the sandy street, the night sounds enclosing them.

"Did you get that?" Ernie leaned heavily against Thomas in an effort to keep them both steady as they walked.

Thomas's tongue was as fat and heavy as a piece of old ham. He struggled to produce pictures in his mind to coincide with the words in his head, and slowly tested his words around his alien tongue. "I dunno, Ernie. Don' walk so fast."

THE FOLLOWING MORNING THE rays of the sun pierced Thomas's eyelids. His head ached and he couldn't close his mouth; his lips had dried and cracked and his tongue had been drained of all moisture.

"Bloody hell," he croaked, knowing that he had picked up the habit of swearing from Ernie, and that he was too ill to feel ashamed.

The canoe had already started to move away from the shore, and his ears were filled with the sound of the paddles on the water and the calling of the brightly colored birds that perched in the trees overlooking the river. He had come to recognize the breeds he saw, but at that moment he couldn't think, and didn't *want* to think. He just wanted them to be silent.

On the shore nearby, a monkey screamed; the cry was that of a woman in distress.

His headache subsided when he drank a quantity of water, and the others left him alone, after giving him a few pokes and jibes, to sleep off his hangover. Ernie, in the other canoe, seemed unaffected; in between fuggy sleep, Thomas heard him singing at the top of his voice.

His dreams were troubled by the way the evening had ended. In one dream the captain said that Santos had seduced his wife; in another he had stolen their children. In still another, Arturo was mad that they were with Santos because he had desperately wanted to accompany them on their journey and Santos had forbidden him. In the dream, Arturo sat down and wept like a child.

Thomas felt ready to get out of his hammock when the canoes bumped toward the shore. A makeshift jetty jutted out into the water, its logs cracked and scarred, whether from misuse or disuse it was not obvious.

"Are we there? Have we arrived?" His voice cracked in his throat.

"Yes, sleepyhead," said George. "We have arrived. Time to get to work instead of lying about all day."

Thomas's legs felt as they had when he reached shore after his voyage across the Atlantic: they shook as he put his weight on the jetty, and his body was not connected to them. The problem was compounded by the swaying of the jetty, and as a rotten log began to give way under him, he leapt off and onto the sand of the adjoining shore. His legs collapsed and he sank to his hands and knees. He stayed on all fours, gathering his bearings, while Ernie jeered at him and the men began to unload the crates. The sand was damp between his fingers and seemed to be alive. It trickled over his skin, tickling him. Then an excruciating stab made him cry out and yank his hand away; another pain shot through his other hand and he jumped to his feet, suddenly steady. He looked down and saw that the sand was alive—seething with bloodred insects, which ran over his boots and tried to scramble their way up his legs. He yelled and drummed his feet on the ground like a child throwing a tantrum. His hands burned as if they had been thrust into the heart of a log fire, and the stings were angry and swollen. He had been stung by ants since he had been in the Amazon, but these ants were different. With two wide strides he was on the jetty again. Antonio was beside him, ready with a bucket of river water to throw over his legs. He began to beat at Thomas's trousers and boots with a rag.

All the men had turned back at Thomas's cries, and now young Paulo and João the guide were speaking to each other in low tones, nodding and scowling.

"Wait," said George, and he crouched down and attempted to catch one of the ants with his tweezers. "Fire ants. They're not deadly, Thomas, don't worry, but I imagine you are in a lot of pain." He gave up trying to catch one, and instead joined the others in stamping on them with his boots. Most of the insects escaped and crawled back down toward the sand. "*Formiga de fogo*," he said to the men. Antonio grunted and nodded, while Paulo beamed at him. George grinned back, pleased with himself.

"Why is it always me that gets stung?" wailed Thomas.

Ernie rolled his eyes. "'*Why is it always me?*'" he imitated in a shrill voice. "Please, Tom, don't be such a *girl*."

"Shut up, Ernie," said John, and the others looked at him in surprise. "You wait until something has a go at you, and see how you feel about it."

Suddenly the rain forest was starting to lose some of its appeal, and Thomas wondered if the feeling he had was homesickness—not for England, but for the relative safety of Belém or Santarém. Perhaps adventure wasn't something he craved after all.

A NARROW SANDY ROAD bordered by towering trees led them a few hundred yards into the forest. Thomas imagined they were being watched—by laughing monkeys and twitching birds, keeping the in-truders in their sights, ready to flee. Perhaps some of the eyes waiting in the gloom were human. After the hot light that bounced off the river, the forest seemed to consume them in its darkness. Despite the loss of the scorching sun, the lack of wind made the humidity al-most unbearable. Sweat rolled down between his shoulder blades in a salty river. A root, snaking out from the forest floor, caught his foot and pitched him into the mulch. He braced himself for another insect onslaught, but instead strong arms pulled him to his feet. The men said nothing, but Thomas felt the sting of their stares on his neck. He mentally kicked himself as the blood pumping into his head carried with it the renewed pain of his hangover. When he wiped his face with his hands, he winced as the salt found his wounds.

The sight of the compound, with four huts facing one another in a circle, made Thomas even more ill. A makeshift construction in the middle, nothing more than a few palm fronds supported by sticks, served as a cookhouse. There was no outhouse. His stomach ached from holding in his regular movements, and now his bowels had backed up and were pressing against the wall of his gut. He had been waiting until they reached their camp to release them, and now saw he had waited in vain—the forest would be his lavatory. He would have to squat, exposed to God only knew how many hazards.

The small settlement, once the temporary home of rubber collec-tors, had been roughly maintained. The huts were nothing more than basic shelters, with holes for doors, but the undergrowth had been cut back to prevent the jungle from reclaiming the palm leaves and poles that made up the building materials. Two of them sloped dangerously off-kilter, crazy houses at a fun fair.

"Four huts," said Ernie as he set his bag down. He raised his arms in a diamond above his head, and pushed upward, stretching. "Per-fect. One each."

"What about the men?" said Thomas. He noticed the dark patches under Ernie's arms, smelled the sharp scent of his sweat.

And something else, sour. He realized with a shudder that it smelled like semen.

"Yes. Of course. They can have one, you and John can have another, and George and I will have one each."

George smiled. The pomade on his hair had melted and begun to creep down his forehead. He took his handkerchief and wiped his face, then pressed it over his nose, sidling away from Ernie. John shrugged.

"Suit yourself, Ernie," said Thomas. The truth was that he would rather share with somebody, especially somebody like John, who could explain the noises in the night and know when they were getting dangerously close.

"Good man," said Ernie. He retrieved his bag and strode off to examine the interior of one of the huts.

Thomas managed to sweep his hut out satisfactorily with a palm frond, and to hang a curtain for a door. He and John slung their hammocks from beams in the ceiling. Antonio brought some balsam to smear on the ropes, to prevent ants crawling on them as they slept, and encouraged them to rub the foul-smelling liquid, like rotten fruit, on their exposed skin. The previous occupants had left behind some hardy basic furniture, which included footstools, so that when they sat down, their feet would be off the ground; the legs of the chairs and stools were doused with the same liquid. Thomas thought the stress of always keeping his feet moving when he stood would drive him mad but he soon got used to it, and they learned to avoid the sandy mounds that signaled ant nests. Unfortunately for Ernie, one of the nests was in front of his hut and he was the only one to get stung regularly.

George was fascinated by the creatures, and collected many specimens, alive—which he fed on farina and anything left over from meals—and dead. He studied the ants' sizable jaws, which latched onto their prey from the front while they attacked with their stings from the other end. In the cookhouse, the men had to suspend supplies in bundles from the ceiling, the cords holding the food smeared with the same bitter balsam, to stop the ants from invading their food.

Ants were not the only problem. Thomas huddled every night under his mosquito net, while insects, unhindered by the flimsy walls of the hut, hurled themselves at him. Ernie had caught a vampire bat in his hut one night and confessed he had almost let it bite him just so he could record the effects. Damp rose up from the ground with every rainfall, and the pages of Thomas's books were beginning to mildew and undulate.

The richness of the collecting opportunities went some way toward making up for the discomforts, Thomas felt. The men slipped back into their routines, but they were sure to take their guides with them, and kept together more; the lack of proximity to a city made them feel less safe than they had previously. The land around the settlement was looped by tracks the rubber collectors used. Each *Hevea* tree stood far from the one before it, but the tangle of paths linked some two or three hundred trees in seven or eight miles of trail. Thick cuts of machete blades scarred the smooth gray trunks, a startling human intrusion in the otherwise pristine rain forest. The incisions were deep but controlled, in regular and deliberate stripes. Rusted tin cups dangled from branches, used to catch the weeping milk, which Antonio explained would later be smoked and hardened by the *seringueiros*, the rubber-tappers, to be shipped off to appease the world's hunger for rubber.

One morning, as Thomas strolled through a sandy path near the river with John and João, the Indian stopped and pointed at something on the ground.

"*Rastro de jaguar,*" he said.

This Thomas understood: jaguar tracks. He fell on the ground beside them, pushing his face as close as he could.

"How fresh are they?" he asked.

John got down and examined the prints, fat scars in the sand, which was damp from the overnight rain. If it had been dry, as it had been every other day since they had arrived, they might not have seen them.

"Since last night, obviously, or they would have been washed away."

Thomas looked around, peering through the gloom into the depth of the forest. Shadows and blurred shapes moved everywhere—in the treetops, on the forest floor—but nothing took the form of a jaguar.

"Perhaps it's watching us," he whispered hopefully. "Will it attack?"

John chuckled. "It's more scared of you than you are of it, Thomas."

They continued on their way, but Thomas couldn't help glancing over his shoulder, and he caught no more specimens that afternoon.

That night, as he lay in his hammock, he heard an unearthly cry just outside their camp.

"There's your jaguar, Thomas," said John, creaking in his hammock as he turned on his side.

It was some time before Thomas fell asleep. He lay in his hammock, listening for the jaguar, picturing its heavy feet treading lightly through the forest, its body swinging. The print had been the size of a man's hand and he imagined holding the velvet paw in his palm. He must remember to tell Sophie about it the next chance he had to write: the black jaguar was so rare.

Though he thought of her often, he found that more and more his head was filled with butterflies—one in particular. He realized he hadn't written to Sophie before they left Santarém, and there was no point in writing now until they got back to the city. His last letter from the agent said the first consignment had fetched a healthy sum, and he had sent details of his bank account to make sure Sophie was well provided for while he was gone, but there it was. That guilt again, at leaving his wife. Not only at leaving her, but at the fact that at times he didn't even think of her; their life together in Richmond seemed so far away. So irrelevant.

But her letters were cheerful enough—full of meals with friends, with games, with walks in the park—and they went a good way toward alleviating these feelings. He even envied her a little bit, for the time she spent in his beloved Richmond Park. He did miss it, despite the fact it would seem quite bare and barren of insect life when he returned.

He remembered his first walk in the park, clutching his new butterfly net, a few days after his fifth birthday. He saw a deer picking its way through the bracken. His father gripped his hand and walked briskly toward the flower beds, the rough tweed of his jacket flapping in Thomas's face. Thomas had to run to keep up with him and his first attempts at swiping at a red admiral failed. He was on the verge of tears when his father put his big hand over his own and guided it. Together they caught the butterfly and Thomas watched its slow struggle in the light netting, its legs as fine as hairs poking through the tiny holes.

His parents hadn't realized that by giving him such an innocuous present they had started a fire. Butterflies began to take up all of his spare time. He was still too small to go collecting on his own, but inevitably his father would get so fed up with Thomas's badgering that he would yank him into the park, stand around smoking his pipe for five minutes, then order him home again. Thomas did not let this deter him. He began to request books on butterflies for all of his birthdays, and whenever the family went on a picnic would take his net and jars with him.

Elderly gentlemen they passed on the way to their picnic spot invariably feigned interest. "Going fishing, are we?" Thomas would shake his head and the men would wander away, no doubt wondering at the impertinence of the boy. He clearly had a net with him; what else would he be doing with it?

"For goodness' sake, Thomas," said his mother, when they were settled and pouring tea. "Sit *still*. You're to finish your sandwiches and sit there and be quiet before you go running off all over the countryside. Really," she said, turning to her husband, "I wish we'd never given him that stupid net."

But his mother had gasped with pleasure when he brought her the chrysalis he had kept on his windowsill. Together they watched the brimstone emerge from its slippery bed, yellow and slick as a newborn calf. Slowly and quietly; they felt that if they spoke or breathed it might disturb the transformation and send the butterfly back into its cocoon. It slipped out, dew-wet, and rested, testing its wings, opening and closing them carefully, feeling for a drying wind that didn't exist in his mother's gloomy bedroom.

"Let it out now, Tom," she said, and he sensed in her the same reluctance he felt to say good-bye to this small miracle. He crossed to the window and opened it, setting the jar with its branch on the sill. The butterfly waited another minute, seemed to be gathering its bearings, then launched itself from the branch and spun away into the garden.

"It's gone," he said, and his mother opened her arms to him. He climbed onto her bed and was enclosed in a rare embrace by her cinnamon smell and the pillow of warm air that arose from under the covers.

For all his father's gruffness and complaints, he still encouraged his son's habit. He took him to London when he was twelve years old to "Watkins and Doncaster, Naturalists" in the Strand. Up until this point Thomas had caught butterflies and inexpertly pressed them into books, where they lasted for only a few months before insects attacked them and they mildewed and rotted away. Visiting Watkins and Doncaster was to Thomas as pleasurable as being in the most delicious sweet shop was to other boys—rows and shelves of all the equipment the serious collector could ever hope for. Instead of the smell of black balls and sherbet, Thomas was enclosed by the stench of killing chemicals, laurel leaves, and the dusky odor of plaster of Paris. He was allowed to select a new net, some corklined collecting boxes, and most important, a bottle of cyanide potassium. Until this point, he had only been allowed to use laurel leaves to kill his insects. The man behind the counter, with a giant belly and fingers like sausages, bent his face down close to Thomas's and said, "Highly poisonous, young man. If you touch this or breathe it, you will die. You must only use it when your father is there to supervise you. Do you understand?" Thomas nodded and pulled his face away—the man's gray muttonchops were tickling his nose. The man gave a nod, satisfied that he had relieved himself of all responsibility should the boy kill himself. Mr. Edgar gripped the back of Thomas's neck and squeezed, just to make sure the message had got through.

The last present Thomas received from his father before the old man died, when Thomas was finishing his studies, was a magnificent set of collecting drawers, fashioned by none other than the Bradys of Edmonton. Thomas could hardly breathe when he saw them; they were the most highly prized drawers that money could buy. Usually, money *couldn't* buy them. The Bradys, a father-and-son team, wouldn't sell them to just anyone who asked; one had to impress Brady Senior with one's connections, and he might offer to make a set of drawers. It was an elaborate game that saw many men leave his premises empty handed, their supply of famous names well and truly exhausted, their countenance defeated.

But here they were: a set of Brady drawers, for Thomas.

"Just remember I will always be proud of you, Thomas, no matter what you do." His father laid his hand on Thomas's shoulder, and his eyes became rimmed with red. It was the most honest display of emotion Thomas had seen from him, and he vowed at that moment not to hide his feelings from his own children for so long. Mr. Edgar died a month later. The doctor said he had a weak heart.

THE SADNESS THAT ROSE up inside him as he lay on his hammock surprised him. He hadn't thought of his father for some time. His gut twisted and a pain shot between his lower ribs. His father had loved the park. And now Sophie was discovering the delights of its shaded walks and the hidden valleys. In her letter, she also spoke of her friendship with Agatha, who he knew would keep her happy—she had a gift for making people laugh, Thomas included. Sophie had also mentioned a retired army captain she had met at church. Some kindly old widower, he expected, who had taken an avuncular interest in Sophie in the absence of her husband and her father.

His guilt was subsiding, along with the pain in his stomach. She'll be all right, he thought. She's strong and likes to be independent.

He turned his thoughts again to the giant swallow-tailed butter-fly he hoped to capture. What if he found only one? He would be re-luctant to kill it right away, but knew that if he didn't it could damage itself and then be useless as a specimen. Would he sell it? Or would he donate it to the Natural History Museum in the name of science? Science. He shuddered. The more he collected, the more Thomas re-alized how far from a scientist he actually was. Ernie and George made that obvious to him every day—not always intentionally. He had to identify many of the specimens he caught with books, and George seemed to be able to recognize those that he couldn't. Thomas had pored over the cabinets of lepidoptera at the museum, but their taxonomic names filled him with frustration at their un-willingness to adhere to his memory. He was still an amateur, no matter that he would make some money from his sales.

No, it was clear to him that the only way he could truly make a dif-ference in the world was as an explorer—he would bring home the *Papilio sophia* and the world would remember him for it. His wife's name would be immortalized, and he would be revered. He would travel the world speaking to entomological societies about the but-terfly. He would relate again and again the adventure of the chase, the triumph he would feel when he caught one in his net, the skill he would use to do so.

The jaguar yowled again, and another blast of pain echoed around Thomas's stomach. Perhaps it wasn't grief that was hurting him after all. Perhaps there was something wrong with him. It seemed the closer he got to the butterfly, the more the dark rain forest tried to hinder him. He would speak to Ernie tomorrow.

THE FOLLOWING AFTERNOON, AS the men returned from their day's collecting—Thomas clutching his gut to try to subdue the waves of pain—Antonio, who had stayed behind, met them on the path.

"You have a visitor," he said, his wide face looking at them for approval.

Outside the cookhouse, a white man of around fifty years was sitting on a chair with his feet up on a stool. He stood and removed his hat before walking forward to greet them. His neat cream suit was remarkably spotless. He was smooth shaven except for a large gray mustache, waxed into thick leaves. There was something unnatural about the face beneath the combed and oiled hair. Thomas couldn't quite place it until they stood face-to-face with him: the skin was utterly dry. While all around him men wiped at their grimy brows, slick with sweat, this man was as cool as if it were an English spring day. He bowed slightly as he shook each of their hands; his palm confirmed Thomas's perception of him—it felt like cool glass, and his nails were clean and cut into neat squares.

"I am very honored to meet you, sirs," he said in almost flawless English. "Your man Antonio has told you who I am?"

"Only that you are a hat merchant, my dear fellow," said George, whose nervousness had deserted him once he had laid eyes on the man; his relaxed hands were folded loosely in front of him.

"My name is José," said the man. "Please just call me José. I am very pleased to make your acquaintance. No!" He held up his hand as Ernie went to speak, "Please do not tell me. You are the doctor,

Ernest Harris?" Ernie nodded and raised his eyebrows, before following José's gaze to John. "And you . . . you must be Mr. Gitchens, I think. The hardy plant-hunter." John nodded, but looked at the ground. Thomas sensed that John was anxious to wander away, to snatch some moments alone with his work. His whole body seemed to be straining toward the hut. "And this must be Mr. Sebel, of course, the learned scholar. And finally young Mr. Edgar."

Thomas had the curious impression they were being welcomed to their own camp; he almost expected the hat seller to stretch his arms out to them. "And how do you know so much about us?" he asked.

"Ah, that would be your man Antonio again. We have been talking for a good two hours in your absence. I trust you had a good day collecting?"

Ernie suggested they sit down. They gave their equipment to Paulo, who staggered away under its collective weight.

"What brings you up the Tapajós, sir?"

"Hats. I have come from Manaus, and I thought I would take a detour up the Tapajós before leaving Santarém for Belém. I have many hats to sell."

"And where are you from?"

"São Paulo. I came to the Amazon to make my fortune in Manaus. I arrived there two years ago, and tried to sell my hats there, but nobody wanted to buy them. I even tried to drop the price, but nobody wanted them. Then I learned something. You see . . ." He leaned forward in his chair, as if about to let the men in on a secret. "In Manaus everything is very expensive. The people there, they don't care for quality, they only want what costs them the most so they can brag to their neighbors about it. Those rubber men! When they would not buy my hats, I put the price up a thousand percent. I sold out within a week. They all wanted my hats! They were the most expensive, you see, and to them that means status! So you see before you a much wealthier man than the man who left São Paulo."

"And well educated, I am guessing, sir, by your excellent English."

"Oh, you know, one picks it up." He laughed. "May I be so bold as to ask if we may have some tea?"

They looked at one another. Tea was a habit they had fallen away from in Belém.

"I'm afraid we don't have any tea, old man," said Ernie, and Thomas wondered if José would be offended by the expression. "We can offer you some coffee. Please forgive us for not offering before."

"*Coffee?*" José looked terribly disappointed. "But you are English! Surely you drink tea?"

"We do, but it has been a little hard to get. And we have developed a taste for coffee."

"Never mind. I have brought a supply of my own. I think it the most charming habit of the English—they want to drink tea at all times of the day."

"Have you been to England, Mr. José?" asked Thomas.

"No," said the man. Then, "Manuel!"

Thomas jumped; he was not expecting the man to suddenly shout out.

A man came walking around from the back of the cookhouse. He was Indian, short and well muscled. His hair was worn in the traditional bowl cut but he was dressed in a white shirt and black waistcoat, with black trousers. Like an English servant, perhaps. Scars marked his bare feet and Thomas wondered how he coped with the fire ants.

"Manuel, bring me some of my tea," he said in Portuguese. "Enough for the gentlemen."

Manuel nodded, but his face showed no expression. He emerged a few minutes later—the water must have been already on the boil for their supper—with a pristine china teapot and five tiny cups and saucers. The cup he set down in front of Thomas had a chip in the rim but the rest were unmarked—an extraordinary sight in the middle of the jungle.

"*Obrigado*, Manuel," said John. "*Você gosta de chá?*"

Manuel eyed John for a moment, then turned questioning eyes to José, who waved him away.

"I congratulate you on your excellent Portuguese, Mr. Gitchens," said José when the servant's back had disappeared again. "But Manuel cannot speak. He is mute."

"But not deaf?" asked George.

"No. He is mute because he has no tongue. I see you looking at me in horror, gentlemen. It is one of the hazards of the Amazon. He lost it in an accident."

"God," said Ernie. "What sort of accident?"

"I would not like to upset you by telling you," said José. "Please do not ask me to explain." He took up his teacup, clutching the tiny handle between thumb and forefinger and cocking his little finger as he raised it to his lips. He gave a satisfied sigh as he lowered it back to the saucer perched on his belly. "I prefer it with milk, but I like it almost as much with a slice of lemon, don't you, gentlemen?"

Thomas's tea was too hot, so he blew on it. He couldn't remember the last time he had drunk tea; the familiar smell coursed through him and made him smile.

"I see you smile, Mr. Edgar," said José. "You are missing England, I think."

"Why, yes," said Thomas. "That is, I am not, but I did for a moment remember tea at home, you're right."

"I should miss England if I were you," said José. "I imagine it is a fine country. I would very much like to go there one day."

"What is it you like about England?" asked George.

"The tea, of course! But you can have that anywhere. I am very much moved by your poets, sir. I am particularly fond of Byron and Shelley. And Wordsworth, not forgetting him! Through them I come to know your landscape. And William Blake. *Such* a wise man!"

"You *are* an educated man," said George. "Just as I suspected."

He sat with one leg slung over the other, seemingly forgetting the threat of ants, and waved a fly away with one hand while holding his tea in the other.

"If one can read, Mr. Sebel, one can be educated."

"True, true," said George.

John stood and excused himself. "I have some work to do before the day's end. I will take supper in my room, so I bid you good night." He sloped off, and the circle was broken somehow—an edge of it now lay exposed to the darkening forest.

"I understand you are under the patronage of Senhor Santos," said José. "Have you met the man?"

"Not yet," said Ernie. "Do you know him?"

"I am aware of him, yes. It would be difficult to live in Manaus and not know of him."

"What is he like?" asked Thomas. An image of Captain Arturo's angry face appeared in his mind.

"You mean you know nothing of him? You have heard nothing?" asked José.

"No, nothing," said George. "All we know is that he has been very kind to us. He has provided us with accommodation and transport, including our passages here, and we are making our way to Manaus to meet him. He was to have met us at Santarém, but he had some trouble with some of his Indian rubber workers upriver."

"Yes, the Indians can be troublesome in employment. It is very hard to find decent men among the Indians or the Negroes. Since slavery was abolished it is even harder. So I am told. They are too proud to work for the white man, and try to subsist on their own." He finished his tea and poured himself another as he spoke. "So nobody has talked to you of Santos?"

"No," said George.

"Well . . ." said Thomas. He paused. He couldn't be sure he remembered what Captain Arturo had said about Santos. Perhaps it was better to keep quiet. But then again, perhaps José could shed some light on it. The others were looking at him, so he went on. "Dr. Harris and I had an encounter with a man downriver from here. I'm ashamed to say we were quite drunk when it happened, so I don't really remember. He mentioned Mr. Santos, I think."

"I see." José leaned forward in his chair, interested.

"I can't be sure . . . only when we mentioned we were under the patronage of Mr. Santos, he became quite angry and all but threw us out of his house." He looked at Ernie for confirmation, but Ernie shrugged.

"I haven't a clue, old man," he said. "Can't remember a moment past pudding. Mark of a good rum, or whatever that hell-water was we were drinking." It was not unusual for Ernie to forget events that occurred when he was intoxicated, and he seemed unconcerned.

"Interesting," said José. He stroked his gigantic mustache for a moment. "What was this man's name?"

"Arturo. A retired sea captain. Do you have any idea what he might have been bothered by?"

"It is hard to tell." He sighed and adjusted his jacket, pulling it over his solid belly. "Some of the Portuguese are jealous of the success of the rubber developers. You may have run into nothing more than a case of petty envy. I would forget about it immediately."

Thomas smiled. "Yes, of course. I will. I don't even know if I'm remembering it correctly. Thank you, sir."

"Do you know what he is like?" asked Ernie.

"Santos?" José smiled. "A good man. But a man to be careful with. He likes to play games with people, I am told. You should be wary of him, but at the same time treat him with respect. And he will do the same for you, I am sure of it."

As they spoke, evening was falling around them. Thomas had setting to do, so he too excused himself and joined John in their hut.

"An interesting man, don't you think, John?"

John sat at his desk scribbling notes. "Yes," he said, without turning around.

His posture invited no more conversation, so Thomas unpacked his day's catches: several of the speedy *Junonia lavinia*, with iridescent green patches on their brown lower wings, which he had managed to catch as they gathered at a mud puddle; some male *Papilio torquatus*, black with pink and white spots, and one precious female, which with its black and yellow markings, had excited him prematurely. He took them from their temporary boxes, where they had been pinned onto pieces of cork. He picked up his pen and card to write the labels for them—the species, the location, and his own name next to the date. He was pleased that he had not had to consult any books—he was as sure of these species as he was of his own name. He thought about what the hat merchant had said—as long as one can read one can be educated. So Thomas had never studied entomology at Cambridge as George had. So what? He had a good general education—the rest of what he needed to know about science he could glean from the books he read. Alfred Wallace had never trained as an entomologist, yet he was accepted by the Entomological Society as a pioneer. He made a mental note to himself to spend more time reading and less time daydreaming, although he had read all the books he had brought with him. He would read them again.

He was also envious of the way José slipped easily between English and Portuguese. Thomas's Portuguese was still very limited. He could give basic instructions to the men, but relied heavily on John to translate sentences for him.

As he set a *Cithaerias aurorina* on its new card, his hand slipped and tore one of its wings. He cursed to himself, then looked up to see if John had heard him. If he had, he didn't react. He lifted the specimen up again and ran a light finger over the tear. It was so delicate that he couldn't feel it on his callused fingers. He placed the wing between his finger and thumb and rubbed harder, and there it was—the velvety texture, seducing his skin. His fingertips came away with stardust on them and he wondered at the jewel-like quality of the butterfly. What woman needed diamonds, he thought, or sapphires, if she had a butterfly to adorn her? He glanced at an unusually small *Morpho rhetenor* he had carried from Santarém, reluctant to leave it behind. He would make a gift of it to Sophie, perhaps set it in resin so she could pin it to her coat or her hat. Its wings would reflect the blue of her eyes, its deep black lines her eyelashes.

He worked on. Paulo brought his supper but it went cold on his desk. Finally, when he had finished his work, he looked up, blinking, surprised to find himself still at his desk. He had mounted and set all the day's catch, as well as labeling them. He had then written in his journal of the place and manner he had caught each one, and sketched the specimens, pausing to fill in strategic whorls of color—a pink spot here, a red stripe there. His paints could never compete with the natural, iridescent colors, but he sat back and took in his work with satisfaction.

John had already retired; Thomas hadn't even heard him, he was so engrossed in his work. He looked at his pocket watch and saw that it was well past midnight. He packed his paints away quietly and went outside for a cigarette. When he drew back the curtain from the doorway, something dark bumped against his face. He threw his arm up in alarm and knocked a huge moth to the ground. It floundered around on the ground, dazed, before righting itself and launching into the night air, in the direction of Ernie's hut. Thomas took a deep breath. He had felt the moth's wings beating on his face, felt its powder brush onto his face and into his eyes. He imagined that he had breathed it in and an involuntary cough welled up inside him.

He heard a noise behind him, and John stood before him in his underwear, his hair standing straight up.

"What's wrong, Thomas? I heard you yell."

Had he yelled? He didn't remember doing so, but he had been smothered by the moth's attack.

"Sorry. It was nothing. Just a moth. It startled me."

John chuckled. "And you call yourself a lepidopterist?"

"No, I don't!" Thomas snapped.

John apologized quickly. "I have noticed, Thomas, that you haven't been collecting moths. Any reason?"

"No," said Thomas, too hastily, he knew. He turned his face away so that John could not see the blush on his cheeks. "Sorry for getting you up. I'm fine."

John stood there for a moment and the silence between them was palpable. Then he let out a grunt and closed the curtain. Thomas was in near darkness again. The moth, which must have been hovering by the crack of light at the doorway, had merely dived for it when Thomas opened the curtain. It was unlikely that he had been attacked. Nasty, ugly thing.

He shook his head at his own morbid imagination and rolled a cigarette. The compound was silent, except for the usual forest sounds. No light escaped from any of the other huts. Thomas had heard Ernie's offer to share his hut with José; no doubt he thought he had found a new drinking partner. Thomas supposed Ernie had warned him about the ants. José's man Manuel was probably squashed into the men's hut.

He inhaled and felt the nicotine in the cigarette enter his veins and make its way to his heart, where the beating had subsided. He hadn't known before that smoking could be such a pleasure, that it would be the thing he craved when he was upset or disturbed in some way. He also thought he wouldn't mind a drink, but he pushed the thought away.

As he stood still, not leaning against the wall for fear of what might crawl into his shirt, he heard a shuffle across the compound and saw a shadow slip from George's hut. He could barely make it out, but the figure stood for a moment, and he nearly called to it.

He stopped himself in case he woke everyone. It must be George, nipping out to relieve himself. But the figure crouched low and scuttled across the yard to the men's hut and disappeared.

Thomas threw his cigarette on the ground and jogged over to George's hut. He knocked on the doorframe. "George," he whispered.

"What?" came a voice from inside. "Who is it?"

Thomas pulled back the curtain. "Are you all right?" he asked. "I thought I saw something."

"What? What did you see? Of course I'm all right."

"One of the men . . ."

"There's no man in here."

"I thought you were asleep. I saw someone come out of your hut—"

"Nonsense, man. I've been awake the whole time. There's been nobody here but me." He turned over in his hammock, facing away from Thomas. "Go back to bed."

Up the Tapajós, January 2, 1904

We are nearing the end of our time in this godforsaken place. I am ashamed to admit that I am longing for the relative comforts of Santarém, but who will read this journal other than myself? Our salted meat has run out. The men took the canoes a little upriver to a village to trade, but all they managed to bring back was a skinny chicken and some fruit. Their fishing endeavors amounted to little—I understand now why the residents of Captain Arturo's settlement were so thin—even fish is not in as much supply as on the main river. We had one fish go around between the eight of us, and though it was large it didn't last long.

Ernie diagnosed my stomach cramps as constipation, and I am not surprised. I was so unwilling to do my business, my body unconsciously held on to it. It took something extraordinary to alleviate the problem. Imagine my horror when João appeared one afternoon with a monkey—a dear little long-haired creature with white hands—a *whaiápu-saí*, as the natives call it. João had the decency to kill it before he brought it back to camp so we would not have to listen to its cries. He carried it by tying its tail around its neck and using it as a handle. He seemed at first to be swinging some kind of purse when he approached the camp, all smiles. Late that evening he placed it on the fire to burn its hair off and I had to leave the compound. With its hair gone, it looked even more like a tiny human baby. Its hands were so like a child's that I imagined it reaching out to me, much in the way the *caboclo* children reached out to me for coins. I'm afraid this thought made me quite sick in the stomach, and I spent the next half hour squatting in the undergrowth, well away from the camp, the monkey, and the nests of red ants. It cleared up my stomach cramps at least.

I couldn't bring myself to eat the monkey; to me it would have been like eating a baby. The locals sometimes have these monkeys as pets—I saw many on the shoulders of the villagers. By all accounts they don't make very agreeable pets—they are not as playful as one might expect and rather tend to sulky behavior—but to me that makes them even more human. The others were hungry enough to eat it. Ernie berated me, said I should keep my strength up or risk falling ill, but I do not see how a few days with less food will hurt me all that much. It is true that I have lost some weight since arriving in Brazil—my clothes are looser—but there is nothing to be alarmed about yet. We have been very lucky in that regard, and I know it cannot last.

It is now a week since José the hat merchant left us. He was gone when we awoke in the morning. Even Ernie, who shared his room, had not heard him leave, but this is not so unusual—he had probably been drunk the night before and could hear nothing over his own snores. It wasn't until after he had gone we realized we had not seen any of his hats.

Tomorrow we depart for Santarém. We have exhausted the collecting opportunities in this area—at least as much as our bodies will tolerate. It is shameful, I know—the great naturalists who went before us spent months up the tributaries: we have lasted barely two weeks. I sense that I am feeling it the most—even George, who appears to be a man comfortable only among civilized people, has not complained as much as I would have expected.

There is still no sign of my butterfly—the people we have met in the area have never heard of it. I am beginning to despair that it has all been for nothing, and that my journey up the Amazon will in the end amount to nothing more than the collection of a few pretty insects and a body's worth of insect bites. I did not manage to escape being stung by the wretched fire ants, and our time here has been punctuated by shouts of pain. Ernie even has a sting on his face, which gives him a clownish appearance, so close to his nose. I vow right now not to allow myself to be made to camp around such a hazard. Alligators and snakes I can tolerate—it's the unseen menace of the lurking insect that chills me to the bone.

FIVE

*I*F ONE BUTTERFLY MAKES no sound, coasting on the air, harnessing it with a flicker of its wings, would a swarm of butterflies be silent as well? Thomas has told Sophie before about the giant flocks of monarch butterflies that migrate from Central America, fanning out across the world. She imagines standing in a field one day while a flock of monarchs looms behind her—a storm cloud, silent. Would the air crackle the way it does before an electrical storm, when a black tempest puffs at the horizon and moves across the sun? Or would she hear the butterflies as she might hear a wind, passing through anything that gives it resistance, stirring, whispering? She imagines the flock of butterflies as a giant sigh, building up behind her and escaping as the monarchs pass through and around her, parting as the river does around a rock, opening and meeting again, liquid.

But the beating wings. Surely, though generally inaudible to the human ear, when magnified a thousandfold they must produce a sound. A flapping as of bird wings, or the steady flick of a deck of cards. Do people in Mexico stop and look up as a dark swarm of butterflies moves overhead? Leaning on their hoes as they work their land, taking their hats off and wiping at their brows, raising a hand to block the sting of sunlight so they might observe the phenomenon better?

All this Sophie thinks of, as she kneels alone in the church for prayer. Her thoughts have spun away from the spiritual and once again to Thomas—meandering sideways to the butterflies. She is lucky, she knows, that Thomas has always shared his knowledge with her, telling her snippets of information that she might be curious about. Such as the monarch, and how people have stumbled into valleys of them in the jungle, where every tree and leaf and flower heaves with them, a tapestry of orange and black, where walking means treading on the beautiful creatures by the hundreds. She should like to see a sight such as that before she dies, but doesn't suppose she ever will.

It is now more than a week since she met Thomas at the station, and beyond his occasional communication through a nod or the shake of his head, she's made little progress with him.

A shuffle of soft shoes catches her attention. The vicar pads down the aisle. She catches his eye and begins to rise.

"I'm sorry, Mrs. Edgar," he says. "I didn't mean to disturb you."

She brushes at her skirts, then pats her hair. "You didn't. I was just leaving."

"And how are you?"

She sits back down on the pew, and he sits too, perched on the edge of the aisle. She is always surprised, when she sees him sitting, that his legs manage to reach the floor. When he first visited her house, he was swallowed by the armchair in the drawing room, and always chose a hard, straight-backed chair from then on. Though modest, he seems very self-conscious about his size. She often wonders if he has grown such thick muttonchops to prevent people mistaking him for a child. His face reminds her of a little pug's.

"I'm not well, I'm afraid," says Sophie. "You know my husband is back."

His eyebrows rise. The beginning of a smile. "No, I didn't. That's wonderful!" He puts his hand to his mouth and glances sideways around the empty church. "Wonderful," he says again, more quietly.

Sophie doesn't look at him.

"Oh, but things are not so wonderful," he deduces. His face collapses into seriousness again. He rubs at his chin.

"I've been meaning to tell you, but I didn't know where to start. I suppose I was hoping it wouldn't be a problem for long." She stops and picks at a loose splinter on the pew in front.

"Are you all right, Mrs. Edgar? Please, do go on. I'm listening."

Sophie sighs and tells him everything that has occurred since Thomas's return—everything, that is, except the part where she lied to her father. She thinks hard about this. By not telling him, is she now lying to the vicar, too? Surely that is a wicked sin? But no. She is simply being selective with her information. Her jaw becomes tight; she is a coward. She knows full well she isn't telling him in order to not incriminate herself. Selfish, selfish.

The vicar listens generously, without speaking. This is his usual behavior—he encourages people to relate their whole story or predicament before offering any comfort or advice. When she has finished, he makes a steeple of his joined hands and presses his face against his raised fingers.

"Hmm" is all he says.

Sophie waits patiently. A cool breeze scratches at her neck; the door to the church has come slightly ajar. She watches the colored patterns on the floor from the stained-glass windows fade in and out as the sun passes behind clouds and out again.

"I'm very sorry for your troubles," he says at last. "This is indeed a test for you. But it has only been a short time . . . perhaps he will come right of his own accord. I trust you will bring him to the service tomorrow?"

"Do you think I should? To be honest . . . I was hoping to keep him away from prying eyes until he is better."

"I understand your reluctance. But who knows what opportunities he had to commune with God in the jungle? Perhaps just setting foot in our little chapel will do him the world of good."

Sophie nods, her eyes downcast.

"You have nothing to be ashamed of, Mrs. Edgar, if that is what you are thinking. Your husband is ill, that is all. It is no different than if he were recovering from pneumonia, or had a broken leg. At least he is able to physically come to church."

Sophie is silent, thinking. She remembers again the time she watched Thomas in prayer. He was enraptured. Surely he has not lost the part of him that can be moved so? But then she remembers the little butterfly that flew out from his hands. Perhaps it wasn't the church or God that had moved him after all.

"Thank you, Vicar," she says. "I will think over what you have said. You are very kind."

"As are the members of our congregation, Mrs. Edgar. I know that people can be judgmental, but I'm sure you will also find they can be kind, that they will only want what is best for you."

She hopes he is right.

AGATHA STANDS AT THE end of Robert Chapman's garden while Robert attacks her neck with wet kisses.

"No, I have to go," she says, and pushes him away.

"You're a brave woman, Agatha Dunne. Imagine if someone saw you here, standing in my garden like this. Unchaperoned!" He takes her hat from her hands and places it on her head.

"Don't tease me, Robert. You know I'm careful that nobody sees me."

"Still, we ought to be more careful. We don't want you branded a wanton woman."

"Stop it, Robert. Is that what *you* think?"

"Darling." He pulls her into an embrace again. "You know I don't. I find your candor exciting. And refreshing," he says as she starts to jerk away again. He laughs as she struggles. Then, "Ow!" as she stamps on his foot.

"I am warning you," she says, and she knows then that she is giving him what he calls her "wild-eyed Gypsy stare." She can't help it. She mostly enjoys his touch but every now and then he clings a little too tightly, his tongue a little too wet.

He is still laughing, and she sighs and pins her hat, allowing herself to relax into a smile.

"All right, then," he relents. "I'll see you in church tomorrow. It's not long to go now, my sweet. We can begin a public courtship at the end of summer. You know it's just too soon after Nellie . . ."

"I know." The truth is, she doesn't know if she wants to begin a public courtship with Robert. That would make things too . . . official. The courtship would lead to marriage, and she's not sure she is ready for that. She has seen what it has done to her friends—turned them from carefree pranksters into serious ladies, all talk of servants and hostessing. Nothing makes them smile anymore; it is a serious business, being a wife. Except Sophie. She at least has retained some of her independence, but that is only because Thomas went off and left her like that. Agatha was the one to encourage her not to care what others thought of her, but she felt bad when disapproving looks were cast at Sophie in the street—looks to which Sophie herself had been oblivious.

Robert walks with her to the back gate and opens it into the quiet pocket of the park. He kisses her once more, dryly this time, on the cheek, before giving her a last, longing look and pushing the gate closed. It always makes her nervous when he starts talking about their future together, and she wonders, not for the first time, whether she wouldn't do better to break it off before he announces it to the world.

She turns and leans against the gate while fumbling in her pockets for her cigarettes. As she pulls them out, a small movement catches her eye. A figure sits on a log in the shadow, looking at her. She curses to herself; nobody ever comes to this part of the wood, except for the odd beetle collector, rummaging among the dead and rotting tree stumps. She takes a step closer, to determine whether it is someone she knows. Did they see that last kiss?

It is Thomas Edgar. She has to stop herself from gasping. This *is* a surprise. He rises as she approaches, and she has no choice but to go and greet him. What is he doing, lurking about in the shadowy, damp corner of the park? Sophie told her that he doesn't go out, that he stays in bed all day and mopes soundlessly.

He looks as shocked to see her as she is him. Agatha looks at the cigarette in her hand, and back at him. It is too late now—he's seen it. She shrugs and sits down on the log, and he drops himself back down. She fumbles with gloved hands to light her cigarette; in her haste, she breaks a match as she tries to strike it, and the next one she drops. A nervous giggle escapes her, and her cheeks begin to burn.

Thomas, with his bare hands, which are brown and callused, takes the matches from her, and she looks at him in surprise. He isn't looking at her; he concentrates on the matches. He strikes and the flame jumps to life. Slowly, he raises the match to her face and she cocks her head and touches the paper to the flame. Agatha looks behind them, to get her bearings, and sees only a steep bank; they are sheltered here, from the wind, and from prying eyes.

She inhales with a trembling hand. Thomas still holds the match, staring at it as if the answers to all the world's questions are contained in its flickering flame. He doesn't throw it away until it burns him, at which point he drops it and immediately puts his thumb in his mouth. It comes out glistening with saliva, and he licks it one more time before replacing his hands in his lap. Agatha realizes he is now staring at her cigarette, where it balances between gloved fingers on her knee. When she raises it to her lips, his eyes follow it, and his stare is hungry.

He wants one, she thinks. She didn't even know he smoked.

She shakes one out for him and he takes it quickly, lighting it in one fluid motion. He inhales deeply, and closes his eyes as he blows out a transparent dribble of smoke; most of it seems to have been absorbed into his body.

"Have you been sitting here long, Mr. Edgar?" she asks.

He shakes his head and goes back to his cigarette. His face has taken on an almost serene appearance, such is the pleasure it obviously gives him. She still has no clue as to whether he saw her with Robert.

"Are you feeling better?"

He nods slowly, still not looking at her.

"I meant to call on old Mrs. Hatchett, but I'm afraid I got a little lost. I was sure her house was through that gate there, but it turns out I was wrong."

He looks at her then, and nods again. Is that a smile curling at the edges of his mouth?

"Mr. Edgar," she says, determined to change tack and swing him away from the reasons for her presence in this part of the park, "Sophie is very worried about you. Can you not tell her what is the matter? You can still write, can't you? Why not write it down for her?"

All trace of the smile leaves him. Instead, his eyes grow wide and sad. How small he looks. He has lost any sign of the youth that once plumped his cheeks. His pert lips quiver before he takes the last puff of his cigarette and flings it away with a surprisingly powerful flick of his wrist.

"I would say, Mr. Edgar, that you look like a man with a secret." She angles her head toward him and blows out her last stream of smoke. It wafts around his face. She drops her voice to a hoarse whisper. "Do you have a secret, Thomas?"

This gets a reaction from him at least. He stands and draws himself up tall, then makes a movement with his head, which could be an assenting nod, or could be a clumsy sort of a bow, dismissing himself. He turns and marches away, his arms stiff at his sides.

Agatha feels a surge of energy. She has really touched the quick. What possessed her to say it? There was something in his face that leapt out at her—he is concealing something; if it were found out, he might talk again. But he has her secret too, probably. She's not bothered about smoking in front of him—if he knows about Robert, then he might as well know about her habit—and it's not as if he would tell anyone, would he? Her breathing calms and she chuckles. She can tell him anything, now, can't she? Perhaps he will become her unwilling confidant. Lord knows that Sophie is too easily shocked.

SOPHIE LIES IN HER bed and watches the line of sunlight move across the floor. When it reaches her she knows it is time to get up and get ready for church. She remembers Thomas telling her how as a child he watched a similar patch of sun in the spring—that if it wasn't there when he woke up, he knew that it was a gray day and the butterflies would be in hiding. Even worse, if it was raining he would have to spend the day inside with his brother Cameron, who would inevitably pull his ear or push him over and make him cry.

She washes and dresses carefully, with Mary's assistance, in tight stays—which emphasize her already substantial bosom and pitch her forward with a concave back; two petticoats; a high-necked blouse with leg-o'-mutton sleeves; and her best Sunday suit—an emerald green woolen skirt with a slight train and bolero jacket that Agatha helped her pick out. At the time Agatha said it was boring. "But if it's for church, boring is probably what you want," she'd said with a sigh. The rigidity of the undergarments will leave her breathless and sore within a few hours, and she will join the rest of the women in the congregation in tottering about stupidly in order not to fall flat on her face from being front-heavy.

Sophie takes time to do her hair, backcombing it into a high bouffant and letting Mary set it with pins that pinch and scrape at her scalp. Dark circles puff under her eyes, and she applies powder to them with little result. The powder catches in her dark eyelashes and in the natural light that falls through the window. Her blue eyes are magnets in her face. Such a contrast, the long dark lashes against her blond hair. She can scarcely admit this to herself, but she is aware that she is taking more care than usual, as if today is a special day. And it is—she will take Thomas out in public; not for the first time, but for the first time into a circle of acquaintances. Perhaps if she is immaculately and fashionably dressed, she can draw attention away from him. She wishes she had thought to borrow one of Agatha's elaborate hats, which seem to get bigger and fruitier every week.

With a last look in the mirror, and a pinch of her pale cheeks, she satisfies herself that she is ready.

Due to the direction of Thomas's window, the sun has not penetrated the edges of his thick curtains, and the room is as dark as dusk. She pushes open the door silently and listens for a moment to his rasping breath as he sleeps. There was a time when this served only as Thomas's dressing room and they spent every night together in her bed—*their* bed, really, though she now thinks of it as only hers. In the gloom, she makes out his arm, covered with his soft cotton nightshirt, flung over his head. Up closer, he seems feverish—sweat darkens the curls that frame his face and she can feel a heat emanating from his body as she sits on the bed beside him. In his sleep, he shakes his head and grunts. Her stomach flutters—this is the first sound she has heard from him. If she sits very still, will he stay asleep and utter some words—the sounds of the bad dream he is having?

Instead, Thomas gasps and opens his eyes.

"I'm here," she says quickly, not wanting to startle him. "Shh. You were having a bad dream."

He blinks at her before closing his eyes as relief passes over his face. He wipes at his brow with his sleeve, then pushes the covers down, letting the cool air touch his body. She lets him lie for a moment, getting his bearings, before she rises and opens the curtains. A dull wash illuminates the room.

"I thought we might go to church," she says. "The service starts in an hour. Enough time for you to bathe and get dressed. Mary will have breakfast ready for you soon."

Thomas doesn't nod as she expects him to, or make a move to get out of bed. Instead, he pulls the covers up again and turns over, pushing his back to her.

"Thomas?" She lays a hand on his shoulder, then pulls it away as if she has been burned. She has touched a handful of sharp bones. "Darling, please. You must get back into society. You've hardly left the house."

She says nothing about it, but she knows he leaves the house when she is not there. She came home from church yesterday to find him in bed, but she tripped over his boots and fresh mud brushed onto her skirts. When she questioned Mary about it, the girl said she assumed that the master had spent the morning in bed; that she had taken him a cup of tea just after Sophie had left and had seen nothing more of him as she went about her chores.

But now he is refusing to come to church with her. She draws herself up and, without another word, leaves him to his mood.

THE CHURCH IS UNBEARABLY hot—the first sign that summer might be on its way. All around Sophie, people fan themselves with hats and Bibles, which create an ineffectual whisper of a breeze. She feels sweat building up between her thighs and under her arms, and her stays are suddenly tighter than they have ever been before. The vicar holds on to his pulpit with both hands. He stands on a box behind it, giving him the illusion of unnatural height. His voice is soporific as he drones on about this or that virtue and sin, and for the first time she can remember, Sophie has stopped listening. A blowfly butts against the window closest to her and in her head the sermon and the insect's buzzing mingle and become one.

Agatha is starting to nod off beside her; Sophie manages to nudge her just before a snore—which she has heard building—is released into the thick atmosphere. If only Sophie hadn't worn the woolen suit, but had chosen a light muslin dress instead. But all her summer dresses are in a trunk, carefully folded away until the weather is more promising.

She is aware of somebody's face turned toward her. Captain Fale is looking at her from across the aisle. He nods at her before averting his eyes.

After the service, during which the rousing hymns woke everybody up, the congregation files sluggishly outside and a collective sigh ripples through the crowd at the cool breeze. It is as if they have been let out from some prison, the tall church doors thrown open like gates. The jailer stands at the bottom of the steps and shakes everybody's hand as he or she leaves. He grasps Sophie's and looks up earnestly into her eyes while his little nose twitches.

"You didn't bring your husband today, Mrs. Edgar?"

"No," she says. "He was very feverish this morning. I think he may be really ill." More lies, falling on top of one another like dead leaves.

"Ah, that is a shame. Be sure to have the doctor look at him, won't you? We look forward to seeing him next time."

And then she is moving past him and he is shaking Agatha's hand with a smile, but the two have nothing to say to each other, and Mrs. Cotton, behind Agatha, is eager to grab him and twinkle at him about how delighted she was, just *delighted*, with the sermon.

Agatha takes the opportunity of the vicar's distraction to grasp Sophie's arm and pull her aside. "What is all that about? I haven't had a chance to ask you. Invite me for tea."

Sophie smiles at her. "Yes, of course." She welcomes the confidence she can bestow on her friend. Agatha understands her better than anyone.

"Mrs. Edgar." Sophie turns as Captain Fale approaches her. He wears his uniform today, which accentuates his strong frame. "So nice to see you on this fine day. I thought the whole congregation was going to faint from the heat."

Sophie touches her cheek and feels the warmth through her gloves. "Yes, it certainly is hot. A nice breeze out here, though." How shadowed his face is always, she thinks. Even at church, for which he must have freshly shaved, his beard is visible beneath the surface of his skin. It gives him a bearlike appearance, although he is never gruff with her. His body is a dark mass compared to her husband's.

She glances at Agatha, who has been sequestered by Robert Chapman. They stand a respectable distance apart, she is relieved to see, and appear to be exchanging polite pleasantries.

"I meant to ask you," says Fale, "how are things with Mr. Edgar? The last time I saw you he was not so . . . well. He is too ill to come to church?"

"It's not that," she blurts, then stops herself. *Damn.* She puts her hand to her mouth in case her thought escapes her mouth and she swears in public. Captain Fale has that effect on her, though. He seems to be able to draw out the things she most wants to keep to herself. But she can trust him, can't she? He always gives her good advice. He is looking at her, waiting, so she goes on. "I tried to get him up for the service, but he refused." Her nose begins to tingle, a sign that she might start crying. She puts her hand on it and squashes it into her face, covering her mouth as she does so.

"Why, do you think?" he asks.

"Oh, it will undoubtedly be the crowds. He seems to value quiet, and in his present condition I'm sure he won't want to face people with their questions and their well-meaning chitchat. You know . . ." She goes to lay a hand on his arm but stops herself. "Nobody really knows about this, Samuel. I would appreciate it if you didn't tell anyone."

Captain Fale's shadowed cheeks begin to flush. He opens his mouth as if to say something. No doubt she has disarmed him with her use of his Christian name. She doesn't know what possessed her, but at the same time it felt right.

"Of course not, Mrs. *Edgar*," he says at last, with an emphasis on her married name. "But . . . are you sure it is your husband's worry about the crowds that has prevented him coming to church?"

"Yes, I'm sure. I will bring him here again later, when there is nobody about. Why? Do you have another idea?"

"Only that . . ." He shifts on his cane. "Do you think perhaps that he has . . . how can I put this? Perhaps he has compromised . . . that is, maybe in the jungle he had his faith . . . challenged."

Sophie is horrified. "Whatever do you mean, sir?"

"Please, madam," he says quickly. "I mean you no offense. Please forgive me. I just meant that perhaps he has fallen away from some of his . . . duties."

"Are you suggesting that my husband is now some kind of *pagan*?" This she says too loudly, and Agatha and Mr. Chapman stop speaking to look her way. Several groups continue to mill about, and she sees gloved hands go to mouths, words whispered behind them and nods in her direction. They know, she thinks. They all know. It is no wonder nobody spoke to her when she arrived; she didn't notice at the time, but now she recalls Mrs. Cotton turning her slightly humped back to her, Mr. and Mrs. Deighton stepping quickly out of her way.

"Please, forgive me," Captain Fale says again. "I meant nothing of the sort. Please forget I said anything."

Sophie finds she is trembling, and to hide it she turns her back to him. "We must be going," she murmurs. "Good day."

Agatha, frowning, disengages herself immediately and takes Sophie's arm. Together they turn up the hill toward home.

. . .

STUPID, STUPID. HOW COULD he be so stupid? The captain's walk home is a painful one. His leg always seems to give him trouble when he is upset. Normally he gives in to it and takes a hansom cab, but today he wants to punish himself. His admonishments come in time with his shuffling gait and the tapping of his cane.

Idiot. *Tap*. Cad. *Tap*.

His house is remarkably cool, given the closed windows and how hot it was in church; but it is always cold. Even in the middle of summer he lights fires at night in an effort to warm the place. He puts this down to the sparse furnishing: a decor he has taken little interest in. There is no doubt about it: the house requires a woman's touch. Mrs. Brown cleans for him, certainly, and cooks, but she doesn't live here; she certainly doesn't interfere with the house beyond her duty, never offering to embroider a cushion for the hard settee in the drawing room, or to cut some flowers from the garden to brighten the mantelpiece. Not that she would find many out there; beyond a neatly trimmed lawn and several rosebushes tended by a hired gardener a few times a year, the garden is as bare as the house. One day, he thinks, one day, it will be filled with blossoming flowers and perhaps even a few children running back and forth on hobbyhorses or with hoops and sticks, or whatever it is that children play with these days.

At least if he had a wife he could widen his circle of friends and stop spending all his time with other bachelors, and with his old army friends, who only keep in touch with him out of pity. He's not the only cripple he knows—Jack Burroughs lost an arm in the war, but nobody feels sorry for him, especially since he pins his empty sleeve up with his bloody medals. Jack got married soon after he returned; the women flocked to him, and his wife mollycoddles him beyond belief. But those men: they never try to introduce Fale to their wives' younger sisters, or their own, as if he's not good enough for them. No wonder he hasn't found anyone to marry. The men enjoy his company, enjoy analyzing politics over a brandy and a cigar, but when they start talking about the war, and the blasted Boers, he feels their shoulders turn away from him, until someone will flick a glance his way, clear his throat, and change the subject. It's not his fault he missed it. It was that bloody horse's. He should have had the thing shot. He'd rather have died in the war than feel the space that blooms inside him sometimes.

He drops, exhausted, into his armchair by the fireplace. It is only eleven o'clock, and already his stomach gurgles. At least he has an hour to get his strength back and to calm his nerves before he is due out for luncheon.

Well, he handled that badly, to be sure. How sweet Sophie looked when she told him about trying to rouse her husband. Her fine nostrils went an endearing pink before she put her hand over her face and composed herself. He thought for a moment she must have known he had met her father at the Star and Garter, when she asked him like that not to tell anybody—he found himself blushing, and his embarrassment at her seeing him in that state made him blush even more. But he had chosen not to speak out about her husband's condition to her father. For now.

It cut him up to see her turn away from him so angrily. Why had he opened his mouth? He reaches for the whiskey bottle he keeps secreted behind his chair and takes a swig. She is mad at him now, but might not his words sow in her a tiny seed of doubt? She seems to be the brooding type; perhaps she will go home and think about what he said, start to read a few signs here and there, and decide that her husband has indeed become . . . a heathen. A nonbeliever, after all.

But he mustn't lose her trust. He will send her a card, an apology, tomorrow. He must proceed very slowly and softly. Perhaps it is time to contact Mr. Winterstone again. As a barrister, surely he would have the right contacts to further proceedings.

He takes another nip of whiskey. Yes, this room is bare. What it needs is some of those lacy doily things that women like to hang over the backs of chairs. Maybe some new wallpaper, something flowery. Is he mad himself? Surely Sophie would never consider divorce. But then again . . . they have no children. Wouldn't her husband's insanity present a perfectly legal case to clear the way to the only woman he desires? All they would need is a good solicitor on their side.

AFTER AGATHA LEAVES, SOPHIE sits for a long time looking out into the garden, where the flowers are thriving in the spring weather. Her roses have had a sudden spurt of growth and the buds sit tightly coiled, ready to open. Daffodils nod their heads in the breeze. Crocuses cluster together in the far flower bed like butterflies gathered to lap at a puddle, along with the pretty little violas and pansies she planted only last month. The lilac and philadelphus that line the garden path have flowered and the orange-tinted scent drifts in through the open window.

Inside, though, Sophie is cold. Thomas hasn't come down, and she can't face going to him. He probably sneaked out while she and Mary were at church on one of his secret expeditions that leave his boots caked with mud and, she has also discovered, his pockets filled with mulch from the forest floor.

Secret. That is the word that Agatha used. *I think Thomas has a secret, Sophie. You should try to find out what it is.* She gave no reason for this new suspicion, but Sophie is not at all surprised by it. Not after what Captain Fale said at church.

What if he is right? When she looks into Thomas's eyes, all that light that burned is gone. It's as if all the muscles in his face have been paralyzed, so devoid is it of any kind of expression. What if he has lost his faith? What would be the point of living without it? What if he wastes away, his soul barren and withered, until he just dies one day, and there's nowhere for him to go but straight to hell.

She begins to cry. Tiny, discreet sobs at first, but as she realizes that Mary is out and Thomas upstairs with three doors between them, she lets herself fall into her grief as if it were a well—deep and black, with mossy brick sides and a stench of fungus.

When she has finished, she feels better, but a new feeling now eats at her. How much Thomas has deprived her of ! When he was away, she felt truly independent for the first time, with nobody to consult about any aspect of her existence. All decisions were hers alone, with no man to override her or take charge—not her father, not Thomas, not even Agatha's father. She rehearsed over and over in her head, as she glided across the park, just how she would explain to him when he returned that she didn't want him to take care of her, to treat her as an invalid, or a child, or somebody incapable of any kind of thought or movement, as so many women seemed to be treated. She planned to tell him she would be needing more independence.

But he has robbed her of that option. Now she *has* to be the strong one; there is no choice in the matter. She is impotent once more, with Thomas dictating how her life is going to be.

She stands and throws down her sodden handkerchief. Blast him! If he has a secret, she'll find out what it is.

The hallway is in darkness. With all the doors to the rooms shut, no light illuminates its creaky corners. Thomas's study is under the stairs and the door has stayed shut since the cabdriver stacked Thomas's crates in there on the day of his arrival. Not even Thomas has been in there.

When she opens the curtains, light falls as a sheet through dancing dust motes. The atmosphere chokes her: a mixture of stale air, dust, and the chemicals Thomas uses to kill and preserve his precious insects. She sneezes, then pushes the window up and takes great gulps of air. She disturbs a thrush outside, which carries a snail in its beak. When it sees she doesn't intend any harm, it goes back to its task of hitting the snail against a rock.

The crates sit where the man left them, assembled in the corner of the room below a wall map of England—marked with flags where Thomas has found this or that rare butterfly—and beside his precious Brady drawers, in which he keeps his best specimens.

They are nailed shut, but she soon finds a metal instrument to prize a lid open. The cracking, tearing sound of the wood and nails clashing startles her and she stops for a moment and listens, expecting to hear Thomas's footsteps on the stairs above. But the only sound is the tapping of the tenacious thrush with its snail.

She lifts the lid off carefully and sets it on the ground. Her hands come away blackened: this is one of the crates tarnished by the smoke from the ship's fire. A powerful chemical odor hits her in the face and she leans away, the back of her hand to her mouth. She supposes the chemical is necessary to stop the specimens being attacked by fungus or parasites or whatever the danger is for them. Inside the crate more boxes are packed together, and when she opens these, still more, this time floating in cotton wool and sawdust, which is infused with the foul smell. When she picks some up and runs it through her fingers, she detects a base note of camphor. In the smaller boxes—some are cigar boxes, others biscuit tins—lie little parcels of paper with twisted corners. She lifts one carefully and unfolds it. Out slips what she first mistakes for a jewel—the most exquisite creature she has ever seen. It is a butterfly, with clear wings speckled with stardust. Two bright spots of the deepest pink appear to have been painted on this morning, they are so vivid. She can see the color of her hand through the transparent wings. The inside of the envelope is inscribed in Thomas's careful handwriting: *Cithaerias aurorina*, River Tapajós, Brazil. She turns the butterfly this way and that, catching its wings in the light.

Sophie opens several more boxes and envelopes. In the sturdiest boxes, butterflies are pinned in rows, with labels etched onto tiny strips of paper below. A few of them have jagged tears in their wings. When she opens one of the boxes, only chunks and crumbs fall out, and she jumps up to brush her skirts off as half a body falls into them, the remains of its wings little more than tiny rags. But most of them are perfect: large butterflies and small ones, some of the most breathtaking, luminous primary colors, others with intricate markings like drawings—all perfectly symmetrical. If she didn't know better she might think they had been manufactured by man, that Thomas made them himself from silk and oil colors. But no—these are a testament to the artistic flair of a benevolent God. She feels a surge of pride.

She opens another crate, and there, on top, is a small tin with her name inscribed on it. She stops for a moment, breathing hard. Should she open it? It has her name on it, but should she wait for Thomas to show her? Her hands itch and tremble, and she finds them pulling her toward the tin, fumbling with the lid, prizing it off. Inside, on a bed of snow-white cotton wool, sits a deep blue butterfly, its wings rimmed with black. She stares at it; she feels it luring her in; it is as if she could fall into those wings. It is the most beautiful of them all. She looks for the inscription. On the inside of the lid there is a note. "Sophie. It reminds me of your eyes. Love, Thomas."

Thomas, she thinks, as her vision blurs. *My Thomas. What happened to you, my love?*

She doesn't think she will find any more clues in these boxes, just more butterflies, as lovely as they are. He told her in his letters that he was keeping a journal. Where would she find that? She closes her eyes for a moment and squeezes the last of the tears out of them. She sees a picture of Thomas on the day she met him at the station, standing on the platform, looking so frightened of her, trembling like a newborn calf—his thin arms wrapped around that Gladstone bag.

She carefully replaces all the lids and dusts herself off. Her hands have left black streaks on her skirts and as she passes the hallway mirror she startles herself: her eyes are wide, and tears have traced intricate patterns through the soot on her cheeks. Her hair, which she carefully set only that morning, is coming detached from its pins. She pauses to smooth it.

Upstairs, she hears Thomas's even breathing and pushes his door open. The bag is where he left it, right by the doorway. With one eye on her sleeping husband, Sophie picks up the bag and closes the door softly. She crosses the landing to her own room and sets it down while she washes her hands and face at her basin. The water turns an inky black. The bed is too pristine and white to risk soiling, so she sits on the little chair she uses to drape her clothes on at nighttime. It gives a shudder under her weight—how long since she actually sat on it?—but holds fast.

The clasp on the bag releases stiffly, and deposits more grit into her hands; it appears that Thomas has not opened it for some time. On the top of the bag Sophie recognizes her own handwriting—her letters, tied tightly with the blue velvet ribbon she sent him with the first one. She fingers them, and lifts the pile from the bag. Seeing them clumped together like that, she realizes she had plenty to say to him while he was away—even after his letters stopped.

Underneath the letters, she knows she has found what she is looking for. She tips the bag out and four journals tumble to the floor, along with a few of his textbooks: *British Museum Handbook of Instructions for Collectors, Butterflies of South America, A Naturalist on the River Amazons*. She picks up the most battered-looking journal; the edges of its red cover have been worn white. It is tied with a band, and bulges thick and misshapen; shards of dried leaves poke out, and a fragrance emanates from its pages, from the flowers that are pressed inside. Sophie unties the band. The first page is headed *On the Atlantic, May 1903*—his outgoing voyage.

She hesitates and closes the book. Does she really want to be doing this? What gives her the right to go through his private papers? But surely, she is helping him. He is unable to speak for himself, and these journals will speak for him. And they are, after all, married—isn't that where her right comes from? But. There is a huge *but*. He would have shown them to her himself if he wanted her to see them. Her head is cloudy with the idea that she might not like what she finds, and that she would be better to leave the books untouched. But it is as if the books call to her, call for the words in them to be let out like caged insects. She can't help herself. She adjusts a cushion behind her back, and, as the afternoon light drains from the room, opens the journal and begins to read.

SIX

Santarém—Manaus, January 6th, 1904

Sophie,

I know I haven't written for a long time, but I have not wanted to worry you with my complaints. Of course, there was no chance to post a letter while we were upriver. I will be brief, dear—I am too tired to write much right now, but I did just want to let you know I am well. I am not feeling as healthy as I have been, but now we are back in civilization, I'm sure my strength will come back to me. Suffice to say we had a stimulating time up the Tapajós. We met some interesting characters along the way, but also came in contact with some of the more unpleasant aspects of life in the Amazon. Do not worry, my dear. I am unharmed. It has been a sad few days for me—a man we met on the Tapajós who entertained me one evening died not long after we left him. His house caught fire and he died trying to rescue his seven children, two of whom perished with him. We are trying to put it behind us as we move upriver to Manaus. Ernie is very excited about this city. I fear it is very expensive, and I understand collecting will be sparse *in the area, but we have been summoned by our patron, Mr. Santos, and, having stayed so long under his hospitality, we are obliged to go and stay with him for a time before moving on to the next camp that he has arranged for us, up the River Negro.*

I will finish this now, as there is much to be seen from the deck, and I am feeling a little weak. Nothing that a sit-down in the fresh air won't cure, I am sure. Thank you for your last letter. I am glad you are making new friends. The weather must be getting colder in England. I confess I am a little jealous, as there seems to be no respite from the sticky heat here.

Thomas

He slipped the single sheet of paper into its envelope. The thinness of the letter admonished him. Intending to go and find a steward to post it for him, he tucked it into his breast pocket, where it sat weightless and insubstantial. It was true he didn't want to worry her—talk of fire ants and jaguars and diarrhea was likely to do just that—but he was also unsettled after his last letter from her. It seemed she had been spending some time with her Captain Fale, who turned out not to be as old as Thomas had originally thought. Not only was she spending time with him, but she seemed to be *entertaining* him. She made a mention of the fact the captain had commented on the state of the drawing room, evidently inquiring as to whether Thomas intended to use the proceeds of his trip to redecorate. There was no mention of anybody else being present.

Thomas had suggested to her that she stay with her father, even though he knew it might make her miserable. When he thought of Mr. Winterstone, an upright man, he remembered the disappointment he had radiated when Thomas declared his intention to marry his daughter. His brother Cameron was a much better suitor in Sophie's father's opinion—the elder brother, the man to inherit the bulk of his father's wealth, while Thomas was to live on a more modest income. At the time, Thomas had felt the full force of his own indignation that this man—whose house was no bigger than the one Thomas intended to move into with Sophie once they were married—should question his ability to look after his daughter. He had made her a good husband, and would continue to do so. Most important, he loved her and cherished her more than he did any amount of money or status. Perhaps even more than he nursed his desire to become a great collector, more than his beloved butterflies.

Sophie had not wanted to stay with her father, and Thomas was secretly relieved. He did not want to give Mr. Winterstone the satisfaction of thinking Thomas had somehow abandoned his only daughter while the ink was still wet on their marriage license. But how headstrong Sophie could be! She insisted on staying alone in the house, regardless of what people thought of them, and now this business of entertaining a man at home. Alone. What would people think? He wrinkled his eyebrows and shook his head, pushing the thought away to the back of his mind, locking a gate to stop it from slipping to the front again.

After giving the letter to the steward, Thomas found John up on deck, leaning over the side with his face to the breeze. His features were grave, with intense concentration, as if he were listening for something. When Thomas caught his eye, he melted into a languid smile, which was soon gone again.

"We're approaching the Rio Negro," said the plant-hunter. "I've something to show you."

Thomas leaned out over the railing as John was doing, and turned his face upriver. The ship churned through the ocher waters. Ahead, a curled ribbon lay on the water, tapering forward from a point until it became a thick stripe. At first it seemed to be an oil slick, twisting and shining on the surface of the river, but as the ship plowed on, Thomas saw that it was simply a dark thread of water, which became thicker and bolder, until the steamer cut through the line where the two colors met, mixing them in its wake.

"What a sight!" said Thomas, and he felt his strength returning. "The waters of the River Negro, I presume? It certainly lives up to its name! How far is it to Manaus, do you think?"

"About fifty miles, I'd say. That's when they start to blend. Look." John faced the southern bank now, and pointed into the clouded water. A creature writhed in the liquid, and Thomas thought at first it was a naked man, but as the creature rose up and dived, he saw it was some other kind of mammal.

"Is it a manatee?"

"Dolphin," said John.

Thomas looked again. Surely not. Dolphins were sleek animals with shining graphite skin. This was pink and rubbery, with features that looked to be malleable, like raw clay. "The river dolphin?" said Thomas. "What a strange creature!" It had no fin, only a misshapen hump like a hunchback's, with a fatty outcrop on his head above its eyes.

"Yes, the *bouto*. It swims where the currents of two rivers meet, where it's more likely to find fish to feed on. I saw some when I swam around the mouth of the Tapajós."

They watched it in silence for a moment. Another joined it and together the cavorting dolphins rose out of the water with gasps and sighs.

"What a melancholy animal," said Thomas. "It seems so sad with its sighs."

"The *caboclos* believe they are some kind of water spirit, that they cause all manner of mischief."

"Like what?"

"It's believed the male *bouto* takes on human form and comes to shore to have relations with village women. It accounts for many an unexplained pregnancy and disease, I'm sure."

Thomas smiled.

"And the female is said to take the form of a beautiful woman who lures men to their deaths in the river." John leaned farther over the rail and his voice dropped to a murmur. "Not a bad way to go, drowned by a beautiful spirit."

"Is it only the *caboclos* who believe this?"

"I think they are the most superstitious of the Brazilians. Perhaps they have inherited all the superstition from their various cultures. I don't think the Indians believe any of it."

The dolphins took a last leap and fell behind.

"That's not all they believe. Anyone who uses *bouto* oil to light a lamp will be blinded if he works by it. If a fisherman kills one, he will lose his ability to fish and will eventually starve."

"And how do you know all of this, John?"

John smiled. "It's simple, really, Thomas. There's no secret. I talk to people. You ought to try it. You can gain a lot of trust from people if you just listen to them. I met a man on one of my walks, a rubber-tapper who had lost a hand in an accident. He told me about his brother, who killed a *bouto* that had stolen some fish from him. He had six children who eventually had to be put to work because the father could no longer catch any fish. He died of a fever. It sounded like malaria, if you ask me, but the man I met was convinced it was because of bad luck from killing the dolphin."

It was true Thomas had made little effort to get to know the local people. This was partly because he could not speak the language very well, but also he had been shy of them. When he came upon an Indian, or one of the mixes, a *mameluco* or a *caboclo*, with their sun-baked skin, he felt a physical barrier between them that he could not bring himself to step over. It was different with the Europeans: the men and women of Belém and Santarém treasured pale skin above all else, and looked to Paris as the height of elegance. They spent all their days trying to imitate the unfortunate French who happened to stumble into their town. There were so few people he had met whom he felt he could relate to. Captain Arturo had been an exception. Although he had been a harsh, drunken man, there was something in his warmth, the way he tenderly held the faces of his children as he kissed them, that reached out to Thomas and made him believe he could begin to connect with the people of Brazil.

But Arturo was gone, burnt. Thomas hung his head, the dolphins forgotten. They had called on the village for Antonio to trade the last of the supplies and had found the people in shock, walking around the village with quiet steps and solemn faces. They had been taken to the charred bones of the house; the table they had sat at to get drunk was on its side in the remains, its legs all but burnt away. The door they had been ejected through was no longer there. A smell hung in the air—of woodsmoke, perhaps the sour smell of scorched flesh. Thomas had vomited at the thought. Unable to make it to a discreet place, he had been watched by a crowd of onlookers as he hiccupped and retched onto the ground. At least the tang of his guts smothered the stench of death.

They had all been quiet on the trip back to Santarém; alone with their thoughts, even Ernie. Upon their arrival, Antonio announced that there was word from Santos to meet him in Manaus.

The two halves of the river continued to vie for space as the ship churned through it. Manaus was drawing ever closer and, despite his apprehensions about the place, Thomas was glad to be finally making the acquaintance of Senhor Santos. Only then, he felt, would their journey seem complete, like the interlocking of the two rivers, black and yellow.

THE LAST THING THOMAS expected to be doing in the sweltering Amazon heat was standing in a shop trying on a dinner suit. But there was the tailor—a small, wiry man with wavy hair tamed by pomade and a thin mustache waxed into curlicues at its ends—in front of him, testing the tightness of the jacket by pulling at the lapels, his head cocked to one side and his lips pursed in disapproval.

"*Non, non,*" he tutted. "This will not do." As a Frenchman, he was, no doubt, the most expensive and sought-after tailor in Manaus.

Antonio stood by, silently observing the proceedings. He had announced upon their arrival that the first thing he had been instructed to do was to take the men shopping to buy dinner suits, top hats, and new boots, to be paid for by Mr. Santos. Ernie and George had already been subjected to Monsieur Pompadour's pinching and pulling, but had perhaps enjoyed it more than poor John Gitchens, who stooped and glowered at his reflection beside Thomas, while the tailor's assistant squeaked in despair.

After an hour of taking trousers on and off and shrugging themselves into ten different jackets with tails—Thomas glimpsed the price tags, which, once he had converted the currency in his head, were ten times higher than in London—the men emerged from the shop and were directed into a waiting carriage. Thomas wondered as he settled into its cushioned seats how the horses had come to be in Manaus, as there were no roads in and out and everything had to be brought in by boat. Then again, a horse was a minuscule concern compared with the lavish building materials and the tramlines, not to mention the trams themselves, which must all have arrived by water as well. Manaus was an amusement park, built in the middle of the jungle, which he half expected would turn out to be a cardboard set at a theater; if he looked behind its facade, he would find flat boards held up with beams.

Senhor Santos's house stood with a vast lawn at the front and dense forest behind. Thomas had come across impossible rose gardens in Santarém, but this was the first time he had seen such a well-manicured expanse of grass in Brazil. Hoops of a croquet set marched across the lawn like the humps of a tiny sea serpent.

"Bloody hell," said Ernie, leaning over the open side of the carriage. "It's like visiting my Aunt Ethel. Where are the peacocks?" In answer, the caterwaul of a peacock cut across the lawn, and a peacock strutted into view, trailing its tail feathers behind it. Ernie collapsed back into his seat, laughing.

They were met in front of the two-story stucco house—guarded by stone lions—by a butler, a tall, thin man, sweating profusely in a stiff white shirt, black tails, and white gloves.

"Good afternoon, sirs," he said in careful English, bowing. "Senhor Santos waits for you in the house."

Dark clouds had gathered and, as they walked toward the house, the afternoon deluge began. The smell of the river carried on the wind, and flies clung to them as if to escape the rain. Despite appearances, Thomas knew he was in the Amazon after all. A monkey howled somewhere out of sight.

The butler led them up the steps to the open door and into a cool foyer with marble floors. Classical statues of white, bare-breasted women with coyly curled bodies dotted the room next to potted palms and heavy velvet drapes. Oil paintings with gilt frames hung on the walls.

The butler bid them wait while he mounted a winding staircase. They milled about for a moment, and Thomas watched with worry as two young men arrived from nowhere and fought over their cases and crates in the rain. He was thankful they had sent the bulk of their collections back to Ridewell from Santarém.

The other men were unusually quiet and Thomas, feeling quite pale, realized they were as apprehensive as he was. They were finally to meet their benefactor. Antonio stood by, his hands crossed in front of him. His expression could only be interpreted as a smirk.

"Gentlemen!"

Thomas turned his face to the top of the stairs, where a man stood, shrouded in wafts of smoke from the cigar he held in his hand. His arms were stretched out in welcome, and he wore a fine black suit. A gold watch chain glinted on his solid belly and his grin, under the thick waxed mustache, was wide.

"We meet again!"

"Well, I'll be damned," muttered Ernie.

The men stood about, stupefied, as Santos danced down the stairs. His cigar was now firmly stuck between his teeth, and a throaty laugh built in his lungs.

"Your faces!" he guffawed when he reached them.

Thomas's face wore an uncertain smile, and inside, he was just as unsure. The man before them was José the hat merchant, and yet here he was in Santos's house—was Santos himself, in fact. What was it the man had said to them in the forest? *He likes to play games with people.*

Santos's laugh built to a crescendo, and Ernie, who slapped a stiff George on the back, had joined in. John shook his head slowly from side to side, and wore a smile that conceded a brilliant trick, as if the man had cheated him out of his life savings but he had to commend the ingeniousness of the scheme. Antonio's eyes were fixed on Santos and he laughed just as heartily as he did, following the peaks and valleys exactly.

"Oh dear," said Santos as he took a handkerchief from his pocket and wiped his eyes. "Please forgive me, gentlemen, for playing a trick on you. But it was worth it just to see the looks on your faces. Come now, Mr. Sebel, Mr. Edgar. Where are your funny bones? Not in your elbows where they should be, I think!"

Thomas was overcome with shyness, and looked at George in the hope that he would speak for both of them.

"We are very amused, Mr. Santos," said George. "Forgive us. We are just tired. It has been a long journey, and a long, hot day."

"Ah yes," said Santos. "You bought the suits? I hope you don't mind, but we have a celebration tonight and I guessed you might not have brought dinner suits with you. Am I right?"

They conceded and gave their collective thanks. Only George Sebel had brought a dinner suit with him, but he hadn't protested when Antonio bought him a new one.

"But you are tired, I am sure. Please come into the dining room. We will have some tea and sandwiches and then my *butler*"—he beamed at them all as he emphasized the word—"will show you to your rooms to rest."

THOMAS LAY ON HIS back, drifting in and out of sleep in the dry, high-ceilinged room. A fan turned lazily overhead, pulling the hot air up and dispersing it. He didn't want to ever leave this spot—for he lay in a proper bed, as firm as his bed at home, with cool cotton sheets and feather pillows. He was astonished to find electricity here, in a town that was essentially in the middle of the jungle. He didn't even yet have electricity at home in England. He had stood for a long time when he walked in, turning the light switch on and off. Not that he hadn't seen an electric light before—of course he had—he just needed to feel it over and over at the tip of his fingers to believe he wasn't dreaming.

His room was relatively restrained compared with what he had seen of the rest of the house, but the wallpaper was still a sprawling map of bursting flowers; thick velvet drapes hung from the windows—which he couldn't understand, as he thought these were essentially to keep warmth in—and the bed was an elaborate four-poster. The room had a slightly excessive feeling about it, rather how he expected a bedroom in a brothel might be. But Mr. Santos had money and he was eager to show it off.

He got up and crossed the room to a small writing desk in the corner, where he dashed off another quick letter to Sophie, telling her of his impressions of the house and the city, mentioning a painting that had caught his attention in the grand entrance hall. It was as ineffectual as his last attempt, and he had no idea when he would finish it and send it. For now, fatigue overcame him once more and he lay down again.

Somewhere outside a woman laughed; the sound floated into the half-dream he was having about Sophie. His prick hardened as he felt her laugh into his ear, her breath coat his neck. He wondered what she was doing now, whether she experienced similar dreams.

The thought was unbearable and he pressed his palm hard against his erection, and felt a jolt run through his body. He snatched his hand away just before he orgasmed, and sat up, flushed and breathing hard. He must be stronger; the heat was getting to him, the luxuriance of the room. His judgment was clouded.

He rose and washed, then shaved with the razor left out for him by a maid. It was some time since he had looked at himself properly in a mirror—there had been a small one in his cabin on the ship, but the light was terrible and he couldn't see more than two inches of skin at a time. His hair had grown since George last cut it with a pair of grooming scissors. A large curl foamed over his forehead, covering two great mosquito bites, the color of ripe raspberries. His lips were dry and perpetually tingling; the irritation painted them a shade darker than their natural color, which Sophie had always referred to as his "sweet, strawberry-stained mouth." Thomas smiled. So now his face was beginning to resemble a fruit bowl. His cheekbones jutted through tanned skin; it was if a new person looked out at him—no, not a person: a *man*. He smiled again as he rinsed the soap from the razor. His hands were light with elation—that he had decided to take this journey, and where it had brought him so far. Where would he be now otherwise? Probably plump on pudding and becoming bored with his quiet life at home.

Santos was taking them to his club for dinner and, as it was "a special occasion," had asked them to wear the full evening dress he had bought for them. Thomas dressed in his new clothes, which he had found laid out for him when he arrived in his room after tea. He pulled on stiff trousers over his underwear and a starched-front cotton shirt that scraped at his skin. The smell overwhelmed him. When was the last time he had smelled such fresh clothes? He had long ago resigned himself to material infused with bodily odors. These new clothes reminded him of his wedding linen, and for a moment he was taken with the associated sense of anticipation.

Next he slung his arms into a low-cut, single-breasted satin waistcoat with sparkling crystal buttons, which perfectly matched the cuff links that had sat on top of the pile of clothes like shiny beetles.

By the time he came to put on his shoes, he was sweating again. Why couldn't custom be relaxed, here of all places? What was it about men who insisted on keeping up appearances in the most wretched of conditions? He had let his own standards drop, and would have happily swanned around in his underwear provided there were no ladies present.

Now there was a sight he thought he wouldn't see in Brazil—his new oxfords shining like fresh spit. It wouldn't be long before the dust from the streets coated them, anyway. He fastened his spats and looked at himself in the long mirror.

He had never worn a suit that fitted him quite as well. The long, narrow trousers accentuated his narrow shape. He would have liked a little more breadth across the shoulders, but on the whole he looked a fine, handsome fellow. If only Sophie could see him now. She would help him button his collar and tie the little white bow tie that still lay on the bed. After he did it himself, he realized he needed a final touch. And, yes, there beside the washbasin was a jar of pomade. It had liquefied in the warmth and was like honey on his fingers. He worried for a moment that he might attract a horde of jungle insects if he put it in his hair, but ignored the thought and combed it through. A middle parting looked ridiculous—his giant curl, once separated, became angel's wings and flapped inanely above his ears. He tried instead a side parting, which George insisted was now the fashion anyway, not that Thomas knew about such things. That was better. He stopped as he gave it a final touch, head cocked to one side and his hands hovering by his ears. He had never noticed before, but now he could see how like his dear old father he had become. He raised one blond eyebrow to confirm the likeness.

. . .

THE CARRIAGE TOOK THEM down long boulevards lined with trees and paved with immaculate stones. Thomas knew not all of Manaus was as clean—down by the river there was a stench of sewers, and rubbish built up in the gutters. But here the streets were pristine, and the only smell was from the fresh manure one of their horses deposited on arrival outside the club. The horses were decorated like carousel ponies for the occasion, with huge, garish red plumes that shook and waved as they tossed their heads. A little man popped out from an alleyway with silver buckets and proceeded to water them.

"Tonight is a celebration!" declared Santos to nobody in particular. Then he murmured something in the groom's ear. The man bowed low, and while the men alighted from the carriage, he scuttled inside and reemerged holding a bottle of champagne.

"Dom Pérignon, Senhor Santos," croaked the man.

"Excellent!" Santos took the bottle and popped the cork, but instead of offering it to anyone, or drinking any himself, he poured it into the horses' water buckets. The horses snorted and nodded their heads as the bubbles frothed up the sides. "And now we can go inside, gentlemen."

The men exchanged glances when Santos wasn't looking. It was clear he was putting on a show of wealth for them, but Thomas felt sorry for the horses. He dropped back behind John, who, with his top hat on, had to bend to get through the door. In his evening dress, he reminded Thomas of a sight he had seen at a circus once: a bear in a bellboy costume, riding a tiny bicycle, the humiliation of which had made him terribly sad. John was trying to make an effort, but though his vowels had rounded slightly and he had combed his hair and trimmed his beard, the back of his neck was caked with dirt, and it was rubbing off onto his cool white collar.

Inside, the club was like any gentlemen's club in London. Potted palms decorated the foyer, which was amusing, considering that in England they were there for fashion, as exotic plants; here in Brazil there were thousands of such palms growing wild within a mile. More healthily than these, which were clearly in need of water: their leaves were curled and browning. The floor was made up of large black and white tiles, and rich leather couches and armchairs nestled in dark corners. Men in white tunics scampered past.

"Guns, please, gentlemen," said Santos. "There are no guns in my club."

A table by the door was piled with pistols, some small and silver such as a lady might secret into a garter belt, others big and black with long muzzles. Santos himself laid such a gun down.

"We don't have any guns," said Ernie. "Only shotguns for shooting birds, and where would we put those?"

"Do we need them here?" asked George, a little nervously.

Santos hesitated. "No, not really, though everyone carries one. It keeps the peace in a city such as this. But you have nothing to fear. Men will just assume you have one."

They were met by an obsequious young man who bowed nearly to the floor and welcomed them in Portuguese.

"We are speaking English tonight, Mr. Reis, in honor of my English guests."

The man's cheeks turned puce; clearly he couldn't speak English. Instead he muttered "thank you" over and over as he seated them in the lounge and sidled away. Thomas tried to give him a reassuring smile, and whispered an "*obrigado*" to him as he passed, but he was careful not to let Santos hear; somehow, he felt it might not be appropriate.

They sank into seemingly bottomless armchairs. Thomas couldn't remember the last time he had sat on anything so comfortable. He sighed with pleasure.

Santos ordered brandy all around and offered cigars. Ernie and John took one, and Thomas followed suit.

"The best cigars, gentlemen, from Cuba. Every one hand-rolled."

"How strange it is, Mr. Santos," said George, "to be in this club. It is almost identical to my club in London."

"Yes, that was the intention."

"Did you have something to do with its construction?" asked Ernie.

"I own it, Dr. Harris. This is my club. These people are all in my employ."

"But you have never actually seen a London club?" asked George. "That's remarkable."

"On the contrary, sir," said Santos, "I have indeed. That little joke I played on you in the forest—I do apologize. José the hat merchant has never been to England, but I certainly have." He tipped his head back and laughed.

George smiled and shook his head. "I should have guessed. Your English and knowledge are far too good. I was completely taken in."

"Yes, and of course I have been to England to meet with the English directors of my company. I have dined in many clubs such as this."

"It's wonderful, sir," said Thomas. He leaned forward as Santos lit the cigar. He had watched Ernie and followed his lead, giving three or four short puffs, without inhaling.

"Thank you, Mr. Edgar. Ah, here is our brandy."

Ernie looked as if he were in paradise. He leaned back, closed his eyes, and gave a satisfied sigh before Santos struck up a conversation with him about his practice in London.

Thomas forgot himself for a moment and inhaled some thick cigar smoke, which scraped at his lungs and made him cough. The coughing made his throat worse. "Excuse me," he spluttered.

"Not at all!" said Santos. "A cigar virgin, I think, eh, Dr. Harris?"

They shared a moment together, Santos and Ernie, and Thomas blushed and took a sip of his brandy. The aroma hit him in the face and cleared his nose, making his eyes water. Or was that the effect of the cigar?

"Tonight," said Santos, "we have in store for you all the delights Manaus can offer!" He made a circular gesture with his hands, as if conducting an invisible orchestra.

George cleared his throat and leaned forward. Santos sat with Ernie to one side, with Thomas, George, and John in armchairs facing them both, a table between them.

"I want to take this opportunity, sir, to thank you for your extreme hospitality and for your wonderful patronage. British science thanks you, as do we."

"You are very gracious, Mr. Sebel. It is my pleasure."

"And we hope to learn about your business in rubber. Evidently you have been very successful in your endeavors. I congratulate you. Can you tell us about it?"

"Oh, there is not so much to tell. I fear I will bore you. I have a few thousand miles of plantation—around here, on the River Negro, some on the Tapajós, but the bulk of it is in the far reaches, in Peru."

"And how many people work for you?"

"Oh, I cannot say. Thousands. I have employed some Negro men from British Guiana—with British interests in my company it seems appropriate, and they are very fair foremen. And many Brazilians, of course. I have whole tribes of Indians on the Putamayo, in Peru, working for me, but they are a constant struggle. I need them to make up the numbers, but they can be a lazy, drunken bunch. And most of them owe *me* money."

"How can that be?" asked John. It was the first time he had spoken since they arrived.

"I provide them with shelter and wages, and other things like cloth and fishhooks, but they end up drinking their wages away and need to borrow more to buy food. Otherwise they would be weak and useless to me, so I give it to them."

"That is very generous of you," said Ernie. "But I see you are a generous man by nature."

"I try, Dr. Harris, I try. But they are ungrateful. I have little choice in the matter. I need men to work my plantations or the rubber will not be tapped and demand will not be met. I'm sure you do not agree with slavery, gentlemen?"

Thomas shook his head, and the others did too.

"Well," continued Santos, "since slavery was abolished here—and it was less than twenty years ago—it has been very hard to get decent labor. The Negroes are too proud now to work in any situation they would once have had no choice in. They have filled the cities, and are now begging in the streets. The government has introduced a law that says they must register as professional beggars or leave town. Can you imagine it? Professional beggars! Anyway, the point I wish to make is, to me, slavery is a natural state, and one that is beneficial to both slave and master."

Thomas shifted in his seat, wondering how Santos was going to justify this speech. He fixed his gaze on the fan turning lazily in the center of the room.

"The role of the owner is essentially that of father, the slaves the children. Slaves have the same rights as children—that is, they must do as their 'father' tells them. They cannot own property, they cannot vote. In return, they are given a roof over their heads, and protection. As a slave owner I would feel the same duty as a father to protect my slaves, and they would be bound to stay with me as their provider. Now slavery has been abolished, we have been forced to employ Indians, who, I add, sirs, have not been slaves for some time—there was some kind of 'protection,' as the monarchy liked to put it, on them. The Indians are not bound by the natural laws of a father and child. The act of paying them has given them a false sense of independence that verges on insolence. Although they can't live without my wages, they no longer have my protection, either—I do not feel as obliged to them because I employ them for wages instead of out of duty. Do I make sense, gentlemen?"

Thomas could see that, in a strange way, Santos was making sense. Did this then mean he agreed with the man, that slavery was not a bad thing? He would need to consider that some more.

"With all due respect, sir," said John, "what natural right is there that you should be the master and they the slave?"

"Oho, Mr. Gitchens. Do we have a socialist on our hands? I suppose you believe all men are created equal?"

"I do, as a matter of fact." John gulped down the rest of his brandy and a waiter stepped forward immediately to refill the glass.

"Don't mind him," said Ernie. "Of course he's a socialist. It is the right of all the lower classes to believe such a thing. I'm sure it keeps them sane."

"And you, Dr. Harris?"

"I confess to being a bit of one myself, old man. But I can see your point of view. I would have to have some time to think about what you're saying, though. I've never been in any kind of position to have slaves under my command. I'm not saying I would want to, but I couldn't speak about it with certainty until I had, I suppose."

George snorted. "Ernest, the British have enslaved people for centuries. The British Empire could not have spread so far without it. You probably wouldn't be where you are today without it."

"How do you figure that?" asked Ernie.

"Now, now, gentlemen. Mr. Sebel, you bring up an interesting point. The British Empire has indeed been very powerful. If only Portugal had been half as strong. What did we accomplish? Not nearly as much as we once thought we would, that's what. Have you ever been to Portugal? What a proud country it once was—so full of hope and expectation! Now it seems to have a sad air about it. An air of disappointment. It never became as great as it once thought it would be. Now the British . . ." He trailed away, deep in thought, and sucked hard on his cigar.

Thomas was beginning to feel dizzy with the cigar, and he put it down in the ashtray in front of him.

"You're very quiet over there, Mr. Edgar," said Santos. "We are not boring you, I hope?"

"Oh no, sir!" said Thomas. He felt himself redden, with all eyes fixed on him. "I am interested in your conversation, absolutely. I'm afraid I don't feel quite worldly enough to join in yet."

"And what age are you, if you don't mind my asking?"

"Twenty-seven, sir."

"Ah! So young! Young enough to be my son. In fact you are all young enough to be my sons . . . except perhaps you, Mr. Gitchens. How lucky I would feel if I had three sons as fine as you gentlemen."

Thomas wriggled in his seat, suddenly feeling like a schoolboy praised by his favorite teacher. He saw Ernie and George glance at each other, pride puffing their chests.

"And do you have any sons?" asked Thomas.

"No," said Santos. His face clouded. "I have no children. My first wife died childless, and as yet my second wife and I have not been blessed."

"We haven't met your wife yet," said George.

"Clara. You will meet her tomorrow. She is a fine young woman, Portuguese. She would be interested to talk to you, Mr. Gitchens."

John started, and looked around as if he had just woken from a dream.

"Me, sir?"

"Yes. She is very interested in botany. I have always encouraged her to have interests, just until our first children are born. She has become very interested in plants. Always with her nose in a book about them. I have to stop her from running off into the forest alone to look at them—too many dangers. But if she could accompany you at any time on one of your plant-hunting expeditions, she would be very happy."

"Of course," said John, and he smiled for the first time that evening.

AFTER DINNER, WHICH HAD been followed by port from Oporto and cheese from Cork, as Santos had proudly pointed out, he led them farther into the interior of the building, which seemed endless. They went through a curtain at the back of the restaurant and then a heavy door. As soon as it opened a barrage hit their senses. Thomas had noticed during dinner the men who had passed through the dining room, but he didn't realize it had been quite so many. The room seethed with the conversation of a hundred men, all dressed in evening dress, standing around long tables, sitting about smaller, round tables, or leaning at the bar with drinks in their hands. Smoke hung like a bank of storm clouds above their heads.

"And now for some fun, gentlemen," said Santos. He handed them each a cylinder of banknotes and gestured into the room. Thomas moved forward and saw the tables dotted about were those of roulette and men playing cards. Gambling.

He began to pick out individual sounds in the roar, much as he had on the first day in the rain forest: the clacking of the roulette wheel, the flick of cards, the laughter of the men, one or two voices raised in anger. Pianola music ground in the corner and somebody whistled along to the tune; somewhere a glass smashed. There were women in the room, too, leaning over the men as they gambled, exhibiting their cleavages. One woman glided past, without looking at him, in a fur coat. Her face burst with color, but she clung to her coat anyway. She stumbled a little as she went past and Thomas expected to see her at some time in the night faint with heat exhaustion.

"I have a table for us in this corner, gentlemen, if you would prefer to sit and watch for a time." Santos gestured to a large cushioned seat, which curved around a table. Thomas nodded gratefully and they started to move toward it, except for Ernie, who had already disappeared into the crowd.

Champagne sat on the table in a bucket of ice. Santos popped the cork with a whoop and poured the frothing liquid into glasses. Thomas was already woozy from the rich dinner and the alcohol but he accepted a glass to be polite. John, beside him, took a large gulp of his and wiped his mouth. Thomas hadn't seen him drink so much before.

"A toast to your expedition, gentlemen!" Glasses crashed together and the smile Santos bestowed on Thomas was so warm he felt it settle inside him. He followed his host's lead and downed the glass in one swallow. After Santos had refilled it, he became bold.

"Another toast, to our gracious host!" He laughed at the unintentional rhyme.

George joined in on the toast with a genuine if slightly serious nod, and knocked his champagne back with the rest of them.

A handsome woman in her forties approached the table and Santos stood and grasped her hand. He leaned down to kiss her gloved fingers.

"Senhora da Silva," he said, "you look quite exquisite tonight. Won't you join us for a moment?"

Her black dress rustled as she sat, and she cast appraising, black-rimmed eyes over the table of men. "These are your English guests, Senhor Santos, no? Which is why you speak English to me."

Santos introduced them by name, while the woman's headdress—a tall feather, which reminded Thomas of the horses that had brought them—waved about above her. When she spoke she revealed large pointed teeth, but when she smiled, she kept her lips tightly clamped over them.

"Would you like me to send some of my girls over for the company of the gentlemen?"

"Why not?" said Santos. "Ask Ana and Maria to join us."

Senhora da Silva rose again with more rustling, gave a courteous nod with closed eyes, and walked away, noisy skirts trailing.

Thomas found that his hands trembled and he asked Santos if he had a cigarette; he had left his back at the house.

"Well, Mr. Edgar, I do have a cigarette, but it is perhaps not the kind of cigarette you are used to. It is a local one, made from a different kind of tobacco. It is from the dried bark of the *ayahuasca* vine. Would you care to try it?"

Thomas nodded. He could see the women—Ana and Maria, he presumed—approaching the table. Santos reached into his jacket and pulled out the cigarette; Thomas took it quickly and lit it. The first inhalation scorched his lungs and he coughed. The woody smell was unusual, like the smoke of a log fire.

Santos laughed. "Yes, it takes some getting used to, I'm afraid. There is ordinary tobacco in there as well. You'll soon like it." He winked.

Thomas had no chance to answer, as the young ladies were upon them. Santos welcomed the girls and they squeezed into the booth, one next to George, as Santos had let Maria in before he sat back down again, and the other next to John. Thomas sat between George and John.

The ladies spoke no English, so conversation was stilted, and Santos soon ignored them and instead questioned George about his life in London. George did most of his work for the Natural History Museum, but Santos was also jealous of the full life he led in London society.

"Do you see much opera, sir?" he asked.

"Yes, some," George replied. "I prefer the theater, but opera can be just as good. I saw a performance of Puccini's *Tosca* not long before we set out here. It was superb." Maria sat very close to George and stared up into his face as he spoke. Her little round face wore a rapt expression, as if she couldn't wait to hear what he said next. Thomas thought she could only be faking it; she couldn't possibly understand him. George noticed her looking at him and leaned his face away slightly, bending his body like a spoon.

"Puccini!" exclaimed Santos. "How wonderful! You know we have an opera house here in Manaus, Mr. Sebel?"

"I have heard of it, yes. It's one of the reasons I wanted to come here. I understand it's magnificent."

"Yes, it is." Santos glowed. "You know I had some hand in the building of it myself. I am one of its patrons."

"How often do you have performances?"

"Alas, not as much as we would like. Some of the performers have died from yellow fever, and it has been difficult getting really talented singers from Europe to agree to come."

"That's terrible," murmured George, with one eye on Maria, who was now leaning into him—the gesture could more accurately be described as *snuggling*—and trying to drink from his glass.

Thomas finished the cigarette. Ana, who sat next to John, gave him a shy smile as he reached for his glass and he returned it. He surprised himself by feeling genuine warmth toward her. John was talking softly to her in Portuguese, but her body language was not as forward as Maria's—if anything, there was more of a father-daughter aspect to their interaction; there were easily enough years between them for it to be so. Her eyes were now downcast, and John appeared to be gently admonishing her. He patted her hands, covering both of hers with one of his. His knuckles were as big as acorns over her delicate pink gloves. He turned heavy eyes to Santos.

"If you please, sir, I think I should like to go home now. I'm very tired, and I have some work I would like to do before I go to sleep. I thank you for your incredibly kind hospitality."

"Mr. Gitchens, you disappoint me. You and Ana seem to be getting on tremendously. But very well, I will not come between a man and his work. My driver is outside—he will take you."

George jumped to his feet, startling Maria, who gave a squeak.

"I'll come with you, John."

"Mr. Sebel as well! You haven't even had a turn at one of the tables. Oh, you do disappoint me, sirs."

Thomas would have liked to leave at that point, too—he was beginning to feel most peculiar—but it was now his duty not to disappoint their host further.

"I hope we have not offended you, Mr. Santos," said George, glowering at John for getting in his request to leave early. Clearly George had been planning it for some time, hoping to slip away quietly, unnoticed.

"No, Mr. Sebel, you have not offended me." Santos gave him a huge smile to prove it and clapped him on the back. "You have had a long day; there will be plenty more opportunities for us to enjoy ourselves while you are here."

George's jaw visibly tightened at this prospect, but he managed a weak smile. "Thank you for being so understanding." As he spoke he removed his glasses, which had become misted, and wiped them on his handkerchief before wrapping the wires around his ears and returning them to his nose.

"Thank you for this." John dropped the rolled-up money onto the table in front of Santos, who accepted it with a nod. George's hand went slowly to his breast pocket to draw out his own money. He looked at it for a moment as if it might beg to be kept, before laying it reluctantly on the table.

After their departure, Santos dismissed the two girls as well, and Thomas found himself alone for the first time with their host.

"How are you feeling, Mr. Edgar?"

"Very well, thank you, sir."

Santos leaned forward, and looking intensely into his eyes, said, "Are you sure? Would you like another cigarette?"

Thomas felt he couldn't refuse under the circumstances, that to reject any more of the man's hospitality would be rude. In truth he wasn't feeling very well at all. His head had become light, as if it might float upward and detach from his shoulders. The sounds of the room startled him at intervals; he heard another glass smash next to his ear, but when he snapped his head around, found that the commotion was on the other side of the room. His sensory perception seemed warped. It was time to stop drinking—he didn't want to lose control of himself, not in a place such as this.

"Another cigarette. Yes, please." He pushed his half-full glass to one side and accepted the offering. "And might I have some water?"

"Will you not have a flutter? Your friends have left, but there is no reason why you should not have a good time. I have been watching Dr. Harris—he seems to be enjoying himself."

Thomas shifted uncomfortably. He flicked the end of his cigarette into an ashtray, and went on flicking when there was nothing left to shift.

"Mr. Santos . . ." He took a deep breath. "Sir, I mean you no offense, but I made a promise to my father at an early age that I would never gamble."

Santos nodded, but leaned forward and prodded Thomas's arm. "Come now, Mr. Edgar. We won't tell on you. Who will know?"

Thomas smiled. Very quietly, he said, "God will know, sir." He pulled the roll of money from his pocket and placed it in front of Santos, who pushed it back to him.

"No, you keep it. I admire a man who sticks to his principles. Please use it to buy something nice for your children. Do you have children?"

"Not yet."

"Ah, you will soon be blessed, I'm sure. There is nothing more important in this world than producing children. I predict you will have many. For your lovely wife, then. I'm sure she is lovely, and that she misses you. Buy something for her. Promise me."

"I will, sir." He could not refuse. "I thank you."

Before he received a reply, a large shape, all arms and legs, stumbled out of the crowd and banged into the table. Ernie Harris stood before them, his arms wrapped around a woman in a blue dress, with startling red hair. He had lost his jacket and patches of yellow moisture spread over his white shirt from under his arms. Sweat beaded his forehead and large red splotches flamed under the skin of his cheeks. His mustache, which had previously been waxed in a miniature imitation of his host's, had wilted over his wet lips.

"I say," he wheezed, "look who I found."

The woman in his arms—trying to disentangle herself and regain some of the composure that had been stolen from her— was Lillie, the woman from the ship that had dropped them off in Santarém. Her dress shone with beads, and a diamond necklace clasped her white throat. It was mesmerizing; Thomas stared into it until he heard her speak.

"Good evening, Mr. Edgar. Nice to see you again." She extended her hand and he grasped the end of her fingers through her pristine white gloves.

"Sir," said Ernie to Santos, "may I introduce to you Miss Lillie. She's French." He bumped down into the seat next to Thomas, uninvited. Lillie remained standing, waiting.

"*Enchanté, mademoiselle*," said Santos as he stood and planted a kiss on her hand. "Please, join us." He kept hold of her hand and moved over so she had to sit next to him.

"I am having a top night, thank you, sir." Ernie fanned himself with an imaginary fan. "But damned if I haven't lost all of your money." His eyes drooped.

"Do not concern yourself, Dr. Harris. It was yours for the evening to do with as you wished."

Ernie took Thomas's cigarette from between his fingers and took a puff. His face screwed up and he coughed. "Christ! What's this you're smoking?"

"Shh, Ernie," said Thomas, but Mr. Santos was deep in conversation, in French, with Lillie. "It's a local tobacco. Mr. Santos gave it to me. You can finish it if you want. I'm not . . . feeling so well."

"No stamina, that's your problem, Tom." Ernie tried the cigarette again, and examined the end of it as he exhaled.

Lillie sat with one hand resting on her breastbone, nodding vigorously. She looked utterly transfixed. Santos leaned in close to her and touched her often—her shoulder, her arm, even her face on one occasion. His finger, with its perfect nails, lingered on her cheek for a moment and traced a tiny circle before he withdrew it. Thomas didn't understand what he said to her, but she looked down, a smile on her face, and nodded again, harder than ever.

The room suddenly became unbearable. Thomas clapped his hands over his ears, but this made the noises around him seem louder. Ernie was uncomfortably close. He was speaking, but Thomas couldn't understand what he was saying. His face was huge and shiny, and his eyes popped with veins, as if he were being strangled.

"Are you all right, Mr. Edgar?" came a voice, seemingly from inside a cathedral; it echoed and bounced around his head. Santos had turned his attention from Lillie, and they both looked at him with concern.

"Just . . . need some air." Thomas stood. He lost his balance and clung to the table. "Going for a walk."

Santos didn't protest; instead, he pointed to a door on the other side of the room, which he said would take Thomas to an alleyway. "Be careful," he added. "Stay on the streets that are lit well. Stay where there are other people."

Thomas nodded and lurched toward the door. He dodged fat men in tailcoats standing about boasting to one another over the din. One man, with a wide, red forehead, caught his eye as he stumbled past. He was lighting a cigar with a banknote and winked at him. The conversations were in Portuguese, but as Thomas caught snippets, he understood as perfectly as if it were English.

"My wife ordered a grand piano from France and she hasn't touched it since it arrived. She just stares at it all day long."

"I have two of the things. So elegant."

"I've imported two lions from Africa. They are tame as long as I keep them well fed."

Beyond the knot of men a crowd was gathered around a bathtub, in which sat two young women in extravagant jewels and nothing else. Two men—all the men in the room looked the same—were emptying huge bottles of champagne into the bath while the women squealed. One of the women looked directly at Thomas and he found that he had stopped to stare. Her small breasts shone with moisture and she smiled at him. He heard a voice in his head: "Come closer, Senhor Edgar." He gasped and took a step back, but the woman had looked away again, and her lips had not moved.

This is a pit of sin, he thought. Sweat ran into his eyes and blinded him momentarily. He tasted it on his lips as he licked his tongue over them, polishing them. He didn't know how long he had stood there, but his whole body willed him to leave. With a final heave he reached the door and tumbled outside onto the street.

A cool breeze carried with it the sandy smell of the river and the forest. He could make out hundreds of different senses: the sharp musk of monkeys, the rustle of palms, the calling of dolphins, the smell of decaying fish, the sulphur odor of the male *Morpho rhetenor*. He stood and allowed the wind to cool the sweat on his face. It stroked him and calmed him. His breathing softened.

He stood beneath a single gas lamp in a narrow alley, not far from the main street. Wafts of music carried back and forth on the wind, getting louder by the second. Now that he was alone, he felt better: warm water trickled through his veins, and the backs of his arms tingled. He inhaled deeply, imagining he was breathing in the music.

He crunched down the alley and out into the street. Below the music he detected a commotion. He glided toward it, his feet light. Rounding a corner, he burst onto a scene of exploding color and vibrations, music and dancing figures. It was some kind of carnival or street party, with masked men and women cavorting to music that emanated from a band of musicians dressed in colored rags. Thomas laughed as the crowd enclosed him; hands fluttered, ribbons waved, flags and confetti filled the air. He had an overwhelming urge to move his feet in time to the music; when he closed his eyes it entered his body and took hold of his limbs. Here were hands reaching out to touch him, and he let them. Masked faces laughed with him. He was in heaven, surely.

Through the dancing bodies a flicker caught his eye on the edge of the crowd. When he looked directly at it, it was gone. But wait—there it was again. He fought his way toward it. Somebody grabbed his hands and twirled him around; his feet pivoted on the cobbled street and he nearly fell down, but righted himself as his assailant spun away. He had lost the flickering object. Which way had he been facing? There it was—to his right. He stumbled after it, and gasped as he found what he was looking for.

In the light of the revelers' torches and the gas lamps, a butterfly hovered in the crowd. He stood only a few feet from it, breathless at its beauty. It hung in the air like a hummingbird, waiting for him. Thomas grabbed his chest and pulled at his jacket. Surely not . . . to have traveled so far and to find it here. Each pair of wings, with its scalloped tail, one yellow, one black, was as big as his hand. The black wings were the darkest things he had ever seen, and yet they swirled with every color. In the yellow wings, Thomas could see his future. He started toward it but the butterfly danced away from him, through the crowd. Nobody else looked at it; all their eyes were only on him as he cried out for his butterfly. As it flitted away from the crowd, it seemed to pause for him to catch up. When he was nearly upon it, it was off again.

He was alone with it now; the party was left behind. He should have felt a desperation, then, that it would get away. Instead he felt an aching warmth in his groin—here was his ultimate chase! His arousal spread through his whole body, to his tingling ears.

The butterfly paused in its flight at the entrance to an alley and, as he reached it, disappeared into it. Thomas was breathing hard now. He turned into the dark alleyway—provided it didn't ascend, he would have it. He didn't know what he would do with it once he had it, or how he would catch it with only his hands, but it would be his.

He rounded the corner and cried out in the dim light. The butterfly had grown to huge proportions—it was as big as a human. Two hands snaked out from beneath the wings, beckoning to him. It no longer hovered, but stood firmly on the ground on human feet. He moved closer and it did not pull away. He reached out and touched skin, painted skin, which colored his hands black. The butterfly laughed and enfolded him in her wings. He pressed himself to her and she kissed him, a flicker of nectar-coated tongue. He drank her

in, shared it with her. His hands moved over her body, found wide
buttocks and wings of shimmering silk that brushed coolly over his
face and arms. Fingers fumbled with his braces, the clasp on his
trousers. His cock was released; straining forward, it slammed into
her. Legs wrapped around his body as he pinned her to the wall, and
he was enclosed in warmth that made him gasp. Repeatedly he withdrew and entered her. She whimpered in his ear and he drew back to
look at her—the fog in his mind told him *a butterfly makes no sound*.

Something was clearing now. He thrust harder but could not fall
off the edge of the plateau. Her face swam into focus. A woman, now, a
woman. Her arms gripped his neck and black paint had worn off her
face to reveal gold skin underneath. Her dark eyes looked into his and
she cried out. The sound was all wrong; he tried to pull back from her
but she had limpeted herself to him. Her face was a triangle, balanced
on its apex, the inquisitive shape of a butterfly's head above its thorax.
He pushed her and she landed on her feet. He groped for his trousers,
draped ridiculously around his ankles, and pulled them up.

"Senhor," she whispered, and touched his face.

She was no specimen. Her wide-set eyes pleaded with him. She
leaned forward and he allowed a final kiss. Then she looked down at
herself, saw that the paint had disappeared from her now naked body,
and crossed her wings in front of her. How could he have mistaken
this makeshift costume for the wings of his precious butterfly?

The woman did not move and Thomas willed her to walk away, to
leave him to his shame. She's waiting for something, he thought. He
wiped his forehead with one blackened hand and reached into his
trouser pocket. He withdrew the money Santos had given him and
offered it to her, to pay her for her apparent services. It was not so
bad, he told himself, if he paid her.

She reached out toward the money but stopped when she saw what
it was. She shook her head sadly and knocked the roll of notes from
his hand. Then she turned and fled, her wings streaming behind her.

Thomas stumbled back out onto the street. The carnival had

moved on—or perhaps it had never been there? He couldn't say. The streets were frighteningly real to him now and his feet rang a tune on the stones as he walked. He recognized the carriage in the street and approached.

"Senhor Edgar," said the driver, a looming figure in a bowler hat; Thomas couldn't see his face. "*Tudo bem com você?*"

Thomas looked down and saw that his hands were smeared with black paint. He had lost his jacket and his elegant white waistcoat and shirt were crumpled and soiled. He caught a glimpse of himself in the window of the carriage; his face resembled a chimney sweep's. He buckled over with a sudden nausea and vomited into the gutter.

"Please," he said to the driver, "take me home. *Para casa.*"

THE ROOM GRADUALLY BRIGHTENED and Thomas's head hurt. He folded himself into Sophie's back, the rough cotton of her nightgown warm against his cheek. So good to be home, he thought—in his bed again. His eyelids drifted open and he waited for them to focus on the dresser and on the pink wallpaper of Sophie's room—*their* room. But something was amiss. The walls were dark and crowded with patterns. In place of the dresser, an overstuffed chair squatted, with a grubby shirt and a pair of trousers slung over the back. When he squeezed Sophie's waist, he found that it gave way under his fingers like a pudding. He lifted his head and squinted around the room.

He was not at home after all. The shape in his arms was nothing more than a pillow in a cotton casing. Disappointment pushed his eyes closed again.

He took a moment to enjoy the luxuriance of the bed, so soft it coddled his aching limbs. But the night's events came back to him and he covered his face with his hands and let out a groan. What had possessed him? He knew he hadn't drunk too much, and by the time he had left the club the rich food would have mostly been digested. It could only have been the strange cigarettes that Santos had pressed on him. Some kind of poisonous root. He tried not to listen to the thought that for a while there he had enjoyed the strange new sensations he was experiencing—no, he must keep in mind that it had led him to do unspeakable things.

Sophie. My poor Sophie, he thought. He had broken his marital vows and would surely be punished.

An insistent knock at the door. Was this what had woken him up? Whoever was on the other side had been kept waiting.

"Come," Thomas croaked.

Santos's butler backed in with a tray of tea and steaming rolls. He still wore his penguin suit—ridiculous in this kind of heat.

"Good morning, sir. Did you sleep good?"

"Thank you," said Thomas, noncommittal. "What time is it?"

"It is nearly noon, sir. Two of your friends have been awake a long time. They read on the balcony. Senhor Santos has business in town."

Thomas didn't have to ask which two. If Ernie had finished his cigarette last night, he would be feeling as bad as Thomas was.

The butler began picking up his clothes from the floor—his underwear, his spats, and his shoes. He paused when he reached the chair and stretched out a cautious hand, as if the shirt were covered in shit, not paint. He lifted it between two fingers.

"I will have these cleaned for you, sir," he said.

Thomas waved a hand and dismissed him.

DOWNSTAIRS HE FOUND THAT Ernie had joined John and George and they were sitting in the shade, drinking coffee. Thomas headed straight for it and poured himself a cup.

"Thomas, you look dreadful," said George. "Sort of . . . yellow. Doesn't he, Ernest?"

"You look like piss," said Ernie, clearly pleased with the comparison.

Thomas slurped the coffee, which had gone cold in its jug. "What about you, Ernie? How do you feel?"

"Perfectly fine, sir. Nothing that a good sleep didn't cure. And some caffeine."

"And did anything . . . unusual happen? After I left, I mean."

"Not that I can remember. Mr. Santos became rather fond of our Lillie, but that's about it."

"Who's 'our Lillie'?" asked George.

"Only one of the most beautiful ladies of the night in Manaus, George. Keep up."

George harrumphed.

"She might be *your* Lillie," said Thomas, "but she's not mine."

"All right, all right, keep your wig on," said Ernie. "It's only an expression. Isn't that right, John?"

John looked up from his book. "I suppose, if you say so, Ernie."

"Christ, what is it with everyone today? So testy." Ernie tutted and picked up a newspaper.

Thomas sat back in his chair and wiped at the flies that had settled on his arms and face. The forest lay on the other side of a high wall, and patches of it had broken through the brickwork and forced their way inside. It must be a constant battle to keep it in check. He longed to explore this new area, where the change in the components of the earth had turned the river so black it was named for its startling color. It surely meant a whole new array of insect life as well. Somewhere out there his butterfly was waiting for him. Despite the horrors of the night before, perhaps it had been a sign. That he would have to do anything to find it.

WHEN SANTOS RETURNED FROM his business, he helped them fill in the rest of the afternoon with a tour of Manaus. The first stop was Santos's pride and joy, the opera house, but the gloom that had settled over Thomas dulled its decadent sheen. It was truly a structure on which no expense had been spared. Santos boasted of the sixty-six thousand blue and gold tiles imported from Alsace that made up the gilded dome; it looked to Thomas as if thousands of Morphos glittered in the afternoon sun and he waited for them to take off and reveal something far murkier below. The building utilized a Florentine design, and the stone had been brought from Italy. A heavy load indeed for any ocean liner, thought Thomas. Inside the building, Santos pointed out and named extravagant chandeliers from Venice, pillars of Carrara marble, and tall vases of Sèvres porcelain. Sophie would have been captivated by it, and he longed to share it with her. Indeed, if she had been here, none of last night's foolishness would have happened.

"You must see it when there is a performance on," said Santos. "This is when it truly shines. It is more magnificent than any building in the whole of Europe! With this opera house, we have proven that we are a truly elegant city. Don't you agree, gentlemen?"

The men nodded, struck dumb, but it was clear they all thought the same as Thomas: that this building was a freak presence in the jungle, as incongruous as an elephant sitting down to tea at the Ritz. As magnificent as it was, Thomas felt uncomfortable in its presence after all he had seen of the forest and the people who lived there.

That evening, when Thomas came downstairs for dinner and entered the drawing room, the others were sitting down drinking brandy.

"I have a treat for you tonight," said Santos. "Some music. Do you like music?"

"Of course," said George. "We have not heard enough music since we have been here."

"Well," said Santos, "I assure you, Mr. Sebel, this is unlike any music you have heard before."

He rang a bell beside him where he stood at the mantelpiece. How curious, thought Thomas, to have a fireplace in a climate such as this.

A short, rounded woman entered the room, followed by two men. One of them Thomas recognized as Manuel, Santos's servant who had lost his tongue. The two men carried guitars and sat in two hard chairs, while the woman positioned herself between them. She pulled a black shawl around her shoulders and stood with her eyes closed. The guitars began to play, mournful notes plucked from the strings by deft fingers. The two players worked in complement to each other, their notes weaving a tapestry of sound.

With her eyes still closed, the woman began to sing in a low voice, sad and throaty. As her voice built, she opened her eyes. She sang in Portuguese—Thomas closed his eyes and tried to make out the words. It was a melancholy song, filled with longing. He understood that the singer craved her lost homeland, Oporto; that there was a great river there. The words sang of drinking wine and dancing slowly. Thomas opened his eyes again and looked around at his companions, who were all captivated. Santos's face held a sad smile, barely noticeable under his mustache. The woman's eyes glistened with tears as she sang. She didn't look at them, but stared off into the far corners of the room, as if looking through the walls and over the ocean to her homeland. Her face, with its golden skin and small chin, its large brown eyes, stirred something in Thomas. As the song came to a close and she held a final, impossibly long note, her eyes slipped to his and her eyebrows twitched. His blood froze and he stopped breathing as if a great fall had winded him.

The song ended and the men clapped heartily. Thomas's hands moved mechanically. The woman bowed low, but there was something strong and defiant in the sweep of her dress as she did so. She spread the fan that dangled from her wrist and hid her face behind it, fanning herself. The two men picked up their guitars and left the room.

"Beautiful, my dear," said Santos. He turned to the men. "This music is Fado, gentlemen. The music of Portuguese who long for their home. This lady is the best Fado singer in Manaus."

She looked at the ground, her eyelashes flickering over the fan. Santos held his hand out to her and she walked forward to take it.

"May I introduce my wife, Clara."

Thomas thought he was going to faint as they all stood. He reached out a hand to steady himself on the back of George's chair. As Santos went around the men, introducing them one by one, Clara would not look at him.

"And this is Mr. Edgar."

Santos turned his back for a moment, to say something to Ernie, who had moved toward the fireplace. Clara angled her fan away from her face and looked Thomas in the eye. Then she raised one black-gloved finger to her lips.

Thomas nodded his quiet assent, the evening collapsing around him.

Manaus, January 7th, 1904

I am but a man. And man has historically been enslaved by his body—what could have brought me to presume I could be any different?

I have now betrayed two people—my wife and my benefactor. Part of me tells myself I am mistaken, but I know I am not. What business does a woman, the wife of one of the wealthiest men in Manaus, have in dressing in costume and joining in on a street party? Does Santos know she engages in such nocturnal wanderings? His behavior is not exactly appropriate, but men are much more likely to behave in such a manner, are they not? Perhaps I am being naive. I know nothing of this city and its customs. Perhaps its inhabitants are as wild as each other. With her silent gesture she implored me to keep quiet, and she has no reason to fear that I will betray her wishes—it would mean betraying myself as well. I will hold my tongue and I pray that she will, too. This journal will now have to be kept safe from prying eyes.

Sophie, will you ever forgive me?

SEVEN

Richmond, May 1904

SOPHIE FLINCHES AT BEING addressed directly, as if Thomas is in the room pleading with her. So *that's* it. It's the last entry in that particular journal, and she feels its note of despair, but has no sympathy. On the page opposite—the last page of the journal—is a colored painting of the yellow and black butterfly. It has been painted with such intricate detail that for a moment she forgets herself and admires his ability. She wonders if he has painted it from life. It is beautiful. Is this supposed to give her hope after what she has just read?

The room is a dark gray now—it's a wonder she's been able to read at all. She examines the entry again in the gloom, trying to glean as much meaning from it as she can, to read it in as many different ways as she can. But only one possibility stands out to her at this moment. She's not stupid; she knows men behave like this, but she could have sworn Thomas was different from other men.

She stands and flings the journal against the far wall, where it clatters onto the nightstand, knocking over an unlit candle, and falls to the floor. Clutching her stomach, she paces the room before picking the book up again and looking at it. The spine has come detached from its body and flaps like a ribbon. She stares at it as if it will give her the answers to the questions she wants to scream at her husband. She throws it back into the bag in disgust and opens the window to breathe some fresh air. The eastern sky reflects the sinking sun; clouds lie with bulging bellies on the horizon, promising rain. Everything is tinged with a lavender light; she even fancies she can smell it on the air. It's a vista she has seen many times, but now the world has changed. Its corners are darker.

What can she do? Her fingers reach for her hair and scratch at her scalp. The edges of a headache press her brow from the inside. There is no going back. She wanted to know, and now she knows.

She stoops and gathers up the books that lie like leaves on the ground, shoves them back into the bag and slams it shut. Next, she edges open her husband's door and slips the bag back inside, making no sound.

Down in the scullery, the last light slants through the window and falls across the bench. She works quickly, cutting bread and ham and cheese. Too quickly: the knife slips and, as it slices through her fingertip, she feels the resistance before the pain. Her gasp in the silence is deafening. Blood drips off her finger and onto Thomas's supper. She thinks about leaving it there for a moment as she presses a cloth to the wound, but throws the stained bread into the sink and cuts another slice.

Thomas sits up when she enters his room with the tray of food. He stretches. He reminds her of a little boy, woken by his mother, but then she remembers what he is capable of and pushes this thought far from her mind.

Without a word, she places the tray in front of him. He catches it as it teeters dangerously, and she turns and marches from the room, feeling his eyes pierce her back.

Downstairs she pauses in front of the hallway mirror to fix her hair. Carefully she curls it over and pins it into place, trying not to dwell on what she is about to do. When she is satisfied, she takes her best hat and places it over the hairdo in the position to best flatter her face—tilted slightly forward, so her brow is covered and her eyes glint mysteriously from below. She takes a deep breath. Her dress is still marked with soot, but she doesn't have the patience to go and change; instead, she selects a light coat to cover the damage—one she won't be compelled to remove in the warmth of the evening. She lets herself out onto the quiet street, where the lamplighters have begun their evening's work.

CAPTAIN FALE IS NOT expecting any visitors, so when the doorbell rings, he jumps a little in his chair. He must have fallen asleep—he is now sitting in the dark. He fumbles for his walking stick and pushes himself up. It's probably a note from Sid Worthing, saying he can't make their engagement tomorrow. But on a Sunday? It really is most tedious to have visitors on Mrs. Brown's day off.

As the door swings open, he has a wild impulse to comb his hair, but it is too late. Sophie stands on his doorstep, looking up at him from under the low brim of a most fetching hat.

"Mrs. Edgar," he says. "This *is* a surprise."

He doesn't say *and a delight*. She has sought him out! Is that desire in her eyes? He barely dares to hope that his plan is working—that *she* has come to *him*. Perhaps his hint that her husband has lost his faith hit its mark. He wants to open the door wide, to pull her inside. His hands itch to embrace her. He has a flash in his mind of her sinking into his arms with a sigh, the feel of the weight of her. But something is wrong. She has forgotten to put on her gloves and a piece of white cloth is tied around one finger, with blood seeping through it like a cluster of jewels on a ring. The sight of her bare hands makes him blush—it feels conspicuously intimate. She shifts from one foot to the other, and her eyes dart about. She keeps glancing over her shoulder at the street.

"Samuel," she says. "May I come in?"

"I . . ." What is he thinking? Already some people have passed in the street and given them curious looks—people he recognizes from church. He can hear their thoughts now: what is a beautiful young married woman doing calling on a withered old single gentleman like this? As night is falling? He cannot act on his urge to pull her in after all. He shifts his weight and a stab of pain in his leg makes him flinch.

"Mrs. Edgar . . ." he begins again. She called him *Samuel* again. And now here she is on his doorstep waiting to be let in. "Mrs. Edgar, I don't think . . ."

She rubs at her hands, pulling on them and flicking them as if they were dripping with water. She steps up onto the threshold and he falls back a pace in surprise.

"Please, Samuel." She stands so close to him he can smell her; the scent of rosewater fills his nostrils and his head. He wants nothing more than to have her come in—in her state, who knows where things might lead? But he stands his ground and when she bumps against him does not relinquish his stance. She is clearly upset about something. Her face is tearstained and slightly grubby, as if she has been standing in front of a smoky fire. She stares resolutely into his eyes and for a moment the struggle of power between them arouses him again. They stand for a few seconds, their faces expressionless—he is anxious not to give away any of his feelings, and she is determined to override him, it seems. But she relents with a sigh and steps down again.

"I'm sorry," she says. "You're right. This is most improper." Her voice is a notch above a murmur, as if she is talking to herself but hoping she might be overheard.

"I can call on you tomorrow, if you wish," he says, but she waves a hand at him. "No, Captain Fale. That won't be necessary." Without a farewell, she turns in a daze—a product of cold anger, perhaps—and floats away from him out onto the street.

He closes the door and leans against it. The wood is cool on the back of his head. His hands shake and he raises one to wrap around his throat. He is disarmed, to be sure—he should be overjoyed at her intentions but after the initial shock and joy of seeing her at his door he is left merely confused. Has he done the right thing by not letting her in? Yes, he has, he is sure of it. It would not do for her reputation to be ruined.

THE RAIN COMES DOWN all night, thudding on roofs and slapping windows with drops like fat tadpoles. By morning, nobody can leave their house without umbrellas turning inside out, coats whipping against legs, and water reaching warm crevices and dry petticoats. Agatha watches the empty street from her sitting room window while her sister Catherine plays the piano, fingers pounding the keys in time to the thumps of rain, and her brother Edwin plays with his new kitten. He is so gentle with it—too gentle for a boy his age—and holds it awkwardly, as if it is made of sand and might run through his fingers.

Catherine has come far in her playing. She is only fifteen and already she has surpassed Agatha's own skills at the instrument. Agatha doesn't have the patience to learn the scales, and suffered many a swollen knuckle from her teacher when she was young, until her father found out and sent Mrs. Rogers crying out the door. No daughter of his was going to be smacked like a common animal, he said, and gathered her to him while she slipped her arms around his enormous girth and smirked into his vest. But Catherine can sit at the piano for hours, running up and down the scales until somebody comes to ask her to stop. It's as if she's in a trance and has sent herself far away; the scales are the sound of waves on the beach reaching and receding in an endless cycle. She inherited the gift from their grandmother, who could play any instrument she touched.

Agatha huffs and steps over Edwin, who now lies on his back with the kitten on his stomach. She can't resist and reaches down to tickle his ribs, giving him a sharp jab and making him scream like a little girl.

"Mummy!" he calls, and she straightens in disgust.

"Mummy can't hear you, *Edwina*." She prods him with her foot and the kitten falls off his stomach, mewling. Then she crouches down again and sweeps her brother up in a quick embrace until he wriggles like a small animal. She drops a kiss on the top of his dark curls and slouches out of the room and up the stairs, heartily bored.

Her Ouija board is hidden under her bed, away from prying little eyes and fingers. Her grandmother gave it to her just before she died, when Agatha was fifteen. Nona had held on for a long time, and it was as if she were waiting for Agatha to fully develop hips and breasts before she let herself go, satisfied that she had been guided into womanhood and her gifts were fully realized. She always said that while a girl went through puberty she was susceptible to the spirits, and certainly Agatha became interested in spiritualism, but the interest waned as she approached womanhood. This old thing—she has got it out a few times with friends, but puts it away again when she sees that it doesn't spring to life as easily as it once did.

It is thoughts of Thomas that led her upstairs. She is tempted to take the Ouija board over to Sophie's and try it out again. What if he has been taken by spirits? If some part of him has gone over to the other side and not come back? The younger Agatha would have believed it unquestioningly, but somehow the adult Agatha stands in the way. She sits down on the bed and runs her fingers over the cool wood of the board. Nona would have known what to do. She would have taken no nonsense; she'd have got Thomas speaking again.

Nona was a Romany who ran away from life on the road and married an Englishman. She didn't fit the stereotype of the Gypsy—she didn't wear scarves and gold earrings—but she had skin the color of strong tea and an accent that could cut glass. And she held on to

many beliefs and gifts. The music she passed on to Catherine—
Katerina, Nona would call her—and to Agatha she passed the gift of
spiritualism. She also taught her never to give in to convention, and
of all her advice (which to Agatha had included a lot of superstitious
nonsense) this was the piece that Agatha took to heart. It colored her
life every day and gave her the strength of her convictions.

"Never care about what others think of you, child. You have only
to answer to yourself and to God. Only those two. And God will love
you no matter what you do."

It was Nona who taught Agatha about the animal spirits that in-
habit people. Agatha was stung on the ear when she was a child, and
her hearing never fully recovered. Every now and then a buzzing
starts up in her head. Nona told her that the bee left a part of itself inside her and when it died, its spirit stayed with her to guide her.

Perhaps she will suggest to Sophie that they use the Ouija board.
Sophie will no doubt refuse. She seems to think there is something
unchristian about communing with spirits.

Agatha tried automatic writing once, and quickly tapped into
two spirits who seemed to linger around her. They never had anything interesting to say, though, and they became like two bicker-
ing aunts. One of them would pop in and disagree with the other's
advice about removing tea stains and Agatha began to wonder,
when she picked up the pen and emptied her mind, if it wasn't the
product of her own imagination, too unadventurous to come up
with any ghosts who had died horrible deaths or who might have
the answer to all of life's problems.

She scoops up the Ouija board and readies herself against the
rain.

SOPHIE SITS IN THE darkened parlor with a cool flannel at her forehead. She hardly slept last night, and her stomach is hollow. The
thought of eating makes her feel sick, as if food will turn to glass

once she has swallowed it and embed itself inside her. She hasn't been able to face Thomas at all since taking him his supper last night. Part of her doesn't trust herself—fears that she might fly at him and scream and slap him, hard. Now her head aches with keeping it all in and her body feels pinned to the chair.

Her husband has been unfaithful to her. Dear, sweet Thomas, who had never so much as touched a woman before he met her. The first time he kissed her he was trembling, and as he pulled her close she felt his heart through both of their clothes, unnaturally fast. His peppermint lips had been furtive, as if they might break her if he leaned in too near.

She has always been good at pushing aside bad thoughts—considers it to be a skill, in fact. She could choose to ignore this set-back, never mention it to Thomas, never even mention it to herself. It may go away, and once Thomas is better, they can all go back to normal.

Sophie gropes beside her for the glass of brandy she poured herself on impulse before she sat down. It stings her throat and she coughs. It forges a hot channel down through her chest to her stomach, warming her.

Should she leave him? Is this what one does when one discovers an affair? How ill-equipped she is to deal with this! She knows of women who tolerate their husbands' affairs as long as they are not flaunted, but those men are successful businessmen, going up to London at every opportunity for this dinner or that business meeting; she even knows of some who have been invited to parties by the king himself and not returned home for days. But these men are not Thomas.

And yet those women are not unhappy. Not outwardly, anyway, despite probable adultery. Has she been naive? Has it always been beating at her world, too, and now she has just released it, like a horde of moths? Is she holding on to some distant Victorian morality, despite a new king and, some say, a new age?

She hears the doorbell ring, but it is a distant rumble that seems to belong to another time and place. The house has been in a thick fog, with only the muffled patter of rain from outside, and with the flannel on her forehead, Sophie has become lost in it. She hopes whoever it is will go away.

"Miss Dunne, ma'am," says Mary, and in strides Agatha, soaked to the skin. She is hatless for a change and her hair hangs like sodden weeds around her face. She is puffing, as if she has been running, and her cheeks are a healthy shade of pink. Water runs off her skirts and onto the carpet.

Sophie pulls the flannel from her face. "Good Lord, Aggie, what have you been doing?"

Agatha looks down at herself and laughs. Despite her headache, and her need for silence, Sophie welcomes the sound as if it were music.

"I was going crazy at home," says Agatha. "I needed to get out. Cat and Edwin were driving me batty. What are you doing?"

Sophie tucks the flannel beside her. "Nothing. I was just thinking."

"Well, don't," says Agatha, removing her gloves. She has something tucked under her arm. "It's not the weather for it." She drops into a chair and sighs, placing her Ouija board in her lap.

"Agatha!" Sophie ignores the instrument; it's Agatha's favorite toy, but if she doesn't mention it, maybe her friend will forget it's there. "You're soaking wet! Let's get you upstairs and changed out of those wet things. Then we'll get Mary to light the fire."

"But it's too warm for a fire, Bear."

"I won't hear another word. Come on."

Sophie is glad to leave behind the dark room, which suddenly seems too small for the two of them, as if their limbs stretch into every corner. Memories of evenings laughing in front of the fire with Thomas are starting to evaporate now, and all she can see is sagging furniture and curtains the color of bruises. Even the roses on the mantel look as if they have been dipped in blood and left to dry. She will go mad if she has to spend the rest of her days in this house. She is glad, too, for something to do—a job to keep her busy, tending to Agatha and making sure she doesn't catch a cold and ruin the furniture all at once.

Upstairs, Sophie helps Agatha remove her outer garments and gives her a robe to wear before going back downstairs to find Mary, who casts her a curious look when she is handed a bundle of dripping clothes.

"Start the fire, please, Mary, and make sure these things get dried." Sophie is all bustling efficiency now, her headache receding.

"So how is it going with you know who?" Agatha asks when Sophie comes back. She sits on Sophie's bed, drying her hair. "Have you found out yet what his secret is?"

Sophie raises a finger to her lips and closes the door, checking first for the possible strip of light under Thomas's door. The hallway is dark.

"No," she says, turning back. "That is, I might have."

Agatha sits up straight, her eyes eager. "Really?"

Sophie slumps onto the bed beside her. "I did what you suggested. I did some digging. I went through his belongings. First of all, I found this." She reaches over to her dresser, where she has placed the box containing the blue butterfly.

"It's gorgeous," breathes Agatha. "How special! Where can I get one? Did he have any others?"

"Well, he had crates and crates of them, if that's what you mean."

"Wouldn't it look just perfect on a hat, Sophie? What do you think?" She holds it up to her hair and Sophie snatches it away from her, suddenly jealous.

That stops her. Agatha seems to choke on her own breath. Sophie is not sorry. How tetchy she is today.

"All right," says Agatha. "Sorry. I only meant it would look very well. I wonder if he would sell me one for a hat."

"It's too delicate," mutters Sophie. "It would blow off and get torn." Can't she leave the subject alone?

"Well, maybe he has collected something else! Don't they all stuff birds and animals on those expeditions? A little bird would be grand! With a tiny nest. What a fine hat that would make."

Sophie has to smile. She never stays angry at Agatha for long. She pats her friend's hand as an apology, hoping she will understand. She replaces the butterfly carefully on the dresser, keeping her back turned. "You and your hats," she murmurs. Then, "There is something else." A whisper.

"What?"

Sophie takes a deep breath and sits back down on the bed. "I read his diary."

"No!" Agatha leans forward and starts rubbing her hands together. "What was in it?"

Sophie's not sure she wants to share, but Agatha is looking so eager. And it will do her good to talk about it, surely. "Mostly he wrote about the butterfly he hoped to find. Just day-to-day things, really, although there was quite a bit that he didn't tell me in letters. Some of the dangers he faced, for instance. Fire ants and jaguars and piranhas!" She chuckles as Agatha looks suitably enthralled. "I suppose he didn't want me to worry. There were pictures, too, of the butterflies he'd caught. They started out quite simple, but they soon became quite expert. I was surprised." She pauses for breath. She knows she is procrastinating. "There were quite a few pictures of the butterfly he wanted to catch, actually—it has one side yellow wings and the other black. A swallow-tailed butterfly, you know?"

Agatha nods, rapt. "So he *did* catch it?"

"That's what I thought at first, but the entries didn't say so . . . not as far as I read, anyway. I think he was just obsessed with it, drawing it over and over, like a doodle."

"Is that it? Is that what you found?"

Out with it. "I think there was a woman."

Agatha's head snaps back. *A woman*, she mouths with big eyes. How beautiful she is. Her dark eyes are so striking next to her white skin; her teeth bite a full bottom lip that is always smooth and red. The Gypsy in her.

"You mean . . . ?" Agatha doesn't seem to be able to say it, but Sophie knows what she means.

"I can't be definite. The entry was not direct by any means, but that is how I read it." She feels her mouth screw up and fill with saliva.

"Not Thomas!" says Agatha. "But he loves you!"

Sophie can no longer speak. Tears hammer behind her eyes.

"Sophie, darling . . ." Agatha lays a hand on her arm. "These things do happen. You mustn't blame yourself."

"Oh, I don't," bursts Sophie. "I blame him! And her!" She slaps a tear away and composes herself.

"Well, what are you going to do?"

Sophie thinks for a moment about telling Agatha of her impulse to see Captain Fale. What drove her there? Revenge? She can't now imagine what was going through her mind—she seemed to move automatically, without thought or feeling, and the memory of the evening is blurred, as if she is remembering something that happened to someone else. Thank God he didn't let her in, though she doesn't have it in her to do anything *really* bad. She just wanted to try it out, she supposes. "I don't know. Do you think this is why he won't speak?"

Agatha grunts. "Hardly. Men do this kind of thing to their wives all the time. It's not something they would lose sleep over, let alone their voices. It might explain why he can't look at you, but he doesn't talk to *anyone*. And he stays in bed all day long. Where has his passion gone? He has no passion."

Sophie turns away, embarrassed to hear Agatha talking of her husband's passion. She can be vulgar sometimes.

"You must keep reading."

"Ugh," says Sophie. "I couldn't. Not yet, anyway."

"Sophie." Agatha grabs her hand. "Look at me. *Look* at me. He loves you. Look at this." She stands and picks up the butterfly where Sophie let it drop onto the dresser. "This proves it. This is hope. You can hate him for what he has done, or you can keep going and find out what is the matter with him. I know it's hard, but you've found out that he's human after all . . . Now that it's out, you're just going to have to live with it."

She's right, of course. Agatha is so often right, even if at first Sophie doesn't agree with her. "But I don't need to know any more. This is bad enough. What if . . . what if it gets worse?" She barely even mouths this last word.

"Yes, well, there's that. The world's not quite the place you thought it was, is it?"

Sophie shakes her head, miserable, while Agatha lays a hand on her shoulder. The hand is shaking slightly—she must be cold, sitting there in damp underwear with only a robe to keep her warm.

"Why don't you go and get the journals?" suggests Agatha gently. "We can look together. I'll be here with you."

Sophie finds herself obeying without question, standing and moving as if on wheels to the door and out into the hallway. No sound comes from Thomas's room. She opens the door a crack. He lies on his side and she is startled to see his eyes looking at her. She expected him to be asleep as usual. Perhaps the rain drumming on the roof is keeping him awake. Or perhaps he simply can't sleep anymore. He must be bored, lying there like that. I must remember to get him up when the rain clears, she thinks, but stops. Where did that thought come from? She is angry with him, and here she is worrying that he needs entertaining, as if he were a child again.

She goes to back out of the room, but as she does so, she notices that the Gladstone bag has gone from its place by the door.

"The bag's gone," she says once she is back in her room.

"Oh, bother," says Agatha. "He's hidden it, I suppose. But you'll keep looking, won't you? Say you will."

"I don't know," says Sophie. And she really doesn't.

. . .

THE NEXT DAY SOPHIE watches Thomas get dressed with his back to her. She knows it would be polite to leave, but she gains some satisfaction from making him uncomfortable. The wounds on his back are healing—it is a good start—and she has removed the bandage from his arm. The cuts are dry now, shiny welts that are sensitive to touch—he flinches when she runs her finger over them—but tightly closed.

They walk down the hill through the gardens toward town. She holds his arm lightly, for appearances, but she feels as if she could crush that bone if she wanted, wring his reedy neck, and nobody would ever know. She strays for a moment from the path; the earth springs under her feet like a sponge, still sodden from yesterday's rain.

"Why don't you unpack your specimens from Brazil?" Her voice cuts through the moist air and a robin flies out of their path in fright. "Why don't you do something? Surely this hanging about in bed all day isn't doing you any good. I know, I *know*." She answers him as if he has spoken. "The doctor says bed rest, but it's not working, is it, dear? Do you even want to get better?" She stops walking and drops his arm. He takes it back and holds it with his other hand, rubbing at it as if she has bruised him. Was she holding him too tightly? His bones are fragile these days. She takes it up again, gently, and they continue walking.

A cricket match is being played on the green; figures in white standing around scratching themselves, waiting for the red ball to be hit their way. She can't understand the game herself. Thomas played when he was at school, but showed little interest in it. To prove it, he continues their stroll without a glance in the game's direction. But then, he's not interested in anything now, not even his precious butterflies. He's probably thinking about *her*. She stops the thought immediately. It will drive her crazy.

Richmond is a busy town. On the weekends, the population swells with Londoners making outings, attracted by the Terrace Gardens and the boating in the summertime. Even during the week, rowboats shunt around beneath the bridge, lovers trailing hands in the water, or teams of boys competing in bunches. If today's walk helps him, thinks Sophie, she will take him to Kew next. He has a friend there . . . what's his name? Peter someone. Crawley, that's it. She remembers because the name conjures up images of crawling insects and whenever Thomas has mentioned him she has glanced at the beetles on the wall. She imagines he looks like one—hard armor and mashing mandibles, or at least a shiny dark suit and a drooping mustache. Perhaps she will write to Peter—a friendly face might be just what Thomas needs.

So far they haven't met anybody they know; Sophie is glad they don't live in a smaller town. Perhaps she should have put the word out that Thomas is ill—she is unsure what she will do when an acquaintance wants to stop and welcome her husband home and finds him speechless. She couldn't stand the awkwardness. Then again, maybe it would pull Thomas out of his muddy condition.

Thomas waits outside the draper's while she goes inside to buy material for a new summer frock—she has decided to treat herself.

"Mrs. Edgar!" cries Molly Sykes, gaudy in red and blue, with rough hands and chipped nails. "We 'aven't seen you in 'ere for such a long time. Is that Mr. Edgar outside? Is 'e back from 'is journey, then?"

Sophie bites her lip. This is it. Mrs. Sykes is the most tenacious gossip in town. If she tells her, it will course through the streets like a flood. But how can she stop it?

"Yes, Mrs. Sykes, he's back. The only thing is . . ." She approaches the counter and drops her voice. She can almost see the ears of the girls working in the back growing and straining. "He's ill. Very ill."

"Really? 'E looks fine from 'ere. What's wrong with 'im, then?"

Nosy witch. "He's had a bad shock. He's not speaking. We're trying to be very quiet with him."

"Not speaking?" cries the woman, clasping her hands, feigning shock, but unable to suppress an excited smile. The whole of Richmond will probably know by tomorrow evening—what has she done?

As Mrs. Sykes helps Sophie select her fabric—a light muslin with tiny cornflowers—she keeps stealing glances at Thomas out the window. He has turned his back to the street and is looking at Sophie imploringly. Mrs. Sykes gives him a wave, a tinkle of the fingers as one might give a baby. He doesn't return it, just looks more desperate, like a dog waiting for its master.

Rounding the corner from the draper's onto George Street, Sophie and Thomas nearly walk into Captain Fale. He steps back in alarm when he sees them, but seems to compose himself. He raises his hat.

"Mrs. Edgar. Mr. Edgar."

Sophie nods, her face burning at the thought of her behavior two nights ago. She means to keep walking, but Thomas—whose arm is linked with hers—has become rigid. He stares at the captain, with his bottom jaw jutting out and his breath coming in quick hisses through his nose.

Captain Fale obviously senses something is wrong and steps quickly out onto the street to go around them, just as a motor clatters past. It sounds its horn at the captain, who loses his composure and drops his cane. He bends to pick it up and his hat falls into the gutter, still wet and mulchy from the recent rain.

"Samuel," says Sophie, and she steps forward to help him pick it up. He takes the hat without looking at her and limps away as fast as he is able. In his haste, his receding figure wobbles like a windup toy. A small crowd has stopped on the other side of the street to watch the commotion. Sophie draws herself up and takes her husband's arm. The beginning of a smile curves his lips and she thinks she hears him chuckle, but it may be the rumble of a passing carriage.

. . .

THE IDEA THAT SHE may have been mistaken in her reading of Thomas's journal grows inside her. She has no way of checking now, anyway, until she finds the bag. She has a quick scan of his room and around his study, while he sits in the garden. She finds the bottom drawer of his Brady chest locked, but has no idea if it has always been so. She pulls open the top drawer and examines its contents—beetles he has collected in the park. She reads the labels aloud to herself, feeling the unfamiliar words curl around her tongue: *Stenus kiesenwetteri, Anchomenus sexpunctatus* (she was with him the day he caught one on the edge of the pond near the windmill), *Lamprinus saginatus* and *Stenus longitarsus*. Her low voice sounds to her ears like a chanting monk's.

A movement catches her eye and she turns her head to find Thomas standing in the doorway. He looks at the crates she opened two days ago and his hand tightens on the doorframe. She feels a stab of guilt, like a child caught stealing sweets.

"They're just languishing here, Thomas."

He stares at the jagged scars in the wood where she prized the lids open. She sees now that it looks like a frenzied attack. She fixes her face with what she hopes is a benign smile, employs a bright tone.

"I just opened a couple to see what was inside, that's all. They're beautiful specimens, Thomas. I'm sure they could fetch a healthy price. I've written to Mr. Ridewell. He's arriving at eleven o'clock tomorrow morning."

He wavers for a moment, as if he is going to come in. Perhaps he doesn't mind that she snooped after all—she has piqued his interest. But then he tears his gaze away from the crates and steps silently back into the dark hallway. She hears his feet drum on the stairs as he takes them two at a time.

FRANCIS RIDEWELL'S HANDS SWEAT in his gloves as the cab pulls in front of the two-story brick house. Already he has shed his coat and would like to do the same with his hat. Moisture beads on his head and he removes his hat to give it a quick wipe with his handkerchief before he meets Mrs. Edgar.

The pretty little housekeeper leads him through to the drawing room, where he finds Mrs. Edgar waiting for him.

"Please, don't get up," he says as she rises to greet him. "So nice to see you again, Mrs. Edgar. Thank you for your letter." A draft licks at his damp head, deliciously cool.

He can see straightaway why she called upon him. The room they sit in sags with neglect. Despite his understanding that Edgar has a comfortable allowance, Mrs. Edgar could clearly do with some extra income. He hopes to be able to provide it: the first two consignments sent him from Brazil fetched a healthy price at auction. His commission made his efforts more than worthwhile. People are still nutty for natural history, even though its heyday was last century. It seems that at every dinner party he has been to, even the ladies know a good deal about the natural sciences, can reel off a list of sea anemones and their habitats; every wealthy man covets the most rare and exotic insects.

He has also managed to find publishers for any papers Edgar may have prepared on Brazilian lepidoptera, but he can't help wondering if he may get his hands on the real prize—the account of Edgar's hunt for the rumored butterfly. Above all, he needs to know whether he found it and brought it back with him. He had been tempted to look through the crates of specimens when they arrived in Liverpool with their silent owner, but he respected his client enough to wait until he was ready to share them. Perhaps the time has now come.

"Will Mr. Edgar be joining us?" he asks hopefully.

"He is still very ill, Mr. Ridewell. He is in bed. I have informed him of your visit, and he will join us if he can, I'm sure."

"I see. And he knows I have come to look at his collection?"

"I told him."

"And the time has come to sell them?"

"I think so, yes."

"But what does your husband think, Mrs. Edgar?"

The lady begins to blush. She looks down at the arm of her chair and starts to pick at some loose tapestry. "How could I possibly know, Mr. Ridewell?" Her voice is a murmur in the gloomy room. "He hasn't spoken a word to me, as you know."

"Yes, of course, madam. I'm sorry." This complicates things. Unless he is sure Edgar has sent for him, he is not comfortable taking anything away. "Shall we at least have a look at them?"

She seems relieved that the small talk has come to an end, and she rises from her chair, nodding vigorously. She is a fine-looking woman, tall and strong. She reminds him of his eldest daughter, now safely married and living in the country. The fingers that scraped at her chair were long, artist's fingers. Good for playing the piano, he thinks, but a quick glance around the room tells him there is no piano. He imagines her selling it to survive while her husband was away; the sacrifices she had to make for him, and now here he is, Ridewell himself, standing in the way of her plans. He shakes the guilt away. Letting his imagination run away again. She probably doesn't even play the piano.

She leads him through the dark hallway to a door under the stairs.

"Just through here," she says, and turns the handle. Her weight bumps against the door and she looks at him in surprise; she expected it to give way and instead it is a barrier between her and whatever is on the other side. She tries the door again, this time prepared, rattling the handle without leaning on the wood.

"It's locked," she says, as if he could do something about it.

"Do you have the key?" he asks.

"No," she says. She stares at the wood for a moment, then knocks. "Thomas? Darling, are you in there?"

There is no answer—of course—but from somewhere deep in the room there is a shuffle and the scrape of wood against wood: somebody pushing a chair. Mrs. Edgar steps back and looks expectantly at the door, but it remains resolutely shut and the quiet from within burns.

Ridewell coughs and shifts his weight. Mrs. Edgar looks at him with drooping features. She runs those long fingers over her face and sighs; not for the first time in the last week or so, he is sure. He takes her elbow and begins to steer her back to the drawing room.

"How about we have some tea? You haven't offered me any tea, Mrs. Edgar." He tries to make his voice seem jovial.

"Yes." She gives him a weak smile. "Tea would be nice, wouldn't it? Forgive me. After your long journey, as well. Where is it you've come from?"

"Russell Square. Near the museum."

"Yes, Russell Square." Her voice is hollow and mechanical.

The maid brings them tea and they chat idly about the weather. Mrs. Edgar makes only a passing comment about her husband's state—how he is missing church to remain in bed—and he tries to find in her words some clue to whether she has solved the mystery of his silence. He thinks perhaps there was some indiscretion on Edgar's part—something he said in a letter once after Ridewell had inquired on Mrs. Edgar's behalf as to why he hadn't written to her. *It is a matter between myself and my wife*, the letter had said, as if Mrs. Edgar was on one side of a quarrel between them, when clearly, at least to Ridewell, she had no idea what was going on. But it is unlikely that this possible indiscretion had anything to do with his muteness; more likely he's had some shock.

He finds himself relaxing around her; the armchair, though worn, molds to his shape with great comfort. Finally, he decides to just come out with it.

"Mrs. Edgar, have you found some clue as to what might be wrong with your husband?"

She bites her lip and shakes her head. He has caught her off guard and her body closes in on itself.

"Forgive me," he says. "I am as concerned as you are. You know your husband and I had a very genial correspondence for a time. Until . . ."

"Until?" She leans forward.

He shrugs. "I'm sorry, madam. Until he reached Manaus, where his letters became . . ."

"Yes? Mr. Ridewell, you have shared none of this with me. I only had one letter from Manaus, and it was unfinished. Anything you can share with me I would be most grateful for. Did he, by any chance, mention a woman?"

A-*ha*. He clears his throat. "No, not that I recall."

"But his letters seemed . . ." She is egging him on.

"Well, they seemed almost to have been written by another man. He became more and more obsessed with finding that yellow and black species he talked about, which frankly . . ." He closes his mouth. It's not his place to say that he thinks Edgar was making a fool of himself. How unlikely it is that such a butterfly exists, with wings two different colors. Really! It goes against all evidence of nature, of symmetry in the world of lepidoptera. It wouldn't even be able to fly—its wings would be of different weight and density.

He tries a different tack. "Many of his letters seemed . . . feverish. As if he were ill or something. Some of them even seemed a little . . . paranoid."

Her hand goes to her mouth. "Paranoid? What do you mean?"

"Oh, nothing to be too alarmed about," he says, his tone as reassuring as he can make it. "He just mentioned in his letters that he couldn't say any more about some matters, that he thought somebody might be trying to hinder him. It's as if he had stumbled onto something he desperately wanted to share but couldn't. Does that make sense?"

She nods at this, and her eyes slip out of focus as if she is listening to his voice across the sea.

"Thank you for being so candid, Mr. Ridewell. You've helped, I think."

No, I haven't, he thinks. Not really. "What did the doctor say?"

"That he'd had a bump on his head, and that he had perhaps had some kind of shock."

"And does he appear to be getting better?"

"Yes, a little." She smiles for the first time a genuine smile, not simply a polite one. It is small, but it is there. "I think it is only a matter of time. Small steps, you know, Mr. Ridewell."

He nods. "I understand." He thinks of his own wife at home, how he could never bear for anything like this to befall him, the pain it would cause her. And the two children still left at home, his married daughter, his sons safely in trades of their own, including young Francis, whom he is training to follow in his footsteps. There is no doubt about it: Mrs. Edgar is a brave woman.

"More tea?" She raises the teapot and moves it toward his cup.

"No, thank you. I should really be going. If your husband . . ." How could he say it?

"I'm sorry, Mr. Ridewell. You came all this way." She stands up, draws herself upright and rigid. "We can at least pass the study on your way out and try the door again."

They don't need to try it: the door stands slightly ajar. From within Ridewell detects the familiar smell of chloroform and naphthalene, used to protect specimens from the damp of the tropics. They both hesitate at the door, before Mrs. Edgar puts her hand up and pushes. The door swings silently on its hinges.

Edgar sits hunched at his desk. Two of the crates are open; tissue and sawdust litter the floor. On the surface of the desk are strewn cards with butterflies on them, scattered like colored rags. In among them, Edgar scribbles furiously in a journal. Only when Mrs. Edgar steps forward and her foot crunches onto sawdust does he look up. His face is gray and stony, but his eyes are clear and alive.

EIGHT

Manaus, January 1904

HE COULDN'T WRITE TO Sophie. How could he? Every time he picked up his pen his mind whited out as if filled with glare, and his hand jerked and trembled. What could he write about, after all? The presence of Clara had filled his waking moments and many of his sleeping ones too. He had collected nothing; instead, he had wandered the streets of Manaus in a fug, along the waterfront with its floating dock that rose and fell with the rain. He ventured only a few yards into the forest. The company of butterflies was thin compared with the forest around Belém and Santarém, or perhaps he simply hadn't seen them, so busy was he walking with hunched shoulders, eyes on the ground. But no—Ernie and George, too, had complained that they needed to venture further afield to find new specimens; there was nothing new for them here. While the lack of insects meant a respite from the mosquitoes that had plagued them on the Amazon, there was little other comfort in the fact.

Thomas avoided conversation with Clara, and she didn't pursue it with him. She was seated each evening next to John Gitchens and they would be deep in discussion for most of the meal. Only John was satisfied with the collecting in the immediate surroundings. The foliage was different on the Rio Negro, where tall palms dominated on the main river, here the scanty Jara palm hardly made a feature of the landscape. Santos looked on with approval— no doubt they were discussing botany, the hobby he sought to encourage in his wife. The first night she had looked up at Thomas only once, but Thomas felt the seconds of the gaze pounding in his ears. He hoped the others hadn't noticed. When nobody was looking, he sometimes followed her with his eyes, trying to reconcile the image of the butterfly—so free moving and graceful—with the woman before him. Part of him told himself he was mistaken, but he knew he was not. He thought her unusual-looking: not what one would call beautiful in conventional terms. She was very small, but buxom and wide-hipped, and her face had eyes that were too big and a nose and chin too small. She waddled slightly as she walked, like an old woman, although by Thomas's estimate she was no more than thirty-five.

On their fourth night at dinner, Ernie broached the topic that was on all their minds.

"We've had a brilliant time here, sir, but we've all decided we should like to move on. If that is agreeable to you."

Santos gulped down a large mouthful of food and nodded. "Certainly," he said, then cleared his throat. "Excuse me. Yes, I was going to suggest the same thing myself to you all. I notice you have not been collecting as much as I thought you might."

"To be honest, sir," said George, "there's not as much to be collected here as in Belém, or even Santarém. Insects are the scarcest of all."

"I see. Mr. Edgar? Do you find the same with your precious lepidoptera?"

Thomas nodded. "I do, sir. I am also particularly interested in finding a certain butterfly that is rumored to be around these parts. Sightings put it north of here, on the Negro. I should very much like to go and look for it."

"Rumored? You mean it has not been found before?"

"No. It is a most unusual species. Nobody has caught it or recorded it—only spoken of it. I don't even know if it exists. It is rumor and hearsay."

"And what does it look like, this rumored butterfly?"

"It is large, of the Papilionidae—a swallow-tailed species. It is most unusually marked, with one side having yellow wings and the other black. Those colors generally indicate that it is poisonous—the yellow and black act as a warning to predators."

"It is an unlikely marking," said George. "Butterflies are by nature symmetrical, so this one would just be all wrong. We've been humoring you, though, haven't we, Thomas?"

Thomas gritted his teeth. What a time for him to speak up. Was George trying to humiliate him? "Yes, George, you have. But I am determined to find it. The source of the rumor is very well respected."

"Yes, but it's like Chinese Whispers, isn't it, old boy?" said Ernie. "Who knows what Wallace or Bates or whoever it was said? They didn't write it down."

"Spruce," said Thomas. "It was Alfred Wallace and Richard Spruce."

"Do you know, Mr. Edgar," said Santos, "I believe I have heard of this butterfly you speak of. It is not just large but a giant. The local Indians have a name for it; I'm not sure what it is. In Portuguese it is '*o beleza gigante*.' They say it only appears at sunset. Local legend has it that there is a valley to the north where they are found in their thousands."

"And yet nobody has ever caught one?" said George, barely keeping the scoff from his voice.

"That's right. The Indians have no use for catching butterflies, sir."

Thomas shot George a triumphant look. That put him in his place, surely. George was too resilient, too sure of himself.

Santos continued. "They think we Europeans are strange for wanting to do so; after all, they cannot be eaten. The only explanation they can come up with is that we use them to copy pretty patterns onto our fabrics. Why on earth would we kill something that is of no use?"

Thomas found that he had begun to tingle. Santos's words filled him with new hope. So he was right. There was even a legend surrounding it!

"This is good news indeed, sir. Might we make our way north?"

"Of course," said Santos. "I have a camp a hundred miles from here that will suit your needs very well. I may even join you myself. My wife also."

Clara looked up from her plate. Her eyes were glossy onyx beads. They slipped to Thomas for a second and he looked away quickly. Did she know of the butterfly? She had been dressed as one that evening, hadn't she? He tried to recall the costume she wore, but he could not; he could think only of his hallucination—that she *was* the butterfly. Now that he thought harder, he saw her fall back off him, both arms covered in black fabric. She was more like a moth. He heard her clear her throat as he shuddered.

"That would be wonderful." Her voice was like cream, thick and smooth; her accent bejeweled her excellent English and made it sparkle. It was surprisingly loud for such a small woman.

John spoke up. "Your wife has expressed interest in my work, sir. Perhaps this is an opportunity for her to learn something about botany. She may even be able to teach me a thing or two. She has already explained to me that the black of the River Negro is due to the nutrients of the rich forest in this part of the country."

"Has she now?" Santos looked amused. "I did not know she knew that. You surprise me every day, my dear."

"And you surprise me, my dear." A mischievous smile curved her tiny mouth and she reached for another slice of meat. She placed it on her empty plate. The woman had an appetite, too; Thomas's meal was only half finished and he already felt full.

"Yes, Mr. Gitchens," Santos went on, "I would be very happy for you to indulge my wife in her hobby. A toast, gentlemen. To your new expedition. To Mr. Edgar's butterfly, and to my lovely wife."

As they raised their glasses, Thomas's eyes found Clara's again, and this time, neither of them looked away.

IT WAS WITH MORE than the usual excitement that Thomas boarded the small boat that was to take them to their camp upriver. All feelings of shame over the affair with Clara were blotted out by anticipation. He could feel it now, the closeness of the *Papilio sophia*. The night before he had dreamed of it again. He had felt the velvet wings fluttering against his skin and all the tension that had been building inside him was released like a sigh.

George fussed around as the porter carried his gear on. In addition to Antonio, their constant companion, Manuel, the mute Indian servant, and a cook came with them, plus a skinny boy who looked no more than twelve or thirteen. The cook, a *caboclo* named Pedro, threw himself into helping load cargo and puffed about like a fat schoolboy chasing a football, while smiling and singing to himself.

The morning light shimmered on the black water. Thomas shielded his eyes before he stepped to the edge of the dock to peer into its depths. His face was reflected back at him; the flesh hanging off it gave him a ghoulish appearance and he drew back again. The heat was rising. The shirt he had put on new this morning scratched at his hot skin. He turned his face upriver to where the *Papilio sophia* waited for him. Finding it would make everything all right. He felt his body straining toward it, as if it alone knew where it was; he would need only to follow its instincts and the butterfly would be his. Naming it after his wife would make it up to her. His life would be complete.

"Where's Ernie?" George stood with a hand holding his new cane balanced on his hip. The few days they had spent in Manaus clearly agreed with him; though he had managed to maintain a relatively pristine state in the jungle, the heat and the insects, not to mention the dirt, had begun to affect his appearance. But now, his immaculate look was restored. He had been shopping for new clothes and they fitted his straight-backed frame well. Thomas wondered how long his new hat would keep its crisp shape before it wilted and drooped like a cut poppy.

"He didn't come home last night," said John. "I passed by his room very early this morning. His bed hadn't been slept in."

At that moment, Ernie strolled up, looking freshly cleaned. He paused from his whistling to produce a handkerchief from his pocket and wipe his face.

"Good morning, gentlemen," he said. "Lovely morning. All ready for adventure, are we?"

"Where have you been?" asked George.

"None of yours, my fine friend. And I shouldn't like to compromise the young lady in question. I say, don't you look smart?"

George puffed out at this, his irritation with Ernie clearly forgotten. He patted his stomach and took a deep breath through his nose.

"Where is all your gear, Ernie?" Thomas whispered.

"That butler fellow—what's his name? He took it. I told him last night I might not be back in the morning. It's all arranged. He said it would be. Look, there's one of my bags now." He approached the men as they loaded the luggage and placed his hands beneath it as Pedro lifted, offering no support at all.

THOMAS SAT ON THE deck watching the emerald of the forest trailing into the water. The vegetation was denser here, darker, and melded with the black water. On the other side of the boat, the shore could not be seen; were it not for the absence of salt in the air, Thomas might have fancied himself on a wide ocean.

Rain approached; he felt the blood in his veins slow down; even the movements of the other men as they wandered past had been reduced to a sluggish crawl. He had come to understand that this was normal before the clouds opened and dumped their burden of water on the world below. He had learned to give in to it, to lie back with eyes closed and enjoy the sensation: the prickle of electricity on his tongue and his body wrapped in dense air. Just before the deluge hit, it would be preceded by a cooling wind. When he felt it on his skin, he knew the downpour was just a few minutes away.

There was a new pleasure on this river—an absence of mosquitoes. He could sit without being harassed; the air was not punctuated by slaps and curses as it had been on the Amazon. Still, he was the only one sitting outside. Mrs. Santos had her own room, where she had remained since their departure from Manaus. Santos, too, kept to himself, and Thomas observed endless trays of tea being taken to his cabin by the young boy. His skinny legs took careful steps, knees raised high, and he reminded Thomas of a heron picking its way through wetlands. His hands were white on the tray, so scared was he of spilling a drop, and he walked with his eyes on the teapot, his tongue poking out in concentration and sweat beading on his brow.

Thomas remained outside, under cover, during the afternoon's rain. He was too excited to be confined inside, and his eyes scanned the shore, as if he would find his butterfly flapping lazily between the trees and the water. He rolled cigarette after cigarette and watched the smoke drifting and melting in the rain.

As evening fell, and the rain had abated, the pilot steered the boat toward a dock. An acrid smell like burning effluent hung in the air. Thomas's nose twitched and George shielded his face with a handkerchief.

"Pooh!" said Ernie. He pointed at the tendrils of white smoke rising above the trees.

"It is the rubber," said Antonio, who had joined them. "The *seringueiros* are smoking the day's harvest in the fire of the attalea palm. You will see it when we arrive in the camp."

During the short walk to the camp, the smell grew stronger, but Thomas was used to it; it even excited him.

When the rubber-tappers saw Antonio, who led the party, they scrambled to their feet; when they saw Santos, they fell to the ground again, bowed in supplication. Santos murmured something to Antonio, who then barked orders at the men. They were to vacate their camp for them, it seemed. Thomas couldn't help but feel guilty. Where were they to go, with night about to fall?

These men were the *seringueiros* he had heard about—men of mixed race, recruited from the workforce around Amazonia, even from northern Brazil—not the Indians Santos employed in Peru.

Only the men standing over the fires stood their ground. One man, with a smooth face like a baby's, bore a flood of tears from the smoke. The fire—more smoke than flames—was piled high with palm fronds. He turned a pole smeared with rubber that grew as the men watched into a large and heavy ball. Weeping ulcers marked his arms; intermittently he scratched at them and smeared his skin with blood and pus.

"I promised you, didn't I, sirs," said Antonio, as the men stood transfixed, "that you would see how the rubber is prepared? Quite a sight, no?"

Thomas looked around him. Ernie and George watched with eyes bright, while John hung around behind them. The look on his face was more pity than fascination, and he met Thomas's eyes for a moment with a small shake of his head.

Santos stood talking to a black man. To Thomas's wonder, they were speaking English. The man, dressed in a light long-sleeved shirt, with a handkerchief knotted at his neck and a felt hat, and a rifle slung over his shoulder, stood rigid beside Santos, nodding vigorously. Though he had an air of authority about him, he was utterly deferential in the presence of Santos. Santos commands so much respect, thought Thomas.

Clara stood by her husband, with her hand tucked into his arm. She wore her city clothes, which surprised Thomas; he had thought she was of hardier stock, and the delicate parasol she twirled absentmindedly over her shoulder looked ridiculous in the middle of the forest, where the sinking sun came in thin spikes through the canopy.

The servants bustled about with the *seringueiros*, loading up possessions on their backs to vacate the huts. This camp was larger than the one on the Tapajós, with more than ten huts facing in a circle and a cookhouse. Gas lamps hung from poles; when one man reached up to take one, Antonio barked at him to leave it.

Thomas's heart sank when he entered his hut. Though it was bigger than the ones he had previously shared with John, a hammock was once again to be his bed. The room, elevated presumably to prevent flooding, and with poles for a floor, was bare, with no desk for him to work at or shelves for his books.

"Is everything all right, sir?" Antonio walked in behind him.

"Yes, thank you, Antonio."

"We have sent for some furniture for you. It will arrive in two days."

Thomas's heart lifted. "Thank you. That is most helpful."

The room held the most basic human smell—old sweat and perhaps waste as well—but a look around the room told him he must be mistaken. Merely a room, with four hammocks, where four men had worked hard and slept soundly, not caring for the niceties of society, or wanting for them.

As he placed his bags in a clean spot in the corner of the room, a movement caught his eye on the wall beside him. He had startled something—an insect. No—an arachnid. He leapt back from the wall, then mocked himself for taking fright. He was supposed to be a naturalist, for pity's sake. The spider was thickset and large, with legs like wide, fibrous cords. A tarantula.

Antonio popped his head through the door again. "Are you all right? I heard a cry."

Had he cried out? He seemed to be making a habit of taking fright and being deaf to his own noises.

"Nothing," said Thomas. "It's just a spider. I'll kill it." He reached down to remove a boot.

"No!" Antonio stepped through the door. "You mustn't kill it, Mr. Edgar. It will drop all the hairs on its legs, and these are more dangerous than the spider's bite. They are like pins, and poisonous."

"Well, what will I do with it?" He didn't want to have to pick the thing up. He was ashamed at his squeamishness, but there—Antonio already knew he was a coward.

"Leave it alone, sir. It will not bother you. By morning it will be gone. You'll see."

He supposed he should call George, but he was taken by a sudden urge to keep the tarantula from him. George didn't seem all that interested in spiders, after all, and he would only come in and give him some lecture about it.

Everybody retired early to get a good night's sleep before a day of collecting. Santos was unusually quiet and Clara ate her supper in her own hut. At first Thomas couldn't see the tarantula in the black shadows cast by the lamp, but when he lay on his hammock he saw it moving around on the rafters above him. Too nervous to turn the lamp off, in case the tarantula crawled onto the ropes of his hammock, he left it on. Every time the spider moved, a wash of cold crept over his skin. It wasn't just the spider that made him tense; only a few flimsy walls of palm leaves separated him from Clara. It was strange to hear a woman's voice—low and husky as she talked to her husband—out here in the jungle, mixing with the trills of the crickets and the cries of the night creatures. Birds that were named for the sounds they made—the *murucututú*—a sort of owl—and the *jacurutú*—sounded at intervals throughout the night as Thomas finally fell asleep, the spider weaving a web through his dreams.

THOMAS SET OUT COLLECTING on the first day with winged feet. Colors seemed brighter, the birds and monkeys in the trees louder. Santos accompanied them, which made things rather uncomfortable; where the men were used to hunting in silence, he seemed determined to converse with them.

"It's just strange to me," he said, "that you worship these creatures you collect—you in particular, Mr. Edgar—and yet the first thing you do when you find them, in their wild, natural state, looking as magnificent as they ever will, the first thing you want to do is *kill* them."

"Well, we are scientists foremost," said Ernie, who didn't at all seem to mind the distraction, despite the fact that their presence scared away birds. Flashes of brightly colored wings sprang up in all directions, but Ernie was focused on Santos.

"Oh, I don't mean you, Dr. Harris," said Santos. "I declare that you appear to have no feelings for these animals at all."

"Steady on," said Ernie. He stopped for a moment, and looked crestfallen at his patron's assessment of him. "I do sometimes feel guilty about killing them."

"Then why do it?"

"If you don't mind my saying, Mr. Santos," said George, "you have paid for all of this. Do you have no conscience about it?"

"But I am a hypocrite, Mr. Sebel, and freely admit it! And anyway, I do not love animals. I love to eat them, but I find them a nuisance at best, and insects I have even less tolerance for. But you . . . I have heard you profess to love your precious ants and beetles. And you, Mr. Edgar, your butterflies."

Thomas considered his answer carefully. Santos had raised an issue he had always pushed from his mind. He was going to make a mess of it, he knew. "I love them as an example of God's work, sir. It is our duty, as scientists—" at this point he thought he heard George give a kind of a snuffle "—as *scientists*," he repeated, louder this time, "to study just how amazing God's work is. I mean, the intricacy of these creatures, the minute and precise workings of them, more complex than any machine—"

"Yes, yes, Mr. Edgar, all very admirable, I'm sure, but I'm afraid you have not convinced me." Santos dropped back to continue the conversation with George, and Thomas, finding his heart pumping faster and his face flushing, pushed on ahead, defeated.

The hottest part of the day came, and Thomas reminded himself what Santos had said about the giant butterfly emerging in the cool of the evening. He contented himself in the afternoon with cataloging and reading.

Clara and John had stayed close to camp, and John seemed to be concentrating on giving Clara lessons in botany rather than collecting specimens. They sat side by side in the shade with piles of leaves in front of them, which they were drawing and painting and writing notes about. Though he was still avoiding Clara, Thomas couldn't help but feel a pinch of jealousy at the easy way they related to each other. He knew that if it wasn't for what had happened between them—he couldn't even bear to name it, not even to himself—he might be able to relax around her, even engage her in conversation, for she seemed a bright and intelligent woman.

As the sun began to fall, Thomas ventured once again into the forest, taking Ernie with him, as he was nervous to go on his own when he was unfamiliar with the paths. He jerked his face toward every movement in the trees, but found only monkeys leaning in for a closer look, or heavy-bodied birds jumping from branch to branch. No other butterflies appeared—they had gone into hiding for the coming night. Though the snatches of sky through the trees were still blue, the light on the forest floor was failing. They would have to turn back.

"Don't move," said Ernie, who was behind him. Thomas stopped, noting the serious tone of Ernie's voice.

"What is it?" whispered Thomas, but he didn't need an answer. Standing on the path ahead of them was a huge black animal, barely visible against the darkening trees. It had seen them, but its look of curiosity was giving way to suspicion. Its ears began to flatten against its head and its legs buckled as it sank to a crouch. It was getting ready to spring if it needed to.

"I can get it from here," said Ernie.

Thomas turned his head slowly, fearing what he would see, and sure enough, Ernie had his shotgun and was readying himself to fire. Forgetting the admonition not to move, Thomas grabbed the barrel of the gun and pushed it upward, just as Ernie squeezed the trigger. The sound exploded in his ears.

"What are you doing?" cried Ernie, but Thomas had already spun around to look back at the jaguar. Luckily, it turned and leapt away from them, making little noise in the undergrowth. Thomas heard only the buzzing in his ears from the gun.

"Idiot," he said. His hands shook and, now the danger was past, he felt his cold blood flooding back through his veins. "Shooting at a beautiful creature like that, are you mad? And with shot. *Shot*, Ernie. You would only have wounded it and made it mad as hell. You're lucky it didn't tear your head off!"

Ernie stood looking at him dumbly, the gun wilting in his arms. "You're right, old man," he said at last. "Crikey, what a telling off!"

He was looking at Thomas with a new respect, and Thomas realized that he had kept his head while Ernie had panicked. The jungle was becoming a part of him now.

That night, Thomas lay in his hammock and pictured the jaguar. It had looked him in the eye and Thomas felt it was staring into his very soul. Ernie had sung his praises when they returned to camp and he had felt himself walking a little taller. But, despite the excitement, he was weighed down by disappointment. No butterfly. The whole idea of its coming out at sundown seemed preposterous, and he convinced himself that Santos had been mistaken about this aspect. He must be patient. He must continue as he had been, and when the time was right, the butterfly would appear.

A WEEK WENT BY, and though Thomas saw nothing of his butterfly, he collected a good number of other specimens. The collecting was not as abundant as it had been in Belém, but it was slightly better than when they had stayed in Manaus. He noticed that when the men mentioned Belém, nostalgia crept into their voices, and he came to realize that they, himself included, had taken their life there for granted. Everything had been new and exciting, but they also had an abundance of food, natural life, and friends. Life was as relaxed as it could get. He missed their chats on the balcony of the comfortable house, while hummingbirds and bees buzzed from flower to flower, and the local girls called out to them and waved. He even missed the young boys George had employed to collect for him, their gap-toothed smiles and their laughter. He scarcely wanted to admit it to himself, but the presence of Santos kept him always on edge. He was conscious of his manners at all times, and Santos regularly tried to engage him in intense discussions to which he felt he had not enough knowledge to contribute. And as for Clara . . . the effort of avoiding her was becoming a strain.

Santos took tea religiously at eleven o'clock and four o'clock, whether they were inside waiting for the rain to stop, or wandering through the forest. Manuel was forced to light a fire to boil a kettle, and to carefully unwrap the precious china. The men felt obliged to take tea with him, and Santos used the opportunity to engage them in discussions about art and philosophy, particularly that of English poets. Thomas would sit and observe him: saucer balanced on outstretched palm, teacup raised daintily to his lips, his giant mustache coming away glistening with tea. Santos recited poems and George joined in, face shining over "Ode on a Grecian Urn" or "Kubla Khan." The two men then fell to discussing the poets, their lives and their work, while Thomas and John listened, and Ernie shuffled his feet and stifled yawns. Santos seemed particularly fond of William Blake. A visionary, he called him. Thomas had read Blake at school, but his masters considered the prophetic works too risqué to be studied.

"But have you really *read* them, Mr. Edgar?" asked Santos when Thomas told him this.

"I have, Mr. Santos, and I must boldly conclude that the man was quite mad."

"Mad? What makes you say that?"

"All that talk about heaven being a place where people lead a torturous existence. His refutation of Swedenborg, who was surely a visionary."

"But do you understand what Blake was saying?"

"He was saying that hell is a preferable place to heaven. That we should deliberately sin to get there."

Santos laughed. "Oh, dear sir, you have had some priest or teacher beat that into you, I suppose."

Thomas blushed. He had a picture for a moment of his old master hunched over a podium, denouncing Blake with spittle groping the corners of his mouth.

What was it Blake had said? *Sooner murder an infant in its cradle than nurse unacted desires.* Being in the presence of Clara filled him with desire; he finally admitted it to himself. It wasn't that he found her beautiful, but rather the opposite. It was her plainness that excited him, her throaty voice that spoke too loudly for a lady, her huge appetite for food and drink. All reason told him he should have been repelled by her, but if he unharnessed his thoughts for even a moment he remembered their encounter in the alleyway, the sweet taste of her tongue, and he became aroused. He took to carrying one of his setting pins in his pocket at all times, and if any wicked thought crept into his mind, he pricked himself soundly on the finger. By the end of a week, his index finger was bruised and bloodied, and he had to write by pinching the pen between his thumb and middle finger.

At night he was hounded by erotic dreams of the butterfly and Clara. Ernie had warned him that taking quinine could provoke vivid dreams, so he ceased taking it in an effort to curb them. He stayed awake as long as possible, thinking of his life back home in England, of the cold and sterile rooms of the Natural History Museum. His thoughts wandered over the butterflies on display in the Insect Room; how he had pored over them in the dim light of the oil lamps and naked gas jets, shivering, never dreaming he would catch such foreign beauties himself one day. Until then, the most exotic specimen he had caught was a purple emperor, as a boy on holiday in Kent.

He had had an unlikely ally in the capture. His brother Cameron, a fat and angry child, was two years older than Thomas. It wasn't until they were adults that Thomas understood that Cameron had been teased mercilessly at boarding school. When he came home, especially when he brought a friend with him, he let out all his pent-up rage and frustration on Thomas. There were bruises from being pushed down, grass-stained knees rubbed raw and muddied, broken toys and torn books. But Thomas never told on him. For one thing, Cameron always threatened him with a beating if he did, but second, he detected in his brother's soft belly and sloping shoulders a terrible sadness, which he felt an overwhelming urge to quell. Perhaps, he thought, by soaking up the punishment he would relieve his brother of some of his pain.

He was twelve years old when he and Cameron went to stay with their aunt one summer. She had a small lake on her estate, surrounded by a meadow with long, languid grass. Thomas spent all day stalking fritillaries while his brother swam in the lake and lay on the little jetty in the sun. Cameron had recently had a growth spurt: the soft belly had been stretched taut and his legs had grown dark and hairy.

"Come on," he said to Thomas one afternoon. "Race you back to the house."

Thomas reluctantly gathered his net and his jars, knowing he didn't stand a chance against his brother. He was about to protest when a flick of color caught his eye. He gave a shout when he saw what it was, though he had spent the morning trying to be as quiet as he could. The purple emperor seemed to weave in and out of the high branches of a yew tree, alternately flapping and coasting on a current twenty feet above them.

"I can't go yet," he told his brother. "I have to get that butterfly." The only time he had seen one in the meadow was two years before, when he had tried to coax it down with a decomposing rabbit he had found in a trap, but the butterfly had not caught the scent, or else was simply uninterested, and his aunt had smacked him for coming home stinking of rotten flesh.

He expected Cameron to pinch him and tell him to hurry up, or, worse, to wrestle his net from him and run off with it. Instead, he watched his brother find the butterfly with his eyes. A curious look fell over Cameron's face, like a man who has made a scientific discovery. As the emperor swooped above them, his stance changed. Every new muscle went rigid in his body, like a big cat, and his eyes darted about with it. Finally, as the unsuspecting butterfly came tauntingly close, Cameron, quick as a spider, snapped his towel into the air and winged it. The butterfly fell to the ground, stunned.

Thomas gasped and fell on it. Thinking no, no, expecting its wings to be torn and its body mangled. He was ready to finally hate his brother.

But the butterfly was still perfect. He was able to scoop it up in disbelief and put it in a jar. He looked up from where he crouched on the ground, and Cameron, with the sun behind him, looked down with the kindest expression Thomas had ever seen: pride mingled with sympathy. Thomas knew that from then on things would be different between them, but at school the following autumn, Cameron pushed him into the freezing pond to entertain Bertie Whitehead, the school bully.

SANTOS ANNOUNCED ONE MORNING that he was traveling back to Manaus to conduct business.

"I have spent too much time in the forest," he said. "I have enjoyed your company immensely, but duty calls. I have spoken to my wife, and she is reluctant to leave while she is learning so much. I hope you do not mind, sirs, if I leave her to your protection. Just for a few days, in which time I will return to collect her."

Santos left with Antonio and the pilot of the boat, with Antonio promising to return immediately with fresh supplies. They had already been forced to eat agouti, a sort of guinea pig, which was dry and chewy, and the cook was threatening to serve them sloth.

Clara disappeared with John for the remainder of the day.

"Maybe our John is teaching her about biology as well as botany," suggested Ernie as they rested in the afternoon.

"Shut up, Harris," said Thomas as he slapped at a line of ants crawling up his boot.

"Yes, shut up," said George. "Even John's got better manners than to fool about with the host's things." Thomas had felt a momentary flutter of camaraderie with him, but it evaporated quickly. His face grew hot, so he stood and busied himself looking in his bag, his back to his companions.

Clara took her supper in her hut. Thomas wished he could make her feel more welcome to join them, but knew that Ernie and George would make little effort with her. Ernie had let slip when they were out collecting that he found her particularly unattractive, and Thomas had come to realize that this was as good a reason as any for Ernie to not speak to her, as he had no desire to flirt with her. George, on the other hand, showed her the same complacency that he showed all women. Actually, Thomas was more than a little relieved that she didn't join them, and that he could blame his companions; in the absence of her husband he was worried she would start paying him attention and he could not predict how he would behave. Even an accidental touch from her under the table was likely to make his face burn and his skin tingle.

After supper, Ernie produced a bottle of brandy Santos had given him, and some cards. The men played rummy into the night, perched on crates in Ernie's hut, while insects hurled themselves at the lamp. Even John joined them to make a fourth and they huddled in the small room under a cloud of cigarette smoke.

"So what do you make of our esteemed host?" asked Ernie as he shuffled the deck expertly. Thomas was starting to have trouble focusing on the numbers and the suits.

"A very intelligent man," volunteered George. "It was as I suspected earlier—he *is* an educated man. In fact he studied in England, which explains his love for all things English, I suppose." He accepted the cards Ernie dealt him and began to fan them out. "I can't make out whether he's well bred or not. I suspect he is of the nouveau riche. As are most of the rubber barons. *Baron* is a bit misleading, I suppose."

"Well, where did he get the money from to start the business?" asked Ernie.

George shook his head and Thomas shrugged as he arranged his cards into neat suits.

"His wife," said John. He had taken to smoking a pipe in the forest, and he sucked on it thoughtfully before speaking, while the others looked at him in surprise. Even in games, he was a silent presence, seemingly there out of politeness to make up the numbers rather than for the social occasion.

"She told you this?" asked George.

"Yes. We have to talk about something while we're wandering around the jungle, don't we?"

Ernie snorted and John shot him a lethal look, which shut him up completely.

"He really was a hat merchant for a while," said John. "Just like he said he was that day up the Tapajós. He went to Portugal to make his fortune and he insinuated himself with Senhora Santos's father in Oporto. The old man died soon after he married her and she inherited the family port wine business. It sold for a mint to an Englishman, and Santos used the money to buy his land."

"Rags to riches, eh?" said Ernie.

"Not quite. I think he comes from a comfortably middle-class home. As does Mrs. Santos. They just got lucky in business, both port and rubber."

"Well, I for one find him quite charming," said George. "So nice to find someone in a colony with whom to discuss the important things in life. I don't care what class he is."

Thomas couldn't help himself. "That's a first."

George looked at him in surprise and Ernie began to laugh.

"But I suppose he's got money," Thomas continued, "so he's all right?"

"And he is an *educated* man," said George. "That counts for something."

Thomas wished he'd kept his mouth shut. John dropped his cards on the table and strode off, banging his head on the low doorframe as he left.

"Steady on, you two," said Ernie. "Play nice. Bugger if we haven't lost our fourth."

THOMAS COULDN'T SLEEP AND lay on his hammock with his clothes still on. Every time he closed his eyes, the room spun mildly, but at least he didn't feel sick. He needed something to focus on, so he rose and sat in his doorway, where he could look at the lamp they kept lit at all times in the middle of the yard. It flickered with the shifting haze of night insects driven to a frenzy by the light. He rolled himself a cigarette with fingers dulled by alcohol. For the first time in days he was able to use his wounded index finger, whether because it was healing, which meant he had managed to keep his thoughts in control, or because it was anaesthetized, he couldn't be sure.

The usual chattering filled the night. It's a wonder we can ever get to sleep, he thought, with that racket. The air was oppressively moist; even now, after all these months, he wasn't used to it.

He didn't see her until she was almost upon him. He heard his name, whispered as if by a ghost, and then she appeared in front of him, a figure in white.

"Thomas," she said again, not to get his attention, but more as a confirmation that this was his name.

"Yes," he said miserably, for he knew the inevitable had arrived.

Her arms were crossed in front of her, as if she were cold, and her bare feet peeped out from under her nightdress.

"Mrs. Santos, I—"

"Clara," she said. "You must call me Clara."

He drew deeply on his cigarette and looked at the ground in front of her. Then he wobbled to his feet.

"I don't think we should be talking like this," he said.

"But I must speak with you," she whispered. "We have not spoken to each other at all."

"No." He felt deflated, and he grasped the doorframe to stop himself buckling toward the ground once more. Get it over with, he told himself. What did she want?

"I'm sorry," he said at last. "For what happened. I wasn't my-self . . ." He trailed away and still could not look at her.

"You have nothing to apologize for. My husband told me that he gave you one of his cigarettes."

"Yes?" Had they discussed him?

"Do not look so alarmed." Her voice was light, amused. "He only mentioned it in passing. Did you feel strange that night?"

"Strange, yes. I saw . . . things."

"It was *caapi*. A drug. From the *ayahuasca* vine. The Indians use it to commune with gods. Usually they mix it with saliva and make a drink from the paste, but it can also be dried and smoked. My husband uses it for recreation."

He let her words sink in, turning over his memories of the night.

"I expect you were not yourself. You mustn't take the blame."

"I see." A layer of guilt peeled, then lifted away. He had not been himself.

"May I have a cigarette?" She startled him by moving forward and sitting in the doorway at his feet. He had no choice but to join her. He gave her the tobacco, but she turned the pouch over in her hands and gave it back to him; he must roll one for her.

He rolled two, then watched her hair, loose and falling over her shoulders, as she bent her head to touch her cigarette to the match he held. He lit his own. The tension was leaving him now. Thank goodness for the brandy.

The back of one small hand faced him as she held the cigarette and exhaled a stream of smoke over his head. They were close now, almost touching, but he didn't move away.

"Your friends don't like me, I think."

"No," he said. "That is, you're wrong. I'm sure they do."

She shrugged. "I do not care. Senhor Gitchens is very kind to me. You have avoided me, but I do not feel the same scorn as I do from the other two."

Thomas didn't know what to say. She was right.

"That Dr. Harris, he is nothing more than a drunken idiot."

He had to smile. Right again.

"And that Senhor Sebel. Well, it is clear, isn't it?"

"What is clear?"

"He doesn't like women."

"Oh, I'm sure that is not true. He has funny ideas about people, that's all. He's a snob, I will give you that."

"No, I mean, he doesn't like *women*. Women are too old for him. And the wrong sex."

Thomas was too shocked to speak.

She laughed. "You look so offended. Surely you have noticed it. Do you not see the way he looks at the servant boy? I'm surprised he has not made it known to you."

He knew she was right, but he had tried not to think about it. George's relationship with the young boys in Belém, which Thomas had thought fatherly at first. The night on the Tapajós when he had seen a figure leaving George's room. Paulo, of course, who had been so upset when they left Santarém; he had begged them to let him accompany them, but Antonio had forbidden it. George had given him a bag of money.

"I don't want to talk about it," he said finally.

"I've made you uncomfortable." She laid a hand on his arm, and he did not move away. Warmth pulsated from it.

"Does your husband know?" He meant about George but she misunderstood.

"Of course not! That first night, at dinner, you and I agreed, did we not, to keep it a secret?"

"Your poor husband. My poor wife."

"My poor husband!" she spat. "I'm sorry, Mr. Edgar. I do not know your wife, but my husband does not deserve your pity. What do you think he has gone back to Manaus for?"

"I thought it was to engage in some business."

"Yes, business. Business with one of the many brothels there. Did you know, Thomas, that every third house in Manaus is a brothel?"

"I didn't, no."

"All these women who have arrived from Europe to make their fortunes. And they do make fortunes, believe me. All a girl has to do is make herself more expensive than the next, and she becomes instantly more desirable. Those men, they try to outdo each other at every turn."

"I'm sorry, Mrs. Santos. Clara. If I was your husband, I don't think I could . . ."

"No, perhaps you couldn't. But he has lost interest in me. He has not touched me for months. I'm afraid when you found me on that night . . . well, I also was not myself. And I did not expect to see you again."

Why was she opening herself up to him like this? He had neither solicited nor desired it. And yet he found himself wanting to listen further. "But why has your husband not touched you?" The question came out like a belch, unexpectedly.

"Have you not guessed? Have you not heard him speaking all the time about family, about the importance of family? We cannot have any children. I cannot give him any children. He does not find me desirable, and to him there is no reason to share a bed with me."

"But he seems to respect you, worship you, even."

"Oh, he tolerates me. Family is sacred to him. It was my father's wish that we should be married. My husband promised him he would take over my father's business when he died, but he didn't. He sold it at the first opportunity."

"I'm sorry."

"I have accepted it. Manaus is not so bad."

"You're lying. I can hear it in your voice."

She bit her lip and looked down at her cigarette, which had burnt out. She turned it over, as if surprised to see it there, before tossing it away. Then she covered her face with her hands and began to cry.

She leaned into his shoulder and he felt his arm move to accommodate her; he had little control over it as it wrapped around her shoulder and pulled her in to comfort her.

Her hair smelt of berries and a warmth emanated from it. He laid his cheek against it, then kissed the top of her head. Her sobs turned to soft hiccups and her shoulders stopped shaking. She put her arms around his waist and squeezed. How long had it been since he'd shared any kind of affection? He swallowed to stop his own tears and coughed. She pulled away and turned her face to his. Teardrops lined her dark lashes like dew and her cheeks were flushed. Her small lips quivered and her eyes searched his mouth.

He couldn't help himself, as he had known he would not be able to. As he kissed her, his free hand found his pocket and he dug the pin deep into his palm until he felt the blood run.

DISCRETION COUNTERED THE GUILT somehow. Thomas made excuses for his behavior: loneliness; that he had lived for so many months out of the sight of God that he was forgotten; everybody knew adultery was mildly acceptable in today's society—not that he had ever approved—so long as it was kept private and not flaunted. And he did not flaunt it.

There was something else: the longer he went without a letter from his wife, the more he was sure he was right about Captain Fale. He imagined the captain striding through Thomas's drawing room, tall and strong, a sheathed sword at his hip, sweeping Sophie into his arms before laying her gently on the floor and taking her in front of the fire. He saw the rapturous expression on her face as he entered her, the firelight dancing in her eyes, her absent husband forgotten.

He still began to hate himself, his lack of willpower. But mostly he hated his body. It disgusted him. How his cock stirred whenever Clara approached him. Even his normal bodily functions made him sick—the way he had to bury his own shit, and how it smelled: worse out here for some reason among the loamy scent of the forest. His sweat smelled acrid to him, too, and his face sprouted coarse hair where it had previously been soft and downy.

Clara discovered the pin in his pocket when he pulled his hand out and blood dripped onto her skirt. She made him throw it away, convinced him with a soft word in his ear and sweet breath that he was entitled to some pleasure, that to go without was both unhealthy and unwise. He began to believe her. After all, he had already done it once and had felt terrible about it; the damage was already done. The idea that what he was doing was wrong only aroused him more, as did the prospect of being caught.

They made love like animals—no, not love, for he certainly didn't love her, but the scent of her body, under her skirts, drove him wild. Clara liked it rough and coaxed him into ramming himself hard into her, which he did with his eyes closed, or fixed on the path to make sure nobody was approaching. He hadn't known he had it in him, this animal lust. With Sophie, it was tender, an expression of his love for her, and he hadn't realized there was any other way until now. The fact that he didn't love Clara made it easier, for he was only betraying Sophie physically, not with his whole being. This had nothing to do with her at all. It was about Thomas, about his time in the rain forest, a time he would never go back to again. She could have her captain, he would have his Clara, and they would never speak of it.

One afternoon, when out collecting together, he took Clara from behind while she bent in front of him. She grunted like a sow and he was forced to put his hand over her mouth when a cracking sound alerted him to someone's approach. He had just managed to pull his trousers up when Ernie lumbered toward them, swinging his prize catch—an umbrella bird.

"I've found a friend," he said, oblivious to what he had interrupted, scarcely even noticing that Thomas wasn't alone.

A bird walked behind him, following him like a lost dog. Its body was about the size of a pheasant's, but with its long legs and neck, it resembled a crane.

"Trumpeter bird," said Ernie. "They call it an *agami*. Bloody thing won't leave me alone. Didn't have the heart to shoot it. Gave it some fruit and now I can't get rid of it."

"What will you do?" Thomas was sweating hard; he didn't care in the least what Ernie was going to do with it, but he was trying his hardest to feign nonchalance. He glanced at Clara. Her cheeks were flushed and her lips plumped with blood.

"Well, the locals keep them as pets. Senhor Santos thinks I don't give a hoot about animals. I'll prove him wrong. Think I'll keep him." He bent down and tried to pick up the bird, but it stepped away from him and arched its wings.

"Bugger off, then." Ernie aimed a kick at the bird, which it dodged. "I'm off to deal with this beauty," he said, holding up the umbrella bird. "See you back there." He strode away, and the *agami* ran after him, making a sound that was less like a trumpet and more like a rumble from deep within its body.

TO AVOID ANY SUSPICION, Clara still accompanied John in the mornings, and after their near miss with Ernie, Thomas discouraged her from coming with him too often. When she did, she helped him collect butterflies, even catching a few specimens of her own, but she was reluctant to kill them, and instead put them in jars, which she kept in her hut. Thomas didn't have the heart to tell her that she was being more cruel than kind; eventually the butterflies would die like that. He suspected she set them free again, anyway.

The afternoon rains were becoming more prevalent. They came every day now, while the men worked in their own huts or occasionally together for company. Thomas had taken to drinking in the afternoon to try to quell the sickness in his stomach that he knew was guilt, and it worked. By nighttime he was fluid and loose, with butter in his joints as he slipped into Clara's room and crawled under her mosquito net.

It was here that she introduced him to another pleasure. She was reluctant at first, but he pressed her to tell him what it was that made her claim that on the night they met, at the carnival, she was not herself.

"It is this," she said, and produced a small bag of white powder, which she measured out and mixed into a glass of tea. "I take it for my headaches. Drink some with me," she said. He drank, remembering that despite what the *caapi* had made him do, he had enjoyed the sensation of warmth through his veins and the vision of his butterfly it gave him.

They didn't make love that night, just lay side by side on Clara's bed. It was still and firm compared with his hammock: it had taken three men to carry it from the boat for her. A sweet warmth came over him, and Thomas felt at once tied tightly together with her in their shared experience and happy to be on his own, staring into the light on the net that lay over them like a shroud and listening to the calls of the night sounds. His body felt bathed in light, and he imagined it emanating from his heart, pulsing to his fingertips, warming him. Surely this is what God feels like, he thought. I have found God at last. Everything will be all right.

Clara moved a foot against him and woke him from his reverie. She rolled over and flung her arm over her head with a small moan, knocking over two jars on the chair next to the bed. They smashed to the floor and the butterflies within sat stunned on the floor for a moment before launching themselves sluggishly into the air. They were drawn to the mosquito netting as if to his net. Clara sat up and put her hands out of the covering. The butterflies—*Morpho menelaus*, their color changing from blue to pink as their wings caught the candlelight—crawled onto her fingers. She brought them back and began to sing to them, her voice low and melancholy. Thomas saw that he had been unkind to her. She was more beautiful than any woman he had seen. Her inquisitive head once again took on butterfly qualities, and the butterflies walking up her arm seemed to sense the pulsing beauty within her.

"Lovely," he whispered, before putting his head down and falling asleep, the sweet sound of the Fado song filling his dreams.

HE WAS AWAKED BY a shaft of sunlight falling onto his eyes. Clara stirred beside him. He sat up and realized the light outside was too strong. He had slept in. He should have gone back to his hut before the end of the night, but now the sun had climbed into the sky and it was mid-morning.

"Damn, damn," he said through clenched teeth as he put his boots on. He was still fully dressed; at least nobody had come in to find him naked.

"*O que é?* What is it?" asked Clara. Her hair had come loose from her bun and covered her face like tendrils of seaweed.

"It's late," he said, and threw the mosquito net aside. He realized too late that the butterflies had settled on the floor—perhaps they were half dead anyway—and he stood on one. He lifted his foot to find it ground into his heel, its blue wings torn and its body squashed.

Outside, he checked the yard. Only the cook was in sight, his back to the huts as he washed dishes from breakfast. Thomas ducked down and scampered across the yard to his own hut. The men had left for the day. He only hoped and prayed that they thought he had merely risen early to go out collecting; this is what he would tell them, anyway. But what about John? He would have been expecting to go out with Clara, and he didn't remember hearing him knock on her door. Perhaps he waited for her to appear and then left her to sleep. Please, God, he thought.

His head ached and his limbs were leaden. The heaviness would soon turn to pain, he knew; he recognized the sensation from when he was coming down with influenza.

Today is the day, he thought, that I will find my butterfly, because I cannot last any longer. The rainy season was fast approaching. It rained every afternoon now, and soon most of the day would be taken by deluge and the butterflies would go into hiding. He would be forced to watch while his colleagues continued with their work and his dried up.

His shaking hands found the whiskey he kept in his trunk. He poured himself a nip, downed it, and then took a slug from the bottle. This will see the illness off, he thought. Within minutes he felt better, and had another gulp just to make sure. Whatever it was that Clara had given him last night left him feeling exhausted but there was no doubt that for a time he had felt exquisite. He had to remind himself that the sensation wasn't real . . . and yet how could feeling good be wrong? In the jungle, his body had come to rule him. For one evening he had been able to leave his body far behind and feed his soul instead.

He thought it best to set out without Clara, to avoid any suspicion. As he left the camp John returned alone. Thomas dropped his gaze, couldn't look at him. What if he had seen him in Clara's hut?

"Where've you been?" John asked, with no greeting.

"I got up early." Thomas's words rolled heavily off his tongue. "I forgot something, though, so I've just been back to get it. Some jars I prepared last night."

He couldn't tell without looking at John what his reaction was.

"Senhor Gitchens." Clara came walking up between them. "Forgive me. I overslept. I wasn't feeling very well."

Thomas took the opportunity of the distraction to sneak a glance at John, whose whole body language had changed. He began to run one hand through his hair over and over again. He smiled a rare smile as he looked down at Clara. She stood close to him, her own smile loose on her lips. Thomas took a step back from them and spun on his toes to face the forest.

"Good day," he said, and didn't wait for an answer. If John had suspected anything, it was eclipsed by the arrival of Clara; Thomas might as well not even have been standing there.

Despite the ache in his limbs, which was getting stronger, he decided to go farther today than ever before. He knew it was unwise without Manuel or the boy to help and guide him, but he needed to get far away from the camp. Cracking branches sounded off at intervals to his right and left. Every time he caught a movement with his eye, when he looked at it he saw only moving branches, swaying as if a great weight had pushed off them. He concentrated on the markers on the rubber trees left by the *seringueiros*, making sure to check the direction with his compass.

He walked for an hour without stopping to catch anything. This was a new path and it started to turn in on itself, to curve back toward the camp. He made a decision to keep going, heading north, for north was where Santos had said the butterfly was. The forest grew thicker; many times he had to go around a thick knuckle of trees. The ground grew steeper, but he would not be swayed from his course. North, north, always north. Finally he had to stoop and use his hands to pull himself up where the forest floor had become a bank.

At the top, he stayed doubled over to catch his breath. His lungs labored and his limbs were filled with water. His clothes stuck to his body, drenched. He dropped to his knees and looked at the small valley before him.

He had stumbled onto a clearing covered with a lush flowering vine that trailed yellow petals from tree branches, blanketing the floor of the forest. A small river trickled its way east toward the Negro, falling first twenty feet down rocks slick with emerald slime and shining with minerals. He waited for the breeze that played on the flowers to reach him, but his clothes stayed moist and warm. His eyes slipped into focus as he tried to determine what might be making the flowers waver and undulate. He picked out one flower, then another. The second one came detached from the vine, rose up on a current, and floated up into the air. It was not a flower; it was a butterfly, flapping lazily through the ether toward him, one side yellow wings, one side black. He drew himself slowly to his feet, wiped his dripping forehead with the back of his hand. The butterflies carpeted the ground; groups huddled around pools of water to drink. The sounds of the jungle had stopped. The valley was bathed in silence; even the brook made no sound, as if the presence of the butterflies muffled it, like cotton wool.

Thomas took a step forward. A cloud of yellow and black rose before him like a small tornado, and a faint noise went with it—a rustling, like leaves caught by a wind on an autumn morning, or the shuffle of tissue paper on a desk. The butterflies made a *sound* in the stillness; he had never expected to hear it. The cloud dispersed, joining mates on tree branches that bent under their collective weight. Each specimen was as large as his outstretched hand.

He wanted to scream; to lie down on the ground and beat his fists and feet against the happy earth; to have the *Papilio sophia* cover him like a shroud while he lay, not breathing. Instead, he crossed his arms over his chest and stared. Finally he poised his net and swiped gently at the air, catching one of the butterflies. What would he do with it? He sat on the ground, suddenly overcome. He had forgotten to breathe and his head hammered. He was reluctant to turn it out into a killing jar. Now that he had it, he knew he couldn't kill it. But here were thousands—no, millions—of the species; surely one would not be missed? He examined it through the net, the exquisite sculpting of the swallow-tail, the black wings like dark velvet, the yellow delicate, like freshly churned butter. He lay back on the ground and held it close to his face. He kissed it, only a layer of fine netting separating him from his heart's desire. With the captive on the ground beside him, he closed his eyes and, as he felt the *Papilio sophia* alight on him one by one, fell into a sweet sleep.

IT WAS THE RAIN that woke him, huge drops that fell into his eyes and his open mouth. He brought his hand up to shield his face but lay on his back, disoriented. He thought at first that the roof of his hut had sprung a leak, but he gradually became aware of the sounds of the jungle around him and the weight of a hundred anacondas inside his head. He tried to sit up, but found that every muscle ached. He groaned and rolled over on his side. A procession of ants crawled past his nose and into his bag, which lay open a foot away; another line exited carrying morsels of fruit. At intervals a drop of rain fell on the parade, scattering ants the way an explosive would. But, limbs intact, the ants shook themselves off and rejoined their army.

He pushed himself up. His net lay beside him and for a moment Thomas knew he had forgotten something. He looked about him. He sat in a clearing with a waterfall running through it; rain fell into the small river and bowed the leaves of palms and epiphytes. Birds and monkeys shrieked in the treetops. The sound penetrated deep into his eardrums and intensified the pounding in his head. Despite the rain, he burned. I have a fever, he thought. I'm done for.

He swayed to his feet, and it was a monumental effort just to stay upright. He tried to get his bearings; behind him was a bank, and he had a vague recollection of pulling himself up . . . and the rest came to him. He began to search wildly with his eyes: no flowers, no butterflies. No *Papilio*. Not one. He fell on the ground beside his net and lifted it with trembling hands. It was empty.

He cried out. Birds rose in fright, calling back, and hammered their wings in the air. Thomas ran his hands through the mud on the ground and sobbed. He brought up handfuls of gloop, smeared it over his cheeks and his aching chest.

"Who did it?" he shouted at the treetops. For this was the only explanation he could think of. Somebody had frightened the butterflies away, then stolen the one specimen he had caught.

He sat for half an hour while the rain fell around him, too exhausted, too angry, too scared to move. But he knew that the heat rising from his body and the pounding inside him was not disappointment but illness, and he had to get back to camp while he could still move.

It was a miracle that he found the path. He stumbled south for half an hour before darkness ate at the edges of his vision and he fell to his knees.

He didn't know how long had passed before he felt strong arms lift him and he was weightlessness itself, soaring through the forest, coasting on a current of air, catching the updraft with a flick of his wings.

He was carried—by John, it turned out—and lowered gently into his hammock. Figures surrounded him. Ernie mopped his forehead and murmured to him, "Just a touch of the ague, old boy. Nothing to worry about."

Clara was there, too, and George. Behind them loomed two large dark figures, conversing in Portuguese: Antonio and Santos. *Santos is back.* The room tilted on its axis and a wave of nausea crashed over Thomas. It was Santos, it had to be. He had followed him to the butterfly valley. He had waited until he fell asleep, then he had played his cruel trick on him. He was punishing him for his relations with Clara.

"I had it," he wheezed. "He took it."

Muttering erupted around him. *What's he on about? . . . He's delirious . . . Get him to drink some water . . .*

Thomas caught Santos's marble eyes looking at him. Then all went black.

NINE

Richmond, May 1904

SOPHIE PAUSES OUTSIDE THOMAS'S study to listen for any sounds. Nothing. She knocks gently, then opens the door.

"I brought you tea," she says, as if she needs an excuse to enter; besides, it's obvious from the cup she holds in her hand.

He looks up from his work and nods, before resuming bending over a specimen with a magnifying glass. Sophie puts the cup down beside him and hovers about. She has been crying and she doesn't care if he sees her puffy eyes. Let him know how he upsets her. There is no doubt he is changing: the color is coming back into his cheeks; his abrasions are healing and he seems to walk more upright. His brittle frame has become more robust.

But still he will not speak to her.

After the agent's visit on Thursday—two days ago—Sophie tried again to find his journals; when she couldn't, she thought about asking him for them.

Another day, though. It was not the right time. Mr. Ridewell spoke of secrets, and hindrances to his work, a fever. But when she studied her husband as he ate his dinner, his eyes downcast, taking the food in neat bites, he was unreadable.

He glances over his shoulder at her, as if to say, *Are you still here?* She folds her arms and moves closer.

"I found the blue butterfly, Thomas." He freezes. He goes on looking at the specimen in front of him, but every muscle has gone rigid. "I meant to say thank you. It's beautiful."

He nods, and his body relaxes once more.

"Did you ever find your *Papilio*, my love?"

He lays his magnifying glass to one side, brings a fist to his mouth and coughs. His throat sounds full of tiny stones. It's the first real sound she has heard from him, and it fills the room and swirls around her. Then he shrugs.

How can he not know whether he found it or not? She's irritated suddenly at his evasiveness, the way he always has his back to her or his eyes down. At least when he was catatonic she could tell herself how sick he was, but now he seems to be willfully keeping silent. Now that he spends all day in his study, unpacking, ordering, cataloging, and writing, she can't make excuses for him. If only he showed as much attention to her as he does for his stupid butterflies. For the woman in Brazil, even. Perhaps a spell in hospital would do him good after all.

What is she thinking? She shakes the thought away and removes an old teacup from beside him. No, the next step is to continue life as normal, as if nothing has happened. *Take him to do the things he loves.* Tonight they will go to the theater. She will make him notice her again.

IT HAS BEEN A long time since Sophie has dressed up properly for an evening out and she takes her time getting ready. She selects the dress Thomas bought her before he left and has never seen on her. The copper-shot lavender chiffon falls in soft folds about her body. She worried at first that it was too daring—the neckline is cut low and her shoulders are exposed through peepholes—but now it doesn't seem to matter. She knows that Agatha must have helped Thomas choose the design, because it is something she can imagine Agatha wearing—the height of fashion—and the sort of thing her friend is always trying to persuade her to buy. She doesn't dare think how much it must have cost: the details are exquisite, with a blouse waist, a plaited belt of Liberty satin, and the sleeves formed from draped pieces of gauze held with satin. She shimmers as she walks and the spangled material and fringe catch the light.

She pins her hair in a high pompadour and fixes a silk flower to the front of it. A matching lavender fan and a diamanté necklace complete the outfit.

Earlier in the day she laid Thomas's evening suit out for him while he sat in his study. She had found it when she unpacked his trunk of clothes. Everything else had been worn thin and filthy. When she sniffed at the rags of his collecting clothes she fancied they smelled of the jungle, and his old boots were muddy, with grit and dead leaves embedded in the soles. He had inadvertently brought back more of the forest than he had intended. In the middle of all that tattered and dirty clothing—which she later threw away—was a glossy black suit, with shirt and tie and even spats. When could he have worn it? She brought it to her nose and inhaled. It smelled faintly of cigar smoke.

He will need protection tonight, that is certain: from the gaping stares of people, from those who try to engage him in conversation, and those who will be scrutinizing him for signs of madness. She has scarcely been able to admit it to herself—has in fact pushed the thought from her head for her own sanity—but it is these signs that worry her the most: his dogged silence; the way he can barely look at her when she enters the room; the way he jumped up, quivering, when a butterfly touched the window that day. His secret disappearances. What if Thomas behaves strangely tonight and somebody reports it to her father? He would have Thomas committed to an institution in a heartbeat, would take Sophie back to live out her life in his care with an "I told you so" look every day.

Dr. Dixon might also be at the theater tonight. He is an avid fan of comedies—he told her so himself. If he sees Thomas is not getting better . . . she stops herself. No, Thomas has definitely improved since the doctor examined him. She will put it all out of her mind and concentrate on enjoying herself—and making sure her husband does too. And if *that woman* is still on his mind, she will make him forget.

When she calls into his room, he sits dressed on his bed. He jumps to his feet when he sees her and his mouth opens so she thinks he might speak, but he closes it again. The look he gives her says it all. Hope spreads through her like warm milk.

The crowd is gathered in the warm evening at the edge of the common, by the theater's entrance. A rumble of conversation and bright laughter meet them as they move in tight formation, the three of them. It is as if she and Agatha are chaperoning Thomas instead of the other way around. Sophie clasps his left arm and on the other side of him Agatha is so close Sophie can smell her scent: lilacs. It is overpowering. The crowd parts for them as they move through it. She expects people to avoid her gaze, to turn their backs as they did at church. Instead, they give her and Thomas sympathetic smiles. Did she imagine it at church that day?

She is glad she told Mrs. Sykes now. At first she regretted it, wanted to keep their private life private, but now nobody moves to speak to them and they are all saved from excruciating awkwardness. She couldn't stand to cause a scene.

Robert Chapman, however, immediately approaches Agatha, who moves away from Thomas and turns her body toward her lover. Her gaze sweeps approvingly over his evening suit, and it is returned with as much admiration. Honestly, the two of them just can't seem to hide their feelings, even though Robert over-compensates by greeting Sophie, not Agatha.

"Mrs. Edgar," he says, taking her hand. "And Mr. Edgar. So nice to see you back from your travels." Agatha must have told him, because he doesn't address any questions to Thomas, whose rigid arm softens in hers.

"I say, there's Captain Fale," says Robert. He waves and beckons to him. Samuel looks desperate for a moment, but he soon composes himself and waves back, without making a move toward them. Sophie tightens her grip on Thomas's arm, steadying them both. She must make everything as normal as possible, to help Thomas. To help herself.

"I was just talking to Mr. Slater, from the council," Robert is telling Agatha. "They're building another almshouse, if you can believe it."

"That's wonderful," says Agatha. "Don't you think, Sophie?"

"Mm." Sophie wonders where this conversation is leading. Thomas is rigid again beside her, staring at the ground as if in a trance.

"Well, I'm sorry, ladies," says Robert, "but I disagree. Richmond is being overrun with the unfortunate."

"What exactly do you mean by 'the unfortunate'?" asks Sophie.

"Those who cannot look after themselves or their families."

Like us, she thinks. He means us. Is this what people think of them? She stares at him defiantly. "Aren't you more at rest, knowing that if for some reason—God forbid—you found yourself in a position to need an almshouse, it would be there for you?"

"That will never happen. Besides, having five almshouses in one town may also have the effect of attracting all those who are doomed to fail, therefore making Richmond a town of failed businesses. Soon there will be no business and the whole of Richmond will be living in almshouses. Then they'll need to open up many more!"

"You're being contrary, Robert, and look, you're making Sophie angry. Stop it at once."

He laughs and throws up his hands in surrender. "All right, ladies. You can be happy in the knowledge that the almshouses are sprouting like mushrooms and we gentlemen will have to see that you never end up in one! Isn't that right, Edgar?" He winks at Thomas, who gives him a blank look, as if he is deaf and doesn't know he is being addressed. Robert's smirk vanishes, and he looks away quickly, embarrassed. He murmurs something in Agatha's ear. She giggles softly and a blush forms on her cheeks. She really should be more careful, thinks Sophie. And is Robert laughing at them now, and making Agatha laugh too?

But it makes her think. If Thomas continues as he is, will they end up relying on the charity of others? Certainly her father would never let them starve, and Thomas's allowance is enough to keep them, but what good will that be if someone decides he belongs in an institution? They will live out their days apart, Thomas rotting and silent, while she visits him on Saturdays and special occasions.

She shouldn't have come, and she shouldn't have brought Thomas. She is opening them both up for scrutiny and judgment.

As they move toward the stairs to take them to their seats, Agatha leans in close to Sophie.

"Ask Mr. Chapman to join us," she whispers.

"Oh, Agatha." Sophie doesn't even want to stay herself, but how can she leave and let Agatha down, and, more important, leave her alone with a man so recently widowed? Her friend cannot afford to behave scandalously.

"*Please*, Bear. For me?"

Reluctantly, Sophie turns to Mr. Chapman. "Won't you join us? That is, unless you have other companions waiting."

"Thank you, Mrs. Edgar. I would be delighted."

They settle into their box and she surveys the crowds below and across on the other side. Eyes flicker up at them. Fans beat the warm air. As the lamps dim, Sophie glances at Thomas. He sits staring at his hands, seemingly oblivious to the world around him.

The performance is a comedy, a very modern play about manners. The audience laughs frequently, but Sophie misses the joke each time; the players speak quickly, firing back and forth, and she cannot concentrate on their words. At times the content of the play scandalizes some of the ladies below—gloved hands cover their mouths, but there are giggles beneath them. Thomas appears to have fallen asleep beside her. So much for taking him to do the things he loves—he seems to have regressed rather than improved.

She finds herself thinking about what Mr. Ridewell said about Thomas's letters. He wrote something about keeping secrets for others. What had he seen? And the journals. She should have kept reading that day instead of throwing the book at the wall and giving up. But what she had found had disturbed her so much, she couldn't bear to think there might be more. She had walked around in a trance those days after, fretting and mulling and making herself feel ill. She doesn't know if she can ever forgive him. The hurt he has caused her twists into her belly like a screwdriver. But what she can do is try and see past it to their future together.

Last night she dreamed that Thomas was wrapped in a sticky film. She could see him beneath it, sleeping, and realized with a shudder that he was a chrysalis. He woke then, in the dream, and began to stretch and shake in the cocoon, which started to tear . . .

Agatha shrieks with laughter and Sophie realizes she has missed a particularly funny moment. She glances over at her friend but looks away again quickly when she sees that her fingers are entwined in Mr. Chapman's. Silly girl. She thinks she is being discreet, but if she carries on like this, the whole world will know. Still, Agatha can rely on her to keep it quiet. Sophie moves closer to her husband. Perhaps she and Thomas are not so different after all.

When the show is over, the four of them join the audience as it flows down the stairs to the foyer. Halfway down, the crowd stops. People build up behind them like a storm.

"What's the holdup?" shouts a man's voice close to Sophie's ear. She flinches and rubs exaggeratedly at her ear with her gloved fingers. They come away damp; the man, in his enthusiasm, has drenched her with spittle.

"It's raining," comes a voice from below them. "They've all stopped at the door."

"Well, tell them to get a move on," the man bellows.

There is a surge behind them and the man falls roughly against Sophie, but does not apologize. She loses her footing and slips painfully down to the next step, twisting her ankle slightly. Thomas catches her arm and holds her steady. She turns to him, ready to smile; despite her discomfort, it is a startling gesture and his hand is strong on her arm. But Thomas is not looking at her. As the crowd boils around him and people shift indignantly on the stairs, he glares at the man who spat on her, looking as if he might murder him.

"What's your problem, mister?" asks the man.

Thomas continues to stare. His cheeks are flushed and his breath hisses through his nose.

"Cat got your tongue?"

Robert just manages to put a restraining arm against Thomas's chest as he lunges toward the man. Then Thomas turns, letting go of Sophie and pushing his weight through the crowd, all elbows. The throng is moving now, thinning out—people have braved the rain and are beginning to leave—but Thomas moves through it at a faster rate. Sophie watches the back of his head disappear.

The rude man laughs.

"It is not funny," she snaps. She bunches her hands into fists and resists the urge to slap him herself. This man will ruin everything. Already people are swiveling their heads to look at her, murmuring to one another, straightening the collars that Thomas has ruffled in his path. They will all think he is quite mad, she thinks.

The man shrugs. "Suit yourself, madam." He hangs back and is absorbed by the crowd.

She glances down into the foyer, scanning the faces for her husband, who she is sure has run outside by now. Instead she finds Captain Fale staring at her, and her stomach lurches. She wishes now she had worn something more modest. She feels naked under his gaze.

"WAIT HERE FOR ME, PLEASE," Captain Fale says to the cabdriver. "I won't be long."

He leans heavily on his cane as he alights from the carriage in a quiet street leading down to the river. A large oak tree stands in Mr. Winterstone's front yard, and for a moment he is reminded of the tree he climbed as a boy. Well, there will be no tree-climbing now, not with this wretched leg of his.

He thought it polite to write to Mr. Winterstone before descending on him, but he did not wait for a reply. The note was simple: *I have some urgent business I would like to discuss with you. I will be in Kingston tomorrow morning and should like to call on you at midday.* Of course, the only reason he is in Kingston is to see the fellow. He will make some excuse about a tailor if he is asked.

An alarmingly fat housekeeper opens the door and scowls at him. She moves quickly for one so large, however, and Fale soon finds himself in the drawing room. He waits by the fireplace, not presuming to take a seat. The room smells heavily of cigar smoke and is furnished with pristine leather armchairs. A photograph of a young woman hangs above the mantel, but it was taken some time ago. The look on her face gives him a fright: the curled lip seems to admonish him for coming. And yet the eyes soften her and he changes his mind about her expression. This, no doubt, is Sophie's mother, although he can find little resemblance beyond the blond coloring. Another photograph sits below it, propped in a silver frame. Sophie, as a much younger woman—a girl, really—sitting on a chair while Mr. Winterstone stands beside her. Their faces are grim, as is customary, but there is a further emptiness in their stance. Winterstone stands rigid, with hands by his sides, when any photographer would have instructed him to put his hand on the back of the chair.

He turns away from the photographs just as Winterstone comes into the room and approaches with his hand outstretched.

"Your note was a pleasant surprise," says the older man. "I enjoyed our chat at the Star and Garter. How can I be of help to you, sir?" He bids him sit in one of the leather armchairs, which squeaks as Fale lowers himself heavily into it.

"I am hoping that it is I who can be of help to you, sir."

"Oh?" Winterstone rises and moves to a liquor cabinet. "Drink?" He holds up a brandy decanter and Fale nods.

"It's regarding your daughter's husband."

Winterstone hands him the drink, his eyes sharp but his expression registering nothing. He sits and crosses his long legs, waving one elegant hand at Fale to continue.

"Are you aware, sir, that Mr. Edgar returned from the Amazon a changed man?"

"Changed? In what way? I haven't spoken to him yet, though I am interested to hear of his travels."

"He came back somewhat . . . disturbed."

Winterstone swallows loudly.

"That is, he is not speaking."

"What do you mean not speaking? Do you mean to my daughter? Have they fallen out?"

"Not just your daughter. He is not speaking to anyone. He appears to be, well, *mute*."

"Mute?" Winterstone roars. "Has he lost his mind?"

"Well, this is indeed the question, sir, and the reason I am here. I thought after I met you the other day that it was my duty to tell you, as Mrs. Edgar had obviously concealed it from you."

"I'm sure she had her reasons."

"Reasons, yes," says Fale. "Perhaps she is planning to tell you. After all, the whole town knows about it now."

"How do they know?"

"You know how people gossip, sir. Personally, I haven't told anyone, even though Mrs. Edgar confided in me."

Winterstone's eyebrows shoot up.

"As a good friend of Mr. Edgar's. Thomas." He takes a deep breath. He must tread carefully with his lies. "Also, they attended the theater on Saturday night, and an acquaintance of ours, a Mr. Chapman, had to restrain him from flying at a chap who had merely jostled him. I'm afraid he has become quite violent, and I worry that Sophie may be in danger."

"Good God. Sophie." Winterstone is lost in thought for a moment, his brow creased.

"He went to church with her yesterday and, frankly, he looked as if he would rather not have been there. He didn't join in on any of the hymns or prayers."

The man snaps his attention away from his glass and looks at him. "That would seem obvious, sir."

"Yes, of course." Idiot. He thought throwing in Edgar's apparent lack of faith might help his case, but he handled it badly. "He avoided all contact with the parishioners, even though many of them tried to show him some kindness."

Winterstone has not moved from his position, but his glass is empty and he now drums it rhythmically on his armrest. He stares at the ground. Fale waits for him to speak.

"Why are you telling me this?" the older man asks finally.

He's suspicious of my motives, thinks Fale. It's now or never.

"I only thought, sir, that by telling you this, we may be able to help the unfortunate couple. I know that Mrs. Edgar is most reluctant to have her husband committed to any kind of hospital or institution. Perhaps with your influence, you could make it a matter of legality. After all, it can do your daughter no good to stay married to a man who resembles a vegetable." He laughs, but it comes out high and girlish and he stifles it immediately. "One prone to violent outbursts, as well. How can the man be expected to support your daughter when he is clearly such a burden on her, and a danger?"

"Captain Fale," says Mr. Winterstone. "You hinted at something when I saw you last. I asked you directly what it was you were meaning. You said something about how terrible it was about him. Why did you not tell me then, instead of inventing some story about how he had a few hives and scratches?"

"I . . . I didn't want to alarm you, sir. And I hardly knew you."

"You hardly know me now."

"I know. I know. But now I am acting in what I believe to be your daughter's best interests."

Winterstone's eyes bore into him. Things are not going as Fale had planned. They got on so well together over a drink at the Star and Garter. But now, admittedly, he has just delivered some bad news, and no doubt the man is in shock.

Suddenly Winterstone's face softens, and he smiles a sad smile.

"You're right, sir. This is a most unpleasant situation for my daughter to be in. I will see what I can do about it. Leave me your details, and I will be in touch."

This is Fale's cue to go—he must leave Mr. Winterstone to deal with his new knowledge. As he stands he says, "I must ask you a favor, sir. Please do not tell Mrs. Edgar that it was I who informed you. It is a delicate matter, and they are both my friends. I would not like them to think I have been conspiring against them. Even though," he adds quickly, "I truly believe I am acting in their best interests."

"Of course. I'll say nothing about it. Good day."

. . .

"BUT HOW DO YOU know ghosts are real?" Agatha's little brother is tucked up in bed, his eyes as round as shillings.

"Because I've spoken to them," says Agatha. "Nona said I have a great talent."

"Are there ghosts in this house?" whispers Edwin.

"They're *everywhere*," she says, and tickles his chest. "But no, we've never seen any here. There are plenty around Richmond, though."

"Like where?"

"Like . . . at Ham House. You've been there. They say there is a cavalier who appears to people. Just when they think it's odd what quaint old-fashioned dress he is wearing, he . . ."

"He what?" Edwin is scrunched down under his covers.

Agatha drops her voice to a whisper, all the better to scare him with. "He *disappears*," she hisses.

Edwin giggles nervously and puts his face under the covers. "More," comes his muffled voice.

"Let's see," says Agatha. "Have you heard about Archway Annie?"

His head pops out from under the sheet, and he shakes his head, even though he's heard the story many times before.

"In the window of the archway to the Old Palace a woman appears to people as they walk below. She's very sad, and people hear her crying as they walk by. But nobody has ever seen her, except through the window."

Edwin squeals. "Why is she crying?"

"Her family has been killed—her mother, her father, and . . . her little brother!" Here she tickles him mercilessly until he screams for her to stop.

"What's going on in here?" Agatha's mother puts her head around the door. "Aggie, are you filling that boy's head with nonsense again? Honestly, you give him nightmares, you have no idea!"

Agatha laughs and whispers in her brother's ear, "You're big and strong enough to scare away the ghosts, aren't you, my sweet?"

Edwin gives a determined nod, with his eyebrows clamped down and his jaw jutting out. Agatha kisses him on the cheek and turns out the lamp, leaving them in darkness.

"Good night, darling," she says.

In her own room, she decides to have an early night. She sits at her dressing table and starts taking down her hair. The loose curls fall in ropes down her back and she takes her brush to start the task of taming them.

She hasn't seen Sophie today, but she still worries about her. Her spirits didn't seem at all lifted by the night at the theater, not after the commotion on the stairs. They found Thomas waiting for them outside and they went home in silence; Sophie was very tense. When Agatha tried to squeeze her hand, she took it firmly away, as if she were mad with both of them, not just Thomas.

At least she didn't just give up, but brought Thomas to church the next day. Agatha knew that the congregation was sympathetic, but blast them! They were all so stiff, and nobody would come forward to speak to them, not even to convey sympathies or to talk about the weather. Instead they cast them pitying looks, which were doing Sophie no good, and certainly not Thomas. Agatha suspects that all he really needs is to be treated normally for a time, for people to bombard him with questions so he is forced to speak up. She didn't tell Sophie, but she had been secretly longing for someone, anyone, to march up to him and say, "What's the matter, Mr. Edgar? Cat got your tongue?" Well, her wish had come true the other night, and it had certainly provoked a reaction from him, which must be a good thing, mustn't it?

She laughs softly to herself, but it turns to a grimace when she catches a knot in her hair and it jerks at her scalp.

Sophie said that Thomas's journals had disappeared, but she gave up on them too quickly. Agatha is sure those journals hold the key. Something has happened to him that he must surely have written about, otherwise why would he have hidden them? Sophie may even find something in there to give her hope.

She stares at herself in the mirror, mesmerized by the light from the lamp behind her. Her mind scrambles over possible explanations for Thomas's behavior. He still has his tongue: she's seen it licking his lips. He smokes cigarettes now, and he has the worn look of someone who has been to one too many parties. Just the effects of jungle living, no doubt. But something must have happened to him. Did he see a ghost? Those Indian cultures are famous for their spirits and whatnot. A wild animal? Maybe he . . . she hugs herself at the thought. Maybe he did something unspeakable. Maybe he killed a man by accident while out hunting. Or better yet, maybe he did it *on purpose*?

Agatha stands and begins taking off her clothes, quickly at first, but, as she reaches her undergarments, she slows. She looks in the mirror as she unlaces her corset, releasing her body. I'm a pre-Raphaelite, she thinks. Somebody should paint me. She unbuttons her chemise and exposes her breasts, imagining she is Robert, seeing herself how he saw her this afternoon. Except then it was by a wash of daylight through the open curtains, instead of by soft lamplight. He wanted the curtains closed and as she reached the window, nakedness to the sky, Mrs. Grimshaw walked by on the road. Agatha knew she should hide, but she lingered there instead, until Robert told her to hurry up before she was seen, and Mrs. Grimshaw happened to glance up and lock eyes with her before pressing a hand to her mouth and hurrying away.

TEN

Rio Negro, Brazil, February 1904

Dear Mr. Ridewell,

By now you will be waiting for a consignment from us. I'm not sure what the other men have told you, but my work has been hindered, by both illness and outside forces. I have been rather unwell, you see, and I am told I have had a malarial illness. I have lately been having periods where I can get up and move about, even write letters such as this one, but any physical activity weakens me and I am easily tired. I have eaten nothing but orange juice and cashew nuts for two weeks. Thank you for your letter, which arrived while I was in the height of my fever, and for your concern over my wife. It is a matter between my wife and myself. I will write to her when I am able, but please in the meantime do not tell her I am ill, as I do not wish to cause her worry.

I am plagued by dreams of a normal life at home—reading the morning paper, strolling in Richmond Park, attending church—and feel wretched when I wake up, even though I cannot imagine going home, where I fear things will never be normal for me again.

At night as well as dreams, I am hounded by moths. They thump against my lantern, against the doors and roof, trying to get in, with their sticky proboscises and their powdery wings, waiting to fly down my throat and choke me. They are ugly brutes in comparison to my gentle butterflies and I can scarcely believe they both belong to the order Lepidoptera. I am so close to my goals here in Brazil, but the jungle and its inhabitants conspire against me. This letter will be taken from me and posted, so I cannot say too much. But I am very close, Mr. Ridewell, and if I can rise above my challenges, we will both be very pleased. In the meantime, thank you for your patience. I am amassing my next consignment to you, but am not yet ready to let it go.

Yours sincerely,

Thomas Edgar

He sealed the envelope and left it on his desk for Antonio to collect on his next mission to town, then lay down, spent, in his hammock. It wasn't just that he grew tired easily; the fever came back to him sometimes and he would wake in the night freezing cold. One night he woke to find he had thrown off all of his coverings and his clothes and lay naked and steaming. A figure bent over him, gently wiping his forehead with a cooling cloth.

"Sophie?"

"No, dear, it's me. It's Clara."

"Your husband," he murmured, groping about him for a sheet.

"Shh," she said. "I am here to nurse you with his blessing. You'll feel better soon."

When he could get up, Thomas learned that George had also fallen ill soon after him, but the others had escaped any fever. Ernie said they were unlucky—there were few mosquitoes in this part of the jungle, but they were almost certainly the carriers of the malaria. Thomas had stopped taking his quinine because of the dreams it gave him, but George insisted that he had not stopped.

One morning, Thomas lay in his hammock while the rain pelted down on the roof and punished the yard outside. He would have little chance now, he thought miserably, of finding butterflies. He knew they retreated during the rains and collecting became sparse. He had lost his chance.

There was a knock at his door and Santos entered. Thomas struggled to push himself into a sitting position, and the hammock swung wildly and threatened to tip him out.

"Do not sit up, Mr. Edgar," said Santos. He drew the chair from Thomas's desk and sat down next to him. He gripped something in his hands—a small box.

Now that Thomas's head was clearer, and the fevers infrequent, he told himself the valley of butterflies had been a hallucination. Santos had only just arrived back at camp that evening; of course he could not have found him and released the specimen. But no matter how much he told himself, chastised himself for believing it, something in his gut ate at him, nagged him. He did want to believe that it existed after all. It *did* exist.

The room had grown dark with the rains, and the air was thick and hot.

"I have something for you," said Santos. "I think you will be very pleased."

He unfurled his fingers from the box and pulled off the lid. He held it out to Thomas, who took it and squinted at it in the dim light. Inexpertly pinned, with a broken thorax and a lopsided setting, a *Papilio sophia* sat dead in the box. Hot tears sprang to his eyes and he squeezed his lids shut to clear his vision.

"You found it," he whispered.

"Yes," said Santos, and chuckled.

"Is it . . . mine?"

"*Yours*, Mr. Edgar? Why, yes. I caught this myself when out with Dr. Harris this morning. It is magnificent, is it not? It is my gift to you. I trust you will name it appropriately."

Thomas's head snapped sideways to look at him. His lungs closed.

"Appropriately? But I have already chosen a name for it." His voice sounded small in the close air of the hut, which undulated with humidity while the rain came down in dark sheets outside.

"Which was surely conditional on your finding it. But now I have found it." His voice was matter-of-fact, betraying no emotion. If he was capable of any.

Santos patted him on the shoulder. "I will leave you with your prize," he said. "If I were you, I would give that name some good thought. My first name is José, as you know, if that helps you." He stood and with two long strides was gone.

Thomas lay back, holding the box still in his hand, and stared at the ceiling. My head is clouded, he thought. I cannot think straight. The turmoil he felt refused to clear so that he could identify his feelings and eliminate them. He had it. And yet . . . he did not have it. Santos had stolen it from him. If he had not stolen the actual specimen, he had stolen the glory. He let the thought sink in, and it burrowed into his bones.

His life was not worth living without this discovery. He had nothing. He would return home with nothing but a collection of insects to sell to fat rich men who didn't know a *Papilio* from a *Morpho*.

He would take this specimen home with him as the only thing to show for the legend that had driven him. And he could not even name it for his wife. The naming was the only thing that had kept him from shriveling with guilt, and now he had taken that away from her. She had been wronged with no compensation in sight, and only a failure of a husband. Another tear fell from his eye and slid down to his ear, where it tickled him. He gave a bitter chuckle. It wasn't even a perfect specimen. He brought it up to look at it again. Its black wing was torn, and the body was broken nearly in half. It was as if Santos had caught it by standing on it, or by smashing it out of the air with a stick. There was something else wrong with it: it was much smaller than he had anticipated. It was not even half the size of his hand. The one he had caught in the forest—even if he had imagined the whole episode—was not what one would call a giant, but it was certainly large for a butterfly. The rumors had made out that it was a giant, and . . . there was something else. This wasn't even a Papilionid; it was from some other family altogether. Instead of the elaborate decoration of the swallow-tail, it was plain: a dinner jacket rather than tails. The yellow was pale, almost white, and the black . . .

Thomas swung his legs out of the hammock. He swayed for a moment as the blood rushed away from his head and the beating of wings filled his ears and fluttered in front of his eyes. He pressed his fingertips to his eyelids to calm them.

The black was dull and watery, not iridescent as he had imagined it would be. It should have been like a pool of oil, black in its base, with greens and blues swirling and shimmering over the top. The black wings hung lower than those on the other side, as if weighted down. He looked closer, and pinched the pin that held it to pull it out. As he did so, the butterfly lost half its body, but Thomas was no longer concerned with this. At the bottom of the box, in the space under the butterfly's black wings, were two smudges. Of *ink*. The butterfly's wing had been dipped in Indian ink and whoever had pinned it so roughly had not even waited for it to dry.

He roared and threw the box against the wall of the hut.

Outside, the rain had eased, and Thomas stumbled into the quickening light. Ernie stood at the door to his hut, took one look at Thomas's face, and doubled over with laughter. Thomas marched over to him, light-headed, with legs as insubstantial as air, his hands bunched together in tight fists.

"It was just a joke, old man," said Ernie, straightening now, wiping the corner of his eye. "It was Santos's idea."

Thomas just stood there, impotent, his rage curling and dying inside him.

One by one, the other men emerged from their huts. George stood unevenly, face pale and sharp from his illness; John filled his doorway, his face cast in shadow from the hand at his forehead. Even Pedro, the cook, stood at the door of the cooking hut, rubbing his hands on a cloth. Only Santos smiled along with Ernie. Clara was a shadow at his shoulder, looking at Thomas with a face pinched with sorrow.

THE RAINY SEASON WAS well and truly upon them. The river swelled, and many creeks they had leapt over became deep rivers to be navigated or avoided. Water coursed into the forest, submerging the trunks and lower branches of trees. Where monkeys had sat and jaguars walked, was now the domain of dolphins and fish. Thomas imagined sitting on the riverbed as they swam through the trees toward him as if they were flying.

Insect collecting had now become sparse and difficult; butterflies in particular hid from the rain, but George complained, too, of coleoptera waning. Only John's work didn't abate—in the rain, plant life thrived.

A languid laziness took hold of Thomas and George, which they attributed to their recent illness, but both knew was a lethargy caused by having too little to do. Thomas slept through the morning until lunchtime, when Clara accompanied John. Santos, when he was about, walked with Ernie or stayed behind to converse with George and, on occasion, Thomas. He also went to Manaus for extended visits, but Thomas again fell to avoiding Clara, so worried was he that Santos had guessed what was between them. He used his time alone to redirect his focus to his wife. He wrote Sophie letters, which was like wading through mud, and could not bring himself to send them.

He decided to take John's advice and get to know some of the locals. Antonio was usually wherever Santos was, and Manuel and the boy, Joaquim, acted as guides and assistants to whoever was out collecting. That left Pedro, the cook. Thomas practiced his Portuguese on him.

"*De onde a sua família é?*" he asked, inquiring where his family was from.

"*De todo lugar,*" said Pedro, indicating with a wide sweep of his arms that they were from everywhere.

Thomas asked him if he could watch him while he worked, and Pedro gave him a look as if he were quite mad, but nodded all the same. He limped slightly as he pottered around the cookhouse, and, on a more intent look, Thomas realized the cook had a toe missing on his right foot. Although it would be impolite of him to ask, Thomas was struggling for topics of conversation, so he pointed to the foot.

"*Como . . . dedo . . . ferir?*" he asked, and Pedro smiled a wide smile at his appalling skill with the language. He proceeded to answer, but Thomas could only make out certain words. He ascertained that Pedro had lost the toe when he worked as a fisherman. The big black variety of piranha, though dangerous, was delicious to eat, and one had jumped off his hook in the boat and taken his toe in an instant.

Thomas must have looked horrified, and Pedro laughed again. His two brothers had lost their toes in the same way. Evidently the piranha was a delicacy worth risking digits over.

Thomas asked him if he liked working for Santos, and Pedro shrugged but would not look at him. Thomas had noticed that Pedro took all his orders from Antonio, but when he served Santos, his manner changed. He walked more slowly around him, and the hand that spooned meat onto Santos's plate often shook uncontrollably. Santos didn't seem to notice, or, if he did, ignored it.

For a week, Thomas came and sat with Pedro for an hour or more a day, and Pedro began to help him with his Portuguese. By the end of the week, Pedro called him "*magro*" for being so thin, and flicked pieces of food at him as he cooked, which Thomas dodged when he could, and wiped away from his eye with a smile when he could not. Thomas's language skills were improving and he surprised Clara and John one night by contributing to their conversation at dinner. John slapped him on the back with a smile, but Clara just stared at him. Her eyes pulled him in and a heat rose in the air between them. When he broke away, John was looking from one of them to the other; he had stopped eating, but held a morsel of food in his slightly open mouth. Thomas looked at his plate, burning. He felt as if he had been caught poaching pheasant, while the gamekeeper looked on.

He stood. "If you'll excuse me," he said, "I'm not feeling very well."

The following morning, Thomas slept late. He was awoken by Antonio.

"Senhor Santos would like you to have tea with him, Senhor Edgar, before the rain starts."

"I'll be there presently," said Thomas. Antonio left him and he lay and stared at the ceiling. He had not allowed himself to be alone with Santos. The others would no doubt be off collecting somewhere, and the man needed someone to talk to. He let himself out of his hammock and put his clothes on with shaking hands.

"Ah, Mr. Edgar." Santos sat in a shady corner of the yard at a low table with an extra chair beside him. Pools of water and mud were dotted around from the recent rain, and the thick air promised more. Manuel stood by, fanning Santos with a large palm leaf. As always, Santos managed to appear perfectly cool. Thomas was used to the damp heat now; he had even begun to enjoy the sensation of a warm bath, provided he could have a swim or a cool bath at the end of the day. His shirts were all marred by the same yellow stains under the arms, and he had given up fretting over them. Santos's shirts, however, were always crisp and clean, as if he wore a brand-new one every day.

"I trust you are recovering well?"

"I am feeling better, yes. I do get tired, though."

"Yes, you will. I too have had malaria. It never really leaves you, you know."

"No?" Thomas felt aged suddenly. He had stepped over a threshold and could not come back.

"Don't look so crestfallen, Mr. Edgar! It will make you stronger in the long run. A brush with death is good for the character."

"I'm afraid my character may be deserting me." He mumbled this, half hoping Santos wouldn't hear him. Was he pushing him? Waiting to see if he knew that he had acted dishonorably?

"Nonsense, my dear sir. I have been watching you . . ."

At this Thomas's stomach jolted.

". . . and I have seen you grow. You feel tired now, I know, and perhaps a little useless." He tilted his head and looked at Thomas as he might look at a sulky child. "Am I right? I think I am right. But I have seen your confidence in the jungle grow. Perhaps you have not noticed it yourself. You are becoming a true scientist."

"Scientist?" Thomas clicked his tongue and could not keep the scorn from his voice. Was the man blind? "I'm no scientist, Mr. Santos. I'm nothing but an amateur. I don't even know what I'm doing here half the time. No—most of the time." He ran a hand through his hair and found knots, grit. He shook his fingers. "You know that I am completely unqualified? I'm surprised they even let me come here. Butterflies have been nothing but a hobby to me."

"No, Mr. Edgar, you sell yourself short. You may not have made a career from the study of insects, but you have something much more important. You have passion. I see a fire inside you. It went dim for a time, when you were ill, but it came back a thousandfold the day I played my little trick on you."

"You did that on purpose?"

"Mm, yes and no. It is all right to get angry, Mr. Edgar. I suppose in my own way I was testing you. And you passed, I can tell you that."

"I did find the butterfly, you know. Right before John found me passed out."

"Oh, I think not. You were very ill. You probably just thought you saw it. It's not uncommon to see things with malaria. Why, I saw my first wife once when I was ill, a baby in her arms. She told me it was my son and when I awoke they were both gone."

"You are probably right. I did so want to believe in it, though." He studied Santos's face. The man had been too quick to dismiss his claim. Could he be lying? Could he know Thomas to be telling the truth?

"I saw the photograph you have of your wife. What is her name?"

"Sophie."

"Yes, Sophie." He seemed to be turning the name over, feeling the shape of it on his tongue. "She is very beautiful, isn't she? And so young."

Where was this going? He didn't want to discuss Sophie with him. It tainted her somehow.

"What is she like?" Santos continued.

"Like? Well, I don't know, I suppose she's . . ." He trailed off, trying to conjure up an image of her standing in the garden, smiling at him. Then he saw her beneath him, in the park as he tried to make love to her. He shuddered.

"Come now, Mr. Edgar, surely you know your own wife?"

"Yes, of course. She is wonderful. Quite wonderful." His voice had become a murmur. If he spoke quietly, she would remain pristine, not sullied by the jungle as he was. "I couldn't wish for a better companion."

"And children? Does she want children?"

"Yes, she does." He realized with a jolt that they had not discussed children for a long time, and he worried that this was his fault. Had he discouraged her?

"Excellent. I am very pleased for you. She is so young; I'm sure she has many years of childbearing ahead of her. Not like my wife. I fear her days are over. She is thirty-four years old and has had no children. I envy you. There is nothing I want more in this life than to father many children, for my name to continue for generations."

Thomas, at the mention of Clara, felt himself begin to blush. He willed himself to stop, but this only made him burn harder. He prayed Santos wouldn't notice.

"I've embarrassed you, sir. I apologize. I am always doing this— talking about people's private business."

· "Not . . . not at all," said Thomas, relief cooling his cheeks again.

"Anyway, I'm sure you will have a fine big family. You must not stay away for too long, I think. You are not like the other men— they have no family, no ties. They are married only to themselves and their work. It is selfish of them. There is nothing to stop them disappearing into the jungle—who would miss them? But you, Thomas, you must go back to your pretty wife."

"I will, in time." Was Santos trying to get rid of him?

"But I do admire you, Mr. Edgar. You have passion, and with passion you can succeed at anything. It was always my intention to fund individuals such as yourself, those who might never have an opportunity such as this."

"And the others?"

"Dr. Harris is an amateur like yourself. But he is a skilled taxidermist, even I can see that. His passions are worn on the outside, and spill over into less, shall we say, virtuous pursuits."

Thomas smiled. The skin on his face felt as if it might crack from the newness of the expression.

"And Mr. Sebel," continued Santos. "He did not need my assistance to come here. He has every opportunity in life. Some he will take advantage of, some he will not. He may be educated, Mr. Edgar, but don't for a moment think him superior to you in any way. I have great faith in you."

"Thank you, sir, though I wish I could say the same for myself. And what of Mr. Gitchens? Where does he fit in?"

"Ah, Mr. Gitchens, yes. A fascinating man. Very difficult to get to know. I couldn't even begin to try to understand him. I can only be certain of one thing."

Santos gazed at Thomas, who did what was expected of him. "And what is that?"

"That he is in love with my wife. Ah, our tea."

Thomas had not noticed Manuel slip away as they spoke, and the servant now returned with the tray of tea things. Thomas was grateful for the distraction because Santos's casual accusation of John had made him blush furiously, and he was able to concentrate on watching Manuel's hands while taking calming deep breaths to try to dispel the blood from his cheeks.

As Manuel finished pouring the tea into its tiny cups, an insect landed on his neck, startling him. He swatted at it while attempting to put the teapot back on the tray, his arms crossing as he did so and his elbows clashing. Thomas saw what was about to happen but could not react quickly enough to stop it. The teapot left Manuel's hands, spun slightly as it landed partially on the tray, teetered, and fell to the ground, striking the leg of the table on its way down.

"Look out!" said Thomas, but it could not be saved. The teapot shattered, and hot tea sprayed over the legs of Santos's pale linen suit.

Manuel froze, but Santos sat with his eyes closed, breathing through his nose. Thomas held out his handkerchief and it dangled from his hand, waving in the slight breeze, while he waited for either the servant to take it or the master to open his eyes and see it. Finally, Santos opened his eyes and Thomas saw a cold anger at work in them. He lowered the handkerchief.

"Antonio!" Santos called.

Manuel began to make a sound from his tongueless mouth; it was as if he were trying to speak, to apologize, but it came out only as the low of a calf. He was shaking his head slowly back and forth, staring at Santos, who would not meet his eyes. Antonio strode into the yard, took one look at the teapot, and grabbed Manuel by the arm. Manuel fell silent as he allowed himself to be led away.

"What's he going to do with him?" asked Thomas, suddenly fearful.

Santos smiled and took his own handkerchief from his pocket. "You needn't concern yourself," he said as he dabbed at his leg. The anger had retreated, dried out like laundry on a hot day. "Sugar?"

THOMAS WAS HAUNTED BY the sound Manuel had made, by the look in his eye as he was led away. He didn't see him for the rest of the day, and Santos—who no longer had a pot for his beloved tea—did not call on him.

Reluctant to raise the incident with the others when they returned from collecting, Thomas approached the only other person he could speak to about it.

"I don't know what happened to him," said Pedro in Portuguese. After only a week, Thomas was already able to understand him better, helped by the fact that Pedro spoke slowly and deliberately, with simple words. Thomas could tell he was lying. He sweated more than usual, and his hands shook as he stirred the pot of stew he was cooking. "But Mr. Santos was very angry. He cannot drink tea without his teapot." He lifted the pot off the flames, but dropped it again when he burned his hands and cried out. He eyeballed the stew, but though it slopped into the flames with a hiss, it did not spill too much. His relief was palpable. He turned his back on Thomas when he tried to look at his hands. "*Não foi nada,*" he said.

"Pedro . . ." Thomas laid a hand on his shoulder.

"I know nothing," the cook said in English, as if he had rehearsed the phrase over and over.

THE RAIN ABATED IN the early evening and Thomas took a walk to mull over the situation. He kept an eye out for the path that had taken him to the valley where he had seen the butterflies, but it eluded him. Pedro seemed terrified of Santos, that much was certain, and knew what had become of Manuel but would not tell Thomas. He couldn't ask Clara about it, not yet. He would have to wait until Santos was gone again; at the moment he still couldn't be near her. Thomas didn't dare risk exposing his feelings for her, especially after the incident with Manuel and the glimpse of his rage—cleverly contained, but certainly there.

As he walked, he was struck by the absence of butterflies. Where once they had crisscrossed his path, even landing on his shoulder if he stood still enough, the rain had driven them away—where to, he could not say.

And what of John? Santos had spoken so clearly of the plant-hunter's fascination with his wife. Though Thomas had not wanted to believe it, there was no denying it in the looks that John directed at her: looks, he noticed, that were not returned with quite the same intensity. He must warn him. But he did not want to lay himself open for suspicion from John or from anybody. No, best to keep it to himself.

The path was growing dim so Thomas turned back toward camp, to be home before it was too dark to see. He had not gone far when he saw a movement off the track, and could make out in the fading light the back of George disappearing into the forest, followed by—leading by the hand—the young boy Joaquim, easy to spot in his white short-sleeved shirt. Thomas didn't know why he did not call out to them; instead he followed, slowly enough that he might lose them. He would call out to them soon, when he was sure he had really lost them.

But he didn't lose them. Instead he came upon them behind a tree. George was kneeling before the boy, whose shorts were down around his ankles. Joaquim's face was sad more than scared; his eyes were closed and his bottom lip quivered, as if he were enduring something bravely that he knew would be over soon. George had both hands on the boy's buttocks, kneading them, while he had the boy's penis in his mouth. A noise arose from his throat, such as one might make to a baby bird to reassure it.

Thomas had no control over his reaction, but he reacted as he had failed to do many years earlier. He ran forward and pulled George off the boy, twisting his hand inside his collar. George uttered a strangled cry as the collar dug into his throat. Thomas had never hit anybody before, but his fist contracted and he planted a punch squarely on George's nose before dropping him on the ground.

"You evil bastard!" he shouted at George, who sat sniveling on the ground. Joaquim had pulled up his pants, and now turned and ran in the direction of the camp. "He's just a boy!"

"Don't, Thomas." George wiped a trickle of blood from his nose, looked at it on his hand, and tried to shake it off.

Thomas aimed a kick at his side, but didn't put his full force into it; he had the overwhelming urge to scare him, not injure him. George leapt to his feet, fumbling in his pocket for a handkerchief.

"Don't tell anyone," he whined. "Please, Thomas, I'll do anything."

"Just leave him alone," Thomas said. "And for God's sake, see a doctor."

George wiped at his bloodied face. "A doctor? Yes, you're right. I'm sick. I need help. Help me, Thomas." He started to laugh, uneasily.

Thomas took a step toward him and George stopped laughing. "Do you want me to tell Harris for you? Or Santos?"

"Shh." George held out his hands. His handkerchief dangled from one like a white flag stained by war. "It's just our secret. Please, Thomas. I won't do it again."

"You're pathetic," said Thomas. He spat on the ground in front of him. He could tell from George's face that he knew Thomas wouldn't tell. He didn't have the guts.

He left George standing as the darkness fell around him and turned back for camp. A sob rose inside him, knocking the breath out of him. Then the tears came with the evening's rain.

• • •

THOMAS HAD BEEN JUST a boy, really, although at the time he felt on the edge of manhood. Since then, any sound of a collection of shoes on wooden floors brought back the echo of boys' voices bouncing down the corridor, which was always cold and smelt of beeswax. Later, when he reached college, the sound came back to him, but the voices that carried above it were deeper, more contained, and therefore quieter. More careful.

It was his Latin master, Mr. Lafferty, who introduced him to sugaring. The first night he had permission from the headmaster to keep four of his boys from their beds, and he chose only his favorite boys. Except Thomas. Thomas had not been particularly good at Latin, did not sit at the front of the class with the other three, but Sir knew Thomas was fond of butterflies, from the drawings etched all over his exercise books, and he invited him along.

First they came to Sir's rooms, which smelled sweet, like toffee, and the other boys—Marcus, with knees constantly grazed and scabbed; Henry, the brain box, whose gift for Latin had it pouring from his tongue like nectar; and David, who was so shy Thomas had never heard him speak a word to anybody outside of class—stood together, shuffling in a group like calves, chests puffed out at being allowed between the hallowed walls. The inner sanctum.

"Come in, boys," said Sir. "First, a drink." Four glasses of lemonade were laid out on the coffee table and the boys fell on them, their eyes huge and alive as they drank, taking in their surroundings.

"And now the magic potion." Sir led them into the cramped alcove with a small stove, where they had to stand single file, Thomas at the end, as Sir busied himself and commentated "for those at the back."

A flame woofed as the fire was lit and a pot clanged down.

"Black treacle first."

Thomas stood on tiptoe and waved his head about to catch a glimpse of the treacle being poured into the pot, hissing as it hit the heated bottom. Marcus, directly in front of him, did the same. A large pimple bloomed on the back of the boy's neck, and it kept appearing in Thomas's line of vision, red and inflamed, with a tiny white eye in the middle, looking back at him.

"Brown Barbados sugar. All the way from Jamaica. Now we stir it." Henry, who stood at the front, was given the wooden spoon, and the line crowded jealously behind him.

"That's it," said Sir. "Just keep stirring until all the sugar crystals are melted. I'll turn it down a bit, so it's not boiling. Don't want you all to be splattered by hot sugar." His eye caught Thomas's then, and he winked at him. Mr. Lafferty had a pleasant face, with a broad, soft nose and large eyes that moistened when he recited a particularly poetic line of Latin. His face had seemed strangely familiar at first, until Thomas realized it was because he resembled his cocker spaniel, Goldie. Mr. Lafferty even had wavy copper hair.

The sugary smell of the flat intensified and Thomas closed his eyes to breathe it in, felt it coat the back of his throat. He poked his tongue out, just a tiny bit, to see if he could taste it in the air.

"That's it, Henry. I'll take it. Now we pour it" Sir paused as he completed the action—"into the tin, and quickly"—the sound of the pot, banging down into the sink—"add two drops of Old Jamaica rum. Perfect. Just give that another little stir, Henry. That's right."

The rum permeated the sweet smell and for a moment Thomas remembered his father's study in the evening. The smell was not the same, but the burning sensation in his nostrils was.

"And that's it. About-face, men!"

Grinning, the boys turned and Thomas found himself staring at the three of them.

"Come on, Edgar," said Marcus, who Thomas knew didn't like him. The boy's sour breath settled on his face, and Thomas turned quickly and marched out of the alcove.

It was a warm spring evening, with no wind at all as they kept marching, all the way down past the playing fields and into the woods at the bottom. They swung lanterns, not yet lit, and carried a net and a killing jar each. Thomas knew he was the only one of the boys experienced in collecting; the others were there only as Latin scholars, trying to please their teacher, and this knowledge kept his head up as he walked.

The sky was not yet dark but a deep indigo, and every tree gave off a mauve light. Rabbits scampered away from them as they approached and a bat squeaked as it flapped past them.

Mr. Lafferty stopped by a larch tree. "This will do," he said. "Quiet now, everyone."

The boys, who had been silent anyway, pushed their fists onto their lips, just to be sure.

Sir dipped a paintbrush into the tin of sweet mixture and smeared a large patch on the trunk of the tree. He stepped up to the next tree and did the same, and then the next.

"That ought to do it," he said.

"What do we do now?" whispered Henry.

"We wait," said Thomas, and Mr. Lafferty nodded and smiled at him before lifting his hand and ruffling his hair.

"I knew we should have brought you," he said, and the other boys looked as if they might just want to kill Thomas. But Thomas didn't give a hoot.

The dusk darkened into night around them. Close by, an owl called, then swooped with a flurry of wings as it caught a mouse. The outline of the larch trees against the sky began to fade and merge.

"That should do it," said Mr. Lafferty. "Hold your lamps out." He lit them one by one and they approached the first tree.

The sticky mixture shone in the lamplight. Caught on the trunk was a collection of writhing insects: wood lice, centipedes, beetles, and huge slugs, which, when Thomas looked closer, were covered with hundreds of tiny mites running back and forth across the vast flanks of their host.

A murmur of disgust arose from the other boys, but Thomas pushed his face as close as he could. In the middle of the mayhem sat a large death's-head moth. The skull on its thorax stared open-mouthed back at Thomas and his heart flipped.

It became a weekly outing throughout spring and into the warm summer. The other boys grew bolder, and began to take almost as much pleasure as Thomas in the catching of the moths. Mr. Lafferty showed them how something so big and brutish could have a delicate iridescence to it, such as the elephant hawk moth, with its shimmering of pink and green, and the startling colors of the red underwing.

One night, Mr. Lafferty bid the boys split up. "So we might discover the diversity over a large area. I'll blow my whistle when we are to meet again."

"On our own, sir?" asked Henry.

David, who never said a word, just hugged himself with definite fright at the prospect.

"You will be fine, men," said Mr. Lafferty. "Just don't stray past the boundaries of the forest and you won't get lost. Follow the sound of my whistle."

Thomas had no fear. The thicket in which they stood was relatively small. He had never been allowed out in the dark on his own, and he relished the opportunity to move through the undergrowth, stealthy as a fox.

They fanned out as the last of the light began to drain from the sky. They each carried their own can of sugar mixture now, as well as a net and killing jar. Thomas walked for a few minutes until the path was too murky to see, and stopped to paint the trunks. Then he waited.

When he had collected four beautiful specimens, he pretended he was a fox and slunk low to the ground, trying to force his senses to the front of his mind to guide him. He sniffed the air but could only smell the sugar and rum in his tin. The moths flickered in the jar in his hand; he felt the vibrations through the glass. Perhaps there wasn't enough cyanide in there to kill them all. His ears, which he imagined pricked in anticipation above his head, caught a cracking sound off to his right. He stopped and crouched lower. His eyes had grown accustomed to the dark now—besides, he was a fox, and he was after his prey. He moved noiselessly along the path toward the sound. As he went farther, he heard a new sound, a low moan, and another, snuffling sound. A large figure stood only a few feet away.

He put down his net and sugar tin and struck a match. In its flare, he saw Mr. Lafferty. He stood tall while a boy—it was David, poor, quiet David—crouched beside him, his hand wrapped around the teacher's penis, moving it back and forth. The boy looked at Thomas in surprise, and his face was wet with tears and snot. Mr. Lafferty's hands were on David's head, stroking his hair, and his eyes opened at the sudden light. The jar of moths slipped from where it was cradled in Thomas's arm and smashed on a tree root. There was a fluttering of huge wings; the moths flew toward the light and hit Thomas in the face. He brushed them away, but they came again, into his eyes, his ears, his mouth. The match fell to the ground, spent, and Thomas ran until he heard the teacher's whistle calling him back. He hesitated for a moment then ran on, back to the school and to his safe bed.

"AND WHAT BECAME OF the boy?" asked Clara. She had come to his room to find him beating at the moths that crowded around his lamp. He had cried then, leaning into her breast, until she asked him to tell her about the moths. He couldn't tell her about George, though; not yet.

"David never looked at me or spoke to me. The other boys went out sugaring a few times, but it all stopped when the weather went cold. Mr. Lafferty had a new team of boys the following year, and the year after that. I could see it in their eyes, always at the end of August. But I never did anything."

"What could you have done?"

"I could have told somebody. A parent. A teacher."

"No, Thomas. You mustn't blame yourself."

"I should have confronted Lafferty about it. Threatened to tell."

"You were only a boy."

"Yes." But he was not a boy now. At least he had put a stop to it this time, saved one little boy. But had he made sure George would leave Joaquim alone? What about the next boy, and the next?

"And the moths?"

"I can't look at them now without remembering. They give me shivers. I actually feel it on my skin. A prickling sensation. They make me feel sick."

Clara moved forward to embrace him but he stopped her. "What about your husband? You shouldn't even be in here."

She made a hissing sound through her teeth. "He's dead drunk. He and Dr. Harris have been drinking all afternoon. He won't be awake until morning."

"All the same, Clara, I don't feel comfortable about this. Not after . . ." He wanted to tell her about what had happened with Manuel, how he feared for his safety. But the words would not come. Clara was neglected enough by this man; he didn't want to worry her further.

"You seem agitated," she said. "Tell me what's wrong." She put both hands on his face.

Thomas grasped her wrists and held them in front of her chest. "I can't. It's nothing. Please, Clara, I need to be alone. I need to sleep." He glanced mournfully at the moths striking against the cracks in the walls, flicking around the lamp.

"Here," she said. He let go of her wrists and she reached into her pocket. "Take this. It will help you sleep." More of her white powder. The last time he had taken it he had become ill the next day. Didn't he see his *Papilio* in the forest after taking it with her? He was now surer than ever that he had hallucinated it; that the butterfly, if it existed at all, was slipping farther from his grasp.

"Don't you think you've had enough?" he asked. She had become sallow in the weeks since he had first fallen ill. Her eyes had a dull glaze to them and her pupils were pinpricks. Her skin was gray, and dark creases etched lines under her eyes.

"Of course not," she said, misunderstanding him. "It is easy enough to get. Antonio brings it to me every time he comes back from Manaus. Those ships, the ones that take all the rubber away. They have to fill up with something before they come here. This is the finest money can buy, and I can have as much as I want." She moved close to him again, and for the first time that he could remember, his body remained flaccid beside her. Her breath smelt of seaweed. He pushed her away, but she clung to his arms.

"Please go, Clara," he said. "Go back to your husband."

She let him go and moved toward the doorway. "He would rather I was dead."

THOMAS'S MOOD WAS A heavy blanket over his body when he awoke. Nothing seemed to carry any purpose in the day—not the urgency in his bladder, not the shouting of monkeys outside nor the clouded light that slipped under his door, reflected in the puddle of water under the floor. He forced himself to rise and shoved his feet into his boots. Who knew what creature would attach itself to him if the yard were flooded? He had already endured bites of leeches and mosquitoes, not to mention the fire ants. His body was covered with hard knots of scars and the red welts of fresh bites.

Ernie and Santos stood conversing in the yard. Ernie's arms were folded and Santos stroked his huge mustache as he talked. The ground they stood on was wet but not underwater; the flood was seeping quickly into the earth.

"Ah, Mr. Edgar," said Santos. "We were just discussing whether we stay here or move back to Manaus. We face the possibility of more flooding if we stay, but Dr. Harris here says he has not finished his business. What about you?"

Thomas's head was slow and dull. He blinked, heavy-lidded. "Yes. That is, I *would* like to leave, yes."

"Scared of a little water?" Ernie bared his teeth at him.

"It's not that." He sighed. Words seemed difficult today. His tongue had become lazy. "My work here is done."

"Done?" said Santos. "But what of your butterfly, senhor? You're not giving up, are you?"

"No. Yes. I don't know." His hands trembled as they pushed his hair off his forehead. A new insect bite demanded scratching. What was wrong with him? The forest had taken on a lackluster sheen; he no longer saw a fertile habitat for his beloved butterflies, but a hot, messy tangle of vegetation, filled with snakes and prickly insects. He longed for a cooling breeze, the light touch of Sophie's hand on his neck. His legs gave way beneath him.

"Steady there." Ernie grabbed him as his knees sank into the mud, and hauled him to his feet again. "I'd say you're still not well, Tom, my friend."

Not well? Or just shriveled by disappointment? He concentrated on putting all his strength into his body, to stand upright.

"I suggest you go back to Manaus," said Santos. "Give yourself the chance to convalesce."

"A good idea," said Ernie. "I won't rib you about it anymore. It's probably for the best. Listen to your doctor."

George Sebel appeared beside them, mud sucking at his feet.

"What's this?" he asked.

"We're sending Mr. Edgar back to Manaus for a rest," said Santos. "And you, Mr. Sebel? Are you still ill?"

"I don't think so," he said. He avoided Thomas's gaze and looked from Santos to Ernie, to the ground.

"Antonio will accompany you," said Santos. "You need a proper bed in a cool room. Some comforts of home."

"Home?" The word hung in the air beside Thomas, close enough to touch.

"Come now, Mr. Edgar! I don't mean England. You mustn't give up now. Do you want to go home defeated?"

Thomas shook his head slowly from side to side. Like a donkey, he thought.

"I thought not. All you need is a rest."

"Can I . . ." He stopped, took a gulp of air before he could continue. "Can I take Joaquim with me?" It came out as a whisper, full of the breath he had just inhaled. There was a palpable tension in the air between him and George, who began to back slowly away.

"Joaquim?" said Santos. "That boy? I suppose so, if the other men can spare him until Antonio gets back. Mr. Sebel? Have you finished with our young friend?"

Was that a knowing look Santos gave George? George nodded and stared at the ground as if it had betrayed him. His ears were a glossy shade of red, but it may have been sunburn; perhaps Thomas had simply not noticed it before.

"Now who's going to help me?" said Ernie. "I've got all sorts of cumbersome beasts to carry."

"I will," said George. "I'm running out of insects to collect with this rain. I can help you with your stuffing."

"God help me," said Ernie.

"Manuel can be your guide," said Santos.

As if in answer to his name, Manuel emerged from the cooking hut. He crept over the wet ground, his eyes on his muddy feet. At first glance, he looked no different from yesterday, and yet something about him had changed. There was a stiffness in his legs and his whole body seemed to droop toward the ground. What had Santos done to him? He moved like a man in a brace.

Thomas excused himself, pleading hunger, and went to find Pedro.

"Tell me what Antonio did to Manuel," he said in Portuguese as soon as he entered the cooking hut.

Pedro looked at him with fright and put a finger to his lips, but Thomas knew everybody was out of earshot.

"No more than can be expected," he whispered. He limped over and stood close to Thomas to speak into his ear. "We have to be careful in this job. But Manuel can be thankful he is a servant and not a rubber-tapper." His head bobbed; he had said too much.

"What do you mean?" asked Thomas. "And why don't you both leave if you are scared to make mistakes?"

Pedro laughed, a dry, hollow sound like that of a wasp inside its nest. "Leave? That is not possible."

"Why not?"

Pedro turned his back on him and began to chop plantain. Thomas noticed for the first time a dead howler monkey, draped over the table like a stole. Its eyes had been eaten by ants; their cavities stared back at him. "I have a family, Senhor Edgar. How will I feed them?"

"You could find another position."

Pedro just shook his head and would not face him.

"What happens to the rubber-tappers?"

Pedro would not speak.

"Pedro?"

The cook pivoted on his heel. The sand crackled beneath his feet. "Do not ask me any more questions, Senhor Edgar, if you count me as a friend."

TRAVELING WITH THE CURRENT, the boat sped toward Manaus. Rain splattered the surface of the water, churning it to a deep black. There was nowhere he would rather be at this time, apart from safely at home perhaps, but he couldn't bear the thought of returning empty-handed. And yet, what was he doing? He was traveling in the opposite direction from the place his butterfly had been spotted, according to Santos, and according to his own sighting, real or imagined.

Then again, Santos was not to be relied upon as a source of information. He could just as easily have made up the facts of the butterfly. What had he said at dinner in Manaus? *There is a valley to the north, where they appear in their thousands, only at sunset.* He had called it the giant beauty. Well, Thomas had certainly found the valley, but perhaps the idea had been planted that night at dinner and the drug and the illness had done the rest.

No, Santos was not to be trusted.

He thought of his companions, huddled in their huts as the rain pounded down. Clara had clung to him when he said good-bye, and he had had to snatch his arm away from her, hitting her on the jaw by accident as he did so, before her husband or anybody else saw. Her small mouth quivered and she ran off, calling for John, and Thomas wondered just how far she would get in the forest before she needed to turn around again to have one of her daily "rests." John's face had come alive at the sound of his name from her lips and the two of them strode into the forest, while Clara cast a look back at Thomas and laid her hand on John's arm.

Thomas shook off the memory, but felt some satisfaction that he seemed to have broken Clara's grip. He tried to concentrate on reading. Joaquim avoided him, and when Thomas tried to speak reassuring words of Portuguese, the boy dumped his plate of food on the table and ran off. Thomas heard Antonio growling orders at him; the gentleman may have requested his company, but he was not going to be kept idle. Later Thomas found his boots polished and his cabin swept.

He realized that though he had spent some months in the company of Antonio, there had been little communication between the two of them. Thomas had preferred to leave himself in the hands of his more experienced companions when it came to making plans and requests to do with their expedition. Antonio had been a solid presence in their lives, always standing behind them, making the going as easy as possible for them, and Thomas had always felt that he was watching their backs.

But alone with him, he didn't feel as safe. Antonio said little at dinner, and he drank frequently from a bottle of clear, strong-smelling liquor. After they had eaten, he offered some to Thomas, who found he could not say no, and the fiery liquid calmed his shaking insides. Emboldened by drink, he tried to make conversation; perhaps he could even take the chance to try to find out what had been making him so uneasy about the Amazon of late.

"Do you ever work with the *seringueiros*, Antonio? Senhor Santos's rubber workers?"

"Sometimes," he said. "But I prefer life in the city. Besides, Senhor Santos has preferences for the type of people who work on his rubber."

"What do you mean?"

"I started out as an overseer for him, but when the British bought an interest in his company he began to import men from Barbados. They are British subjects. And as for the tappers . . ."

"He uses Indians in some of his plantations."

"That's right. Senhor Santos has found the Indians to be more . . . pliable. On the whole they have helped to make him successful."

"On the whole?"

"That camp I took you to, up the Tapajós—"

"It was abandoned."

"Yes, the Mundurukú tribe believed the area belonged to them, that they could harvest the rubber as they saw fit."

"What happened to them?"

"Most of them ran off, back into the jungle."

"And the rest?"

"They tried to fight. Senhor Santos still has camps there, but he is not welcome. He was lucky when he came to see you that he did not get a dart in the neck. But they are probably scared of him. His men, the overseers, they enjoy their work." He chuckled and showed stained teeth.

Thomas thought of Captain Arturo and his tribe of acorn-skinned children. His wife with her quiet eyes. Perhaps Santos had even known him. A terrible thought came to him and then another, following like a hiccup: it was Thomas who had alerted Santos to Arturo's hostility.

Thomas took another swig of his drink. "And what about the fire? In the village?"

"What fire?" said Antonio. His eyelids drooped until his eyes were lazy slits.

His demeanor made Thomas cold and did not invite further inquiry. The smell of the blackened house came back to him, the scent of burned wood and flesh. He turned his face away from Antonio and took out his last cigarette. The sulphur of the match was a welcome barrier to his imagination.

ON HIS FIRST DAY back at Santos's house, Thomas stayed in his room, rousing himself only to drink some water. An electric fan turned overhead, sucking the warm air upward and leaving Thomas cooled. He kept the curtains closed, and for a time he was able to re-treat into the world of a dreamless sleep, his limbs spread across the bed like butter.

By the second day, he began to feel a little better; the heaviness in his neck and shoulders had lifted, and the prospect of getting out of bed did not exhaust him as it had done upriver.

Antonio offered to accompany him on a walk around town, but Thomas declined, saying he would take Joaquim as his guide. Antonio shrugged, as if to say suit yourself, and Thomas was relieved the man didn't push him further.

Joaquim no longer avoided Thomas, but a chill hung about him, and his eyes held extra years. He walked beside Thomas, silent. Thomas didn't want to ask him about what had happened with George—to save not just the boy's embarrassment but his own also, for he could not think about the incident without blushing and wanting to disappear into the earth. He knew the world could be a cruel place, but he had always thought he could live his life without encountering it head-on. He should have known that the Amazon would change all that.

The streets, washed by rain, shone with their neat cobblestones and swept gutters. If it weren't for the heat Thomas could have imagined himself back in Lisbon, not in the middle of the jungle. The sight of the tram wheezing past and the smell of its brakes on the lines were incongruous after his weeks in the forest. Women who passed him on the street met his eye and looked at him with curiosity—hunger, even. He tipped his hat and moved along, remembering Clara's words about every third house containing a brothel. No wonder the women stared after him like that; they hoped to get some of his money. From what he had heard, he doubted he could afford them even if he wanted to.

From out of a shop came the smell of freshly baked bread. Thomas closed his eyes for a moment to savor it before removing his hat and ducking into the bakery, while Joaquim waited for him outside.

It was unbearable inside, and Thomas fought the urge to remove his jacket in the heat. The poor baker, trussed up in a white suit and apron, was sweating so hard Thomas had second thoughts about buying from him. But one look at Joaquim's face pressed to the window decided it for him. He bought two round custard tarts, as yellow as fresh paint, which cost him more than a meal at the Star and Garter would cost him at home. Outside, he gave one to a disbelieving Joaquim and sank his teeth into the other. The pastry gave way perfectly between his lips, with just the right amount of flakiness; the custard was sweet, but not too sweet. Heavenly. They stood on the street, munching the tarts as narrow-waisted women with enormous bosoms and backsides stepped around them, raising their parasols to avoid knocking off Thomas's hat. Men in starched collars and white suits, with huge mustaches like Santos's, shot him uncomprehending looks, as if they had never seen a man and a child enjoying themselves.

On a whim Thomas decided to buy a broadsheet to practice his Portuguese.

"I can only give you an old one, from Belém," said the shopkeeper, a tiny man with rolled-up sleeves and a dirty apron. "The local paper has not been available for some time."

"Oh?" Thomas took the paper and handed him some coins. "Why is that?"

"The printing press burned down two weeks ago."

"That's awful. How did it happen?"

"I don't know. I suppose they printed something they shouldn't have. It wasn't an accident."

"What did they print?"

"Are you joking?" The man folded his arms across his chest. "Do you want my shop burnt down as well?"

"Who would do such a thing?"

The man narrowed his eyes. "I don't know," he said. "How would I know?" The man shrugged theatrically, his hands out as if to show they were empty, so how could he be hiding something? Thomas shifted his weight and glanced outside at Joaquim. He's scared of me, thought Thomas. He thinks I'm something I'm not.

But what?

"The article—"

"Good day, senhor," said the man, turning to dust the shelves behind him.

"Joaquim," he said when he came out of the shop, "do you know where the printing factory is for the newspaper?"

Joaquim nodded.

"Will you take me there?"

They waded through the rising heat of the narrow cobbled streets. The crowds were thinning as residents sought the cool interiors of their homes.

Joaquim let out a long, low whistle when he saw the charred skeleton of the warehouse.

"Did you know about this?" asked Thomas.

"No, senhor," said Joaquim.

Thomas stepped into the ruins. Clouds of soot puffed upward with every footfall, coating his trousers. He walked aimlessly about, crunching on charcoal and stepping over twisted metal. What was he looking for?

"*O que você quer?*" The voice, though loud, was muffled by the wreckage, as if dampened by smoke.

Thomas ducked his head, suddenly ashamed, as if he had been caught stealing. Well, he was trespassing. He approached the owner of the voice, a bald man in his forties, who stood mopping his brow. His skin sagged, as if he might have lost a lot of weight; it hung in loose folds under his chin, and his trousers hung from their braces like a windless sail. Thomas was reminded of a sloth that George had tried to stuff, but had made a poor show by not using enough stuffing.

"*Você fala Inglês?*" asked Thomas. He couldn't face having to communicate in his bumbling Portuguese.

The man turned his eyes to the nonexistent ceiling. He sighed. "Yes. What do you want? This is private property, you know."

"What happened here?"

"As you can see, the building burned down."

"Are you the owner?"

"Who are you?"

"Forgive me. My name is Thomas Edgar. I heard what happened."

"Then I do not need to explain it to you," said the man.

"Do you know who did this?"

"Of course I do. A man who didn't like what I printed in my paper." He gave a bitter laugh. "Look at the good it did me. Now I have no paper at all."

"I wonder, sir. Might I ask . . . was that man José Santos?"

"Not him personally. But one of the many men in his employment. You cannot move in this town without bumping into someone who is paid by Santos." He stopped. His hand went to his hip. Thomas realized he probably had a gun back there. "Why are you asking me all this? You work for him, too, do you?"

"No, sir, I assure you. I have the acquaintance of Mr. Santos, but I do not work for him. He has funded a group of naturalists to collect specimens to take back to England, but we're completely ignorant about the man's business. We are told nothing. I am beginning to have my suspicions, though, and I would like—no, I *need*—to find out more, sir."

"Hm. You're English? He will respect you for that. How do I know you have not been sent by him?" He glanced at Joaquim, who had lost interest in a conversation he couldn't understand and was playing in the mess; already his hands were black and his clean shirt filthy.

Thomas thought hard about what he could say—some proof he could offer to show he was not an enemy. But he had nothing to use to gain his trust. "I give you my word as a Christian," he said eventually.

"A Christian!" said the man and laughed. "Well, I suppose that still means something to some people!"

"And also . . . I lost a friend of mine recently, on the Tapajós. A Captain Arturo. I'm not sure, but I think that Santos may have been responsible for his death and the death of his family. His house was burned down."

Something in his face must have touched the man. His arms relaxed and he nodded sadly.

"All right, Senhor Edgar. God knows why, but I will try and help you. I like your face. No doubt it will be my downfall." He grimaced and put out his hand for shaking. "My name is Rodrigues. Benedito Rodrigues. You'd better come over the road, to my office."

AS RODRIGUES TALKED, THOMAS stood and stared out the window at the river. The clouds rumbled together and the first rain of the afternoon began. The vultures that had been circling a spot on the dock broke their merry-go-round and wheeled away. A steamship loomed in the port and he watched men unloading cargo, running with awkward loads to escape the downpour.

The room darkened. Rodrigues leaned back in his chair, his boots on the table. He clasped his hands behind his head. Two sweat patches the size of bowls darkened his underarms.

He told Thomas about a man who had come to see him, an American, begging him to run an advertisement asking for testimonials about the treatment of the Indians in Santos's employ upriver, near Iquitos. It seemed that everybody was on Santos's payroll up there, and nobody would speak to him. The man, by the name of Roberts, had been sent to oversee the building of a railway through the Amazon; at Iquitos he and a companion had befriended one of Santos's men—the railway was to cut through some of Santos's land. The man had taken them into the forest to show them the operations up the Putumayo River. There they witnessed the most terrible atrocities against the Indian workers. When it became clear the men were horrified, they were robbed and beaten, then imprisoned. Even the police were under the influence of Santos.

Thomas listened with a growing sickness in his stomach. When Rodrigues mentioned the men's imprisonment, he snapped his eyes away from the river.

"Yes, Mr. Edgar, you must tread very carefully. If Santos gets wind of the questions you've been asking, you will be in great danger."

"Surely not," said Thomas. "The man would not dare let any harm come to me. The British government would never allow it."

"And yet they allow thousands of Indians to be mutilated and murdered. You don't know what he is like. The men he employs . . . he lets them run amok. They are not paid wages, but commission on the rubber, so they drive the Indians and threaten them. They're bloodthirsty. I've spared you from describing what they have done to them, but perhaps it's better that you know."

Thomas took a deep breath. "Yes. Go on."

"Mr. Edgar. They tie them to trees and cut off their limbs, leaving them to bleed to death. The women are raped while their children watch. Babies are taken from their mothers and their brains dashed out on trees. The company pretends to employ the Indians, but they are slaves. They bully them into working for them, then keep them in debt by providing food and shelter for them and charging them more than they earn. If they try to leave, they are hunted down for sport, and tortured."

"But that's disgusting!"

"Yes, it is. And your Senhor Santos is the cause of it all."

Thomas pulled at his collar. How hot the room had become. He threw open the window and thrust his head out into the rain. He'd known that Santos was powerful, but he'd thought people revered him for his wealth, not out of fear.

Finally he pulled his head back in. Water ran down his face and into his eyes. He rubbed at them. Sweat and rainwater made them sting.

"How can they get away with this?"

"Half the rubber barons are just as bad, and the others are too scared of Santos to do anything about it."

"Then why run the advertisement?"

"Roberts promised me the protection of the American government." He spat on the ground. "He convinced me I was doing the right thing. You see how gullible I am? I shouldn't even be talking to you like this."

"Senhor Rodrigues. I'll write to the British directors of Santos's company: they must know what is happening here!"

Rodrigues laughed. Thomas had come to realize that he did so when he was anything but amused. "And you're so sure they don't know about it? Think about it, senhor. Indians! Cheap labor! They are lining their pockets with gold. Do you think they want to hear from you?"

"Then I'll tell the government."

"You don't understand, do you? You will be *dead* before you can tell them anything. Santos controls everything in this town. Any letter addressed to the authorities in England or America will be intercepted and you will be killed. The only thing you can do is keep your mouth shut until you are safely out of this place."

"And what about you? Aren't you scared?"

"Of course I am. They have ruined me. It is only a warning. If I do anything else—so much as criticize Santos—I will be food for the piranhas. I shouldn't even be talking to you. But you see that ship out there? In three days I will be on it, bound for Portugal."

"And this Roberts? You say he and his friend were imprisoned?"

"Yes. They didn't kill them. They can't risk that yet; the railroad is too important to them. At the moment there is nothing to link the robbery and the imprisonment with Santos. Roberts managed to bribe his way out—don't ask me how—and he thought by coming to Manaus he could gather further evidence against Santos. But anybody who talked to him refused to sign anything in front of a lawyer. All the lawyers here are probably on Santos's payroll."

"So he did find people to talk to? Do you know who?"

"He promised them confidentiality, so no, I could not tell you. I only know of one, a carpenter by the name of Assis, who once worked for Santos in Iquitos. I don't know where you would find him now."

"And Roberts? Where is he now?"

"I warned him against it, but he has gone back to Iquitos to try to free his colleague."

"Is that wise?"

"He'll be dead before he gets there."

. . .

THE SUN WAS OUT and hot light bounced off the wet road. Thomas squinted and shielded his eyes from the blinding flashes as he moved with slow steps back to the house. What could he do? He wanted more than anything in the world to find his butterfly before he left. At times it seemed so close he could smell it; at others it became nothing but a rumor, not even a legend. But today his petty obsession shrank under his touch, shaming him. Santos was the key to finding the butterfly, but how could he be indebted to a man who was responsible for such crimes? Did it mean that Thomas, too, had blood on his hands? But again, what could he do? To confront Santos about it, even Antonio, could be dangerous. But could he just slip away? Jump on the first boat back to Europe? That would take time; after all, he had no money on him, and without Santos's help a ticket would have to be organized for him at the other end. Besides, what would running away achieve? He could go to the government and inform them about the treatment of the Indians, but what proof did he have? And would they even care? It wasn't so long ago that the British enslaved natives of all kinds in their colonies. They would dismiss him as a bumbling do-gooder scientist who had failed in his quest.

His only chance was to return to the camp and persuade the others it was time to come home, without letting on his reasons— if one of them were to mention Thomas's fears to Santos, they might all be done for.

Joaquim walked beside him, matching his sluggish gait. His shorts were blackened by smears of soot from where he had wiped his hands. Thomas reached out a hand and rested it on the boy's shoulder. He flinched, but didn't move away, and Thomas gave him a pat before dropping his hand again.

Passing a hotel he saw a familiar figure moving down the steps onto the street: Miss Lillie. She was accompanied by not one but three men, all poised with hands ready to guide her off the steps. One held a parasol over her head, shading her from the sun. Thomas attempted to step around her without being noticed, but Lillie spotted him.

"Monsieur Edgar!" she said. "What a pleasant surprise! Back so soon from your travels?"

Thomas feigned astonishment. "Miss Lillie. How nice to see you." She put out her hand, palm down, and he took it, unsure whether he was expected to shake it or kiss it. He squeezed her fingers and bowed slightly before letting her hand drop.

"And your companions? Dr. Harris? Is he with you?"

"No, I came back alone."

"Senhor Santos?"

"Still upriver as well. I have disappointed you."

"Oh no," she said, but the smile she gave was forced. Her three companions stood silently by, looking at Thomas with contempt. She must have noticed Thomas's nervous glances at them because she turned to them and said, "Would you excuse us for a moment, gentlemen?"

They murmured their assent and moved a few paces away.

"You seem to have become very popular," said Thomas, as warmly as he could.

"I have Senhor Santos to thank for that. He graced me with his patronage, and everybody in this town wants what Senhor Santos has. I am now the most sought-after girl in Manaus."

And the most expensive, I'll warrant, thought Thomas. The light fell fetchingly on her red hair, making it glow, and her pale face had developed more freckles than she'd had earlier—an effect of the tropical sun. The tip of her nose was slightly pink.

She asked Thomas for a cigarette, and he obliged. Lillie removed her glove to take it and, as he lit it, he noticed two brown sores, the size of pennies, on her hand.

"Did you burn yourself?" he asked.

Lillie looked away, and Thomas admonished himself. "Forgive me," he said.

"No, that is quite all right. These marks, they just appeared one day. I have them elsewhere." With her other hand, she pulled down the neck of her dress to reveal another sore at her throat. "This heat, and the lace on my collar. I am foolish, I know, but I just couldn't let people see me like this."

"Have you seen a doctor?"

"No. The truth is, I am too scared. If there is something wrong with me, I think I would rather not know. There are so many deaths here, Monsieur Edgar. Nobody speaks of them. They live such a fine life; everybody pretends to be happy. But this place stinks of death. My mistress, Senhora da Silva, she died two weeks ago. Cholera."

Thomas remembered the sharp-toothed woman at the club, the rustle of her skirts. He took an involuntary step back. Lillie chuckled.

"You won't catch it from me, I'm sure of it." She exhaled smoke slowly. A patch of it drifted upward from her mouth and wound about her face. She waved it away. "I would leave this place, but what is there for me back in Paris? Here I am treated like a queen. There I was merely a courtesan. Oh, I'm making you uncomfortable."

Thomas was indeed uncomfortable. He wasn't used to having a woman speak so frankly to him of such things; but then again, nothing in his life was as it once was.

"Will you see Dr. Harris again soon?"

"Soon I think, yes."

"Would you pass on my regards? Tell him . . ." She blushed. "Tell him he is very lucky to have Senhor Santos as a friend. And that I will see him very soon."

Thomas clasped his hands behind his back. "Why do you say that?" What did she know?

Lillie laughed. "Dr. Harris is in love with me, Monsieur Edgar. Surely you knew that."

He *had* known about Ernie's feelings for her, but he had turned away from the thought, for surely this woman, and those like her, had nothing to do with love. He wasn't even sure that Ernie was capable of such emotion, something so sublime. The doctor inhabited his body so fully, abusing it, taking pleasure in it—not even caring if anyone saw him do it. Love was what Thomas felt for Sophie, not what a man like that could feel for a woman like this. He gave a shudder. For he had admired Ernie so much when they first arrived in Brazil, and perhaps he had let himself be influenced a little too much.

"Monsieur? Are you all right?"

"Yes. I . . . I hadn't even thought about it. But what does it have to do with Mr. Santos?"

She tilted her head and looked up at him through her eyelashes. Her eyes were nearly obscured by the brim of her elaborate hat. "If it weren't for Senhor Santos, your friend would never be able to afford me."

She tossed her cigarette, half smoked, into the gutter and put her glove back on.

"So nice to see you," she said. *"Au revoir."*

Thomas managed to get back to the house before the rain started again. He went straight to his room and lay down; not only did he still tire easily, but the heat saturated his body today, and he needed to lie down to absorb what he had learned.

He watched the fan turn sluggishly overhead. Images of the mutilation walked before his eyes; he remembered the scars he had seen on a couple of workers at the camp up the River Negro. He had wondered about them—hoped that they were merely tribal, but now he knew the truth. He had seen backs thatched with healed welts—how many more had not healed, and had been infected with gangrene or worse?

And Santos. The man had shown his cruel streak to Thomas, but no harm had been caused. With all the violence happening upriver, how could he make the connection between his bene-factor, who had so far been incredibly generous to Thomas and his colleagues, and atrocities he could only imagine?

He should speak out about it, confront Santos. Surely Thomas's British citizenship would protect him. But what if it didn't?

I'm a coward, he thought.

A soft knock at the door brought him out of his reverie. Antonio entered, carrying a tray of tea, which was surprising—he never waited on anyone like this; he usually gave the orders to others.

"I trust you had a good morning?" Antonio set the tea things on the desk.

"Yes," said Thomas, alert.

"And what did you do?"

"Do? Oh, I just wandered about a bit, looked at the opera house, things like that."

"Magnificent, isn't it, sir?" Antonio finished pouring the tea and handed it to Thomas. "Did you manage to find anyone to talk to?"

"Only a young lady. A friend of Dr. Harris's."

"Oh yes. I thought that was you I saw. In front of the hotel."

The tea burned Thomas's lips as he took a sip. So that was it. Antonio had been following him. His eyes flicked to Antonio's and for a moment the two men just looked at each other.

"Yes, possibly," Thomas said at last. He handed Antonio the teacup, surprised at how steady his hand was. "Might I have a touch more milk?"

"You know," said Antonio as he handed it back, "you should be careful who you talk to."

"Oh?" Thomas kept his gaze straight ahead and tried to appear as if he was concentrating on his tea. He wasn't going to push the man. If Antonio knew he had talked to Rodrigues, Thomas wasn't going to let on that he knew he knew.

"I only mean . . ." Antonio chuckled. "Those women. They will take all your money if you let them."

"I think I am quite safe, thank you, Antonio. Thank you for the tea."

Antonio bowed his head in a slow nod. His eyes were hard. Thomas noticed for the first time how black they were, like tar, with no definition between the pupil and the iris. The man's tongue flicked out like a knife and licked his lips. "Dinner will be served at four, sir."

THE NEXT DAY, THOMAS knew what he had to do. He wrote a letter to the American Rodrigues had described, Mr. Roberts. He wasn't quite sure what to say, and spent long minutes gazing out at the garden where two black men squatted, pulling out weeds and wheeling them away in a barrow. Finally he put his confused thoughts into the most basic terms. *I would like to speak with you and look at the possibility of helping you in your investigation.*

He went downstairs to the dining room, where breakfast was laid out for him, but nobody was about. He pocketed a bread roll to eat along the way and set out.

It wasn't hard to find his way back to the printing factory. The route was etched on his memory like the scratch of a pin, and when he was close, the stench of ash and soot wafted over him. He didn't know how to get the letter to Roberts, but Rodrigues might know. Thomas had to be prepared for the possibility that he wouldn't be able to help him; after all, Roberts could be back in prison by now, or dead.

The door to Rodrigues's building stood open. Inside hung a smell that Thomas couldn't place—sweet and sickly, tinged with metal and candle wax. His hand trailed on the banister as he walked up the stairs, and he felt grit beneath his palm. He stopped and pulled his hand away. It was black with the soot that had drifted over the road from the fire.

At the top of the stairs he tapped on the closed door. Nothing. He knocked louder. The sound seemed to rise sharply, then be absorbed just as abruptly by the walls. The door was unlocked, so he pushed the door open and stepped inside.

Rodrigues lay facedown on the floor in front of his desk, wearing the same silk-backed waistcoat as yesterday, with patterns that swirled like a watermark. Papers littered the floor around him and an inkpot was smashed at his feet. He had not fallen without a struggle.

"Senhor Rodrigues?"

There was no movement, and with a sickening feeling, Thomas crept toward him. He walked through ink, and paper stuck to the soles of his boots. Part of him wanted to turn and run from the room, but he forced himself to carry on. He crouched down and reached out a hand to where Rodrigues's fist lay curled like a flower. Cold. Thomas snatched his arm back, leaving a black smudge on the man's thumb. He closed his eyes. He should leave now: the man was clearly dead, and there was nothing more he could do, but something—a sense of urgency? Decency? Morbid curiosity?— made him open his eyes and bend closer to the body.

Smudges of blood marked the papers beneath Rodrigues's face. And something else, which at first looked like pale honey that had hardened and crystallized. Thomas recognized one of the smells he had detected earlier: wax. A sound erupted; it came from Thomas's own mouth, a gasp of horror. The wax had dribbled down the side of the man's head, from his ears. Thomas touched it and a flake came away under his fingernail.

Who could do this? Somebody had poured hot wax into Rodrigues's ears, torturing him before shooting him with one clean bullet through the head. There was something else about his face. Thomas spread his fingers over the man's forehead and pulled. If he'd had any hair Thomas would have used that. The head was as heavy as an anchor and the face was inky and terrible. Blood caked the cheeks where it had oozed from the wounds around Rodrigues's mouth, caused by the thick crisscrosses of twine that had been threaded through his skin in order to sew his mouth shut.

ELEVEN

Richmond, June 1904

THE NEWS OF AGATHA and Robert Chapman's indiscretion is all over town within days. Sophie overhears Nancy Sutton gossiping to Mrs. Silver, and when Agatha comes to visit, she tries to think of a way to broach the subject. As if she doesn't have enough to deal with, with Thomas. But she cares about Agatha. It won't do to have her reputation ruined, to be snubbed by the whole community, not at this stage in her life. Perhaps it's not too late and Sophie can talk some sense into her friend.

As they sit together in the garden, Agatha chatters on about her idea to start up a millinery, to make the most fantastical hats. Ladies will come all the way from London to buy them—she'll be the talk of the town. She hasn't once asked Sophie how Thomas is. Selfish girl. Selfish, irresponsible, *stupid* girl. She's succeeded in being the talk of the town all right, but not for her hats. Agatha keeps on, oblivious to Sophie's silence and unfriendly thoughts, and Sophie has an urge to put out a hand and cover her mouth, to have nothing but the sound of the breeze in the plum tree and the blackbirds singing.

But Agatha stops speaking abruptly and stands. She closes her eyes and basks in the midday sun for a moment before going on.

"You'll never guess." She opens her eyes but doesn't look at Sophie, who waits for her to continue. But Agatha has gone red and, with a confused smile on her face, stares at the ground.

"Well?" Sophie's impatience is complete; she is getting ready to ask her friend to leave.

"Robert's proposed."

Sophie's hand goes to her chest. This she did not expect. "But, Aggie, that's wonderful!" Everything will be all right after all. He will marry her, and she will be redeemed.

Agatha screws up her face and hunches her shoulders. She slouches back to the bench and sits down again. She inches over until the sun finds her face.

"Or perhaps not so wonderful," says Sophie. "What's wrong? Aren't you pleased?"

"Well, I do like him, but that doesn't mean I want to *marry* the man."

"Why ever not?"

"I just don't like him that much."

Sophie grabs Agatha's arm with both hands, resisting the urge to shake. "But if you were to be engaged to him, it would make people more accepting of . . . your situation." Can't she see? Why can't she see?

"Our affair, you mean? You don't have to talk around the subject, Sophie, we're both adults."

Sophie looks down at her skirts and smooths them over. Impetuous girl. She has to marry sometime; it might as well be Robert, if she likes him. She stands up. She doesn't have time for this—she has troubles of her own, speaking of lies and secrets.

"You disapprove of me, don't you?" says Agatha.

Sophie sighs. "Yes, I suppose I do sometimes."

"I knew it. At the theater the other night you were angry with me about something."

"I don't know. No. Yes, I suppose I was. Mr. Chapman was laughing at us. And you were doing nothing to hide your feelings for him."

"Laughing at you? Not true." Agatha stamps her foot. "Sometimes you can be so . . ."

"So . . . yes?" Sophie looks down at her, casting a shadow over her face.

"Self-absorbed. And oversensitive!"

"I'm not self-absorbed! It's *you* I've been worrying about! Everyone knows about the two of you now. You're the gossip of Richmond. What were you thinking?"

"Oh, blow what anyone else thinks!" says Agatha. "If I were married to someone else nobody would think anything of my having an affair. It would be expected of me. But no. Everyone's all . . ." She raises her hands in mock horror, then begins fanning herself with an imaginary fan.

"It's all about discretion," says Sophie.

"Lying, you mean? Keeping secrets? Like Thomas and his mistress?"

The loudness of her own voice surprises Sophie. "How dare you bring him up like that? How dare you even mention her?"

"Why? So you can pretend it hasn't happened?"

"He is my husband. It is not your business."

"But *you* are my business. Look at you! You're moping around. Get angry with him! Cry! Do *something*! If you just push it aside and pretend it hasn't happened you'll end up like all those other women who are married and miserable and who spend their days looking out windows and wishing they could breathe. You'll throw parties and never speak to each other again. And he certainly won't get any better."

"How can you say these things? I'm trying! I'm . . . just . . . trying." The tears come then, and she collapses back on the seat.

Agatha puts out a hand to her shoulder but Sophie pushes her away with a fierce "No!" as if Agatha is the problem, the one who has torn her body in half. She feels Agatha's gaze on her, her friend who will not give up on her, will not be pushed away. When Agatha reaches out again Sophie lets her, falling into her embrace and sobbing until her chest aches and liquid comes from her nose and her mouth as well as her eyes, all over Agatha's dress and in her hair, but she knows Agatha of all people won't mind.

She cries for herself this time, for Thomas's unfaithfulness, for his not speaking, and for what it means for her. For the life that she had taken for granted and that has been taken away. They sit for several minutes until Sophie feels the heat inside her cooling and her breathing subsiding. Tears must be finite, she supposes. A body might explode from such violent crying if it went on for too much longer. And Agatha is right—she has been becoming catatonic, just like him. His illness has been threatening to suck her in as well, to paint her life a dull shade of gray, and she must not let it.

She pulls back from her friend's shoulder and wipes her eyes. As she does she glances up at the house and sees a quick shape move away from Thomas's window. Let him see, she thinks.

They sit in silence for another minute. Agatha squeezes her hand. Then she speaks.

"My darling, I am so sorry. I didn't mean to say such hateful, hurtful things, but you were—"

"It's all right. I know. I was judging you when I should have been looking at myself. I'm sorry too. All that talk of discretion. It doesn't matter what other people think." She thinks of her own behavior, going to see Captain Fale that day, and cringes. She had not been discreet. But she had been upset, not herself. How easy it is to make excuses for one's own behavior.

"I know it was hard for you taking Thomas out like that," says Agatha. "And that incident on the stairs—"

"Oh. Don't remind me." Sophie leans back onto the seat and covers her face.

"But don't you see that it's a good thing, Bear? It's good that he got so angry like that. Robert said afterward he thought Thomas was going to punch that man in the face."

"And you think that's a good thing? It's worse now! The whole town thinks he's mad. My father will find out, and then he'll be here in a shot to get Thomas put in some hospital for the dangerously insane."

"Oh, tosh. Thomas would never hurt you or anyone."

"I know that. But other people don't. They'll think he can't take care of me."

"You've got to stop worrying what others think of you. He can still work, so he can still take care of you."

Sophie crosses her arms. "*Still* work? He can *only* work. He stays in that room all day. Sometimes he disappears to the park—I suppose I can be thankful that his strength is returning—but it's like living with a ghost. That is *not* taking care of me."

But Agatha is right, as she so often is. Sophie must stop worrying about what others think. It is only distracting her from dealing with the real issues—Thomas's illness, his infidelity, and whether she can forgive him enough to try to help him.

"I suppose you're right," says Agatha. "But I still think you did the right thing by taking him out. Will you do it again?"

"I'm not sure I could bear it. It was hard enough in church, with all those pitying looks. But I do have another idea about somewhere to take him. I'm hoping it will help."

"Good! You see: it's much better that you try to help him instead of leaving him to rot in bed. What will you do?"

"I wrote to his friend at Kew, Mr. Crawley. I just got the reply this morning. We're going to meet him this afternoon."

"Good luck," says Agatha. "Now I have to go and see Robert and talk about this silly proposal. Are we still friends?"

Sophie smiles, defeated by her friend's optimism. "Of course we are."

Dear Mrs. Edgar,

I was shocked to get your letter. Nobody has spoken to me of your husband's condition. I did not even know he had returned so soon. I haven't seen Mr. Ridewell for some time, and I have not heard of any of Thomas's companions returning either. By all means bring him to visit me. I would very much like to see him. We could take him to the Palm House, where he will feel at home—it is, as you know, the closest to a rain forest one can find in England. The experience may help him in some way, and perhaps we can find out what happened to him and get him talking again. I am very saddened by this news. Your husband is a bright and interesting young man, whom I have taken great pleasure in knowing. Please call on me today at two o'clock. Simply come to the front gate and I will meet you there.

Peter Crawley

THOMAS DOESN'T RESIST WHEN she tells him of her plan, and she is heartened. He is not exactly eager, but he lays down his tools like an obedient child and allows her to help him with his coat and hat.

They wander down the hill to the station and catch the penny tram to Kew. It has been some time since they took a tram together, and the smell of the brakes and stale air remind her of their courting days. She reaches over and takes Thomas's hand, but it is a limp jellyfish in hers. She does not pull away; instead her fingertips trace the shiny calluses, the bumps of his scars, as she looks out the window at the world moving by, everything so normal: passengers alighting from omnibuses; young women shopping with their mothers; men in straw boaters and candy-striped jackets.

Peter Crawley looks nothing like she imagined—he doesn't resemble a beetle at all. His shoulders are narrow and his arms and legs like sticks, and yet a soft belly protrudes through the buttons of his jacket, reminding Sophie of photographs she has seen of native people in far-off lands, where malnutrition has distended their stomachs in an almost comical disproportion to the rest of their bodies. His receding hair falls in thin brown curls but his face is sharp; both his nose and chin point exaggeratedly toward the ground. Small black eyes flash behind small wire-rimmed spectacles. Mr. Crawley has his teeth clamped together and his lips drawn apart in a parody of a smile, and he stares at Thomas with worry.

He manages to tear his gaze away from her husband to greet her.

"Mrs. Edgar." He nods, but does not take her hand. Instead he reaches for Thomas's, grasping it with one hand while resting the other on Thomas's shoulder. "My good friend," he says. "What's become of you, hn? What *have* they done to you?"

Sophie is taken aback by his forthrightness, but she is also glad. For too long people have tiptoed around Thomas, Sophie included, and not addressed the problem directly, as if they could ignore it and it would cease to be an issue. But she shouldn't be surprised. Peter is a good friend of Thomas's. Even though she has never met him before, Thomas has always spoken of him with great warmth and admiration.

Thomas will not meet his friend's eyes.

"Can he hear me?" Mr. Crawley asks Sophie.

"Yes, he can hear you. You just won't get much of a response. You can try, though, please, by all means."

"Right." Mr. Crawley rubs his hands together. "Come in." He leads them through the gates. "I've got just the place for us to go today."

The sky appears huge and white above them. The Palm House looms like the upturned hull of a luxury liner. Men and women promenade up the sweeping pathways, the women spinning colored parasols and the men brandishing unnecessary but fashionable walking sticks.

Silence hangs between them as they walk and Sophie feels an urge to smash it with a hammer. Instead she turns to Mr. Crawley to break it gently.

"It's so nice to finally meet you," she says. "Thomas has told me so much about you. How kind you have been to him, and encouraging. He couldn't have made the trip to Brazil without you, I understand." She realizes as she says this that her voice is harder than she intends. It's not that she blames Mr. Crawley, but the tightness in her belly, the stress of the meeting, forced the words out like hard kernels of grain.

"Mrs. Edgar," says Mr. Crawley, "if I'd had any idea he would return like this, I promise you I never would have put him forward for the expedition."

Sophie tries to stop him, to reassure him, but he goes on.

"I seriously believe Thomas has great scientific aptitude. He had expressed to me his regret he was only ever able to collect a few beetles and butterflies from the park. I really thought this was the opportunity of a lifetime for him. I'm only sorry it didn't appear to work out that way."

We're talking about him as if he's not here, Sophie thinks. She steals a glance at her husband. Though he keeps pace with them, his head hangs as if in shame, and his feet scrape on the ground as he walks. They are talking about him as if he is a failure.

"On the contrary. It *was* the opportunity of a lifetime, there is no denying it. I don't know if you have seen the specimens he brought back but they are magnificent. He has been paid a tidy sum for them. Please don't think that this has ruined him for life . . ." She takes Thomas's arm and gives it a reassuring squeeze. "This condition is only temporary, isn't it, my dear?"

Mr. Crawley seems startled at her addressing him directly, as if Thomas is a photograph she carries in her pocket. It seems to bring him to his senses and he stops talking altogether.

Even as she makes such a bold statement, Sophie knows it is for her benefit as much as Thomas's. In reality, she can see his condition stretching far into their future, a bleak and dusty future where the two of them become strangers and she depends wholly on her father for support. At least her anger has retreated, for now.

The Palm House's curved glass walls stretch above them. Sophie has been here before, both as a child and with Thomas, but the architecture has lost none of its magic. Inside, the humidity hits them like warm meat. Thomas gulps air beside her. She can't imagine what it must have been like for him, enduring this wet heat for months on end. Here, the warmth is produced by boilers under the floor and she wonders how accurate a representation of the tropics it is.

Thomas's eyes dart about and his face is lifted to the ceiling, where palms soar and seem to touch the sky through the glass. About them is the murmur of guests, talking in whispers as if inside a museum, but otherwise it is still and quiet. She remembers the letters he sent her, about the overpowering sounds of the jungle, with screeches of birds and monkeys and frogs and insects. It must seem quite dead to him in here.

"Thomas," says Mr. Crawley. He lays a hand on his arm. "Talk to me, friend. How does this place compare with the real thing, hn?"

Thomas shakes his head slowly.

"Not quite the same, hn? I expect it's a bit devoid of insect life."

Thomas's eyes follow an imaginary butterfly from the canopy down to the ground, his head moving back and forth as the insect zigzags through the air. A sheen of sweat is forming on his forehead, but he doesn't wipe it away.

"Well, what about this?" Peter leads them along the path, beneath the spiral staircase where a woman has lifted her skirts to ascend. She holds tightly to the railing and giggles nervously while her husband stands behind her and supports her, pushes her, even. The smell of damp earth rises from the pots and beds, and a sweet perfume crosses their path. Above them fruit that Sophie has never tasted drips from a vine. She imagines reaching up and plucking one, sinking her teeth into it, and feeling the juice run down her chin and through her hands.

Mr. Crawley stands proudly in front of a tall young plant with finger-like leaves. "*Hevea brasiliensis,*" he says.

Thomas nods again, staring at the plant. He reaches out a hand and touches its smooth trunk.

At Sophie's blank look, Mr. Crawley smiles. "It's a rubber tree, Mrs. Edgar. Thomas will be very familiar with this, I expect, seeing as how it was rubber that paid for his expedition."

Thomas grabs his hand back and puts it in his pocket, as if to control it.

"You'll be used to seeing the trees scarred by machete cuts, I expect. These ones are not bound for rubber production. They'll have a nice quiet life in captivity."

They fall silent and Sophie thinks she can hear water dripping somewhere. The heat prickles on the back of her neck and under her arms. Her thighs are ready to stick together. She opens her mouth to suggest they move back outside.

"Of course," says Mr. Crawley suddenly, stopping Sophie's thoughts, "you went at the right time, Thomas. As we speak, plantations are being cultivated in the East Indies. These rubber trees are from seeds from Brazil, which were, I'm ashamed to say, smuggled out some years ago by a chap called Wickham. We've managed to grow them successfully here, and we shipped off a ton of seedlings to Asia. They'll be planted in nice ordered rows, not like in Brazil where the trees are miles apart. Must make tapping them somewhat difficult, I'd say. This is going to revolutionize the rubber industry. I'm afraid the bottom's about to fall out of the market for poor old Brazil. Your man—what was his name?" He looks at Thomas, forgetting perhaps that he will get no answer from him, so Sophie steps in to provide it.

"Mr. Santos."

"Santos, yes. I'm afraid his fortunes might very well take a dive. Sorry if that's bad news, my friend. I say, did you ever find that butterfly you were going to look for? Please say yes. What a breakthrough it would be!"

Sophie is so interested in Mr. Crawley's speech she has taken her eyes off Thomas, who stands to her left and slightly behind her. There is silence after Mr. Crawley's question, and she sees his face change from joviality to worry again.

"Are you all right, Thomas?"

Sophie turns to look at her husband. His fist is in his mouth and he bites on it, hard. Tears well in his eyes.

"Wrong question, I think," says Mr. Crawley. "I *am* sorry."

Thomas closes his eyes and nods. Then he flicks at his arms and spins around to look at the floor, as if tormented by insects. A grunt escapes him.

"Do you want to wait for us outside, Thomas?"

It is all the encouragement he needs. Scratching his hands, he turns and marches away from them and outside.

"I didn't mean to upset him like that," says Mr. Crawley. "A sore point?"

She sighs. "I really don't know anymore."

"Perhaps the news of his friend's imminent failure came as a shock. I should have been more tactful."

"You weren't to know."

"I do wish he had written to me while he was away. I heard from one of his companions, Mr. Gitchens."

Sophie leans forward. "Really? Which one was he?"

"He was a plant-hunter for us. He has provided us with many seeds and specimens for study. A fine man, in my opinion. His letters are always brief, though. A man of few words."

Sophie feels deflated. "Oh. So he offered no insight into Thomas's circumstances."

"Well, I could write to him, you know. I have an address in Manaus, in the care of Mr. Santos. I haven't heard from him for some time, but as far as I know he is still there."

"Could you? Oh, Mr. Crawley, you don't know how much this means to me."

"Well, you mustn't get too excited. It takes six weeks for letters to travel, and even then I have no idea when it will reach him. You are looking at many months before we hear anything."

"I'm sure he'll be better by then, and can tell us himself. But just in case . . ."

Mr. Crawley closes his eyes and cocks his head, a shy gesture. "I understand, madam. Shall we . . ." He indicates the door.

Outside, couples and groups stroll or stand about chatting; there are no lone figures skulking in corners or sitting on any of the benches. Thomas is nowhere to be seen.

IT STARTS TO RAIN as Sophie arrives home alone. While Mary serves her tea in the drawing room she stares out at the street. She tries not to worry. He probably went for a walk, took the route home through the park. It's a walk they have done together on occasion and he knows the way well. But he will be getting so wet. She imagines him huddled under an oak tree somewhere while the rain crashes onto the branches.

An hour later the rain stops, but a heavy gray blanket lies over the earth. The front door opens and Thomas stands dripping on the tiles. Mud creeps up his legs and his hands are dirty, but he seems perfectly calm. Serene, even. He sucks air in through his teeth.

"Thomas, you're freezing," Sophie says. "Let's get you upstairs."

He walks in front of her, leaving muddy footprints on the carpet, but she doesn't care.

"You shouldn't have gone off like that. I've been worried." She stands behind him and helps him out of his jacket. "Honestly, Thomas, you're like a little boy sometimes."

There, she said it. Thomas turns around, his face only a few inches from hers. He raises a hand and touches her cheek. His skin is icy. Then he pulls it away again and looks at the floor as he unbuttons his waistcoat. Sophie is stunned for a moment by the gesture, by the electricity that passed between them from the touch. She still holds his wet jacket over her arm, and he hands her his waistcoat as well, then his shirt. When he removes his undershirt, she has a glimpse of his translucent underarm hair as he turns away from her. Water smears across his back, catching like jewels in the goose bumps that shiver over his skin, and she catches the smell of him she had conjured up while he was away. She realizes he no longer smells of peppermints, so what she can smell now is entirely his own. She feels a tingling in her arms that she knows is desire.

His boots and trousers come off next, but he leaves his long underwear on.

"Get into bed now, you're shivering."

He does as he is told and she gathers his soiled clothes and boots—her arms are stuffed full of them—and exits the room.

Later she sends Mary up with Thomas's supper—hot soup to warm him up. She tries to sit quietly and read a book, but the chair feels as if it is made of needles, and the words on the page seem to play leapfrog. She keeps finding herself standing in the hallway, looking up the stairs at Thomas's closed door. Finally she convinces herself it is late enough to go to bed.

She undresses quickly in her cold bedroom and reaches for her nightgown. She catches a glimpse of herself in the mirror. Her body is flour-white, even in the caramel glow of the lamp. She stands up straight and turns to the side. She has lost the swell in her stomach as well as the plumpness in her cheeks; her hip bones are solid beneath the skin. She should have children by now. This thought should make her feel younger—that her time has not yet come—but instead it makes her feel like a barren old maid.

My heart and my womb make a fine set of twins, she thinks.

She thinks about her conversation with Agatha this morning—what she said about doing *something*, anything but ignoring the problem and hoping it will go away. All this taking him for walks, tiptoeing around him—it's not helping so far. She has spent too much energy disapproving of Agatha—after all, isn't it the things that are different about her that make Sophie want her as a friend? Perhaps she has always liked her because of, not in spite of her behavior—and a part of her wishes she could live life as free from pettiness and the strictures of propriety. After all, Thomas has changed, perhaps irrevocably. Maybe she needs to change as well, and then—only then—will they make some progress.

She runs a hand over her breasts, still full and rounded, the nipples cold. She thinks of her husband in bed wearing only his underwear. The smell of him, his naked back. What would Agatha do right now?

Thomas's room is dark and smells slightly of beef soup. His breathing is even but loud. She creeps to the side of his bed, pulls back the cover, and slips in beside him. He wakes with a start as her hand finds his chest, where his own are neatly folded.

"Shh," she whispers. "It's only me."

If she could see him, she pictures his face full of alarm, but she imagines as she caresses his chest that she is rubbing his fear away.

"Everything will be all right." Fingers tracing circles on his chest, around his nipples, stroking his hands. She moves her hand lower, to his stomach and the woolly line of hair that rises up from his underwear. It quivers under her touch. She leans over him and kisses his neck, then his cheek, then finally his mouth. It remains

slack under hers for a second, then his lips part and she lets the tip
of her tongue fall in and touch his. He responds, with his mouth
at first, and then his hands are on her back as she moves on top of
him. Her whole weight is on him now as she uses both hands to
push his underwear down. She is in control and she feels a surge
of power and arousal. She pushes herself up and brushes her nipples over his. With her hand she guides him inside her.

A moan escapes him. Is there a word waiting there too?

"Say my name," she whispers, but he is silent. She moves forward and back until she feels him tense beneath her. She places
her hand where she can touch herself every time she moves forward and as his grip on her thighs tightens she feels another surge
of power through her, this time warmth and tingling, shooting up
her abdomen, through her scalp, and down the insides of her
arms. She cries out for both of them and falls forward onto the
sweating chest of her mute husband.

SHE AWAKES IN THE night after dreaming she is lying on the edge
of a deep well. She reaches out a hand—Thomas is gone. After they
made love he turned his cold back to her and her joy dropped like
a barometer. Now he is not in bed; he is nowhere in the room. Her
body is replete, arms and legs limber, her bones liquid. But a
crackle of doubt is growing inside her again; she feels it physically
as a hard, round pebble in her gut. How long will this go on? Wa-
vering between hope and crashing despair? She wants—no, she
needs—to remain optimistic for him, but she can't keep building
up her hopes and having them pushed back in her face like this.

Stop it, she tells herself. We have made progress: we *have*.
Three weeks ago she wouldn't have dreamed of creeping into his
bed like this. His body was as brittle as dried grass then; now it
is filling out and the wounds have healed. She can still feel the
warmth of his cracked hands on her back, the jagged edge of

broken skin that traced a line down her spine. He is getting better. *He is getting better.* He made a sound, too, didn't he? It is only a matter of time before his moans turn to words.

She sits up and listens, but the silence and the darkness are absolute. Thomas has left the covers on his side pulled back and the bottom sheet is cold and damp. She gets out of bed and wraps a sheet around her.

Her feet make no sound on the stairs as she pads down. The rest of the house is dark as well, apart from a faint glow in the hallway, coming from under Thomas's study door.

She pushes the door open, and there is her husband, crouched over his work again. The clock in the corner tells her it is two o'clock.

"Thomas? Darling? It's so late." She rubs at her eyes. He doesn't turn around.

She goes to him and puts her hands on his shoulders, but gets no reaction from him. One of his Brady drawers lies on the desk in front of him, half filled with butterflies, seemingly all the same breed, with only slight variations in size and coloring. Labels in Thomas's scribbly hand sit neatly below each specimen, and his hands tremble as he places a new one beneath a freshly pinned butterfly with a scalpel. She can't make out the Latin name in the poor light. They all look the same, though. Why on earth is he bothering to have so many the same? Surely he should sell them, not keep them all for himself like that? She stands behind him, offering him warmth and love through her hands, but he keeps his back to her, no acknowledgment even of her presence, giving absolute attention to a drawer full of insects. He even left the bed they shared, after she had given herself to him like that, to be with the horrible things.

She pushes off with the heel of her hands, making him falter and drop the label. But still he doesn't let her in, just goes back to picking it up and reapplying it. Sophie backs away from him, giving him one last chance to do something—say something—before she walks upstairs, clutching her stomach, and returns to her own bed.

She sleeps a sort of half sleep, always aware of the sounds in the night, the tapping of the plum tree against the window, and eventually the growing light, but it is interspersed with thoughts that turn absurd. An image descends on her of Thomas's back at his desk, but then it becomes her father's, and she feels the bony touch of Nanny's hand on hers, before it is gone again and she is awake. Butterflies flick at her ears and disappear. She feels Thomas's hands on her back but she is not herself, she is another woman, and Thomas is making love to her as he should only to his wife. She mulls over the little hints Thomas has given her, the journals, the agent's words about the letters he had received. But as her half sleep clouds her brain, she loses a grip on the thought, forgets it, and moves on to the next. One idea comes to her again and again: *He loves the butterflies more than he loves me.*

Just before dawn she hears Thomas ascend the stairs and go into his room. As the ash-gray morning light pushes through the curtains, her waking dreams have darned her insides into tight knots. All sleep deserts her as she rolls onto her side, onto her back—nothing gives her comfort in her bed; her skin itches and every position pushes some part of her body against another. She may as well be sleeping on hard ground, with ants crawling up her legs. Perhaps then Thomas would notice her.

She brings a knuckle to her mouth and puts her head under the covers. She lets out a muffled scream—anything to let out the tension inside her. Her legs thrash under the covers. Thomas and his butterflies. Thomas and his other woman. It's as if he thinks of women as butterflies to be collected and pinned, lifeless, pretty objects to look at, like the blue that he gave her. She doesn't want to join his blasted collection just so he'll pay her some attention, alongside this other woman and who knows how many more?

Well, she can't do anything about *her*, but the butterflies are just sitting there, in her own house, tormenting her.

Without bothering to wash, Sophie walks in her nightgown with sure steps down to Thomas's study. The crates, now half empty, are not as heavy as they once were, and she drags the first of them through the scullery and out the back door. She tips it on its side and the remaining boxes tumble onto the grass. Sawdust spills onto them.

It takes her several trips—the rest of the crates, even the empty ones, the Brady drawers sitting on his desk. The rest are locked, and she thinks about dragging the whole set, but quickly realizes she won't be able to lift them. Assorted boxes of specimens are still scattered around the floor and sitting on shelves. She has made a temple of butterflies in her garden and for a moment regrets what she is about to do. But she knows it is for the best.

She sets a kerosene-soaked rag at the base of the pile—the sawdust will catch easily, and the crates are dry as paper. Her hand shakes as she strikes the match and it goes out. Another thought passes through her—she made love to Thomas, but he was probably thinking of her, the woman in Brazil. It was dark. He could have imagined that it was her on top of him, not Sophie.

She lights another match. This time the flame takes and she holds the match until it nearly reaches her fingers before crouching down and setting it to the rag.

The sun alights the garden just as the flames take to the nearest crate and it blackens, like a spreading ink stain, before burning. Sophie stands facing the house, and she catches movement in Thomas's window. His face appears, a white smudge in the gloom. She sees his mouth open, but no words escape. She feels a twinge of guilt and takes a step toward the fire, which spreads through the sawdust that is scattered on the ground. Then Thomas throws the window open. His face is frozen and a look of sickness passes over it before he opens his mouth again and yells.

"No!"

The word bounces around the garden, off the brick wall behind the roses, off the plum tree and the old oak. It passes into Sophie's ear and causes a ripple through her brain. They stare at each other for what seems like minutes, and the last echo of his voice is the only thing she can hear. Then another sound—the cracking as the first crate is engulfed. The noise snaps something inside her. She looks back at he window, but Thomas has gone.

She runs to the other side of the fire, where the Brady drawers still lie untouched. She dives toward them and begins pulling things out of the line of the fire. She pulls off smoking boxes, some with their corners glowing with sparks, and then her husband is beside her and they are pulling together. Thomas is stamping and she tries to do the same but her feet are bare. She barely registers the pain as her feet blister.

They pull off all they can save and Sophie finds she is crying; great fat tears stream down her cheeks. They may be caused by the smoke or by the regret that looms inside her. She makes a last dash for the flames, but Thomas's arms are around her, strong now, and he pulls her back violently, and together they collapse on the ground, crying. Her face is in his chest.

"Why, Thomas?" She doesn't even know what she is asking of him, but it seems to be the question to all the answers she needs.

Thomas makes a choking sound, and then his voice comes, soft and cracked.

"He killed her."

It seems enough for now, and she stays on the ground in his arms as smoke rises into the sky, and the fire, with nothing more to feed it, dies away.

TWELVE

THOMAS HAD KILLED RODRIGUES, just as he had killed Arturo. It would have been better if he had lost his tongue in an accident and was mute, like Manuel. Then he never would have put either man in such danger. He leaned over the side of the boat, watching the turgid black water churn and feeling the leaden weight of the letter to Roberts in his pocket. He had no choice now but to go and warn the other men about Santos, and persuade them to leave. His tongue was numb and heavy in his mouth. Nowhere was safe for him anymore. If Antonio had had him followed the day before then he would have had him followed again, and known that he had discovered Rodrigues's body.

Thomas had stumbled from the office and through the streets, tripping over gutters, down to the river. A stench of drains had reached him and vultures scratched circles in the sky above him, waiting for him to drop dead so they could feast on his carcass.

People passed by him, flinching at the state of his

vomit-stained clothes and the smell of him, but he found some-one to pay to take him back up the river to the camp. He left with nothing but the clothes on his body and all his money gone.

Now he drummed a fist on his forehead while the roaring in his ears told him it was time to breathe again. What had he done? He took thirsty gulps of air and thought about what he was going to say once he got there, with no luggage and without Antonio to accompany him.

The camp appeared deserted when he arrived. The ground squelched under his feet and the smell of damp bark rose with every step. A lingering smoke drifted through the huts, bringing with it the sour smell of burnt meat. He couldn't help but be reminded of the smell that had permeated Arturo's village after the fire that killed him. He felt his stomach heave, even though he hadn't eaten for a long time. If Pedro had burned the dinner, he would really have something to worry about.

He called out; his voice bounced off the trees and rose into the air. A bird took flight, drumming the air. A figure appeared in the doorway of Santos's hut, small and quiet. Clara. She put a finger to her lips, eyes darting about, and shuffled toward him in her thin nightgown. Her hair was greasy and her face gray and speckled with spots. Dark circles hung below her eyes and her pupils were pinpricks behind a murky film. She gripped his arm.

"Shh," she said. "My husband is asleep. He's unwell." Her voice sounded strange, as if her mouth were full of liquid. An unpleasant odor, like sour milk, rose from her as she moved.

"What's wrong with him? Where are the others?"

"Shh," she said again, though he had spoken softly. She's gone mad, he thought. Her face had about it a tormented look, and her head wouldn't stay still, nor would she look at him; instead, she seemed to be following the erratic flight of a bumblebee, or checking the undergrowth for spies.

"They'll be back soon."

"Mrs. Santos," said Thomas. He clawed at the formal name, brandished it like a weapon. "Are you all right?"

She tapped her temple. "I just have these headaches. The doctor won't give me any laudanum. He says he's run out but I don't believe him. He doesn't understand how much it hurts. I can't even sing anymore."

She touched his hand and her fingertip was clammy against his skin. "But I'm glad you came back for me."

"Clara, no." He drew his hand away. He sensed that he didn't have much time and that Clara would be no help to him. She was safer than any of them; after all, she was Santos's wife. He turned and sniffed at the air, which was damp and crackling with electricity. Rains were coming, and soon.

He set out to find the others before they returned to camp, not really sure of which direction to take, and wandering south. Butterflies crisscrossed his path, as if daring him to catch them. In the warm moist air they moved sluggishly, and he could have reached out and caught any number of them if he had brought his net with him. He tried to look past them, to focus on the task at hand—and to push out of his mind the thought that he was taking a last walk among his beautiful creatures; he felt as if he were saying good-bye to a lover. What a contrast, he thought, between now and the excitement and arousal he had felt early on in his time here, like the beginnings of love, as he had felt with Sophie; as with her, expectancy and thrill had given way to a constant affection.

Beyond the lepidoptera, dark columns of trees stretched into the gloom. Cuts marked the rubber trees he passed, weeping sap. He stopped to touch the sticky stuff and rolled it around in his fingers. Yes, this was very fresh. Santos's workers must have set up camp nearby. He thought of the disgusting circumstances of the workers on the Putumayo and a panic gripped him suddenly.

He should avoid the camp, for fear of what he might witness.

As he stood there silently, deciding which direction to turn in, he was startled by two human figures running through the trees toward him. A man and a woman, Indians, their bare feet making no sound on the forest floor. They stopped when they saw him, frozen like the jaguar, eyes wide. They started to back away slowly.

He put his hand out. "It's all right," he said, for they looked at him as if he might kill them. They both had high, wide foreheads and wide-set eyes, angular jaws. The woman, naked to the waist, was young and still beautiful, for Thomas had thought since he arrived that the women became more like men as they got older. The man held tightly to the woman's arm. He was much shorter than Thomas, but stocky and strong.

A shot rang out and the woman's stare didn't leave Thomas as she fell to her knees. Her hand went to her stomach, and he saw that it swelled with early pregnancy and her nipples were large and dark. Her face screwed up in pain and terror. Her companion tried to pull her to her feet, yelling at her, Thomas forgotten.

Then the men were upon them, four rubber men, kicking them both as they lay on the ground. They hadn't yet seen Thomas, but what could he do? The men's skin was the color of old blood, their faces held terrible smiles as they kicked, as if they were playing a children's game and winning. Thomas edged closer to the rubber tree and hid his face behind it, while his heart sent blood shooting into his tingling fingertips. He covered his face and winced with each sickening sound of boot meeting body. Then it stopped. The men jabbered at one another; they might have even been speaking English, but he couldn't be sure.

He dared to look out from behind the tree but immediately wished he hadn't, though he found he couldn't move or look away. The woman lay still on the ground while one of the men crouched between her legs with his trousers down. The other two, who held the Indian man as he struggled feebly, laughed as the man pumped himself into her. Then they picked the Indian up and dragged him

backward to a tree, where they tied him tightly. The third man
had finished with the woman and came over to help them, secur-
ing the Indian man's limbs while they were bound. The woman
lay motionless, probably dead.

What happened next Thomas knew would torment him forever. One of the men, shorter than the others, with dirty sleeves
rolled to his elbows and bandy legs, raised his machete high and
brought it down on the Indian's upper arm. The Indian screamed,
but his arm was still attached. The rubber men laughed at their
bandy-legged accomplice, who shook his head with a smile and
dug into his pocket. Thomas watched him drop a few coins into the
outstretched palms of the other men, then take up the machete and
swipe again. The Indian's arm fell onto the ground and he passed
out.

Thomas thought he would too. He gripped the tree and swooned;
a buzzing filled his head and replaced the screams of the poor man.
He realized that the rubber men were indeed playing some kind of
game—betting to see who could sever a limb in one go. His mouth
filled with saliva and his stomach heaved. As he vomited, he couldn't
help the rasping sound that came from his throat.

He didn't have time to run; by the time he even considered it
one of the men—the broadest one, with a large mole on his cheek—
was upon him, grabbing him roughly by the arm and shouting
at him in fast Portuguese.

I'm done for, thought Thomas, but he was listless, uncaring
about what happened to him. He had seen it coming all his life.

Mole-face shook his arm and his whole body rattled. Thomas
found the strength to raise a hand. "Please," he said in Portuguese.
"Senhor Santos . . ."

The man dropped his arm as the others arrived. Thomas looked
beyond them to where the Indian slumped against his bindings,
his body slick with his own blood. Bandy-legs poked Thomas in
the chest with his gun, hard, as if to break his sternum.

"He knows Santos," said Mole-face in Portuguese. "Where are you from?" he asked.

"I am English," said Thomas. "I am here with Senhor Santos."

The men looked at one another and lowered their weapons. They conversed quickly and Thomas couldn't make out what they were saying. Finally Mole-face said to him in English: "Friend?"

Thomas nodded. "Yes, friend," wanting to kill himself for the shame of calling these men his friends. They took turns shaking his hand, and none of them mentioned the two violated bodies only yards from where they stood. Thomas started to back away. A wind had started up; it would rain soon, wash the blood off the bodies.

"I go now," he said. Did he have a chance to save the Indian? What could he say? One man's voice would surely have no effect here—why would they listen to him? He would be like a lone butterfly, its wings making no sound. He turned and started to walk, with each step telling himself to stop and go back, to try to help, but his feet carried him back toward the camp, just as the sky opened and the rains came.

LATER, AS THE RAIN fell in steady sheets onto the roof of his hut and he watched water rush under him through a hole in the floor, glinting in the lamplight, he heard his name. John stood in the doorway. Thomas didn't know how long he had been sitting there, alone in the dark, his hands clamped between his knees.

"So you're better, then," said John.

Thomas shook his head sadly. Better? He was worse now, much worse. But what could he say? He beckoned John into the room with a shake of the hand. The big man's huge fingers enclosed Thomas's thin ones.

John lingered awkwardly for a moment before Thomas motioned for him to sit on the one chair. Thomas sat in the hammock as if it were a swing.

"Are you all right?" asked John. "You're very pale. And look, you're trembling. Should I call Ernie?" He stood again. Thomas put out a hand as if to push him back into his seat.

"John," he whispered. His throat was tight; he had to squeeze the words out. "We have to get out of here. We have to leave."

"What is it? What's happened?"

Thomas felt his face crumple and his shoulders sag. His stomach still churned and he couldn't rid himself of the picture of the woman's face, the man with his arm cut off.

"Santos. He's dangerous."

John leaned forward to catch what Thomas was muttering. "It's as I expected. You've seen something, haven't you?"

Thomas nodded.

"Tell me."

"I . . . I can't. It wasn't Santos, but . . . the men he employs. Santos knows about it."

John nodded. "Have you told the others?"

Thomas shook his head.

"They'll never believe you, Thomas. They're enthralled by the man. He might as well be paying them in diamonds for the hold he has over them. We must do something. We'll confront him about it."

Thomas's arm shot out. "No!" he croaked. "It's too dangerous."

"Then we'll leave and speak to the authorities in Manaus. We have to do something, Thomas, we can't just stand by. I saw the scars on the backs of the rubber-tappers. And Manuel . . . I'm sure it wasn't an accident that cost him his tongue."

"There's worse," said Thomas. "Much worse. You have no idea. But nobody will help us here. We must leave and return to England. We'll be safe there."

"Perhaps you're right," said John. "We'll leave in the morning. Santos is too ill to follow us."

"What's wrong with him?"

"Harris says . . . well, he hasn't told Santos yet, so I'm not sure I should be telling you."

"But you know?"

John nodded. "Ernie's not very good at keeping secrets, not even for his patients. He seems worried for himself over it. I don't suppose it will hurt to tell you."

Thomas leaned forward and squeezed one hand inside the other. "Go on."

"Thomas, he's got syphilis."

IN THE EARLY DAWN, Pedro had already lit the fire and smoke hung over the yard. Thomas had stayed in his hut all night and avoided George and Ernie, for what could he say to them? He tried to push away the disgusting memories of the day, but they threaded themselves through his dreams. On top of that was another fear—if Santos had syphilis, might he not have passed it on to his wife, and thereby on to Thomas? How could he go back and face Sophie if this was the case? Was he to die a mad and lonely death?

As he stood in his doorway, looking out at the other huts, Santos emerged and shuffled into the middle of the yard. He was dressed in his white suit, but his face was very red. His cool exterior had slipped for now, and sweat dampened his hair. His mustache drooped. Ernie emerged behind him, his sleeves rolled up, wiping his hands on a cloth. He looked at Thomas in surprise—clearly he hadn't realized he had returned—but said nothing. His face was solemn.

"Clara!" Santos roared. He stood where he was, steadying himself on the table, looking at her hut. There was no answer from inside. Thomas threw an alarmed glance at Ernie, who shook his head, as if warning him. A shape emerged from the adjacent hut— George stood in his doorway, wiping at his neck with a towel, watching. Where was John? Finally Santos strode toward his wife's hut and disappeared inside. He came out a moment later, dragging her by the arm. She tried to walk but slipped as if on skates and could not get a foothold in the mud.

Thomas was sickened. He wanted to rush forward to help her but something held him back. Fear. Or cowardice, he thought wretchedly.

Santos pulled Clara to her feet and glared at her. Ernie stepped forward. "Steady on," he said, his palm facing the couple. Santos turned the glare onto him, which stopped him. Ernie folded his arms, waiting.

Santos's attention was back on his wife, who looked around, bewildered. "Look at me, you whore," said Santos in Portuguese. His voice was calm, but his teeth were clamped together.

"What's he saying?" George appeared beside Thomas. "Can anyone understand him?"

Thomas stayed silent, straining to hear, dread gnawing at him.

"Syphilis," Santos now said in English: he was playing to his audience. "I have syphilis. Look!" He pulled up his sleeve to show her the welts on his arm—welts, Thomas saw with a jolt, like the sores on Lillie's body. Clara shook her head and answered him in her native tongue. "I'm sorry. But why are you angry with me?"

"You? How else did I contract syphilis, but from you?"

"Your whores . . ."

"You are the only whore here! I know what you do when you take your opium and join the carnival. My men have *seen* you, bitch!" Thomas's head spun at this piece of information. "Do you think I'm stupid?" Santos continued. "I know what you have been doing here, with these men, when I am gone. Am I right, gentlemen?" He turned to look at them. Nobody spoke. The edges of Thomas's vision went cloudy. A thought came to him: that Santos had left her alone in the hope that she might commit adultery. And he was right.

"You, Mr. Sebel. It is my wife you have been seen with in the forest, is it not?"

George gasped. His hand went to his mouth. Sweat beaded on his forehead and his gaze darted back and forth between husband and wife, then at Thomas.

"Come now," said Santos, "it's not your fault, I don't blame you. I blame my whore of a wife. Just tell me and we'll get it out in the open."

George, with wide eyes, gave a small dip of his head: a nod. Thomas looked at him in amazement. This couldn't be true. Could it?

"Dr. Harris, you too, I'll warrant?"

Ernie was standing very still. He groaned, as if finally understanding something. His hands were in his pockets and he raised himself briefly onto his toes and back again. "That's right, old man. Yes."

"It's not true!" Clara sank to her knees, Santos's hand still a vise around her arm.

"And you, Mr. Edgar? You too?"

Thomas looked at Clara. She was getting to her feet once again, her nightgown smeared with mud and gaping at the neck, revealing more flesh than was seemly. So he had been caught, as had they all. First by Clara, crouching like a Mygale spider in her web, luring them all in. Now by her husband. Thomas hung his head.

"It's not true, Thomas!" cried Clara, and Thomas flinched at the sound of his name.

"Shut up!" said Santos.

Thomas found he could not speak. He nodded.

"You see?" said Santos, triumphant. "And you carry on with Mr. Gitchens when you go into the forest. You have even made the poor man fall in love with you. You are a whore. *Puta!*" He struck her with the back of his hand. For a moment after she had spun in a perfect ballerina's pirouette she seemed to hang, upright, before she fell backward. As she fell, her head struck the corner of the wooden table. Thomas, rooted to the spot, watched her go down and not get up.

"Christ!" said Ernie, and sprang forward to the fallen woman. He squatted down beside her while everyone looked on. Thomas's feet were bolted to the ground. Ernie put his fingers to Clara's neck.

"Is she dead?" asked Santos. His voice was light, free of remorse.

"No," said Ernie. "Her pulse is weak; she's taken quite a blow. Help me turn her so I can examine the wound."

A dark stain of blood was already haloing out around her head.

"Please step back, Doctor," said Santos. There was something tense in his face that Ernie seemed to respond to. He stood abruptly.

"You're quite sure she is still alive," said Santos.

"Yes, but we must—"

As he spoke Santos turned and picked up a chair, which, though Ernie lunged at him, he brought down with force onto his wife's head.

Still Thomas made no sound. He couldn't cry out because he didn't believe what his eyes were seeing. George gasped and ran, not toward Clara but away from her, into the forest.

"What have you done?" cried Ernie. "Have you gone mad, man?"

Santos pointed a finger at him and said in a low monotone, "Dr. Harris, I am warning you." Ernie's shoulders slumped. He turned and looked at Thomas, who found he was shaking uncontrollably, and for a moment their desperation passed between them.

"Now is she dead?"

Ernie dropped onto both knees and again felt for her pulse. He stayed there for ten seconds, moving his fingers, now dark with blood, to different points, searching. Finally he laid his head on her chest and listened.

He came up again, nodding. "She's dead." He pulled a handkerchief from his pocket and wiped his hands, shaking his head slowly, avoiding Santos's eyes.

Santos gave a satisfied nod, turned, and walked back to his hut, just as the first drops of morning rain fell. Within seconds the yard was enveloped in sheets of water and Clara was drenched.

THOMAS AWOKE ON THE floor. He must have fainted—or did he lie down right here and go to sleep? His body had shut down and could cope with no more. The air was hot and moist and dreams of Clara had been dancing through his mind. He saw her face again and again, pleading with him: "It's not true, Thomas." In another dream he saw her on her knees in front of George, as he had seen George and Joaquim, while Ernie took her from behind. He felt sick again. When had he last eaten? He had nothing left to vomit and was weak. And yet, no matter what her behavior, she did not deserve to die, and a part of him knew he missed her already.

He crossed an empty yard to John's hut. The rain had stopped, and Clara no longer lay on the ground, though there was an impression of her body in the mud, which had taken on a ruby tint. John's hut was empty, but his collecting equipment—his machete and bag—was propped in the corner.

Thomas went to find Ernie, who lay on his back, snoring, an almost empty spirits bottle on the floor beside him. The room smelt of alcohol and stale tobacco; the odor seemed to emanate from the man.

"Ernie." Thomas shook his shoulder. Ernie opened his eyes, then quickly closed them again and clutched his head.

He groaned. "Go away. It's too bright. Oh, my head."

"I need to talk to you about what happened."

Ernie sighed and nodded. "All right. Get me some water, would you?"

Thomas fetched him some water while Ernie rolled a cigarette. He lit it and closed his bloodshot eyes as he inhaled and blew the smoke out. "Right," he said.

Thomas could barely contain himself anymore. "What are we going to do? He murdered his wife, Ernie!"

Ernie just shook his head. "It's best not to get involved, Tom. Things will run their course, you'll see. People will ask questions when he returns to Manaus. In the meantime, what can we do? Nothing. Just forget about it."

"She was a *person*, Ernie, a human being. How can you be so callous? Especially after you and she—"

"Don't be ridiculous. *Me* with *her*? I hardly even noticed her."

Thomas's stomach lurched and he tasted bile in his mouth. He stared at Ernie, who carried on smoking, staring at the ground. Now he was just confused. "What do you mean?" He didn't know if he even wanted an answer.

Ernie said nothing.

"I don't understand," said Thomas.

Ernie harrumphed. He shook his shoulders and rubbed at his forehead. He stared at the ground. "That's nothing new."

"But before, in the yard. Clara. You said—"

"I know what I said."

"But it wasn't true?"

"Wasn't true."

Thomas couldn't decide whether Ernie's tone was ashamed or amused. "And George?"

"George? He doesn't have any interest in women. Haven't you noticed?"

It was starting to make sense. Horrible sense. "Yes, of course I have," Thomas admitted, surprising himself. "So why would he say that? Why would either of you say that?"

Ernie looked at him through squinted eyes. "Santos has given me something I could never afford on my own. I'm not a poor man, but this was way beyond my reach. He said he would need a favor in return, and I guess that was it. I'm not proud of it, Thomas, but we all had our reasons, I'm sure. Why did *you*? I just assumed you were coming along for the ride, like you always do, but maybe you had something else in mind."

Thomas looked away. This changed everything. Santos had Ernie and George in the palm of his hand. He must tread carefully. He must try to speak without stuttering. He felt his cheeks flush. "I don't know." The words fell out of him, heavy and solid.

He turned without another word and went outside. He needed to walk now, to be alone in the forest. If Ernie had done this to repay Santos for funding his whore, why had George? He thought hard back to the moment when Clara was on her knees in the mud, imploring. What had Santos said to George? *It is my wife you have been seen with.* George barely even spoke to Clara, let alone went anywhere with her in the forest. But Joaquim was another story. Perhaps Thomas wasn't the only one who had seen George abusing the boy; Santos had merely been waiting for the right moment to use the information to his advantage. George had said it to protect himself from the threat of exposure. It was blackmail.

He realized he had spent all this time in the forest with these men, and yet he knew nothing about them. He knew them no better now than he did at the beginning. He might as well have been alone all this time.

And what of himself? Antonio could have followed Clara and Thomas at any time—after all, Santos knew about George's transgressions somehow. Would Santos believe that Thomas had really committed adultery with Clara, or think he was lying like everybody else? Perhaps he was sure that Thomas would just go along for the ride, as Ernie had suggested. That he wouldn't have the strength to protest or that he was worried about being left out somehow. Thomas hated himself at that moment—that he had been so predictable. And weak. So weak. And when Clara had fallen, he had let her. He could have spoken out, denied it all, helped her. But he had stayed silent, and his silence had killed her.

He found himself down on the riverbank just as more rain started up. It was incessant. Why was he still here? He needed to leave, to find John and get out of here. The others wouldn't listen to him—Ernie would want to stay for Lillie, and George was too much of a coward to leave now. He let the rain wash over him, run down his face and through his clothes. He hadn't bathed since Manaus and the water felt cleansing. It hit him, then: the memory of Clara and Santos's blow to her head, the feeling he'd had of his legs being made of iron and riveted to the ground. He had done nothing to save her and now she was dead. Killed for being an adulteress when he was the other party. And as for Santos's anger that she had given him syphilis—Clara had said herself that Santos hadn't touched her for months. He desperately wanted children, but because she would not give him any, he had found a way to justify killing her. Now he was free to marry again. A sob welled in his stomach. He slipped and landed painfully on his tailbone, but didn't get up, just sat there on the mud while the rain poured onto him and he cried for the dead woman and for the man he should have been.

Through his tears, which felt like hot, angry stings on his cheeks, he looked out over the black water of the River Negro. Something large floated near the shore. He thought at first it was an alligator, and his body tensed, ready to jump up and run. But it was the wrong shape for an alligator, too stunted.

As the rain began to ease and soften, Thomas wobbled to his feet and stepped down to the water's edge. It wasn't a log either; it was human. A bulky body floated facedown, not three feet from where he stood. He launched himself into the water and grabbed at it, pulling it by cold pale arms back onto the mud. Long straggly hair plastered itself to a face with a thick beard. Thomas cried out: one of the cheeks had been eaten away by fish, and beneath the closed eyelids one of the sockets was empty. The skin was as blue as a duck egg. This was more than Thomas could bear. He gathered John in his arms and silently rocked him.

HIS ARMS WERE WEAK and his back griped with every effort as he pulled the body back toward camp. He wanted to call out for help but could manage barely more than a whisper. His voice seemed to be deserting him.

Pedro was the first to see him, still a hundred yards from the compound. He ran forward and took one arm while Thomas dragged the other.

"Is he . . . ?"

Thomas nodded. "Dead." His voice crackled and was swallowed by his breath, which puffed with every exertion. He wouldn't be able to take much more; his arms were losing their feeling.

Pedro nodded. "The *bouto*, Senhor Edgar."

Thomas stopped and dropped John's arm. He squatted on the ground to stretch his aching back and to calm his breathing. "The dolphin? What of it?"

"This is what they do. They take the form of a beautiful woman and come onto land to lure men to the water."

Thomas remembered the day on the boat, on the way to Manaus. What was it John had said? *Not a bad way to go, drowned by a beautiful spirit.* He pushed the thought away. It was ridiculous.

"You don't really believe that, do you?"

"No." Pedro looked in the direction of the camp, where Antonio was moving silently through the trees toward them.

"Senhor Edgar," the big man drawled with a nod. "What has happened?"

"As if you don't know!" Thomas's hands were trembling. As Antonio bent over John's body Thomas took the opportunity to run; once again his legs took him in their own direction, back to the compound and into John's hut, the two men and the dead body of his friend far behind him. He grabbed the gun that leaned against the wall and checked that it was loaded. It was only shot but it would have to do.

Without stopping to think about what he was about to do, he sprinted through the mud for Santos's hut, his feet slapping the ground.

"Get up!" he shouted at him. Santos was concealed behind a mosquito net and said nothing, so Thomas presumed he was asleep. He stood for a few seconds, tempted to back out, but Santos pulled the net aside.

"Mr. Edgar, what do you think you're doing?"

"You killed him!"

"Who?"

"John, you blind idiot. Don't deny it!"

"But I have been ill in bed, grieving for my wife." His tone was smug. Thomas, dripping wet, with water running into his eyes, gripped the gun tighter in his anger and pointed it at him. If he closed his eyes when he squeezed the trigger, he would be spared the sight of more blood.

"Mr. Edgar, put that gun down. You don't want to have a murder on your hands, now, do you?"

"Like you, you mean?"

"You cannot prove that."

"But I can prove you killed Clara . . . your wife. There are witnesses."

"But who would believe you, sir? When you all lied about her adultery?"

Thomas wavered for a moment, and the gun drooped in his hands.

"Yes, I am indebted to you, my accomplice."

"No!" Thomas was crying now, and his hands shook again. His shaking finger moved to the trigger. Then he heard a crack and felt a blow to his head. His vision went black for a moment and he found himself on the ground, on his knees, the gun fallen to the floor. A hand reached out to pick it up.

"Mr. Edgar," said Santos. He beckoned him closer. Thomas, realizing it was all over, nodded, feeling his throat contract and a sigh escape like a whistle. He crawled along the ground toward the man's hammock. His wet clothes stuck to him, making his movements sluggish.

"You and I need to have a little talk. Antonio took the liberty of booking you a passage home before he left Manaus. You leave in two days, which gives you just enough time to go back and gather the possessions you seem to have left behind at my house in your hurry to leave. Please don't say anything." He raised a hand. Thomas had no intention of speaking. He couldn't have if he tried. "Antonio has written to your agent, Mr. Ridewell, is it? He should be there to meet you at the other end." He paused. His skin was sallow and a sore on his neck looked like a burn from a hot poker. Thomas felt a small satisfaction at this; he hoped it caused the man pain. Santos went on. His voice was low and menacing. "I like you, Mr. Edgar. You remind me of myself when I was your age. Go home to your pretty wife and have a family. Tell them stories about your wondrous butterfly. It doesn't matter that you didn't find it—make it up. I don't know exactly what it is that you think you have seen here, Edgar, but if I were you I would stay very quiet once you get back to England. After all, your friends have chosen to remain here. You wouldn't want anything to happen to them."

Antonio appeared at the door and Santos gave a nod of his head.

"Here now. It's time for you to go. I wish you all the best, Mr. Edgar."

Antonio, a bag slung over his shoulder, walked behind Thomas as they left the camp and moved toward the river. The rain had stopped again. He could feel the stares of the other men—Ernie, with Lillie, who must have returned with Antonio, by his side, his hand on the waist of her bright white dress as she spun a parasol; George and Pedro. Thomas stared at the ground as he walked, not quite believing that he was still alive, that he was escaping with his body intact, with only a bit of blood crusting in his hair. Antonio held his elbow when his step faltered. A yellow and black swallow-tail flitted in front of them and he gave a cry and lunged for it, only to find it was nothing more than a female *torquatas*, black with yellow spots, a mistake he had made before. His heart collapsed. His butterfly. His *Papilio sophia*. How he had betrayed it. It had all been for nothing, and so many were dead because of him. His silence had killed Clara, and it had killed John. Now, it would save his friends.

THIRTEEN

SOPHIE AWAKES WITH HER feet throbbing. She pulls back the sheets to look at them in the weak morning light. Her nightgown and legs are filthy with dirt and soot, her sheets smeared black and gritty. Blisters bubble on her soles, the skin tight and red, but they could have been much worse, considering she was trying to put out a fire with them. She curls herself into a ball and closes her eyes again, remembering the dark shape of her husband at the window, his yell that echoed around the garden. This day, everything has changed. When she gets up, nothing will be as it was, and for now she's not sure if this is a fact to be celebrated or dreaded. The longer she stays in bed, perhaps, the longer she can put off finding out.

His first words, after that first yell, were *He killed her.* They had lain crying in each other's arms after that, then he had carried her upstairs and put her to bed. Had he spoken again after that? She does have a vague memory of him murmuring to her. Afterward he went downstairs and she heard him outside, dragging his crates back inside.

He killed her. Who was *he*? The woman he referred to could only have been that woman—Mr. Santos's wife. But who had killed her? And why? For having relations with Thomas? This might be true. Was this why Thomas had been struck mute? She supposes he could be feeling terribly guilty about it; that his actions led to her death.

There is a soft knock at the door.

"Thomas?" She sits up.

"Only me, ma'am," says Mary, coming in with tea on a tray. She sets it down on the bedside table. Her face is bright. "You'll never guess . . . or maybe you will. But the master—"

"He spoke to you?"

"Yes! I got such a fright. He came and asked me to bring you tea in bed. Said you weren't well." A look of concern fell over her. "Are you feeling all right?"

Sophie sighed. "Yes. Oh, I've only done something silly to myself. I've just burned my feet."

Mary is clearly shocked but too polite to ask her why. "Should I send for Dr. Dixon?"

"No . . . actually, yes. I'd like him to see Mr. Edgar as well."

Mary looks at her sideways. "And isn't it good news? That he's speaking?"

"Yes, Mary. It's wonderful." She manages a wan smile. If only she could enjoy it. But she senses that they have a long way to go before they have a cause to celebrate.

AFTER DR. DIXON HAS left, Sophie finds she can still walk, if a little painfully, on newly bandaged feet, but he has told her to stay off them for a few days, so she returns to bed. Thomas had his wounds examined in the privacy of his own room and when the doctor came in to see Sophie, he smiled warmly at her.

"You must be very pleased, Mrs. Edgar. His wounds have healed nicely and we had a conversation. He seems much more alert and present. I wouldn't say he was verbose, but he answered the questions I had for him."

"And how did he seem otherwise?"

"Fine, fine. It's a wonderful start. He still seems very nervous, and I wouldn't call him completely healthy just yet, but I do believe he is recovering, and I'm sure you have yourself to thank for that. You must have cared for him well."

Sophie nodded, but didn't say what she was really thinking—that it was her own act of madness and rage that brought him back, not her kindness.

Now she lies in bed and waits for Thomas to come to her. Mary has changed her linen, trying to hide astonished noises at the state of her sheets, and it is cool against her skin. The day is muggy and a starling's song drifts through the open window. A motor purrs past and horses' hooves ring out on the road.

Eventually there is a tap at her door.

"I was beginning to think you wouldn't come," she says.

Thomas shuffles forward. "I nearly didn't." His voice is husky and he clasps his hand to his neck as if these new words hurt him, like beetles scratching inside his throat.

"Come closer," she says, and pats the bed. He sits down. "How are you feeling?"

"Dreadful," he says. "What you've endured because of me. I'm so sorry."

She doesn't know what to say, and they sit in silence for a moment. She wants to ask him about the woman, about what can have happened to him to make him this way. But she hasn't had an answer from him before now—what makes her think she'll get one just because he is speaking?

"Your butterflies," she says at last. "The fire . . ."

"Don't," he says. "There's no harm done. God. I *drove* you to that. I'm sorry."

She nods without meaning to, and chews on her top lip. "Thomas . . . darling. What on earth was going through your head when you wouldn't talk to me . . . to anyone?"

"I don't know. It's so hard to explain. I wanted to, so many times. Even to write things down . . . you won't believe how many times I started to, when I was alone in my study. But I simply couldn't. There's no other way to describe it. It was as if my tongue didn't work, or my hands, when it came to writing. Something in my head told me that if I opened my mouth, I would say terrible things, that people would get hurt, that I would confess to a crime I hadn't committed. I was so scared of what I would say once I started—"

"Like what? What happened to you?"

He hangs his head and shakes it. "I still can't," he says. Then he stands and apologizes yet again, before making for the door.

"Thomas, don't walk away!" She can't believe they have come this far, only to have him run away from her yet again. But this time he stops. He stands by the door, fidgeting with his fingers on the door handle.

"Please," she says. "Come back." She tries to keep the desperation from her voice, but can hear the whine. "You don't need to tell me everything at once. Just what you're comfortable with."

He looks at her like a child through his fringe, which has flopped over his eyes, contemplating her offer, before nodding and taking small steps back toward her.

AND SO IT IS that Sophie learns about Clara Santos; the drug Mr. Santos tricked Thomas into smoking and the effect it had on him; his last desperate attempt to find the butterfly before he gave up in despair. The loss of his friend John, and the danger his other two companions could now be in. He also tells her about the murders—of the newspaperman, Captain Arturo, and the poor Indians—but he spares her the details.

Part of her wants to reach out and pull him close, tell him that nothing is his fault, comfort him. But the thought of him with that woman stops her. For now.

He sits in a chair, looking away and speaking in a low, cracked voice. Sometimes he has to stop talking as he bends his head and sobs.

"And then?" she keeps saying. She wants to keep him talking, for fear that if he stops, he will stop forever. On one level she is triumphant that he is on the mend. Her patience and perseverance have paid off. She also knew all along that whatever caused his muteness might be something she didn't want to know about. And she was right. It hurts, this knowledge he has been carrying around with him. It hurts both of them.

After he finishes speaking, it is duty that moves her toward him, makes her take his hand.

"Why didn't you write to me of any of these things?"

"I couldn't. I didn't want to frighten you—and besides, I couldn't voice my suspicions of Santos. It would have been too dangerous. And . . ." He looks at the floor and his voice drops to a whisper. ". . . I was ashamed of my behavior."

Sophie just nods at this, surprisingly devoid of emotion. And so you should be, she thinks. She is hard now; these things bounce off her like hailstones on the road. She should have known when his letters stopped that something was amiss. The last one she had from him was so thin, as if all his self-censoring left him with nothing to say.

But what can she do? She can't leave him—what a scandal that would create! People would start speculating, prying . . . But she has vowed not to worry about what others think, to act only in the interests of herself and her husband. So much of what hurts comes not from the fact that he has betrayed her, but that he is a man *capable* of betraying her. In other words, he's not the man she thought she married. She knows what men are, women too, but she somehow believed that she and Thomas were different: that they truly loved each other and could never hurt each other. This is what she will now have to grieve for—the Thomas who never really existed. She will have to learn to love this new Thomas, who looks like the old one but more aged, more hollow. Even his hands feel colder when he takes hers, his eyes set farther back into his skull. A different man indeed.

TWO DAYS LATER, CHARLES Winterstone pauses outside his daughter's front door. He has not warned Sophie he is coming, and he wonders if she will even be at home. The maid answers the door, eyes wide with fright at seeing him. As he crosses the threshold, broken tiles in the entrance hall crunch under his feet. They should get somebody to repair those, he thinks, before the others become scratched and ruined.

Mary shows him into the drawing room, but when she disappears to fetch Sophie he walks to the parlor. Through the window, he sees his daughter outside in the garden, holding a basket of cut roses. She wears a gardening hat with a veil concealing half her face. He sees a hand, encased in thick gloves, go to her mouth as the maid approaches and speaks. Sophie's head darts about, looking for what he can't imagine. A small groan escapes his throat. There is something in the gesture that reminds him of Martha, who had a habit of looking everywhere when she was upset, as if the answers to all her problems lay in the flower bed, or under the table. He can't help it: every time he thinks of his wife, even twenty years after her death, he feels a gaping hole in his stomach like hunger. He had always been too close to her. She was taken away from him so early in their marriage, before they had had a chance to become bored with each other, before age thickened her waist and pinched her face, before she had a tribe of children to tend to and before she became a hostess so seasoned that she lost all joy for entertaining. Before they ran out of things to discuss at breakfast.

When she died, the house had descended into iciness. The nanny and the housekeeper tiptoed around him, barely raising their voices above a whisper, and he became used to the quiet. He even fancied he could hear his wife in the silences between the soft closing of a door or the shuffle of Nanny's feet on the stairs. He would stand in Martha's beloved garden and listen for her in the wind that rustled the overgrown roses.

He sees a picture in his mind of Martha in her garden, dressed in exactly the same manner as his daughter is now, while the young Sophie squats in the flowerbed, getting herself far too dirty for a good little girl. Martha laughs at her, turns her back to her, and waves a red rose at her husband.

He knows that he left Sophie alone to deal with the loss of her mother; he should have been there for her. But she needed to learn independence. He would far rather he had never been close to Martha than have his heart buried with her. He wouldn't wish that on anybody, least of all his own flesh and blood. Nobody should love so hard and have that love taken away.

"Father?" Sophie is in the room with him now, removing the pins that hold her hat on, pulling the hat off her head and grasping it tightly. Affection bubbles inside him like boiling toffee but he dampens it down.

"Hello, dear," he says. "I was just passing."

She eyes him suspiciously and he drops his head. She becomes more like her mother every day.

"Actually . . ." He gestures to the chairs by the window. "There is something. Can we sit?"

"Of course. Mary?" Mary appears and takes away her hat and gloves.

Sophie smooths her hair down as she perches on the edge of the chair.

"There's no easy way to say this." He has become hot suddenly and fights the urge to loosen his tie. "I know about Thomas, Sophie."

Sophie collapses back into her chair with a sigh. She is relieved, he supposes, that she no longer needs to keep the secret from him, as if the lie has kept her tightly coiled.

"How do you know?"

"It's not a secret anymore, is it? Doesn't the whole of Richmond know?"

She shrugs. "And Kingston now, too, I see." Is she angry with him?

"Where is Thomas now? Is he in bed?"

"Come and see for yourself." She pushes herself up and stands over him. He has no choice but to rise also and follow her into the hallway.

She knocks at a closed door—two raps: one, two—but doesn't wait for an answer.

"There's someone here to see you," she says to the room, and when Charles enters, he sees Thomas sitting at a desk. The air is heavy with a chemical smell, which reminds him of his school days, mixed with dust. Thomas is surrounded by piles of papers, several inkwells, and stacks of small boxes. Charles glimpses a flash of color in the dreary room—a pink and white butterfly, and a pallet of paint beside it, with a jar of dirty water holding a paintbrush.

In the corners of the room, dust creatures crouch, undulating in the draft from the open door as if ready to pounce. Thomas has not yet looked up, and Charles pokes discreetly at a book on the shelf next to him. It moves, leaving a ghost image of itself below.

Finally Thomas looks up from his work, and Charles crosses the room to greet him. The young man stands reluctantly. He stares at the hand Charles has extended before raising his own slowly and offering it. His hand is surprisingly rough, like a gardener's, dry and papery. Charles examines his face for signs of the violent nature Fale described to him, but Thomas's eyes are more timid than dangerous.

"Nice to see you again, Thomas," says Charles. "We won't keep you from your work."

"Not at all," says Thomas, and Charles drops his hand in surprise.

"Good God. But I thought . . ." He lets his voice trail away.

Sophie places her hand on her father's arm and begins to steer him from the room.

"I know what you thought, Father. We'll leave you now, Thomas."

Sophie is walking awkwardly as she leads him back into the parlor, as if on hot coals.

"Are you all right? Have you hurt yourself?"

"It's nothing." She waves him away and sits down. "Too much gardening. As you can see, Father, Thomas is quite well."

"Well then, tell me. Tell me why it is that I heard otherwise."

"Who told you?"

"A Captain Fale came to see me. I believe he is a friend of Thomas's. He was most concerned for you both. He said Thomas . . . I know this sounds extraordinary: he said he was mute. Not speaking. And violent, too. He feared for your safety, in fact. He enlisted my help to have him sent to . . . to hospital."

"Did he now?" Sophie presses the back of her hand to her mouth, thinking. "I see. Well, I'll tell you, Father, he was ill when he returned, and I *was* rather worried about him, but as you can see he is much better now. As for his being violent, that's preposterous! You know Thomas. You know how gentle and kind he is."

"So why would this Captain Fale have told me, when you did not?"

"I didn't want to worry you. You can understand that, can't you?"

"There was something else I want to ask you about Fale. Could it be that he has reason to hope for some kind of separation between you and your husband?"

"Oh, Father, no! I love Thomas with all my heart. Things have been difficult, yes, but you see they are improving."

"Well, whether you know about it or not, this Fale clearly has plans for you, and for Thomas. I would avoid him at all costs."

"And you . . . you don't think I should have Thomas sent away? You don't agree with the captain?"

"My dear, I hardly know the man. When a complete stranger comes to me with such an unusual request I can't help but be suspicious. At first I was angry with you . . . how could you not have told me?"

"I was worried about what you would say! I know you have never liked Thomas—"

"This is not true."

She bites her lip again. "Oh, I'm sorry. Forgive me. I'm tired." Indeed, she has dark circles under her eyes, clearly from lack of sleep. She must be worrying. She has never spoken to him so boldly. He is surprised that he does not mind.

"I couldn't tell you. You would have thought Thomas had failed me. You might have insisted on sending him to hospital."

How well she knows him. This is precisely what had gone through his mind—how to get Thomas as far away from her as possible. But now he can see that Thomas is on the mend. How fiercely she defends him! He is reminded again of Martha—how loyal she was to him, when he wasn't always the ideal husband. He knows what it is to be separated from the object of one's love. How could he have considered inflicting this on his own daughter?

"I would never have you left alone like that." This is only a small lie. "Do you understand me? Do you?"

Sophie pauses before nodding. Her chin wrinkles with the effort of holding in tears.

Charles suddenly has an idea. "Why don't you both move in with me for a time? Just until Thomas is better."

She starts to cry then, and he gives her his handkerchief.

"May I think about it?"

"Of course." He looks at his pocket watch. "And now I must be going." The truth is, she has never cried in front of him so openly. The sight makes him uneasy.

But as he walks out into the street, his feet are light. He has done the right thing. He tried to raise her not to rely on anybody but herself, so she could never be disappointed, as he was, but the time has come to stretch out a hand and claim her as his daughter.

SOPHIE NEEDS TO GET out, get some air. It's all she can think of now: that she has to escape this dark house. She waits a few minutes to be sure her father will be well away, picks up her hat and parasol and walks out the door.

The catch on the gate eludes her shaking fingers and she curses at it before it gives way. Her chest begins to ache with keeping the tears in, and when she reaches the street, she can't do it anymore. She opens her parasol and drapes it low over her face as she walks painfully on her blistered feet.

She wipes her eyes with her glove and sniffs to try to contain the trickles escaping her nose. She grunts at herself, clears the phlegm from her throat. Why can't she hold herself together? It's still not safe to take her parasol down and she knows she will be drawing curious looks from passersby.

Did she lead Captain Fale on? Yes, quite possibly. When he first came calling she told herself she felt sorry for him; he was lonely and would be good company for her. But his conversation was stilted—and always going on about the war and his injury, when everybody knew perfectly well he had hurt himself falling off his horse in the park.

But he was so strong under his uniform, and being with him aroused feelings that were so different from her feelings for Thomas. Where Thomas's eyes looked into her heart, Samuel's looked under her corset. In turn, she had found herself examining the shape of his body as he walked ahead of her. Broad shoulders, long thighs, rounded buttocks. She even imagined his naked chest with all that thick hair, imagined running her fingers through it and burying her face in it. A smell surrounded him, too—sweet and lemony, with a hint of perspiration. It should have disgusted her; instead, it drew her in. She became fascinated with her body's response to it, seemingly independent of her mind. The fact that she didn't even particularly like Samuel only made the feelings easier, for it couldn't count as a betrayal if she wasn't in love with him—could it?

The day she had read Thomas's journal and gone to see the captain, she'd had a vision of throwing herself at him. She'd wanted to walk in there, take his face in her hands, and press her body into his. If Thomas had done it, why couldn't she? But he'd been so resistant, and in the end it just wasn't in her to have an affair. Not when she loved her husband so much.

And she *does* still love Thomas, she realizes. Even though she wants to slap him. To keep on slapping him until her palms ache. She will not let Samuel come between them. The thought of the captain's body disgusts her now, and so does the idea that he somehow thought he could get rid of Thomas and have her for himself.

Her stinging feet have carried her to the park. She passes through the tall gates and sits down on a bench to compose herself and to rest. The tears have stopped now but it feels as if her stomach is full of rocks.

She gazes out at the people entering and leaving the park: a young mother with a pram, pulling a small child roughly by the hand; an elderly couple moving slowly but regally, dressed more appropriately for church than for a stroll; a fat nurse trying to placate a little girl who has dropped her ice cream and is crying while attempting to scrape it up with her fingers. And—no!—Captain Fale, coming through the gates toward her.

She lowers her parasol over her face again but it is too late: he has seen her. She hears the *tap-tap* of his cane as he approaches. She stands, detours around the back of the park bench, and begins walking back the way she came, keeping the parasol so low she can only see his feet as she passes.

"Mrs. Edgar."

Sophie falters, then stops. She raises the parasol a fraction and looks at him. He stares back. She calmly collapses her parasol, keeping her eyes on his hopeful face. Then without a word she turns and continues on her way, his gaze heavy on her back.

Thomas is leaning on the wall by the gate as if he has been waiting for her. He silently takes her arm and turns her around, back into the park, and she finds she doesn't resist. She suspects he has followed her here, but she has no idea whether he has seen her exchange with Captain Fale.

The captain hasn't moved from where she left him, stupid man—why doesn't he walk away? Sophie fears suddenly that there will be a confrontation: whether initiated by Samuel or Thomas, she's not sure. But Thomas steers her past him, and as she averts her eyes her husband tips his hat at the captain.

"Fale," he says.

Sophie allows herself a small turn of the head, in time to see Samuel, red in the face, nod dumbly and take a step back, stumbling slightly on his bad leg.

Thomas leads her up the path toward the wood—the same path they took when he first arrived home. Though they walk in silence, it is the silence of being alone with their thoughts: the way they used to walk before Thomas went away, when his mind was on the butterflies he would catch.

The wood is cool and dark. Soft pennies of light litter the ground. The only sound is the crunch of acorns underfoot. A red admiral flicks across their path and Sophie glances at Thomas. He is watching it, but sees her looking at him and places his hand over hers and squeezes.

"Red admirable," she says, and smiles.

He smiles back, shyly.

They come to the fork in the path and both move without question toward their private hollow, which winds around the oak tree and into the undergrowth, hidden from view.

"Shall we sit?" Thomas takes off his jacket and lays it on the ground for Sophie.

She sits, and picks one foot up to nurse it in her lap.

"How are they?" he asks. "Your feet."

"Much better, thank you. But a rest is good."

He crouches beside her, takes her hand, and brings it to his face. His breath is warm on her skin and she is surprised—this is the most forward gesture he has made to her since he has been back. Thomas kisses her hand gently. It is sweet of him and she is touched. She responds by patting his hair, which has become quite long. The soft curls remind her of a child's and make her wonder for a moment whether their children will have curly hair or not; certainly they will be blond.

"My love," whispers Thomas, and now he lays his cheek against her fingers. "Will you—can you—ever forgive me, do you think?"

Will she? She doesn't like to admit it to herself, but she does now understand the lust that can drive one to act against one's conscience. They both need time, now, to get to know each other again.

"Yes, I think I can. You've been through so much."

He nods and looks at the ground.

"My father . . . he offered to have us stay with him for a time. Just until you're feeling better."

"Very kind, but we'll be all right now."

She looks at him, doubtful. She wants to believe him.

"I've got work to do," he says. "And we have so many specimens still for Mr. Ridewell to sell."

She feels a wash of shame. Some of the specimens were ruined in the fire she started, but they did manage to save most of them.

He shifts his legs so he is kneeling and looking down at her. He leans over and takes her face in his hands to kiss her. It is the first kiss he has initiated in so long, and she feels it through her body, between her legs. She opens her mouth in response and he kisses her harder. Then he pulls back, surprised at the intensity that is passing between them. But Sophie lies back on the ground and pulls him with her. She feels dry dirt rubbing on the back of her neck, falling into her collar, but she doesn't care: she is kissing her husband and he is kissing her back and this is all that matters.

He lifts her skirt and puts his hand on her leg, but suddenly stops and looks at her.

"I'm sorry," he says, and starts to move his hand away.

"No," says Sophie, and places his hand back where it had been. Her skin crackles where he touches it. She pulls him closer so that his body presses against hers.

A twig breaks nearby. Sophie pushes Thomas off her and sits upright, horrified. What has she been thinking? She keeps her eyes turned away from whoever it is that has come upon them, and her face burns.

Thomas starts to laugh, an alien sound. She has forgotten how it swoops, low, then high. "Hello," he says. "Look, Sophie."

She turns slowly. A doe stands a few yards from where they sit, ready to take flight. It breathes quickly, heavily. Sophie is relieved; the blood throbs in her cheeks.

"Thank God," she says. "I thought we'd been caught."

The deer turns and leaps away, but Sophie is not ready to resume their embrace, not yet.

"I saw another doe around here once," she says. "It was the strangest thing, Thomas. I was thinking about you, and how I was missing you, and this deer . . . it looked at me, and it was crying. It was so sad."

"Crying?"

"Yes, real tears. I didn't know it was possible. What do you suppose it was so sad about?"

"Oh, sweetheart, animals can't cry. Deer's eyes have oily secretions, that's all. It's nothing to do with feeling sad."

She nods and sighs. He takes her hand and begins picking twigs and leaves from her hair.

Finally, Sophie speaks. "Thomas, I have to ask . . . that is, you haven't mentioned your butterfly. Did you find it?"

He shakes his head. "I thought I had. There were times when I was sure I had it. But the forest—it played tricks on me. I don't think my butterfly ever really existed. It was just a dream." His voice sounds wretched; she thinks he might start crying. "It drove me mad, Sophie. I think I actually might have gone mad."

Sophie says nothing.

"I'm glad to be home now," he says. "I think I'm ready to put it all behind me."

"But what of that man Santos? What are you going to do about him?"

"What can I do? My friends are still with him. He'll kill them. Or worse."

"You must contact the British directors. You must. Be brave if you have to."

"Brave?" He drops her hand and wipes at his face in disgust. "Things aren't as simple everywhere as they are in Richmond, Sophie."

Something is wrong with his voice. It trails off and she is suddenly gripped with a fear that he is losing it again—that the mere thought of speaking out is making him retreat once more into silence.

"We'll find a way," she says, and puts her arms around him and pulls him close. Butterfly wings unfold and flicker in her belly.

Malay Archipelago, September 6th, 1912

Dear Sophie,

I will be very brief, as I am soon due to go out to dine, but I wanted to reply quickly to your letter, which you must have sent some weeks ago now. There is something I find soothing about writing to you, as if you are in the room with me and I am holding a real conversation with you.

It was with some amusement that I read your letter. That Agatha has turned out to be such a splendid hostess is wonderful, of course, but I can't help but laugh at how different she seems now that she is married with children. I know she's your friend and I mustn't be unkind, but wasn't she always lecturing you about social evils and the whims of society? I wonder sometimes how poor Chapman copes with her, now that she wants to throw parties every night for her new friends. I am glad I am not in Richmond, otherwise I would have to find excuses not to go—you are much better at that sort of thing than I am. I'm pleased Agatha's hat business is doing well, though. Tell her I have a few specimens she will be very interested in.

   Finding all the new species here has made me think of the Papilio
sophia *I never caught in the Amazon. What a fool I was—no doubt
Wallace and Spruce were playing a joke by starting the rumor. Perhaps
it wasn't even them who started it, but some prankster at the Natural
History Museum. What an idiot I was to believe it, when a butterfly
like that is an impossibility. To think of all I nearly lost on its account.
To think, too, what I put you through, and how you've stood by me—
encouraged me even—to get back into the saddle and become a professional collector. You have my word, dear Sophie, that I will never do
that to you again, and neither will I keep things from you as I did back
then. I received a letter yesterday from Mr. Roberts, the American, for-
warded to me by Mr. Ridewell. Roberts informed me that Mr. Santos
died before he was due to stand trial. I don't know how to describe how
I feel about that. Part of me is glad that he is dead—is that terrible?—
the other part is disappointed that he wasn't prosecuted for his crimes.
If only things had moved more quickly, but with nobody believing
Roberts—especially the British directors of Santos's rubber company,
the blind fools—proceedings were certainly slowed. I'm very grateful
that you encouraged me to write to Roberts, Sophie. Some might call
me weak for deferring to your good counsel so readily, but no matter.
You are my strength, and I will always listen to you. The way you now
voice your opinion so strongly fills me with pride and admiration.*

   *I only wish that George and Ernie had spoken out as well before
they died. At least their disappearance made our government sit up and
take notice. I thank God that they died of natural causes, although perhaps we'll never know what to believe. I sometimes have nightmares
that Santos found out about my giving evidence and killed them, just as
he had implied he would do. Cholera was rife, though, and Ernie was
looking ill even when I left. I was fortunate not to catch it myself, so
weakened by my malaria bout, which still comes back to me, as you
know. How many sweaty, delirious nights you've nursed me through!*

   *Roberts has only just told me how Santos tried to blackmail him—
had in fact set him up while he was in Brazil, by getting one of his*

lackeys to offer him money—and that the British directors almost believed it until someone tried to bribe them too. Then they realized that Roberts was telling the truth about it all, and gave in. They sent their own inspectors out there who managed to gather quite a bit of evidence. I suppose the directors thought they could be absolved of all blame if they investigated and found their own company corrupt, and it looks as though they have been. What this means for the trial, I do not know.

Mr. Ridewell has been encouraging me to revisit my journals and bring them up to a publishable format, but I am so busy with other projects—the butterflies in the archipelago wait for no man!—that I am reluctant to start that difficult task. I could scarcely bring myself to read them and remind myself of that time in the Amazon. Perhaps, if it weren't too hard for you, this might be a project you could help me with upon my return? Think about it, anyway, my love, and say no if you want to.

Well, I must run now as Frederick, my new assistant (and an enthusiastic one at that! He keeps me endlessly entertained—you would like him very much), has just come to tell me that we are soon expected. How I wish I could send him off to dine without me, and continue my conversation with you. I ache for you and the children, to be back with you again. Nine months is too, too long, and I promise not to be away for such a time again. Give my love to the children and my regards to your father. I do appreciate the time he spends with them when I'm not there.

My next assignment is to be Australia, next year. I hope, my dear wife, that you and the children might accompany me on that trip. You say the children are running wild in the park—well, in Australia they could be free to be the intrepid little ragamuffins they are. Wouldn't that be an adventure?

I am, as always, yours.

Thomas

While this is a work of imagination, some of the characters are loosely based on real people: the character of José Santos was inspired by the Peruvian rubber baron Julio Arana, who lived in Manaus and had thousands of Indians tortured and enslaved in the Putumayo region (but who did not murder his wife); an American, Walter Hardenburg, provided the starting point for the offstage Mr. Roberts. The story of the clash of these two men deserves a whole book of its own—I urge anyone interested to seek it out. While every care has been taken to get historical details right, I repeat, this is primarily a work of imagination. In regards to the art of butterflies and collecting, I have used information that was available at the time, much of which I'm sure has been superseded. To my knowledge, no such collecting expedition took place in the Amazon at that specific time; however, there were many expeditions before and after. Among my many research sources, I would particularly like to acknowledge authors Peter Raby and Anthony Smith for their books *Bright Paradise* and *Explorers of the Amazon,* which I found invaluable and inspirational.

ACKNOWLEDGMENTS

This book wouldn't have been possible without the following people, so my gratitude goes to:

Laurie Chittenden, Vivien Green, Gaia Banks, Harriet Allan, Sam Humphreys, and Rachel Scott.

Jonathan King, for too many things to mention, but, as a start, telling me about the rubber barons and setting me on the path.

The NZSA (PEN NZ Inc) Mentor Programme supported by Creative New Zealand, and Chris Else for his incredibly valuable advice.

All my Zoetrope buddies, especially Richard Lewis, Paul Cunningham, Hannah Holborn, Thea Atkinson, Joan Wilking, Judith Beck, and Anna Sidak. Special thanks to Mario Ribeiro for Brazilian advice and translation.

Insightful readers and support crew Susan Pearce, Kate Duignan, Katy Robinson, Tim Corballis, and Mary Parker.

Helpful staff at the Natural History Museum in London and the Richmond Public Library. Rob and Joan Marshall for introducing me to Richmond Park.

Friends and family for all manner of help, support, and enthusiasm: Ros Henry, David Elworthy, Harriet Elworthy, Rebecca Priestley, Bill Manhire, Anna Smaill, Carl Shuker, Jason Hebron, Gemma Gracewood, Marianne Elliot, Tanya Fretz, Annette Cotter, Jon Bridges, Janelle Rodrigues, Paula Morris, and especially Peter Rutherford.